The Deaths of Berlin

Jim McDermott

Prologue: 27 July 1941

All cities die.

The words rose from memory like stale air released by the violence around him. A faded image of his *mittelschule* classroom returned - an afternoon's oppressive heat, his schoolmates unusually engaged, throwing out examples to make the lesson pass more quickly. But for Trier their tutor had thrown back *Nineveh*, for Dresden *Ur*, for Mainz *Hattusa*, for Swinemünde (their home) *Persopolis*, *Jericho*, *Babylon* or *Thebes* - take your pick, he'd told them, time would prove all. They declared this to be a cheat, an appeal to faith not evidence, like loaves and fishes, water to wine, resurrection. The boy – the man, now – had not expected to be called to witness its proof.

In front of him the skyline burned, ochring the summer day's straw light. Outlined against its glare, dozens of German dive-bombers plunged into the inferno and climbed again, glowing blackly as if in a super-charged, newsreeled state of being. Flak was thin and sporadic, the target a compact, compliant press of hovels, apartments, churches, villas, military and government buildings - a quarter of a million mortal ambitions with the miserable luck to stand between Army Group Centre and Moscow. So far the city's walls were keeping the business tidy, containing it like an archery ring; they were tall, thick, apparently impervious, but it was an illusion he had seen dismantled before. At their ashlar core ancient fault-lines would be moving, opening, awaiting the slight further pressure that would end their centuries-long command of the open ground below.

He knew too little about the place to make a proper valediction. It lay upon the route from the Varangians to the Greeks, a refuge at which epic travellers had rested, bartered and re-caulked their boats' hulls before pressing on to the north or south. It had been much greater once than now; the Mongols had spared it, Napoleon had not. Its ordeals had made it an icon of self-identity for the *Rus*, though they had been masters here for fewer than half the years since its foundation. But these were big things to know, not the countless tiny elements of a pulse, a story. Its name had been Smolensk.

All cities die. That did away with guilt, at least. An historical imperative made it an irrelevance, an indulgence of tender consciences. Still, the feeling of loss persisted, surprising him; it belonged in another place, a much different time.

A flare rose to his left, and the artillery captain to whose recollections he had been half-listening excused himself politely, turned and blew his whistle. For the past three days the encirclement had been extended in the face of ferocious resistance to an iron, choking grip upon the city and its remaining inhabitants. Now, a brief bombardment would keep heads down while the armour got close enough to the walls, and then the gun crews could sit back while the door-to-door business proceeded. It was hardly *blitzkrieg*, but the Ivans had a way of confounding assumptions and military theory. Every day's fighting was different; a seer couldn't predict whether the Ivans were going to panic and flee like sheep or cross themselves and die, careless of it, in one-man stands against massed tank assaults. The Führer himself had said it – a primitive, awkward enemy, one to whom the rules didn't - shouldn't - apply.

Almost a hundred guns, massed the length of the low ridge above the Dnieper, opened up. He lifted borrowed binoculars and examined the fall of his adopted unit's fire along the ramparts, allowing the noise and its bludgeoning of the senses to excise his moral distractions, to distil the world to the purely mechanical, a matter only of observation, trajectory and rhythm. What he thought of all this no longer mattered; the flare had transmuted the man into a minor instrument of a vast, semi-divine purpose, his pale faith justified by a pressure headache and ringing ears. He observed, absolved of intent.

It shouldn't have been a fight, the enemy here still, defending the city. Every time they tried something like this it went badly for them, yet always they returned for more, willing to contest every ruined alley, to take a German or two for each of their own. It was hardly a plan, much less a strategy; but it made best use of the only commodity they couldn't exhaust, the one upon which Russia had always relied much too heavily. Dig in, hide, kill, die - above all, make time to allow others to find a way to stop the tide. The men behind the walls had pulled the mother of short straws, been written off already, accounted for upon some vast manifest of war materiel.

But what did yet another encirclement matter, when the next fat harvest of poor bastards was assembling to the east, ready to be scythed down?

Four minutes, and another flare signalled the bombardment's end. The armour and troops that sheltered behind it had reached the near fire-point; beyond it, their artillery would kill as many Germans as Russians, even with pinpoint gunnery. As the aural assault faded around him, his thoughts reassembled and identified the paradox that had been tugging at his attention. Their tutor had said that a city died when the God-cult that established it was superseded, or if its trade routes went elsewhere, or because sand replaced fertile soil and water in its zone of sustenance, or at the moment when self-identity ceased to be defined by a particular concept of *civitas*. But none of that was the case here. Here, men had come from elsewhere and rushed into a city even as it collapsed, men who were determined to die to deny an already ruined ground to the enemy, and this struck him as anything but the mark of an ending. Of all possible causes of the deaths of cities, the students had not been offered the obvious one - their wilful destruction at human hands. At the time they had been puzzled by the omission; but now, with the intention before him, spread as wide as the horizon itself, it occurred to Leutnant Otto Fischer that the old man had been wiser than they'd known. If only two stones remained, one upon the other, a city couldn't die while such a savage will to life endured.

Part One

1

A December evening, 1944, the Heilandskirche, where outdoors made its case as the latest fashion in interior architecture. About two hundred people were gathered in the ruined nave, almost surrounding a small ensemble of elderly women who leafed busily through tattered music sheets, searching for something that shouldn't have been there. A stranger might have been touched by the generally make-do, patched quality of the civilians' clothing, the yellow-tinged translucence to their complexions that hinted at nourishment recalled rather than experienced, and the sour odour (pervasive even without a roof to contain it) of flesh liberated from the vanity of hygiene, as if the church had become a sanctuary for retired country priests. But to native Berliners such things were too evident to notice. Everything was of its time, a state of gradual undoing.

After a cursory tuning and momentary stillness the opening bars of Mendelssohn's String Octet drifted out into the ruined spaces, filling them with something other than the unlovely Now. No one cleared a throat or coughed (though there were many weak lungs attending), or shuffled to keep thin blood circulating in numb extremities; no vehicles negotiated the once-busy intersection of two major roads over which the church's battered tower and half-steeple loomed precariously. The banned, sunlit masterpiece sang of a life apart from the present one, and only a few discreet sniffs, an occasional sigh, a solitary cabbage-induced fart and the mute pain of kinder memories marked time with it.

Among the few uniforms stood a Luftwaffe officer who wore his war more visibly than most. His field coat was draped over the shoulders of the old woman standing next to him - a gentlemanly gesture, regretted since the moment he had thought to make it. Occasionally, he put his arm around her shoulder, as much to steal back a little warmth as to steady her as age, diet and the frosty night worked upon fragile joints. At her other side another old woman, less obviously uncomfortable, swayed slightly. Her eyes were closed, her chin raised; a hand moved delicately, following each bar, rising and falling as the music took it. Her neighbour (her sister) found this practised familiarity irritating as she herself didn't recognize the piece. But that was just like Else - she couldn't bear folk to be ignorant of what she knew.

The officer felt the familiar tension in the old woman's thin shoulders. Two months earlier, news had broken of the atrocities inflicted by the Red Army upon the villagers of Nemmersdorf. He recalled her reaction then, a lung-deep groan he had mistaken for pity for the fallen. In fact, it had been a shrewd glimpse of a more personal future, one that rapped on the front door of Jonas-Strasse 17 less than forty-eight hours later. Frau Else Ostermann, widow of Konigsberg, had side-stepped the several threats of molestation, murder and (if rumours regarding Tartars were true) cannibalism by mounting a personal evacuation to Berlin-Moabit. An unhappy decision, but as with every other bitter fortune of the present war one had to learn to make do.

The Octet ended to grateful applause, enough to encourage the players to an encore, the *andante* from Schubert's String Quintet. There were far more tears now, and even the shivering officer, a staunch non-believer in anything other than a warm bed on such a night, was moved to a certain difficulty in swallowing. The frail old lady - her name was Frau Traugott - knew this piece as well as any other German and wept openly, occasionally wiping her nose on the sleeve of the borrowed coat with what she imagined to be a decorous subtlety.

At the close of the music a small bag circulated, a collection for the players. Some members of the audience passed it on quickly, embarrassed by their revealed poverty; others visibly resisted the urge to pluck something from it. The officer, who had been forewarned of the arrangement (this was his first concert in the Age of General Want), donated two tins of cho-ka-kola that he had liberated from the Air Ministry's officers' dining room earlier that afternoon. The sisters, deprived of any prior opportunity to stake their own, obviously superior claim, glared furiously at the treasure as it disappeared.

The crowd dispersed quietly, moving out into dangerous shadows. The officer and two old ladies nodded their goodbyes and hurried the few hundred metres back to their home as quickly as the unlit streets and Frau Traugott's bad joints allowed, though there was time enough for familiar complaints about rationing, crime, the darkened streets, hooliganism, beggars, ausländers, refugees (Frau Ostermann did not maintain a discreet silence on this subject), the broken hips that threatened elderly ladies walking blindly over broken ground - and God knew, that was what most Berlin ground was these days. Like verses of a well-loved psalm, these observations warmed the sisters and gave the officer a faint longing for a billet in an Allied *stammlager*. But he kept an engaged expression on his face and made appropriate noises whenever a pause in their parallel diatribes suggested he was being invited to sympathize. It was a small part of his atonement for an inexcusable sin of admission.

Three weeks earlier, loosened by a couple of shots from Frau Traugott's ancient bottle of apricot brandy, he had let slip word of a creature the police had christened (if that was the appropriate verb) the Suburban Strangler. He had claimed two victims to date, both respectable middle-aged females, taken in the darkness around the Botanical Gardens at Lichterfelde, throttled and then molested post-mortem. The intelligence had been casually offered but privileged, word from an acquaintance at Alexanderplatz. Really, he shouldn't have opened his mouth. As a former kriminalkommissar, a *kripo*, he knew perfectly well what old ladies were capable of.

The sisters had been horrified (rapturously so), and the efficiency with which they spread the word made leaflet-dropping air raids seem crudely ineffectual. Within days, almost the entire silver-haired population between Tiergarten and Sickingenstrasse was losing sleep over the matter of the Moabit Garrotter, a simian grotesque who wandered their darkened neighbourhood, executing decent ladies with their underwear (the mechanics of this atrocity remained unclear), molesting their corpses and then feasting upon parts of their bodies not to be spoken of. A discreet panic had settled like fog; every strange male face excited a faint arrhythmia, every foreign accent an expectation of the sort of savage violation that was much finessed in the retelling. Already, sightings of the creature were legion, and countless lucky escapes had been reported to local *blockhelfers* who had to admit their absolute ignorance of the situation but promised to seek instructions that, for some reason, weren't forthcoming. The wellspring of this distress took up his several penances without complaint. He tried to calm the anxieties of Frau Traugott's friends, adjudicated increasingly bizarre theories (an English degenerate, parachuted into the city; Peter Kürten, reprieved and escaped during a prison transfer; a bachelor who lived next door and never spoke except to himself and an imaginary comrade), pretended a deep understanding of the diseased criminal mind, and, whenever wanderlust overcame his landlady and her sister after dusk, pulled on his boots and provided a military escort (like all adept gossips, they had come to believe absolutely in their invention).

This evening they arrived home a few minutes before the curfew. Jonas-Strasse 17 was a modest property near the Arminius Markthalle, a red brick box unmemorable other than by reference to its neighbours, which had taken the hint from British ordnance and mostly departed. Formerly an end-terrace, it now enjoyed an enviable quality of detachment, being supported on its once-sociable side by large wooden struts. Its yard and garden had been obliterated by the consequences of several direct hits upon the neighbouring street, and the front prospect acned by aerial debris attempting to move on elsewhere. Anyone who knew the street from pre-war days would have called it the sort of shame with which they were all becoming far too familiar, but as a good German Frau Traugott accepted her lot without complaint. Indeed, as the views from her windows lengthened, her complacency was becoming quite unchristian.

They entered to regulation darkness and a cold softened only by the absence of the cutting wind that had chased them through Thusnelda Allee. The officer went ahead, feeling his way along the wall-rail to the table upon which a kerosene lamp awaited duties. As his hand closed upon it something shuffled ahead of him, and before he could attempt evasive manoeuvres or the sort of tactical withdrawal much frowned upon by the Führer a small body had rubbed against his leg, affectionately launching another assault upon his immune system.

'Marlene! Mutti's home, darling!'

How, absent light or helpful mewl, Frau Traugott could identify one beast from another was a mystery that only the Inquisition might have resolved. She fumbled for a moment and struck a match; the lamp spluttered feebly, barely illuminating the hallway, and in its gloomy underworld Marlene (a street-worn tortoiseshell) was joined by Sigi (tabby) and Chancellor Bismarck (too nondescript to be guessed at), three familiars taking turns around their adopted mistress's legs with the grace and coordination of carp in a palace pond.

The officer sneezed violently. Else - a self-proclaimed *doggie* person - tutted and went to fill the kettle. From Konigsberg she had brought a kilo of black tea, her only offering, and eked out the memory of this largesse by rationing herself and her sister to a cup each day - to settle the soul for sleep, she proposed. The officer (who neither enjoyed stale tea nor laid claim to a soul worth settling) dabbed his eyes, excused himself and retired for the evening.

He had few possessions and rarely used the key to his second-floor apartment. The door into his small sitting room was slightly ajar, as he had left it earlier that evening. He felt his way to the table, found a matchbook and lit his table lamp. The P08 Parabellum lay next to it, un-holstered, on a few notes he had been making for a briefing the following day. The papers were also exactly as he had left them, but he had no recollection of placing the pistol upon them. In fact, he couldn't recall owning a P08.

The room was as cold as the rest of the house, but the large, hard-featured man in the armchair had made himself comfortable. A thick grey coat lay over his lap, and a glass half-filled with what the officer suspected was his remaining personal stock of *slivovitz* was cradled carefully in hand. On the floor next to the chair an artificial leg for an above-the-knee amputee stood upright, anchored by the Luftwaffe boot it wore like a lucky find in one of the city's stranger junk shops.

The free hand's knuckles - solid, purple instruments - were beating out a slow tattoo on the chair's leather flank, and in its deliberate rhythm the officer recognized the chorus from *Bomben auf Engelland*. Even in the shock of the moment it dragged a part of him back to those happy days when the war had been going somewhere hopeful, when the gamble had yet seemed a little short of lunatic.

The apparition moved slightly - a gesture, something between a squirm and a shrug.

'Hello, Otto. How are things?'

It was what war did and always had done. Still, she pitied all those poor boys, condemned by their gender and what society expected of them, told that they must be heroes by leaders who would never face the same things themselves and then forgotten, or worse, when they returned from the war.

She thanked God that she had not married, had no sons to see mutilated. It was hard to imagine the pain that a mother must endure; inconceivable that the beautiful memories could outweigh the terrible burden of having them replaced by something … else. As lonely as her life could be, she much preferred to live with gentle regrets for blessings not received.

In her street alone she knew of three women who had lost more than one son, dead or wounded horribly, during the past year. It seemed sometimes that mourning had become as much a part of their daily bread as bread itself - more so, perhaps, as the official ration dwindled to an amount that would barely keep a mouse fat. She caught herself - *no, don't think that.* Everyone had to make sacrifices these days, and given what was happening in the east - the very *near* east - it was hardly insufferable to go hungry occasionally, to make do with less. *A little want is good for the soul* as her mother used to say, and as a cobbler's daughter she'd known something about not eating much.

But the way that some people complained about food one would think there was a plot to starve the nation. The worst of them were the professional scroungers, the ones who turned up regularly, week after week, to demand their share and then complain about every kilocalorie - *there's not enough of this, or that, and why wasn't it done this way, rather than that? Look, they've given her more than me! Well, that isn't a surprise, is it? We all know how she earns her portion!* To have to listen to this never changing nonsense, like a record glued to a gramophone - it was hardly worth the trouble. If it weren't for the temporary warmth and the comfort of knowing that company could still be found (however pinched and sour), she wouldn't have bothered.

The very worst of them, casting around for fuel for their gripings, made a point of complaining about the invalid soldiers who came to eat. *Why are they here? Haven't they got families? Why should we have to look at that?* When she heard such talk she couldn't hold her tongue; it was disgraceful, the lack of charity in those who accepted it for themselves with not the slightest shame. On several occasions she'd told them so, loudly, and had the satisfaction of stemming the bile for a little while at least. She recalled that one lad - blind in one eye and hardly a left arm to speak of any more - had smiled at her and bowed slightly when she'd slapped down a particularly obnoxious *sow*. It had made her cry almost, that someone could be grateful for not being despised.

And yet she went back, again and again, for more of the same. The food *was* terrible, she couldn't pretend otherwise, but at least it filled a hole, and afterwards she always slept well as long as she remembered to put both her coats on the bed to help her only eiderdown do its job. They had all learned that they must eat whenever the opportunity offered. The coming winter was going to be a bad one; she felt it in her shoulders already, and they never lied.

Even so, she almost persuaded herself to miss that evening's sitting. The place was becoming popular, a lure for too many people in their part of Berlin. She couldn't blame them, but the previous week she'd been obliged to queue outside in the cold for almost half an hour before managing to get inside. It was hardly worth it, to eat to restore the warmth you'd lost by waiting to eat. There was half a loaf still in her apartment, and a piece of bratwurst, and a kohlrabi - enough for today and most of tomorrow too, if she ate only what the body needed. But then she recalled that this was a Friday (of course it was!) and she had Sunday to think of also. If she ate out that evening, the rest would last the weekend.

So she washed herself from a bowl in her cold kitchen, put on her best of two dresses and least worn coat, and arrived early to get a place near the head of the queue. This evening she was fortunate; as she arrived the doors were opening, and she was inside and warmed within minutes. Even better, some miracle of God or man had made the food almost palatable for once. She could taste mutton (though she couldn't find any with her spoon), and the vegetables weren't outnumbered too heavily by the coarse variety of rice that seemed to have become a German staple in the past year. Naturally, the old woman next to her had something to say about it that didn't sound complementary - a bicker about meat being withheld, or sold to the rich. She didn't bother to listen; it was background noise, like wind blowing through trees.

She stayed for the music and sang along with the rest of the room, but as always she was ready to leave before almost anyone else. She had never been a night bird, and it was a cold evening, not likely to become less so if she dawdled. Some of the others wouldn't move until the ersatz coffee had been served, but usually it was foul enough even to make *her* complain. So she was happy to say goodnight to the strange faces at her table, pull her coat closely around her body, offer just one word to an old acquaintance and step out into the street. It wasn't far, a matter of a half kilometre, and she had good legs still - seven minutes, usually, if she set herself to it.

She put her head down and leaned into the wind that wrapped around every street corner, hating what this weather did to her tired body, telling herself that it was a minute less, and then another one, and soon she'd be snug in a nearly warm bed. One couldn't rush in a blackout of course, but there was a half moon and she knew the route intimately - it was only necessary not to let a kerb surprise her or a new piece of rubble punish her shins. She concentrated on the ground, trying to make out its hazards, keeping her mind on the coming indoors, her ears deaf to anything but the breeze.

She saw his feet first, and only a moment before his hands were on her neck, lifting her almost clear of the ground with shocking force into the scaffold he had made of the rest of him. A cry of outrage rose from her stomach but halted at the blockage, strangled there like the rest of her; one of her feet twitched as if searching for a stool that had been kicked away, but it found only an ankle upon which it had no strength to make a mark or influence the course of a vanishing history. If she had a final thought there was no time to recognize it for what it was, to shape it into a penance, a plea for enduring grace, before the darkness became something else and took the sum of Gisella Mauer, spinster of Lichterfelde, into its keeping.

3

'Sit, please.'

The doctor was a well-padded gentleman to which a Party badge and expectations of unearned respect were pinned prominently. He waved his visitor to the only unoccupied chair, summoned a frown and with great precision capped and placed his gold fountain pen parallel to the desk's inlaid inkpad. The palms turned upwards, self-absolving.

'Had you remained under the care of your physicians at Potsdam, I'm sure that they could have done something considerable. But it's a matter of doing it at the right time, you see? You've allowed the tissue to harden irreparably, as I'm sure they warned it would, *in time.* As it is, I doubt there's anything to be done.'

The diagnosis concluded with a sigh, as if mild exasperation was the only prescription for the stupidity that had brought them both to this.

Fischer had hardly listened - it was all entirely expected. In any case, he had been distracted by the manicured fingers flitting in front of him, a pleasant vision of smashing them with a heavy paperweight.

'So, no chance of my becoming beautiful again?'

'None whatever. You'll take to the grave what you have now.'

Fischer began to rise from the chair. The doctor seemed hurt, a cabaret act whose audience was gathering its coats before the curtain fell.

'Wait.' He opened a drawer in his desk and removed a pair of surgical gloves. 'Your tunic and shirt.'

The patient employed both hands and arms to demonstrate a point. Broad fingers prodded an area of burn tissue suspiciously, as if a cut of dog was offered as prime pork.

'There's suppleness here. What's your regime?'

Reluctantly flattered, Fischer told him about the weights and pulleys he had somehow wedged into his tiny rooms, the hour each evening he devoted to increasing his wasted muscles' strength. It was a tiresome, noisy routine, but had bothered no one since the elderly Shultz sisters, his neighbours in the apartment immediately below, had spiced a supper with rat poison some months earlier. At the time he'd prayed his exertions hadn't hastened them out of the world, but Frau Traugott had assured him that the act had been looming since Passchendaele, where their husbands had lost an argument with the Tommies over the matter of a trench. It was probably the shrinking ration allowance and no dentists, she told him; there was always a final straw with that sort of thing.

The doctor nodded as he listened. 'Your back flexes fully? Is there restriction?'

'For anything I have the chance to do at my age, it works.'

'Throat and lungs?

'Adequate. I no longer smoke, but winters are … interesting.'

'I see.' Doctors always said it as though they meant it, but Fischer doubted that this one had ever inhaled razor blades, which would be roughly equivalent.

'Put on your clothes, please.'

A brief note was made in a very slim file as the patient dressed. It didn't seem to comprise anything as substantial as a case history.

'May I ask why I'm here?'

'Mm?' The doctor looked up. The frown that kept his heavily pomaded hairline in place deepened slightly. Forgetting himself, Fischer almost shrugged.

'Your time must be rather pressed at the moment, if *moment* isn't putting it too generously. I haven't been examined since the summer of 1943. Why was I summoned today?'

'This is for a Potsdam colleague. He was curious about how you'd progressed, though *that* …' the file closed with a slap … 'is certainly too generous a term.'

'Could I be of interest still?'

It was an insolent question, but Fischer, dragged to a meaningless appointment, was in a mood to be difficult. No German physician could possibly find his wounds *interesting* as the tragic, bloody year staggered to its close. From every horizon, the toll of disasters compounded remorselessly. In the west, the Americans and British were poised to push their large, lavishly provided armies across the Belgian border into what remained of the Reich's industrial heartland. To the east, Romania, Bulgaria, Hungary and half of Slovakia were gone, drowned beneath the advancing wave of Soviet shock armies, and a slice of the ancient *ostmark*, East Prussia, had been violated by the Red boot (if *violated* was how a rapist felt when one pressed up his own arse). To the north, plucky little

Finland had got herself plucked, begged a quick armistice to keep out the Ivans and evicted her former allies. And then there was the happy south, Italy, where National Socialism held on still to what would make a fine city-state for a prince with no great territorial ambitions. With all of that good fortune falling like a light spring shower there had to be mutilations enough for a million skin specialists.

Herr Plump Party Doctor returned the half-shrug. 'You were one of his first. And significant, apparently.'

'Why?'

'You really shouldn't have lived.'

Fischer departed the lazarett through its main gate, a pointlessly correct manoeuvre given that the perimeter fence had been removed some months earlier for recycling as armour. Distracted still by the day's strangeness he went to the s-bahn station at Alt-Reinickendorf and availed himself of the age's least dependable mode of urban transport. Bomb damage at the next station, Schönholz, kept his train halted for almost an hour before it was waved through – and then raced – by a *fremdarbeiter* work gang. Further clearances interrupted the journey between or at almost every subsequent station, and by the time they reached Orienenburgerstrasse mounting blood pressure had lit up the flayed portion of his face. He disembarked hastily to walk the remaining kilometre to his office.

Dislocation plays tricks with memory, and he found it difficult to recall a time when Mitte's disordered streets and gaping facades had been otherwise, when Berliners hadn't been surrounded by reminders of how sowing becomes reaping. It was wiser to let the mind disengage from the visible evidence until things altered for the better, but his eye was drawn to all of it still - the ruins that had become reliable landmarks, the new wounds that rouged the familiar grey, the hunched figures negotiating the many obstacles, searching for fragments of their former lives. It was a near-medieval spectacle, compelling and poignant, framing the wonderful jest of the Air Ministry, his workplace. Sixteen months earlier the building had lost just eight windows during the RAF's first big raid on the city. Later, at the height of the Battle of Berlin (as her citizens optimistically recalled it), a nine-hundred-bomber onslaught had managed to blow out a further dozen or so and scour a tiny section of the building's pretty granite facing on its Leipzigerstrasse flank. But that was as close as the war had come to Wilhelmstrasse 97. The building in which men had devised the modern methods of aerial destruction and introduced them to Europe's non-German cities continued to taunt the Allies with broad, undamaged roofs that were clearly visible at ten thousand metres. Common sense said that it couldn't last - that at some point a British or American aircrew (no doubt aiming for something else) would drop their load into one of the Ministry's inner courtyards and terror bombing would have come full circle. But the longer the moment deferred itself the more it seemed to be suspended indefinitely. Several men of Fischer's department with no family in the city had begun to spend nights here on a number of flimsy pretexts - a report that needed a final tweaking, an inconveniently late meeting, a strategically vital card game. He couldn't blame them; the one time he had done it himself, trapped during a heavy air raid, he had enjoyed several hours' uninterrupted sleep under his desk. The subconscious had felt itself secure.

At the Ministry's main entrance he momentarily forgot his rank and nodded at one of the two elderly guards who had come half to attention at his approach. The man gave him a slight shrug and a slow, deliberate wink as he passed by, code that conveyed more than an hour's worth of acute observation on things and where they were going.

The echo of his heels traversing the massive reception hall carried like birdsong in a foggy dawn. The other half of the jest was that this huge edifice was more than half empty, and, like most of the men who guarded it, a shadow of its times. Back when Germany had been thrusting out one foot in front of the other, a dozen sweeping projects had buzzed around the corridors on any particular day, demanding to be actioned the previous day at the latest. *These* days it was difficult to arrange a collision in the same corridors. On the third floor he passed several rooms, each large enough to house an entire department; all were empty, their former occupants reassigned or fled to OKW's subterranean headquarters at Zossen. One door still bore the name of his old unit, *Kriegsberichter der Luftwaffe* (or 'Lie Division'), an honourable institution devoted to gross improbity, a child of the days when there had been good news to manipulate. A counter-intelligence unit - *LuftGeheimStelle* IIb - had risen from its grave, and the Liars had been redeployed from misleading their own people about the enemy's weaknesses to deceiving the enemy about Germany's.

He entered his new department. A few colleagues - his subordinates - looked up from their work and nodded. No one stood or saluted. Their commanding officer's door was locked.

'Is Karl around?'

At the nearest desk, Hauptgefreiter Detmar Reincke dragged his attention from a report he was heavily altering with his only hand (the left, which wielded a pen like a butcher's cleaver and much to the same effect), smiled broadly and clicked his heels together under the desk. 'He's being briefed at Prince-Albrecht-Strasse, *Herr Major*.'

'Idiot.'

He should have remembered - it wasn't as though Krohne complained about anything else for days before shuffling off to that particular meeting. He released the doorknob and went into his own office, a small, unventilated internal room lacking any natural light. From a desk drawer he removed a cigarette, lit it and immediately stubbed it out in an ashtray - a ritual, though unintentional. His fingers spent a few moments pushing papers away from where his eyes might accidentally light upon their content and then he sat, taking comfort from the press of his walls, and tried to order his scattered thoughts.

His head had ached since before dawn. A futile doctor's appointment and near-stationary rolling stock had added to the pain, but the principal torque was applied by the return of an old problem and how he had allowed himself to think it gone. *Unwise* didn't quite do him justice; having disobeyed the cardinal rule of war by looking for trouble and then thinking himself blessed for having survived it his sin was to be at least doubly stupid. Some men – Generals, top Party officials – seemed able to bear that affliction bravely, but Otto Fischer was a nobody, with no friends of rank, no ability to pass unnoticed (how could someone with half a face be faceless?) and no store of native luck. What remained, what any defenceless creature with sense seized upon, was camouflage.

For fifteen months now it had seemed to work. He had avoided the company of all but his workmates and those with whom he lived, allowed no part of his work to be notably bad or good, invited neither praise nor censure and kept a sharp eye upon every horizon, waiting for incoming ordnance. When it hadn't arrived, anxiety had eased gradually to the point at which, on some days, he almost congratulated himself upon his success. He wondered now if von Paulus had done the same as he hurtled towards Stalingrad under unbroken sunshine.

His hand was considering the prospect of reaching for another cigarette when the door crashed open, which at least deferred the problem of dealing with the Problem.

'Unbelievable! Really, unbeliev …'

'Hello, Karl.'

Breathless, Karl Krohne paused in the doorway, his arms twitching like a seized windmill in a squall. The oberst's uniform that wore him was almost new but still he managed to look unkempt, as profoundly out of place in it as former newspapermen generally were in martial attire. His good eye rose to the ceiling for a moment and then fixed beseechingly upon Fischer; the glass one, as always, stared indifferently to one side.

'Otto, I must report that we're fucked! Penetrated earnestly! Taken from behind like bathhouse towel boys …'

The small desk, resenting a vigorous kick, released its pile of files to the floor.

'Ach! Sorry …'

'Never mind, Karl, leave them. What is it?'

'I've been at Prince-Albrecht-Strasse. '

'Yes.'

'I met with Kaltenbrunner.'

'Yes.'

There was a point to this, but its magnitude seemed to have overwhelmed Fischer's boss. His mouth, a reliably limber instrument usually, made several attempts before the words poured out.

'The bastard's started to wear one! They all have! It's mad, the end!'

'Wearing what, Karl? Please, calm yourself.'

'Real soldiers' uniforms! Everyone at RSHA who doesn't mop up the blood and piss has signed for fighting Generals' tabs! You know why, don't you?'

'Yes, of course.'

'Covering their arses for when it all topples!'

'Yes.'

For months now it had been known the length and generous breadth of Wilhelmstrasse - surely, this couldn't be the news?

Krohne took a deep breath but nothing more emerged. His attention had turned to the floor, a motionless reverie upon the threadbare carpet's faint pattern and stains. It was a habit, a nervous reaction; Fischer assumed it to be a legacy of his newspaper days, a mental tool to search new depths to which to sink a storyline or test the closest shave an outright lie could bear.

'Karl …?'

'I was late, fortunately. Kaltenbrunner was into the agenda already, smirking around the table, flashing his new Knight's Cross, handing out the good news about a fresh batch of July plotters he and Müller have dangled recently. And then he launched into some Amt VI shit about growing social unrest - food riots - in the Home Counties! I didn't want to be the one to say anything, naturally. But the rest of them just sat on their hands, mouths open, so it was left to *me* to pull the Obergruppenführer's head out of fucking Croydon and ask the question that everyone had come to hear the answer to.'

'And?'

'There isn't one.'

For a moment Fischer assumed that Krohne was joking, even if his face said differently. 'I'm sorry?'

'As of today, there isn't one. Nor is anyone working on it, apparently. The Führer waves away the subject every time someone locates his balls and raises it. His own balls I mean, not the Führer's. He says it won't be necessary, once the new divisions get into the line.'

'But…?'

'Why *should* there be one? I mean, really, the Ivans are far, far away on the Vistula, with only two million men, ten thousand tanks and God knows how many aircraft, ready to fall on us like the Assyrians upon that place we mustn't mention. Why *should* we be thinking about plans to defend Berlin?'

'Kaltenbrunner really said it?'

Krohne looked nervously at his subordinate. 'You'd think he'd know, wouldn't you? It couldn't be that they're planning something tremendous and he hasn't been told?'

'The head of almost every surviving intelligence service? Is it likely, Karl?'

The Russians were coming for Berlin. It was evident to anyone who cared to think about it, and what stood in their way - whatever the Führer said or believed - wasn't capable of stopping them. If

Stalin didn't secure the capital his boys couldn't push on westwards to keep the Americans and the British on the Rhine, so he was going to do anything, sacrifice anything, to make it happen. Like gravity this was an irrefutable truth, and even the meanest cadet knew what was needed. Germany had to let go of the slightest ambition and make time to settle with people they could deal with, rather than wait for those they'd be massacred by.

But no one was being allowed to plan the defence of Berlin. It was inconceivable and yet Fischer could have scripted the routine from instinct. Their fellow with the balls, summoning an uncommon degree of courage, would have urged that proper preparations be put in hand immediately. With a single exception, those within earshot of this excellent suggestion would have concurred heartily but remained silent, waiting for another foam-flecked prediction of stabilization, turnaround and miraculous victory snatched from seemingly certain defeat. This they would have applauded with well-practised enthusiasm, perhaps even experienced a brief, unreasoning optimism about the coming catastrophe. Like all Germans, Fischer knew how persuasive the man could be. When one finds oneself in a pit with an orator, hopes of no pit can be raised considerably.

The carpet was getting Krohne's attention once more. The pause seemed charged, as though nudging Fischer to get on with it. He felt a slight pang, the guilt of applying necessary pain.

'Karl?'

'Mm?'

'He's back.'

'What?'

'Freddie's back. He's here, in Berlin.'

Krohne closed his real and glass eyes and clutched his head. Dispassionately, Fischer noted the slight but immediate lifting of his own spirits as he dispensed the bad news.

'Oh, for Christ's … we need a drink!'

4

For Fischer, Krohne and their colleagues, the sort of drink a man *needed* was the sharpest reminder of how dark life had become. Three months earlier, on the afternoon that the death of the Lie Division had been announced, its orphaned staff had fled to their beloved *Silver Birch* (a small establishment defacing an alley off Potsdamer Platz) and to what had been more than one sort of farewell. Later that evening, after the Liars had staggered away to barracks or a desk-bed at the office, the old bar had departed also, redeployed skywards with several adjacent properties and their unfortunate night-watchmen - proof, if it were needed, that the British had no more soul than they had functioning bombsights.

Unlike the seemingly immortal Air Ministry, the *Birch* had been the proverbial sparrow, flitting through the banqueting hall from one window to another. It had given a mere three centuries' service, enticing and poisoning the livers of Prussian peasants, Huguenots, Jews, cuirassiers, would-be revolutionaries and, once Berlin expanded beyond her customs walls, the urban Undiscriminating also. All the while the German nation had grown larger, mightier, more organized, disciplined and joyless, but the *Birch* had stuck to its mission of soothing wounds and curating a vast corpus of Middle European philosophy that abstainers mistook for drunken bullshit. It had been a womb - comfortably shabby, warm and forgiving, a place where timepieces halted themselves politely as their owners shuffled through its front door to hide from where the world was going.

There was a distance in Krohne's eye, and Fischer assumed that he was back at the bar of the *Birch*, buying yet another round for his parched boys, calming the foul language, trying to stem Freddie Holleman's flow for just long enough to ask what his poison was, making a commander's strategic decision to write off the rest of the working day (this at mid-afternoon, usually). It was like watching an old man recall his first night with two girls, and all that Fischer could offer to ease the pain was 'What about *Tomi's*?'

Krohne sighed, resigned to it. *Tomi* - Thomas Beitner, unterfeldwebel, XIV Reserve Corps - had been fertilising ground somewhere east of Verdun for almost thirty years now, but his anima lived on in his bar, a few doors from the Wertheim Store's rear façade on Voss-Strasse. Unlike the *Birch*, *Tomi's* quality of seediness was more straightforwardly of its time, but as the only remaining venue in the district with any proper sense of its role it drew the ex-Liars like the last corpse on the field draws flies. Regrettably, it enjoyed much the worst location in central Berlin. To get there from the Air Ministry a prospective customer had to walk past almost every window in Wilhemstrasse that outranked him, so the real enemy knew exactly when he signed off for the day. Worse, its entrance was directly opposite the New Chancellery, so if the wrong curtain twitched at an unfortunate moment the Man himself could mark the truant's card. The trick, as Krohne had pointed out (had actually rehearsed with his subordinates, up and down their third floor corridor), was to frown while walking purposefully between *here* and *there*, to give an impression of the kind of urgent official business that hadn't time to explain itself even to those whose business it was to know the business of everyone else.

The two officers deployed this tactic briskly as they departed the Ministry and had time only to make a start upon the Problem before they were in Voss-Strasse. Tomi's widow, the establishment's proprietor, manager and sole employee, was unlocking the door at the moment that Fischer's hand reached for it.

'Gentlemen.'

'Hello, Margret.'

She followed them to the coppered counter, placed her generous rear behind it and pronounced once more upon the horrors of a protracted war.

'No beer.'

Krohne smiled sadly, trying to taste the word. 'Two special cocktails, Margret.'

She poured them slowly from an earthenware bottle. Her only product was fermented just metres from where it was served - a foul concoction, possibly poisonous if taken in quantity (though both men had seen enough recoveries from apparent comas to suggest she was at least trying to keep the mix pure). For a few weeks after the last of the Berliner Weisse disappeared, residual supplies of cherry syrup had made the brew almost palatable. Now, only need and iron will kept it down.

Krohne gasped at the first mouthful. Eyes watering, his free hand gripped the bar tightly.

'So - *why*?'

Having taken a tiny sip from his own glass Fischer was unable to reply immediately. He swallowed hard. 'Why would you think?'

'The twins?'

They paused and glanced at their hostess, but it was instinct rather than caution. Frau Beitner was equally oblivious to gossip, speculation and high treason, not so much discreet as taciturn in the manner that rocks attempted to be. Her more maudlin clientele assumed this to be a symptom of the abiding grief she felt for her vanished Tomi; others, the mark of an earlier career as matron at the Charité, where generations of angry infections had been soothed by her cold, uncaring stare. A self-proclaimed expert upon the female condition, Krohne declared her to be an anti-muse, an Aryan *Euterpe* for men whose sense of discretion had been chemically excised. Whatever the true nature of her condition, no one believed that heated tongs would ever drag out anything as voluble as a sentence.

'A neighbour who lives somewhere on the lake, saw the boys gathering wood and called the local *Hitler Jugend* camp as soon as she found a telephone. Freddie had their fake birth certificates ready - they're both a few months short of age yet, so they couldn't be taken. The bastards blustered and said they'd send a *Deutsche Jungvolk* colleague around the next day, but they moved smartly. Freddie went into Lübben to try to arrange some new accommodation. By the time he got back to the lake house *DJ* had come, gone and taken the twins. Kristin's insane with worry, naturally. He swore to her he'd find them, so here he is.'

'Where?'

'At my lodgings. I said he could stay for as long as he needs. It's safe enough, really. My landlady talks constantly but takes care to say nothing.'

Krohne shook his head. 'It's shit, but is he surprised? Is there a *pimpf* in Germany who isn't being trained up to ride a bike and handle a panzerfaust?'

'But you know what Freddie thinks of his lads. He says he's been out of his mind about them since Normandy.'

The fate of 12th SS Panzer Division *Hitlerjugend* was engraved upon every German parent's soul. Pulled out of the line after Falaise the previous August, its fighting strength had fallen from twenty thousands to about half that, the survivors battle-hardened types who couldn't have grown a beard between them. And these were lads of the fortunate class of '43, who had been given proper training and time for their sacs to fill before being deployed. It wasn't hard to understand what could torment a father to stupidity.

Krohne slammed down his glass. 'Bloody Freddie! He's more pain than a wire enema.'

Holleman had been disappeared from Berlin because Fischer had urged it upon men he could trust - men who had willingly placed themselves squarely in the path of an execution should it ever be discovered. For more than a year now they had diverted forged ration cards and Holleman's thoroughly unearned Luftwaffe pay, kept his family alive and safe for no better motive than camaraderie. Krohne was probably thinking the same thing as Fischer – that he should have had the sense to remain disappeared, to have done what German parents did when the Regime came calling to take their children, which was to light a candle and open their mouths only to pray.

Fischer stared into what remained of his poison. 'Where would we start looking? A KLV? An Adolph Hitler School? God forbid, a *volkssturm* unit? And where? How can we start a search without drawing attention to it?'

'Wouldn't the twins be kept in the local *kreis*? That's Lübben, surely? Why is Freddie in Berlin?'

'He doesn't know anyone down there. Here's the only place he can make a start on asking questions.'

'Yes, but ask *who*, and *what*?'

'I doubt that he's thought that far. If he has a plan it doesn't go beyond marching into the Youth Leadership offices and burying something in Reichsjugendführer Axmann's skull.'

Krohne caught Frau Beitner's eye. 'Two more please, Margret. Well, he only has to wait and his kids will be in Berlin anyway. We're all going to be squeezed into a perimeter that doesn't exist, that there isn't a *plan* for. Christ!'

'Who do you know at *Hitler Jugend*?'

Krohne scratched his chin. 'I don't *know* anyone. I know *of* a few people. I once shared a dinner table with Axel Neidermann - he heads Service PR, their Press and Propaganda Amt.'

'Approachable?'

'Hard to say; he was rather surrounded by his good opinion of himself. I think he edited and then closed down two small newspapers in Dortmund before the war, so he's risen pretty far. I recall that he preferred talking to listening.'

To Fischer he didn't sound like promising material, but the Reich's cloths were cut perversely. The nation's supreme leader and prospective deity was a disappointed artist, its most feared security agency the fiefdom of a failed chicken farmer, its air force the plaything of a man who had married money in order to fund a morphine habit. If Herr Neidermann had seized his bootstraps and joined the company of the spectacularly resurrected he knew at least how to work the system. In any case, a former newspaperman would possess one precious quality - with curiosity running through his veins he might be willing to overlook a degree of the same in others.

Reluctantly, Fischer allowed an idea to surface. '*Die Adler*.'

'What?'

I could be writing an article on *Hitler Jugend*'s flak training programme, for *Die Adler*. I still have my Lie Division ID. I doubt that news of its demise has reached Lothringerstrasse.'

'Would that be plausible? It was news from the Front we mutilated.'

'Jesus, Karl. What *isn't* the Front these days?'

Krohne nodded slowly. 'It would get you into the building at least. I could confirm the story, if they bothered to check. How will you bring up the matter of the twins?'

'I won't, but a tour of the place should get me talking to other people. It might keep Freddie from going mad if he knows we're doing something.'

Krohne smiled down at his feet. 'Can you imagine him going after Axmann? A one-legged murderer and a one-armed victim? Like novelty hour at the Roman Circus.'

Fischer, already working the dialogue in his head, said nothing. After a few moments' forlorn contemplation his boss sighed and pushed away his glass. 'Back to work then.'

They should have moved, made an effort at least. Their job was one that most men in uniform would have given both arms to secure - undemanding, as safe as any could be these days, enjoying a prestigious address that suggested *LuftGeheimStelle* IIb was as vital to the war effort as an intact ball-bearing factory. But Freddie Holleman's shadow was cast too long today to pretend any enthusiasm for their pretend work. Krohne tried out his sigh once more. 'Margret, some water in the next one, please.'

It was almost dusk when they emerged on to Voss-Strasse. Across the road the New Chancellery was blacked out already, but slivers of stray light bled from high windows the entire length of the Marble Gallery. Another vital meeting would be coalescing inside to discuss measures to be taken after the fact of a new reverse, to deploy non-existent army groups to smash the enemy fronts, reverse the tide and somehow put the *raum* back into *lebensraum*. It was something about which any German could be proud. The Americans might have the most and biggest of everything, but Reischsminister Speer's masterpiece had long since supplanted Paramount Studios as the world's premier home of romantic fiction.

Ignoring the half-regiment of heavily armed SS troops that guarded the columned entrance, they kept to the opposite pavement, heads down, voices low. It was colder now and they were coatless, but the more obvious ravages of Frau Beitner's special cocktail demanded to be walked off. From the corner of Wilhelmstrasse they turned north rather than return directly to the Ministry.

They paused briefly by the railings of the far more modest Old Chancellery. Krohne lit a cigarette and gave some more attention to his boots. Nearby, two more SS guards set their chins aggressively, tilted their heads slightly higher and glared furiously at some point in the darkening sky.

Fischer watched his boss play with his smoke, preoccupied still. It was Freddie Holleman of course, but also the Berlin thing and what it meant. For two months now they had lived in a deadly pause, a half-concussed daze inflicted by the previous summer's unremitting disasters. A very few Germans could convince themselves that something worse wasn't coming; for the rest, the looming *next* was concentrating minds wonderfully upon what mattered, what really mattered.

'What about Magda and Peter? You're getting them out of Berlin? To her parents?'

Krohne shrugged hopelessly. 'She won't go. She agrees we should send Peter for Christmas and have her mother keep him there. But if I'm staying …'

'You've told her she's being stupid?'

'I've told her more than that, but she cries every time I start. What else can I say? You know how it is - you live twenty years together and it's like trying to detach a major organ.'

With the greatest will, Fischer couldn't say he knew how it was. The sum of his own marriage comprised three years of undeclared war, a coldly efficient separation and then a loss of contact so profound that the relationship might have been a fleeting hallucination. It had been entirely her fault and his, too; they had married as many do, because not marrying seemed other than in the spirit of things, and they had paid the slow, hurtful price to the last pfennig. He tried not to think about it too much either way. It was why he had avoided the subject until now.

He had often made a start on envying Karl Krohne's better fortune - his rutting bull's predilections and the beautiful wife who blinded herself to them, a woman with family in blessed Bamberg, its pretty roofs and nineteen breweries all as yet magically untouched by this war. He was certain that if he had a family still he would have wanted them in a place like Bamberg, or Buenos Aires. But that would have been a different world and a much different Fischer, both of them projections upon a canvas of fanciful contentments. It was a part of the human condition, he imagined - to wish for something *else* without ever comprehending the price of it.

From three directions sirens blared like a chorus of demented *erlkings*. Krohne dragged deeply upon his cigarette and scanned the skies for an enemy that was hundreds of miles away still. There was good, low cloud cover, a perfect opportunity for the RAF to practise its blanket technique upon the suburbs while the intended objects of its ardent attention carried on their work unmolested. It was a bloody waste of time, men and aircraft, but the equation was so one-sided now that it hardly mattered. The war itself was over; the Allies had only to continue going through the motions until the Reich consumed its very last drop of synthetic oil and then it would be a matter of setting out a table for the surrender ceremony. But it was Germany's curse and the Fuhrer's last, desperate hope - that the enemy were no longer fighting for victory, only the biggest share of the corpse.

5

Hans Lutze had seen some things in his life, as he was known to say often. For the price of a drink and sometimes for free he would tell you about his time in the trenches and what he had seen there - the rats, the filth, the comrades blown inside out, the collapsing mud walls, the pieces of horses everywhere (they made for good soup, at least), the remorseless, mind-twisting horror of a world governed by the high explosive shell. It was a hideous canvas, upon which nothing was executed in broad, impressionist strokes. Hans was a details man, who believed his audiences required the gratification of a forensic survey.

If he was of a mind and mood he might talk about times since, of what he had witnessed in early 1919 during the Battle of Berlin, when hastily re-mobilized squads of veterans had fought street by street to retake the city from the Reds. He had been one of them - ragged, confused, still stunned by the way things had gone and not entirely sure of what it was exactly that he was now fighting for. But like many of his comrades from the old regiment he had picked up a rifle, taken a handful of ammunition and been happy to forget that the new enemy were Germans also. It had been a bloody, treacherous time, emptied of pity, when quarter was often sought but rarely offered (as everyone knew - and he made the point remorselessly - there was nothing like a civil war for bringing out the least civil side of men); Hans had fought hard, buried friends, learned to treat bricks as mattresses, and, when ordered, lined prisoners against a convenient wall and put them out of their misguided political principles. It all made for a good story, but he had to choose his audience carefully before telling it. You didn't always know who had stood where back then.

Most often, Hans would talk about the things he had seen in his years as a uniformed policeman in the suburbs. These were not the generally acknowledged attractions and idiosyncrasies of southwest Berlin, obviously. Anyone interested in the city's topography could, as far as he was concerned, buy the guidebook if such a thing existed still. No, Hans preferred to divert his listeners with details of a particular genre - the murder victim *in situ*. With a weary, slightly wondering shake of his head, and a breathless tone that conveyed slightly more than the full horror of the incidents in question, he would describe the preferred *modus operandi* of the less well-balanced members of Berlin's criminal fraternities - the stabbings, the bludgeonings, the mutilations both frenzied and winsome and the sexual embellishments that sometimes seasoned the main event. Yes, he had seen it all and even things he couldn't speak of, not with ladies in the room …

Hans admired the sound of his own voice tremendously, but he was aware that it held a finite attraction for those who had heard his stories several times. Some of his drinking mates had even tried to change the subject when he embarked upon a particularly familiar anecdote, as if their own observations upon the present war and its attendant inconveniences could be as interesting as his monologues. So he was always glad to broaden his repertory, to dish up something new and untested for the palates of friends, acquaintances and strangers alike. Sometimes he poached tales from other jurisdictions, as in the previous year when a brief but gratifying rash of rapes had scared most of Karlshorst and Adlershof into early nights to bed (though not remotely involved in the investigation, Hans had illicitly researched every absorbing detail from the records of victims' examinations and related them with considerable elaboration, ensuring that for almost a week's worth of evenings there had been hardly any interruptions). At other, leaner times he artfully re-blended details from several of his old stories and presented the distilled result as an as-yet untold tale, relying upon his friends' poor memories and poorer attention to keep the free drinks coming. It wasn't always easy to keep the spotlight directly overhead, and someone less confident of his power to fascinate than Hans might sometimes have been tempted to let it drift elsewhere, even at the cost of having to buy his own drinks.

But this evening - a pleasant, unseasonably warm evening – there was a definite spring in his heavy tread, a slight dancing lilt to his habitual lumber as he walked the half kilometre from his Schönberg home to the café that had replaced their bombed-out bar as the lads' clubroom. He carried with him a gem, a great, terrible secret that would not only make his mates' remaining hair stand on end but dance electrically when they heard that *he*, Hans Lutze, had discovered both the crime and its dark meaning! Most exquisitely, he could in all honesty refer to the victim as merely the latest of several, almost certainly the prey of a method murderer, a beast, a *Golem* (though of course no one used that term any more). A few hours of gruesome elucidation loomed, and for once Hans could be absolutely sure that no one would speak except to ask things that would keep their attention wholly upon him.

Three nights past he had been on duty, the Lichterfelde beat, with one of the new, old idiots (Hans himself was almost sixty, but regarded the recent civilian drafts as a geriatric insult to his profession). Like everyone else at the station they had been told to pay particular attention to the streets around the Botanical Gardens following the recent murders. The precise details of these atrocities had eluded Hans to date (though he had done his best to pin them down and had been quite chasing one particular lead), but at least the business offered a prospect of more excitement than did their usual perambulations. His enthusiasm hadn't last long, however. He and the shuffler - a morose individual from whom a name had been dragged and little more - had made only two circuits of the Gardens when light rain became something worse. As far as Hans was concerned, that should have been it for the night, murders notwithstanding. But Vinegar Face started whining about their duty, and, rather than give him an excuse to tell tales at the station, Hans allowed himself to be persuaded into a further lap.

Her feet protruded from beneath a rhododendron bush, metres from the road. They had only small torches to light their way, so it was chance alone that illuminated the crime scene on their third circuit. They might have made a dozen more and seen nothing, but there she was, captured like a photograph in the random sweep - about sixty years old, strangled, her skirt around her waist and undergarments covering her upper face. Hans felt for a pulse and found none, but her skin wasn't entirely cold, so almost certainly she had died while they had been at some other point on their evening's perambulations.

By the time the *kripos* arrived Hans was hardly able to contain his excitement. Naturally, he pulled rank on his partner, made the report from his expert perspective and offered to help search the area with them. They refused as he had expected, but the disappointment was no less intense for that. It almost spoiled the thrill of the evening, and even now he might have thought the less of it had he not made his brilliant discovery the following day. In almost every hour since then he had been imagining his friends' faces and what they would say when he told them - Christ, when he told them that *they* were the first to hear of it! Of course, regulations were perfectly clear, and Hans was aware that he should have reported his findings immediately to the duty officer at Steglitz station. But the temptation to astonish and shock his friends, to excite their admiration for his policing skills, was far too great to resist. Other men might have worried about such a serious dereliction of duty, but Hans merely added it to the sum of his many others. After all, he was a necessary man, an experienced police officer in an underprovided city, and his superiors had no way of knowing *when* he had stumbled upon his little jewel of information.

This evening he was far ahead of his usual time. The café was nearly empty, still about its afternoon trade, and none of the lads had arrived yet. That was fine - another half-hour of sweet anticipation of their shock and titillated horror wouldn't kill him; in fact, it gave him time to consider and refine the casual manner in which he would drop his astonishing revelation into their laps. The girl who managed the place started pouring a *muckefucke* for him without being asked, and as his cup filled he had the tremendous idea that he should first practice the story upon her. She was very attractive - though much too young for his tastes - and her astonishment and revulsion would be just the thing to pamper a man's sense of importance.

But she was already in a conversation with a couple of off-duty wardens, and Hans was hardly able to grab her attention and give her the necessary preamble (hinting delicately at some awful, imminent revelation) before she wandered back to them. It was frustrating, and he had to add to his story piecemeal over the next few minutes as she moved around the counter, serving new customers. He much preferred attention to be undivided, especially when he had such a story to tell, but he kept at it doggedly, knowing that once she got the proper gist she would be all ears and pert, heaving breasts.

The manageress - Mona - did her best to stay away from the old man, but he was notoriously persistent. He was off on one of his stories about killings - at least, the odd word she caught suggested that it was the usual, foul business. She wasn't interested, naturally. There was more than enough news of death to go around right now, and like everyone else she found his fascination with the state both morbid and boring. So she kept her attention on what the two wardens were saying about the fires in Dahlem the week before, and didn't notice when one of her other regulars went up to the old sod and started talking to him. Nor did she see them leave the café together a few minutes later, the one holding the other's arm companionably.

When Hans' friends arrived a little later she was able to say that he had been in, but that was all. They were mildly surprised (though not displeased), and made do as best they could without him. They did the same the following night, and the one after that; weeks passed, and gradually Hans acquired the sort of pre-eminence in their attentions that he had strained for years to attain. In time, when things settled down once more and the Americans permitted their cafe to re-open, they came to find the memory of Hans far more congenial than ever they had his company. And memory being what it is, they convinced themselves that they almost missed the days when he sat in his usual corner, boring them all to death and resurrection with the same gruesome stories, over and over.

6

In the sitting room of Jonas-Strasse 17, Friedrich Holleman perched on a stool, his head a minor acoustic baffle to the sisters' seemingly endless prattle. The smile on his face was not so much fixed as cemented in place. On the small dining table behind them three well-wiped plates awaited the sink. The conversation - two irreconcilable opinions expressed as fact - was dwelling upon the best way to cook horse, and whether Frau Traugott had quite managed it.

When Fischer entered Holleman's smile remained where it was, but the eyebrows rose in desperate, silent enquiry. They received a small nod for their trouble, the sort that tries to encourage without raising too many hopes.

'You're late, Herr Fischer.'

Else Ostermann admonished him with the frown that her late husband had taken up fishing to avoid. Within hours of arriving in Berlin she had noticed that her sister's home lacked domestic discipline, displayed a *laxness* that didn't sit well with what she considered to be a proper landlady-tenant relationship. As a dutiful sibling, one who spoke as she found, she considered it only right that she comment upon symptoms of this malaise whenever she noticed them. Frau Traugott treated such naked plays for ascendancy as they deserved, and variously expressed her displeasure by suffering them dumbly in the manner of a kicked mule or by contradicting whatever Else said. This latest thrust she played dismissively.

'No, it's precisely his usual time. Would you like your supper here, Herr Fischer? Or perhaps in your room?'

Suspecting horse or worse, Fischer told her that he had eaten at the ministry and handed over a greasy paper package containing four small *blutwurst*. He had calculated that the distraction would get him and Holleman out of the room and upstairs without the customary interrogation on the day's rumours and events, a daily ritual whose consequences he had rightly come to fear.

Holleman's leg made the two flights a slow process, though he was the impatient one.

'So...?'

Fischer closed the door to his apartment and lit the gas lamp. He noticed with concern that both the level in the Slivovitz bottle and the bottle itself remained where they had been that morning. Abstinence, in Holleman, was a particularly accurate indicator of a mood to climb walls.

'I'm going to get into the Reich Youth Leadership headquarters: an interview with someone. I'll try to find out how we can make a start. But Freddie, it's difficult. With the *volkssturm* units being trained up …'

Even if someone at Lothringerstrasse was willing to oblige Fischer and could open a file that told him where they were holding the twins, the information might be useless. The whole system was in flux, every resource sucked into replacing what they were losing on the front lines. Whatever a file said, the boys could be anywhere - a training camp, a school, a depot in Breslau being shown the front from the back end of a rusty Karabiner '86. The longer the search went on, the less chance there would be of narrowing it.

Holleman's eyes were red, haunted by a prospect he had been feeding and watering in his dark hours.

'Otto, I don't care, I'll do anything. I'll kiss every arse inside the *Zollmauer* if I have to. We have to get them out of there before … you know what happens to these kids. Six months, and they're strangers to everyone except the Party.'

'Shh, Freddie. Decent lads wear the uniform, too.'

'Not for long, and then they're something else. All that's good in a boy gets bullied, kicked or indoctrinated to death, or it dies at the Front. You think I'll let Franz and Ulrich end up like that?'

There was an art to arguing an impossible case, and Fischer hadn't acquired it. Parents with children in the *HJ* were strongly discouraged from trying to contact them while on 'deployment', so the mechanism was built to confound the effort. Inter-camp transfers were not notified until some weeks after the event, correspondence was examined (and, if necessary, censored or destroyed), telephone calls to or from home were strictly forbidden absent a death in the family, and boys who chose not to take their full leave allowance gained leadership credits. It was all a fairly big hint, and anyone who ignored it was going to attract a deal of attention.

Holleman turned and threw a punch at the apartment's wall, pulling it at the last moment to preserve his fist and the plasterwork. '*Shit!* Can we go out? Walk for a while?'

Fischer's mouth opened to make the sensible reply, but he sensed an imminent detonation in a man who had never practised suppressing his feelings. The firm refusal somehow became a shrug, a finger to the lips.

They departed the house like burglars, emerging from Jonas-Strasse's northern end, walking at Holleman's awkward, faltering pace towards Beussel and the rail yards. Occasionally, a slight disjoining of shadows and the tap of heels on unbroken ground hinted at a passer-by, a ghost, going about some business that even the blackout couldn't defer; but for the most part they could have imagined themselves translated to the centre of a vast, empty stadium, like worshippers arrived much too early for one of the Führer's epic rants.

On Oldenburgerstrasse Holleman paused for a moment, propping himself against a wall to adjust the straps on his metal leg. Fischer, his voice church-low, asked about the Spreewald. In more than a year's worth of idle moments he had imagined the Holleman family's desert island existence barely a hundred kilometres from the heart of the Reich, and wondered how it could be done. Almost every month he'd expected to hear the worst - that the remorseless bureaucracy of National Socialism had followed like stoats through a drainpipe and dragged the fugitives back to Berlin for terminal correction. But the longer they remained in their state of unbeing the more natural it had come to seem that they might get away with it. It was a delusion of course, even if obvious mistakes had been avoided and files expertly misplaced. Germany was going to win or lose the war, and either fate couldn't help but fall upon the Hollemans in the form of an official - a German, Russian or American - knocking upon their door one day, asking who the hell they might be.

Holleman shrugged. 'We stayed inside and kept the curtains drawn, to begin with. I'd brought rations, and the boys were too excited to care about not seeing too much daylight. But you can't go on like that. So Kristin and me, we talked and she was right, I couldn't wander around showing off my face and leg. We decided that once a week she should go into Lübben for food, but apart from that no towns, villages or even neighbours. Strange, it was. I taught the lads to swim, kill squirrels and mend clothes, and Kristin showed them how to cook. We camped out a lot in the woods, so they'd know what to do if …'

'And no one saw you?' Fischer couldn't believe there were parts of modern Germany where any of this could happen.

'Of course they did, it isn't the fucking Amazon! There were always walkers, and sometimes *pimpfen* on camping exercises, but we weren't bothered. The lads knew to say that they were having a short holiday with their uncle if anyone asked. Anyway, you've seen them. I don't know where they get their eyes and hair, but anything *that* Aryan in the woods is taken for kosher, if you see what I mean.'

They came to Union-Platz. It was too close to the Westhafen basin and Moabit's marshalling yards not to have taken bomb damage, but locals had done their best to keep the small park cleared of debris. Some grass remained, and where it didn't fresh allotments had been dug and winter crops planted. It was neat still, ordered to a purpose, putting on a face for passers-by. Near the brutal concrete mass of the park's *luftschutzbunker* they found an extemporary bench, salvaged from a shattered tree trunk, and sat.

'It was a neighbour?'

'Name of Frau Wuersching, a real bitch. She came around the second week we were there, full of smiles and greetings, the sort who *has* to be your friend, you know? When we didn't return the favour she got cold, and then sullen, and then talkative. She's a widow, with no one at home to slap her down, tell her not to mind other folks' business. Another neighbour come to visit, an old fellow, decent bloke, one of the King's Mounted Rifles in the First War. He told us she'd been telling folk in the nearest village that we were communists on the run, or *widerstanden*. That was when I should have done something, but we'd got complacent - I just assumed she'd be laughed down, or ignored like old women are. Dumb, eh? So, one day we got a visit from the *orpos*. It wasn't a problem, I gave them our Hamburg papers, said we'd evacuated after the firestorm. They got a good look at the tin leg, handed them back and went away. That was *really* when I should have done something.'

'But they still think you're …'

'Kurt Beckendorp and family? Why wouldn't they? The poor bastards went up in Hamburg smoke along with just about anyone who ever knew them. There'll be the odd relative still, but they aren't going to be touring the Reich with a photograph.'

'At least Freddie Holleman isn't on anyone's list of people to see.'

'Not yet, no.'

'We'll keep it that way. Your boys are alright with it?'

'Having a secret identity? They love it. I doubt they think of *Holleman* any more than they do of Berlin. They won't talk, if you mean that.'

Fischer couldn't share his certainty. A false identity was like a British grenade with the pin pulled - it had to be clutched tightly or flung as far away as possible. He feared that his forthcoming visit to Lothringerstrasse would be akin to slapping the hand that held the thing.

From across Union-Platz they heard the groan of a loaded cart's axle and hushed, anxious voices - probably some poor bastards moving what remained of their earthly goods. If they saw uniforms they would notice, possibly even ask for help, so Fischer and Holleman abandoned the bench and moved east, out of the park and on to Birkenstrasse, a wider, busier street but the quickest route home.

Their luck held almost to Frau Traugott's house, but at the corner of Jonas-Strasse and Bugenhagenstrasse they collided - literally - with the local *blockhelfer*, Herr Amon Dunst. Dunst was a retired schoolmaster, a most assiduous man who haunted his allocated streets, checking that blackout regulations were being observed, ensuring that local residents rushed to air raid shelters immediately upon hearing the siren and noting precisely any defeatist or anti-Party statements he encountered. Some might have considered such duties onerous, particularly when discharged in the cold and dark, but Dunst applied himself to each with the careful, precise manner that had distinguished his career in education. It would have been easy to regard him as a typical specimen of petty swine who staffed the *block* system, but Fischer had come to realise that Dunst was much more dangerous. He simply liked to be needed, to do things well, and if there were consequences then it was the transgressors' business, not his. Frau Traugott had been one of his early victims; her chance remark (delivered as indiscreetly as most of her opinions) that *certain officials* probably weren't going short of margarine had been reported and brought a stern rebuke from the office of the district *zeelenleiter*. After that, it was apparent to everyone in their part of Moabit that Herr Dunst did not have a blind eye or deaf ear to turn.

The torch barely had to flit across Fischer's distinctive, ruined face before Dunst greeted him respectfully, but Holleman he didn't know and so took his time. Freddie didn't flinch, or try to hide his face, or snatch the torch and beat the old *blockhelfer* to death with it, but the light playing over him did for his hopes of anonymity what searchlights did for men going over the walls of Moabit Prison. Even in December 1944, there still weren't too many one-legged Luftwaffe officers wandering around Berlin. If a question was put, there was now at least one person who could answer it.

Dunst peered at Holleman just long enough to be satisfied that his memory wasn't going to let him down on this one and then dipped the torch. 'Ah, well, goodnight, sirs.' He shuffled on and turned into Bredowstrasse.

Fischer took his friend's arm and felt the tension in it. Holleman was probably thinking it wasn't too late; that in the darkness a swift, powerful blow, the sort that any piece of falling masonry would be willing to take credit for, would simplify things wonderfully. The grip tightened and held until Dunst was safely gone.

'You're going to be seen, Freddie. We can't do anything about that.'

Killing people was easy. It took no great effort nor even will. It required little planning except in the matter of getting away with it, and even then one could usually rely upon the fallibility of those charged with understanding *why*. Killing wasn't a problem; it was living with it that required a certain skill (or perhaps art), and *that* was something Fischer was fairly certain his friend hadn't acquired.

7

At a glance, the *Reichsjugendfuhring* building at Lothringerstrasse 1, Prenzlauer Berg was a cliché of National Socialist architecture - sprawling, intimidating, unpleasantly squat despite its eight storeys and tall roof masts. But to most Berliners over the age of thirty it occupied two worlds and they regarded it with only half the fearful prudence it demanded. They recalled it when it had been *Kaufhaus Jonass*, a proudly Jewish department store that had stocked the proletarian necessities, available to take home for a quarter of the list price, the balance to be paid in interest-free instalments. During the very worst of times the store had helped folk of every faith and none to keep their feet out of the gutter, to stave off the moment when desperation becomes destitution. It had been the best of Germany, a practical embodiment of *guter geist* and thus poison in the veins of National Socialism. The Aryan managers foisted upon its Jewish owners promptly betrayed them, killed off the business and gifted the empty building to the Party. For months it had been ignored, a granite ocean liner becalmed (Prenzlauer Berg was too far from Wilhelmstrasse for lips to reach the right buttocks); but then an organization dedicated to moulding healthy lads into killing machines and girls into breeding mares had discovered that it needed a home in the city. So *Kaufhaus Jonass* was dusted down, repainted and rededicated to a future unanticipated in the darkest dreams of Herren Golluber and Haller.

Fischer gave his name and appointment at the main reception and was told to take a seat on a bench directly beneath a beaming, four-metre Führer accepting flowers from children. The hall - he couldn't help but think of it as a foyer still - resembled a badly organized ants' nest. Staff bustled constantly in front of him, fetching and removing quantities of boxes from the building to a rank of trucks that almost blocked one side of Lothringerstrasse. It struck him as strange, too early for an evacuation even given the present military situation; but he recalled that the *HJ* was no longer what it had been. The inculcation of National Socialist values, the gradual moulding of boys into soldiers, girls into mothers, belonged to a happier time. This was now the general staff headquarters of just another military resource, charged with getting its troops to where they could best be used, and as quickly as possible. No one here was playing at war any more.

The mess, the confusion, reassured him that any effort to check his credentials probably hadn't been carried out too assiduously. Only moments before leaving the Air Ministry that morning he had learned of the death of *Der Adler*, the journal he allegedly represented for this interview. The October 1944 issue had been its swansong, a farewell to heartening stories of air supremacy, dashing aeronauts and technological innovations that would obliterate the Reich's enemies. He was genuinely sorry for its passing. However absurd the written content the photography had been consistently excellent, and he had tried never to miss an issue. But most of all he regretted his elementary error, his failure to do the research. Strategies half-thought out on the spur of the moment, requiring a wing, a prayer and an enemy looking the other way, was what had brought them all to where they presently were.

'Herr Major?'

A flabby middle-aged unterfeldwebel was standing in front of him, attempting to come to attention - an unfamiliar manoeuvre, apparently. The man gave an overall impression of crumpled, and carried a quantity of dust on both sleeves of his uniform for which, absent a ditch and an approaching enemy tank, he should have been kicked. The regretful *moue* was as military as the rest of him.

'I'm sorry you've had to wait, sir. As you see, we're in the middle of changes. Standartenführer Neidermann can see you now.'

Fischer frowned and nodded self-importantly, as he imagined some jumped-up service reporter might dismiss the minor inconvenience. They passed through the main doors into what had once been *Kaufhaus Jonass* 's principal lobby, the point from which its customers once had scattered in search of bargains. There were boxes everywhere, with new ones being added to the mess constantly. The staircase (a double sweep only slightly less grand than Wertheim's) was half-blocked by stacks of paperwork and almost-packed office gewgaws, leaving a narrow passage being contested by roughly equal numbers of ascending and descending staff, none of whom seemed to be enjoying his morning.

The unterfeldwebel sighed. 'We'll take the lift, sir.'

Neidermann lived on the seventh-floor, a carpeted sanctuary. An adjutant in his outer office stood and came to attention smartly as they entered. Fischer returned the salute and was shown through immediately.

'The Press!'

Standartenführer Alex Neidermann was a youngish, good-looking fellow in a bespoke uniform that said more about the tailor than the man. He smiled broadly at Fischer, waved away his adjutant and came around his desk with the grace of a fencing club secretary. A one-handed sub-manoeuvre removed an expensive looking cigarette case from the breast pocket and was offering a choice before the objective was quite in range.

'Bulgarian on the left, ration to the right.'

Fischer declined politely. Neidermann's eyebrows rose. 'A war hero who abstains? Astonishing!'

'My lungs surrendered a while ago, sir.'

'Ah! I'm afraid you're dealing with an idiot.'

Neidermann was doing his best to be pleasant, but then he had a very a nice office to smooth his temperament. The seventh floor was not a victim of the turmoil that plagued the rest of the building. There was no dust on the large, embroidered carpet covering most of the polished wood floor, no fingerprints or stains upon the glass-fronted bookcase that hid one entire wall, nor, impressively, a single piece of paper disfiguring the broad, leather-insert desk upon which several pens awaited either employment or an excursion in a commemorative Mercedes 540K holder.

They sat on amply upholstered leather chairs. The standartenführer leaned back and placed his feet on the desk, displaying barely scuffed soles.

'So, flak emplacements. You must have covered this before, surely?'

Very probably, yes. Fischer cleared his throat. 'We did, briefly. We thought it might be useful to put together the stories of our pilots and those of the emplacement crews, to show how everyone's working to defeat the terror raids.'

Neidermann nodded. 'The nation pulls together, very good. But you know that we're not the best people to speak to about this?'

'I'm sorry?'

'The chaos you came through downstairs? We're having most of our administrative functions taken from us. As of two days ago, 17 December, all fully trained *HJ* units fall under operational direction of the Wehrmacht. The reserve and cadet formations …' (Fischer assumed that he meant half-trained boys, but couldn't say so) '…are to be drafted into *volkssturm* units. At least, that's our assumption. The paperwork is leaving with the authority, as you must have noticed. If you want to see anything, you'll have to apply to Zossen. I'm sorry, Major.'

Zossen. It would be easier to petition Stalin for news of a captured comrade, or Whitehall for a case of Glen Garioch - this was, to conscript Karl Krohne's favourite expression these days, *the end.* No one got into OKW headquarters unless summoned, and no one asked questions there that weren't to do with orders. The story of Franz and Ulrich Holleman was being carried out of the building along with that of almost every other hope for Germany's future.

Fischer tried to appear bewildered, which at that moment required no great effort. 'I'm sorry, sir, but if all of that's going, what remains here? *Is* there a *Reichsjugendfuhrung* any more?'

Neidermann laughed sourly. 'A good question. Ostensibly, we continue to provide the organization that captures and trains the lads and girls as they come of age, and we'll be obliged to maintain our existing facilities until Wehrmacht can make their own arrangements and steal them from us. But that's it. We won't be doing anything further. We are now a sub-office of state without a substantive purpose. Really, I feel I ought to be donating my salary to the Winter Relief.'

'But you'll still have information on *HJ* lads who'd be ... interesting subjects?'

'In what way, *interesting*?'

'You were a newspaperman, sir, so you know what it's about. There are any number of stories of worthy, forgettable characters that don't make good copy. I was looking for the exceptional, the unusual, something that might seize the attention. An inspirational tale, perhaps.'

'Badly Injured Son of First Man Into Fort Vaux Shoots Down British bomber?'

'Precisely, sir.'

'Oh.' Neidermann tilted back further and stared at his ceiling. 'We had a deaf-mute a little while ago, a fifteen-year-old farmer's boy with the smell of cow shit about him still. It was at the height of the Battle of Berlin - heavy nightly bombing, terrible confusion, a lot of people losing their heads in every sense. The lad carried a wounded comrade away from their burning emplacement and then went back to remove the shells to a safe distance - thirty-eight of them, I recall, manhandled one by one. If they'd exploded, half of Herman-Göring-Strasse would have gone north with all those lovely ministerial gardens. Naturally, he should have been decorated, but the Fuhrer couldn't be seen to reward someone who was so obviously a life unfit for life. So the thing was dropped. A shame, really.'

Fischer nodded. *A shame*. 'Other than acts of bravery, what about the unusual biography?'

'The Boy's the Story, you mean?'

'Yes, something like that. The brilliant young pianist who now wears the steel helmet, or the prize-scholarship lad who volunteered to put his studies aside for the duration. Identical twins, of course - they're always good for a photograph, and triplets would be wonderful.'

The standartenführer frowned. 'Really? Aren't litters a token of inferior species?'

'Not if they're solid Aryan stock. It sends a message to women who care more about their figures than they do the Reich.'

'Mm. We must have a *lot* of twins.'

Fischer waved his pen as hacks do. 'Of course, they'd have to be *together*. There's no story in two boys stationed a hundred miles apart who just happen to be indistinguishable. And if you had anything current, that would be better still. It's only one suggestion, though. I'd still prefer a boy prodigy if you know of one, or a hero, naturally. But I wouldn't wish to take up your time. Perhaps one of your men could help with it?'

Neidermann slapped his table and jumped to his feet. 'Well, as I say, the paperwork's disappearing to Zossen, but someone might be able to think of something. Let me see what I can do, Major.'

Naively, Fischer had been hoping to move the thing while he was in the building, but its current state of bureaucratic *dishabille* made that a faint prospect. In any case, to persist would have raised any number of flags. He stood, forcing a smile and his thanks for the standartenführer's time.

Neidermann's adjutant escorted him as far as the stairwell, in which he beheld six flights of clerical mayhem, a Breughel's *Triumph of Stationery*. For a moment he considered waiting for the obstinate lift, but time pressed badly. Trusting to his pink epaulettes he launched himself down the stairs, loudly demanding passage. His face helped, of course - a livid, mutilated stare, thrust closely into an unsuspecting junior's field of vision, invariably induced a backwards lurch into another man, or box. Without quite creating an avalanche, the growing, disordered momentum swathed a path down to the entrance lobby with little more hindrance to its perpetrator than if he'd attempted the same at midnight on a Sunday. It was the first undeniably satisfying experience of the day, but in the lobby he noticed something, an odour absent when he arrived, that killed the brief pleasure and made the risks he had taken seem pointless, even absurd. Downstairs, in what had once been a school clothing department, someone was burning the evidence.

8

It was almost three kilometres from *Kaufhaus Jonass* to Wilhelmstrasse, so Fischer walked to Alexanderplatz's half-ruined station, and, with much the same enthusiasm that he formerly departed airborne fuselages, took the u-bahn. The failure of Germany's domestic supply of toilet soap and toothpaste had transformed what was once an unthinking convenience into a feat of endurance, an assault upon the nose and stomach that would have triggered a mass migration in a saner mammalian species. The ordeal was offered *gratis* to members of the Armed Forces, but that neither raised it in his expectations nor lessened the abuse of his senses. The odours in the staircase that descended to the track were merely unpleasant; on the platform, pressed in by bodies, he felt as though he was sharing a steam bath with the Lemnian women. The interior of the train was beyond plausible comparison. Many of his fellow passengers held their hands unselfconsciously over their faces, preferring the concentrated essence of their own effluvia to molestation by others'. Fischer, trained to fly at unpressurized altitude, managed to hold his breath between stations, for once grateful to be hosting only one working lung.

Emerging into Kochstrasse felt a little like being transported to an Alpine meadow, and he inhaled deeply all the way to the Ministry. Krohne was waiting for him in his office. The morning's appointments had been cancelled or deferred, and a small, fully packed shoulder bag sat on his table. Without a word to any of their subordinates they descended to the Ministry garage, where an Opel OL38 was waiting to be released by Krohne's signature. They dismissed the driver.

'Was nothing more modest available?' Fischer stared doubtfully at the battered, near-geriatric bodywork. Its colour scheme identified it as a regulation Luftwaffe vehicle, but the mutilated trims and much-cracked shine on the front seats (impossible to have been perfected by less than ten thousand arses) hinted at a lend-lease arrangement with goat-herding Serb partisans.

Krohne shrugged. 'You want to be noticed?'

The car started first time, its engine revving like winter mornings in a tuberculosis ward. Less than five minutes east of Wilhelmstrasse they pulled up and reversed carefully into a small yard near Spittelmarkt, the sort of entry that in an earlier age had accommodated a small stables or commercial stores. Most of the walls enclosing the space belonged to buildings with addresses on neighbouring streets, but there was one frontage, a solitary, boarded-up house, sporting a door and two windows, the one over the other. A touch of domestic architectural detail in their frames distinguished them from the utilitarian facades to either side, but the legacy of a century's aerial pollution made any distinction a faint one. Had a little more colour bled from the cobbles the scene might have come from the pen of a German *Phiz*.

'Where are we?' In the past year Fischer had seen many houses similarly unoccupied. Usually it was the result of bomb damage, but this one seemed unscathed.

'A *Germania* clearance. The entire block should have been demolished in 1941, but something may have distracted Herr Speer's schedule.'

Thousands of ordinary Berliners, uprooted from the city's centre between 1938 and 1941 to make way for the refashioning of Berlin as a capital fit for the Thousand Year Reich, had been offered a take-it-or-leave-it option of new housing on the outskirts. The old blocks closest to Unter den Linden and the ministerial districts had been emptied first, but the demands of a two-front war intervened before demolition work could begin in earnest. It had required the fraternal assistance of the British and American air forces to make a serious start on remodelling the area.

Krohne sorted through a number of keys and placed one into a rust-covered lock that appeared wholly unused and unusable. It turned smoothly.

'Haven't the owners tried to return? Nothing's going to be built here now.'

'I believe their name was Rosenthal.'

'Is it safe?'

'It should be, yes. The yard's entirely unoccupied, and the street outside has a single civilian enterprise, a fabrication shop staffed almost entirely by foreign workers. The Luftwaffe's held the leases on every adjoining property since 1942. W*hy*, I don't know. Perhaps this section of *Germania* was going to accommodate a Flying Officers' Club.'

The entrance hallway was as dusty and decrepit as the exterior, but a door to their left opened into a small sitting room that was perfectly clean, warm and furnished with a comfortable supply of domestic furniture. Freddie Holleman occupied its only sofa.

From the moment *blockhelfer* Dunst saw his face the fugitive had been marked as surely as if his file sat on a desk in the Alex, so a rudely surprised Plan B had been deployed. Back at Jones-Strasse 17 they had gathered his few possessions, crept out of the house and hugged the wall as far as the gloomiest corner of Arminius-Platz. Krohne had arrived less than ten minutes later in a Ministry car and whisked away the offending item without a nod or a word. It was all done as efficient as any improvised manoeuvre could have been, and Fischer was fairly certain that no one had witnessed them. But he had expected his boss to organize a definitive removal to somewhere outside the city - the Grunewald, at least. This place was barely a spit from the Führer.

Briefly, he reprised his meeting at Lothringerstrasse. Holleman's face, never hopeful, dropped further as he listened. The problem was obvious, and large. Given its nature and purpose the *Hitler Jugend* was not as rigorously centralized as other institutions of the National Socialist state, and now it was fragmenting further as its resources were distributed or seized to shore up the military effort. Blindly, they had hoped for a functioning registry, a convenient place where a man might be persuaded or bribed into accessing a piece of information. It had seemed something of a fantasy the previous day, and Fischer had been handed the proof of it.

He desperately didn't want to give the news. 'It's not that the twins idea didn't work - I think Neidermann was interested, actually keen to help. But he'll get his people to look at boys who've been in *HJ* a while, not *pimpfen* who've been taken recently. Freddie, I'm sorry, but we need to know exactly what happened after they came for your lads, and I can't think how we're going to follow that track without any number of eyes fixing on us.'

He watched Holleman's face as he spoke. The famous wit and fixer, the crony of Berlin's grafter-elite, was a fled spirit, his seat taken by a frightened father in sight of a future he could neither influence nor employ a bullet to avoid. Freddie could bear – had borne - a bullet as well as anyone, but stoicism drew a hard line upon the matter of a man's sons.

Embarrassed in the uncomfortable pause that followed, Krohne opened his bag and placed a few tins on the mantelpiece - preserved pork, condensed milk and a nondescript oily fish, the best that the

Air Ministry's stores could provide without requiring an inconvenient paper trail. He offered a cigarette to Holleman.

'Look, Freddie, *Forschungsamt* has an intercept station at Lübben, just down the road from where they must have taken your boys on the day they pounced. I know a few people at *FA* - they might be able to tell me something about the local *DJ* organisation, at least let us know what we could be up against.'

'They'll ask why, Karl.' Fischer wished fervently that his boss had considered things before pouring hope into the wound. Putting a question - *any* question - to an intelligence agency was to demand attention. It was their business to be interested, and *Forschungsamt* were all ears - literally, the Reich's principal eavesdropping agency. Worse, they did a great deal of business with RSHA, the very last people sane men would wish to stir.

Krohne shrugged. 'It's a risk. But if anyone noticed and wanted to make a noise about it they'd have to go through *Forschungsamt* headquarters, and at the moment I doubt that anyone in Breslau cares about anything but getting out of the Ivans' path.'

'It's a *risk* you'll be adding to all the others.'

'I know, but …'

Cravenly, Fischer held his tongue, said nothing more of what needed urgently to be said. Of course Krohne would try to do work any possibility, however foolish. He was probably living every frame of Holleman's nightmare.

'So you know someone at the Lübben station?'

'No, but there's a fellow, Martin Paetzel, at *FA* Abteilung VI here in Berlin. We used to have a drink together when there were drinks to be had. He might be able to give me a name.'

Holleman still hadn't spoken. His eyes were wandering, looking for something a thousand kilometres away. Awkwardly, Fischer gripped his shoulder. 'Keep out of sight, Freddie. Do you want us to contact Kristin, to let her know what we're doing?'

'Tell her … not to worry.'

Neither man spoke during the short drive back to Wilhelmstrasse. Fischer desperately tried to think of an alternative to Krohne's proposal, but nothing occurred that wasn't equally uncertain, equally capable of turning that solitary, deadly light upon them all. The bureaucratic machine was unravelling unevenly all across the Reich; information was disappearing into boxes, fires and memory, yet all the risks of accessing it remained. The entire edifice was a wet leper - rotting but acutely sensitive to the slightest touch.

At the office no one had noticed his hierarchy's absence. As usual, the place had an atmosphere of quiet, polite bewilderment, of men struggling to come to terms with a form of deception that required an absolute suspension of disbelief. Fischer counted four of his colleagues, heads down, frowning, searching for the vocabulary to make plausible cake from night soil. They were clustered together, the better to test out ideas on each other's sense of credulity.

There was no reason to put off the least pleasant part of a bad day. Fischer sighed, rubbed his eyes and wished he were elsewhere - the Front, perhaps, or Nova Scotia. 'I'll let Kristin know.'

'How?'

'A message, the hotel in Köthen that Freddie used two years ago. Somehow, he and the old lady who owns it became friends. I think she got used to his language eventually, or imagines that beneath his unpleasant skin he's a sweetheart. It'll get to Kristin.'

Detmar Reincke came over from his desk. His only hand held a piece of paper.

'For you, Otto. Someone at the Alex.'

A *shit* balanced on the tip of Fischer's tongue, but the name on the paper scraped it off. It was from kriminalkommissar Gerd Branssler - a *mensch*, a lamb disguised as a steel-press, one of the few remaining undamaged souls at Police HQ Alexanderplatz. He was Freddie's closest friend, part of the inner circle who had done their time on Berlin's streets before the old world ended. He was also the samaritan, the link between the Air Ministry and Spreewald that had kept the Holleman family alive for more than a year.

Fischer went into his office and called the Alex. Branssler was in a briefing, but came to the telephone as soon as he received the message.

'I heard.'

'How?'

'A friend in the south.'

Kristin hadn't waited, and Fischer could hardly blame her. With Freddie in Berlin she had three little boys to worry about.

'What did she …?'

'Not now. The *Birch*?'

'Gone.'

'Fuck, I'll miss it. The street, then. You know the flea market on Kurststrasse? One hour.'

Kurststrasse was a few streets to the south of Unter den Linden, only five minutes' brisk walk from the parlous 'safe house' that held the fugitive. There was no way Branssler could know about that, but even so the proximity made Fischer more nervous than a coincidence should have done. He reminded himself their rendezvous was roughly mid-way between the Air Ministry and the Alex and an entirely logical choice, nothing in it to cause him to be anxious. Still, he checked his service pistol before leaving, and he couldn't recall the last time he'd thought to do that.

9

The market on Kurststrasse had been badly damaged during the previous year's bombings, but it was open for business still. Damage, in fact, had become its business. People whose homes and possessions had suffered during the raids came here seeking bargains, spare parts or orphaned fragments to rebuild their nests. Some had money; most of them brought unwanted pieces that might retain value for someone else. Pictures frames, cigarette cases, lengths of fabric, utensils, dead relatives' clothing were all recognized currency, things that bought things. Silver was always good of course, damaged or not, and gold could buy anything for those lucky enough to own some still. People came to rummage, to haggle, to barter, to take it or leave it; some came just to share the pain of material loss and derive some comfort from its generality, from knowing that the same sort of luck was spreading its blessings indiscriminately. Like all good markets, Kurststrasse had a bit of something for everyone.

Gerd Branssler was leaning against a lamp opposite the market, watching the thin bustle of thinner customers. Fischer hadn't seen him since the summer of 1943 but he seemed the same - squat, clad in the semi-official Bull's hat and coat, looking like he could open a tin by staring at it. The patrons of the market had identified the object already. Every few seconds, eyes glanced surreptitiously at him and then averted quickly, pretending to find the meagre offerings more fascinating than they were. Twelve years into the new order, they'd all learned it was best not to notice what couldn't be ignored.

The two men shook hands. Branssler tried to take Fischer's left, but the right was functioning well enough now for the formalities. The big man's eyebrows rose, like he was impressed.

Fischer shrugged. 'Things get better.'

Branssler snorted. 'Not the best fucking time to put *that* good word around. Can you do anything for Freddie?'

Fischer told him about the visit to Lothringerstrasse and Krohne's intention to stir the nest at *Forschungsamt*. It didn't add up to much, and the *kripo*'s face darkened as he listened.

'What about you, Gerd? Any thoughts?'

'I wish I had, truly. But can you think of any reason why someone at Alexanderplatz who isn't Gestapo would be asking about the twins? Unless, of course, I let it all out about Freddie's little adventure in the Spreewald, in which case *everyone's* going to be asking questions. Where have you put him?'

'About four hundred metres from where we're standing.'

'Jesus!' Branssler took off his hat and rubbed his bullet head. 'Well, keep him there. Freddie isn't someone who passes through crowds unnoticed, even when - *if* - he keeps his mouth shut. Is there anything I can arrange? Food?'

Fischer shook his head. 'We can't hide him for long, not in Berlin. And this thing, it isn't going to be drawn out, is it? Either we're lucky very quickly or the boys go somewhere we can't follow. They're only thirteen, but ...'

But no one was going to regard them as too young any more. Thirteen was what seventeen had been the previous year, or perhaps the one before that - Fischer couldn't quite recall how quickly standards had slipped, but Napoleonic recruitment policy was beginning to seem tardy by comparison. Worse, the fact that Holleman had managed somehow to keep the twins out of the *DJ* for four years would incline some proper bastard to make sure that they caught up for lost time. Branssler looked to be thinking something similar. His own children were old enough now to have little worries of their own.

Fischer turned to face the Church. Some of the market's clientele were getting too nervous, drifting away, and it wasn't as though German Commerce needed a helping boot in its present state.

'I shouldn't have asked him to disappear the Peenemünde file. If he'd stayed in Berlin ...'

Branssler waved it away impatiently. 'Crap. Freddie was going long before that thing ever happened. It's the twins - it's *only* the twins, has been since '39. You think he gave a damn about some General's secrets, or the toys they're building up on the coast? Believe me, if he cared he'd have shot the bastard and put the gun in your hand.'

Fischer smiled. It wasn't unlikely.

'Where *is* the file, by the way?'

'We burned it last night, at my lodgings. I can't think of a circumstance in which *that* bluff could ever be called.'

'Good, it's better gone. I have to get back to the Alex.' The Bull put on his hat and shook Fischer's hand once more. He had a habit of treating the tail-end of conversations like doors, and this one was closing.

'What about you, Gerd? Plans, I mean?'

"Plans? Greta and thc grandchildren are in a village outside Düsseldorf, praying the western front moves east before the eastern one moves west. That's it.' Branssler shrugged. For a moment Fischer saw the familiar desperation in his hard, life-punished face - and something else, something that was trying very earnestly not to come out. But the pause lasted a moment too long, and gave it a push. The big man glanced around, moved closer.

'Look, this thing that Krohne is doing? If it doesn't ...'

'What?'

'There's a thing I know, it might be useful. But you'll wish that it wasn't, I swear. I'm saying, if there's *nothing* else, if you've begged, threatened, bribed and offered your arse to anyone who might help and still it's all-to-fuck for Freddie, call me.'

He thought about memory a great deal - how it worked, how it didn't. The most satisfying analogy that occurred to him (if something so terrible could possibly *satisfy*) was that his mind was becoming a hotel clerk's rack, a place where everything was open, accessible in a moment, but where only certain boxes contained anything.

He could recall his parents, but not his life with them. Memories of the occasional beating from his father - a strap, nothing vicious - remained, but not the reason for it. His mother's embraces he almost felt still, but he was no longer sure that she had loved him or how the emotion might have been expressed other than in that physical act. Certain moments of his childhood came to mind occasionally, unexpectedly, but they were without context and again, he had only analogies. They were mental photographs lacking captions, fence posts with no connecting wire to corral their meaning.

He certainly remembered his schooling, the virtues it had taught him. Duty, loyalty, selflessness and sacrifice were no more abstractions in his life than were blood, or air. The firm kindness of his teachers, their refusal to countenance weakness or baby-softness in their pupils, their contempt for false intellectualism, moved him still to a profound gratitude. But qualities weren't memories; they held no facts in themselves, only perspectives.

His present life, such as he could recall it, had begun with the Army. Belonging to something tangible, sharing a cause, a rigid set of beliefs and goals - these were the iron rails upon which he plotted his course. If more things were falling from the carriage than was normal, at least he knew that as long as he was among friends he would be cared for.

The campaigns also blurred in memory, but that was because of their number. Poland, France, the Balkans, Russia - it all seemed to matter less as time passed and new enemies arose as if from hydras' teeth, scattered upon a continent that couldn't yet accept the inevitability of a German victory. It was frustrating, and undoubtedly he and his comrades had sometimes let themselves down with bad, undisciplined behaviour - who could be entirely innocent in war? But these were things to be judged by history, not by the letter of conventions fashioned to protect and preserve mediocrity. He felt this as a certainty, and had no guilt upon the matter.

If he had any regrets they were for the present, and not for anything that memory failed to keep clear in his mind. Of his many wounds only one troubled him, the one that had brought him to this, unmanning him (though sparing those parts whose removal defined the condition), the final, catastrophic injury that had extracted him from the company of his own kind. Who wouldn't regret something like that?

He sat on his bed. In a few minutes he would report for breakfast, and then for his duties. He had been a soldier; now, he was a mover of paper from one point on a desk to another, a processor of other men's intentions. He thought often of his former comrades, wondered what they were doing, where they were dying, how well they were living up to their ideals. He had been a part of that, and now he merely observed, stamped, filed and waited (though for what, he couldn't say). He was losing himself, adrift in a place where memory was accorded a status and called tradition.

His trunk, which should have been locked and stored under his bed, was open. His legs straddled it and he was staring down, trying to think. He didn't recall opening it, or ruining the precise arrangement of his few possessions. On the day he arrived here he had removed everything he needed before pushing the trunk under the bed, so there was no reason he could imagine, much less recollect, for removing the thing. It was a mystery whose solution he couldn't really find the enthusiasm to attempt, but the things that shouldn't have been there intrigued him. In turn, he lifted and examined the small, crude rouge-stick (hardly more than a fragment), the fake-jewelled clasp that didn't quite clasp, the genuine silk scarf with a cyrillic label (much-worn and faded), the mother-of-pearl edged notebook without a single entry, the small gold medallion with the image of a saint who was either St Cecelia or St Catherine. All of them were little puzzles, mysteries, placed carefully upon his disordered effects as if intended to be discovered.

He wondered who could have done it. He worked with serious, sober men, none of whom would have played silly pranks. In fact, most of his new colleagues - veterans who had long served as clerical staff - were in awe of his more recent experience in the field and showed him great respect. In any case, who would wish to draw attention to himself by employing such absurd, feminine artefacts?

His alarm clock rang. He closed the lid, locked the trunk, pushed it under the bed and with it, for the moment, went the conundrum. He fastened the collar of his tunic and straightened, taking care to flex the muscles of his stomach - or rather, those that remained to him. He couldn't *eat* breakfast, of course; his diet had been entirely liquid for some months now, a disgusting medicinal broth taken cold and often, in minute quantities. He had been told that there was no prospect of him eating real food again, ever, and even to have its aromas in his nostrils was a torment. But others would be in the canteen, and he would welcome their company and conversation even if it dwelled upon matters that were to him incomprehensible or frivolous. Having been part of a fraternity for the greater part of his short adult life, he found the prospect of solitude unbearable.

11

Karl Krohne's brilliant idea collapsed on the starting line. A brief telephone call revealed that his drinking acquaintance Paetzel had packed his bags and followed *Forschungsamt* headquarters to Breslau. The revelation offered the perfect opportunity to drop the matter, to think of something else or wash hands of the Freddie Holleman problem. But bulldogs with a good grip on things had much in common with Krohne, so without consulting his deputy he invented a minor Intelligence crisis and booked a flight to the East, directly into heavy flak. Fischer found out about it when he returned to the office and read the short, scrawled note. It left him nominally in charge of the department, the first time in years that he had commanded anything.

Appalled, he tore the note into unreadably tiny pieces and tried to distract himself. As acting head of Luftwaffe Counter-Intelligence (Ost) his first duty was to review its ongoing business, a task that his immediate superior was notoriously content to put off to an increasingly proverbial tomorrow. It was a heavy, settled pile. There were transcriptions of telephone conversations translated from English and Russian that attempted to analyse Germany's remaining airpower (all of them gross over-estimations); an intercepted intelligence report, drafted at Tito's ever-advancing headquarters, accurately assuming that Soviet air cover in the northern Balkans would prevent German interference with the partisan advance into Slovenia; a memo from the top floor, urging all departments still located in the building to complete contingency plans to remove files to Zossen; a docket marked *Most Urgent!*, demanding a signature to release a batch of ruled notepaper from the Ministry's central store; a greetings card, signed by most of the department's staff, offering wishes for the speedy recovery of a colleague whose resident shrapnel had decided to recommence its travels (he had died two days earlier). Fischer assessed their relative importance, placed the reordered pile into his pending tray, the card into the bin and gave himself a few hours' leave to think.

He emerged into a crisp, clear day, rare for Berlin in December. For a while he walked vaguely northward, almost aimlessly, his attention caught between two loads of ordure - the personal and the general - that threatened to fall imminently. But then his adopted

Berliner's homing instinct laid a course for his favourite part of the city, the Gendarmenmarkt, the transcendent creation of an age in which Prussia and France had inclined to mutual affection. It was a while since he had been there, a self-exile of sorrow. On the morning of the previous 24 May he had stood at one of its perimeters with hundreds of his fellow citizens, saying farewell to the dome of the French Cathedral as it burned. Facing it, the German Cathedral, an identical twin without any pretensions to primacy, had stood undamaged, bereft, mutely observing its precise reflection being consumed by the peevish gutterings of British incendiary ordnance. A half year on, the ruined French dome was a cold, thrusting stump, and it occurred to Fischer that if one turned from south to east and then north, the square as a whole offered a monumental narrative of the path from one thing to another, from then to now.

But life's grip persisted. Even during a raw winter, the sixth of the present war, people came still to draw some sense of a half-forgotten normality from Gendarmenmarkt's torn beauty. For a few moments, pausing on the west side of the square, he sipped the same medicine, feeling a slow pulse revive. Heavily-wrapped men and women sat on the steps of the long-closed *Schauspielhaus*, their faces tilting upward to catch the sun's meagre warmth, or risked their rears on what remained of the ornamental lawns, indulging memories of a time when picnics involved food and the hours to savour it. Some of them were deep in that last, un-rationed pleasure of German life, a book; others talked, argued, held hands or just enjoyed a brief indolence (one of the Seven Deadly National Socialist Sins). Above all of them, Schiller, swathed in his famous blanket, stood shivering on his plinth, inviting passing birds to unload their opinions of his vision for a German *eutopia.*

At a brazier Fischer paid too much for some stunted chestnuts and perched upon a low wall to eat them, using his lap to catch the edible shards. Within seconds a thin mongrel bitch, her flank pitted with sores, wandered over to pester for the husks with all the nonchalance of a first day offensive. For a while they sat companionably, chewing thoughtfully, contemplating life, wasting nothing. When everything was eaten he folded the greasy paper and returned it to the vendor. His new friend followed him closely, and for a moment he feared he had signed adoption papers. But then a young woman with two children came up to the brazier, and the bitch transferred her hopes and affections seamlessly. As close to amused as his present mood permitted, Fischer watched the play. Tongue lolling, she squatted on her hindquarters as if that particular spot were as good or bad as any other, looking around with a native Berliner's disinterest in what was on offer. But the moment a bag was passed to one of the kids her head tilted, a paw raised and a gentle whine reminded the child of his duty to another innocent victim of the present troubles.

He smiled, looked at the woman's face to gauge her reaction, and wished that he hadn't. Her eyes - almost vacant, distracted by something over the horizon - gave the lie to the illusion of normality, of people making do with a bad situation. They were like instruments calibrated to record the bounty of war: its ever-worsening diet, its air raids, its black-edged envelopes in the post, the remorseless, crushing presence of a Regime that had nowhere to go but was determined to take the nation with it, the excision of hopes for a future that could be called such. What absorbed all of this could have been mistaken for stoicism, but Fischer recognized it as something else. He'd seen similar in dozens of villages and towns in Byelorussia, where civilians found themselves in the path of one or more offensives. Usually they had time to evacuate, to make a dash for the forests where they could be safe for a while. Yet more often than not they remained, awaiting the storm, knowing that they couldn't possibly survive it. It wasn't courage, dullness or stupidity - only a mind-set that had yet to grasp the protocols of panic.

Anxiety pressed upon him suddenly, given an edge when he realised that plotting an eastward course out of Gendarmenmarkt would have put him straight into Kurststrasse once more. He turned northwards, towards Unter den Linden, pretending that the manoeuvre was placing distance between his preoccupations and their cause. The illusion persisted for less than half a block. At the corner of the Crown Prince's Palace he was stopped by a three-man patrol of the *Geheime Feldpolizei* whose unteroffizier glanced indifferently at Fischer's mutilated face and held out a hand.

'Papers.'

Incredible - they saw the wounds, the rank, and still they assumed him to be a deserter, or a spy, or whatever else required hordes of healthy men of fighting age to be stationed in Berlin to counter. Not for the first time Fischer cursed the 20 July plotters for conceiving their business and then not succeeding; for finally giving the Party an excuse to declare *everyone* the enemy.

It would have been entirely in order for him to humiliate the dead-eyed boy who had issued the challenge without salute or the correct address. Instead, he stood, fumed and said nothing, grateful at least that the photograph on his identity card was unambiguous. The unteroffizier checked the papers briefly and returned them. Belatedly, he came to attention. 'Thank you, Herr Major.' He nodded at his two subordinates, who relaxed their grip on their machine pistols

Fischer couldn't resist a feeble retaliation. 'Have you caught *many* absconding Luftwaffe officers, Unteroffizier?'

The boy looked him straight in the eye. 'Not yet, sir, no.'

Ridiculously, the encounter made Fischer feel like the habitual truant he had once been, a world ago. He stood only a moment, watching the patrol withdraw in the direction of Unter den Linden, and then reversed his course abruptly, crossing the broad span of Gendarmenmarkt without once removing his eyes from the ground. He walked quickly, Wilhelmstrasse-to-*Tomi*'s-style, trying to think of nothing.

There was a military ambulance parked in front the Air Ministry's main entrance. Fischer glanced at it without curiosity, but was held by a glance from the old guard on the door, his winking acquaintance.

'Hello, Ernst. How are the knees?'

'As always, Herr Major.'

'You're keeping them warm?'

'I've deployed the last of Selma's hosiery.'

Ernst Körner sighed deeply and glanced up into the sky, searching for some hint of God's purpose in placing him here, in the cold, a mere three hundred kilometres from parlous danger. His previous helmet - dropped somewhere northeast of Amiens - had been spiked, so his feelings were strong. To Fischer and those other members of staff who seemed unlikely to put him in charge he often confided his conviction that sixty-two birthdays, a frail heart, ruinous joints and a professional armchair-warmer's aversion to the outdoors were not qualities that should have recommended themselves to the most enthusiastic scourer of Germany's manpower reserves. But here he was nonetheless, a retired chemist's assistant thrust into field grey once more, a hapless victim, a dupe and -

subject to discreet prior arrangement - the purveyor of certain pharmaceutical commodities misdirected from his brother-in-law's warehouse. To those who believed that a nation's prowess could be assayed by the quality of its rear-echelon troops he was stark proof that the Reich's pot had been emptied and kicked away. To everyone else he was Kondom Körner, or Friday Ernst.

Ernst was presently keeping a professional eye upon the ambulance, it being on his patch of responsibility. In order to more efficiently rub his hands he had propped his rifle against his leg, inviting any passing officer to kick him the entire length of the courtyard. There was a hint of lugubrious satisfaction in the way he was slouching (Ernst had many slouches), and Fischer recognized what might almost have been mistaken for a good mood.

'Who's ill?'

'No one, Herr Major.'

'What is it, then?'

'Generalleutnant Wegener, sir. He's discharged himself. He's done an Udet.'

Wegener was - had been - a senior liaison officer, whose military life had been spent at the Ministry, or Zossen, or on the road between the two. To Fischer's knowledge he hadn't served in the field during the present war.

'Are you sure?'

'Nice clean shot, roof of the mouth. It won't be an open coffin.'

Three years earlier, Generaloberst Ernst Udet's lovelorn suicide - artfully reinterpreted as a test flight tragedy - had given the Regime an opportunity to lay on the spectacle. There had been interminable radio retrospectives upon his career, a full honour guard, dour music and the obligatory slow tramp to the Invalidienfriedhof where the entire Leadership had waited to stare down into the hole for the benefit of the cameras. That had been a closed coffin affair, too (as a breed, senior Luftwaffe officers seemed to be unimaginative, inconsiderate self-murderers), but even allowing the similarities Fischer couldn't see Wegener getting the same treatment. He didn't have the sort of profile that made for good copy.

'Do you think it was a girl this time, Ernst?'

Korner was rubbing a troublesome knee reflectively, and the shrug sent his rifle clattering to the ground. 'Or the latest briefing from OKW. Biting wind, isn't it?'

12

Freddie Holleman tried to ration his hours in the safe house. He gave a few to troubled sleep, a few more to every possible permutation of the many fates that might have taken up his boys and most of the rest to a sightless scrutiny of his view of the courtyard through the half-boarded sitting-room window.

He ate sparingly, without appetite. His longing for alcohol, a near life-long companion, had faded to the point at which even nostalgia couldn't sharpen its absence. Waiting was an unbearable ordeal that he was obliged to bear, time without distraction, enough to savour every stab of his helplessness. He began to understand how men went mad.

He hoped, hour upon hour, that Krohne and Fischer would return with the best of news, but if not that at least to return, to fill this small place with more than himself. They couldn't, of course, not every day; he understood perfectly that their lives were not going to be reordered on the matter of the twins or his fears for them, however much they sympathized. The Holleman family was the centre of a very small universe in a vast, darkening continuum, around which only his fears revolved closely. They would come when they could, and he was going to have to learn to love his own company.

He tried to interest himself in the terrain, but the effort backfired badly. On his second morning in the house, he went upstairs to what once had been a formal dining room. The table and chairs were in their proper place still, covered by three years' accumulation of dust. Place settings were laid neatly; a meal, perhaps a special occasion, had been in prospect for the family when they became ghosts, when *it* happened. To one side, a solid dresser held display plates, carefully balanced to show off their ornate edgings. Facing it, the small, well-maintained fireplace was inlaid with Dutch tiles carrying scenes of bourgeois domestic life from past centuries. Propped on its mantelpiece, Holleman discovered the Rosenthals: Father, Mother and three little *Rosenthalen*, the youngest proudly holding a violin that looked like a cello in her tiny hands: a good, slightly prosperous family of trade, pleased with itself as it was but dutifully ensuring that the new generation climbed the ladder a little further.

Where did they go? Their eyes followed him, trying to answer. To a *Judenhaus*, probably - a filthy, vastly overcrowded tenement in one of Berlin's rougher districts, where those who had murdered Christ and enervated Germany with their poisonous presence could acclimatize to their new situation. But they weren't there now, for certain; Holleman didn't know what had happened next, but like everyone else he was perfectly aware that there were no Jews in Berlin these days, perhaps not in the old Reich at all. They'd all heard of the camps in the East, where the dispossessed had been given an opportunity to expunge their historic guilt in useful labour, but as Germany's 'east' moved remorselessly west once more no Jews had returned, even as refugees. That would have been puzzling, had Holleman allowed himself to think about it. He hadn't, of course.

The bedrooms were on the floor above, but the photograph had killed any desire to know more about their stolen lives. As he gazed around at the dining room's frozen, lost moment he became aware of faint noises to one side, from almost precisely behind the dresser. In the gap between it and the door he pressed his ear to the wall and heard labour: the sounds of everyday toil, men at some physical business, chattering, sometimes laughing, not bothering to place large objects upon the floor too carefully - an ordinary workplace, an enterprise of the living.

He retreated from the noise, through the kitchen (too small a space for the Rosenthals to have entertained largely), into a short corridor at the end of which stood a locked door. The key was on a nail, hammered into the side of the ascending stairs. The lock was substantial, not the sort that kept one part of a house from another, and for a moment he paused, fearing what lay through the door.

Afterwards, he wished that he had curbed his curiosity. Every one of the empty wooden boxes in the long, iron-pillared room bore the fading legend *Werkzeugmaschinenfabriken Rosenthal*. The plant and machinery were gone, appropriated to enhance the Reich's non-Jewish-sourced production elsewhere; only the ranks of empty bolt-holes that had held it firmly to the floor and electrical sockets, hanging from the ceiling precisely above, hinted at its former presence like plough furrows would a plague village. This had been the main fabrication room. Below, probably a dispatching warehouse. Above, the offices, with a view down into the courtyard to check upon despatches, deliveries and time-wasters taking a casual break. An efficient arrangement, everything situated where the boss could best ensure that things moved as they should - a small enterprise, probably employing less than a hundred people, the sort of painstaking, precision concern that had taken Germany from rural stagnation to industrial supremacy in barely two decades. All gone now, expunged, dismantled in a day or two at most, its highly skilled workforce scattered, the very memory of *Werkzeugmaschinenfabriken Rosenthal* razored from history for no more profound reason than that its proprietor's cock had lacked some skin.

He limped the length of the room, to the three tall windows in its furthest wall. They were boarded up, but several years of neglect had opened generous slats. He looked out and down on to a narrow street, one of the many short passages between Kurststrasse and the river. He was facing east, towards the Kupfergraben canal, though buildings obscured it from his sight. It didn't matter; having a sense of his orientation was a relief in itself.

Below, the only traffic was to or from the enterprise he had eavesdropped upon from the dining room. A truck, backed into and blocking the entry, was being loaded by foreign workers who had detached themselves from the laws of physics and were moving tectonically. The driver was supporting one of the walls, smoking, in no apparent hurry to be anywhere. It might have been a Saturday afternoon in 1932, the last shift.

There was a door to Holleman's right, sufficiently recessed for him to have missed it from the other end of the room. He pushed it open. A men's lavatory, with a urinal, two shitters, a sink, lockers and a drooping poster of Renate Müller in men’s clothes, probably the most interesting scene from a long-forbidden film. The only sign of a human presence lay on the edge of the sink - a dead, half-smoked cigarette, silent witness to the moment that men in hats had arrived to draw the line beneath its owner's world.

Slowly, he returned to the ground floor sitting room, his fears whispered and amplified by the unelapsed time his wake disturbed. If they could do this without any testament to what had passed, if an entire way of life could be removed and leave less than a dusty imprint, what chance was there for two naïve, unworldly boys, stolen away to a place where childhood was cut out like a tumour? Would they even recall who they had been, a year from now?

All the rest of that day he sat by the window, staring into the yard. He ate nothing, drank only a little water, waited. When the light failed he returned to the sofa to strip, clean and reassemble his pistol once more.

13

Karl Krohne flew into Tempelhof at first light, supercargo in a crowded JU52. Every one of his fellow passengers was *Forschungsamt*, en-route to their tracking station at Jüterbog. They had been based at Breslau for just four months, and now, remarkably, they were being evacuated westwards once more. It had been one of their masters' more cunning decisions, to transplant an entire secret intelligence division from Berlin to the east, to a city already declared a fortress - *Festung Breslau* - and heaving with a mass of refugees fleeing the advancing Soviet Armies. Naturally, the idiocy of it had dawned almost immediately upon some thinking head, and in fine German fashion resources that were needed desperately elsewhere were being consumed to put things right. The men around Krohne looked deflated, bureaucratically shell-shocked by their latest redeployment; they reminded him of the peripatetic monks of Lindisfarne, hopelessly wandering a Norsemen-ravaged landscape with the bones of their revered St Cuthbert, seeking a place where life's new-found horrors couldn't find them.

Tempelhof was eerily quiet. Krohne's papers were checked at the Luftwaffe desk by one of just three attending staff, as if he had arrived at some remote outpost in one of Germany's former African colonies. He managed to catch only the day's second u-bahn service into Berlin (it stank no less for it), and arrived at the Air Ministry at 7am, probably before any of his subordinates had thought of rousing themselves from their cold beds. He showered, went back to his office and read once more the short, depressing statement of a *Forschungsamt* deputy signals officer, a man with three young sons in the DJ who had been willing - anonymously - to discuss a hypothetical case:

> *All statements relate to the example provided:*
>
> *- Thirteen-year-old boys being registered with the DJ for the first time would represent an extremely rare case of evasion of the system. The following comments are provisional, therefore.*
>
> *- At that age, they would no longer - in my opinion - be inducted into the DJ's programme (though formal registration would still be made*

through that organization). Rather, they would join the Kern Hitler Jugend directly, with an accelerated course of instruction in the Heimabende curriculum to make up for lost time. Typically, boys entering the system later than the norm are required to 'catch up' with some urgency. They are also likely to be treated with disdain and even physical prejudice by other members of their squad, particularly where there is evidence that familial affections remain strong. 'Mummy's boys' do not have an easy life in the HJ.

- Given the suggested lack of ideological rigour in the boys' background, or of indications of academic excellence (you posit that they have been taught largely at home, outside of the main educational system), it is highly unlikely they would be considered for a place either in a Napoli or Adolph Hitler School. In any case, present circumstances dictate that priority is given to physical and occupational training over schooling, so it is likely that the boys will placed directly in one of the HJ's military service camps in the Gau.

- Certainly, the boys will be subject to the HJ's full military training programme, but this would not necessarily lead to immediate deployment (i.e., to flak battery support or volkssturm unit). It is probable - particularly in view of their age and the fact that 1944 has been designated the HJ's 'Year of the Volunteer' - that they would be allowed to choose a non-military posting: for example, Winter Relief work or agricultural service, though this will of course depend upon the developing military situation.

- Any attempts to locate the boys will be identified swiftly and investigated - in this case by HJ Gruppe Ost, which has responsibility for the Brandenburg region. There is no mechanism, formal or otherwise, through which unauthorized, non-HJ personnel may track individuals in service. This is a tested fact (not least, by this writer).

'Well?' Fischer stood in the doorway. Krohne looked up into his subordinate's remarkable half-face. He had long since given up trying to read emotion in it, but the weary slouch, the unmilitary use of the door frame to support the shoulder, reflected something of his own mood. He pushed the piece of paper across his desk and waited for the good news to be absorbed.

'No one could suggest anything?'

'No one wanted to *think* of suggesting anything, other than forget about it.'

'What do we tell Freddie?'

'What *can* we tell him? *Take heart, Freddie, the chances are they're digging turnips from a frozen field or practising anti-tank measures*? We've come to the end, Otto. This is all the news we can give him. He'll just have to hope for the best.'

They looked doubtfully at each other. Friedrich Holleman wasn't the sort of material from which nature's silent sufferers were carved. The prospect of him allowing fate, fortune and National Socialism to work upon his heart's twin delights while he and Kristin bided their time in the Spreewald was about as likely as Churchill begging an armistice. It was far easier to imagine him strapping on his P08, politely asking the loan of Fischer's Belgian FN and Krohne's Walther PPK also and taking a terminal stroll to Lothringstrasse 1.

Fischer cleared his throat, knowing that there was time still not to speak, that the consequences of what he might say deserved to be pored over for a while - a great, thoughtful while.

'There may be something still, I'm not sure.'

'We kidnap Arthur Axmann?'

'Gerd Branssler said something … curious.'

'About what?'

'I don't know. He said it might help, but we might come to wish that it hadn't. He said it was a very last resort. But that was *all* he said.'

Krohne considered this as he tried to out-stare his carpet. 'No hint about what it might be?'

'Nothing. If we trust him, it's probably a matter of closing eyes and stepping off the cliff.'

'Branssler's as close a friend as Freddie has. He wouldn't point us towards something bad.'

Fischer shrugged. 'What if he doesn't have all the facts? This is something from the Alex. Would you trust anyone to be certain that they'd seen both ends of it?'

'Oh Christ. Talk to him, Otto. But try not to ask more than you have to.'

14

'I called *you*, remember?'

'About five weeks ago, yes.'

Gerd Branssler threw back his full measure of Frau Beitner's Special Cocktail without flinching and still found his voice. 'A bit strange that, after a year and a half.'

Fischer pushed his own glass towards the Bull. 'I thought you might have been lonely, needing to talk.'

'A fatal sort of *need*, these days.'

'It seemed a little unlikely.'

'So what did we talk about?'

Fischer considered this. 'Nothing much, that I recall. How things were, generally. News from the Front, my wounds, the usual sort of catching up.'

'I must have been bored that day.'

No one was bored any more, not in this world. Branssler reached for Fischer's glass, thought better of it. 'What else?'

'Work, I suppose. That business in Lichterfelde.'

'Now why would I do that?'

A case in progress, a capital crime - the obvious answer was of course that he wouldn't. Fischer had done the job at a time when there hadn't been a war to make things a hundred times more sensitive, and even then it would have been unthinkable unless it was one Bull talking to another, professionally. Fischer hadn't been in the business for seven years now, and he didn't do old times' sakes.

'How is it going, the case?'

'It isn't. It wasn't then, and it isn't now.'

'A pity. No leads?'

'How would I know? I'm only the investigating officer.'

Outside a siren wailed. Fischer suspected that it was Karl Krohne's voice, wafting up Wilhelmstrasse.

'What do you mean?'

'When we spoke, it was two victims, women of a certain age. Now it's three at least, but no one's looking any more. In fact, everyone's looking anywhere but at it.'

'This was an order?'

'It was, but I don't know who closed the door. The day before, everyone was pressing for a quick arrest. Suddenly, it was forget it, never mind. When my boss gave the word he looked as edgy as I felt, and he kisses more Party arse than a chair in the Chancellery.'

Fischer didn't need the good half of his nose to recognize the smell. 'But how does this help Freddie?'

Branssler stared at him. 'Think about it. Three old women, strangled and fucked. Who did that? Not a woman, obviously. A man then, but what sort of man? About ninety percent of adult males in the Berlin area are over sixty. This is someone who kills from the front, with his thumbs. He doesn't surprise them, so they must have time to struggle. If it were someone of the same age, there'd be noise, a lot of noise. It takes real effort to choke the life out of someone, yet no one heard anything at all. This is a strong guy, he probably lifts them off their feet. He's one of the ten percent.'

'That narrows it to about sixty thousand.'

'But he must have taken them within a square kilometre, his hunting ground. Does he come here from somewhere else, and risk being stopped for his papers every time?'

'He lives in Lichterfelde.'

Branssler nodded. 'He lives in Lichterfelde, or very close by. And who in Lichterfelde - Lichterfelde *West*, to be precise - would give the shits to someone at Alexanderplatz, enough to scrape us off the case like the same from a shoe?'

For a moment Fischer couldn't see it, probably because he didn't want to.

'Jesus!'

'Doubtful. But you get what I'm saying?'

They stared at each other, the one smiling faintly at the other's astonishment as if an *aprilsherz* had worked splendidly.

Lichterfelde West - a pleasant garden suburb on Berlin's south-western border. Almost a village still, though a part of the metropolitan borough of Steglitz since the 1880s; full of well-to-do sorts in their planned colony of villas, a sprinkling of Generals among them (at least *they* could be absolved, being somewhat preoccupied at present by a small war), home to a famed Botanical Gardens and the world's first electric tram service, now decommissioned. A fine, comfortable place in which to clear the mind of present discomforts and delicate nostrils of the scent of Berlin's lumpen proletariat. And then there was the reason why

Lichterfelde West had been graced with such bounty in the first place - its kaserne, the former Prussian Military Cadet Academy, where the elite of the elite came to learn the business of making the French pay over and over for 1806. They had gone away for good in 1918, but fifteen years later the kaserne had reopened its doors to new tenants - National Socialism's Praetorian Guard: 1st SS Division, *Leibstandarte SS Adolph Hitler.*

'But … they're at the Front.'

'Belgium. It was probably the last thing I checked before everything was placed in a sealed box and carried away. But the home administration's still on site, obviously. I can't see who else would have that sort of pull, to stop an investigation like bricks stop faces.'

All the mundane business involved in allowing a division to carry on, busily slaughtering non-Germans without having to distract itself with irrelevances: its equipment, training and medical facilities, the politics of maintaining a position as the Führer's showcase military formation, day-to-day liaison with suppliers, OKW, soldiers' families - all of that remained with divisional administration at home barracks. Hundreds of support personnel, dedicated to letting the Best get on with their job, and all of them utterly untouchable.

Fischer's mouth, which had opened to say something he hadn't quite decided upon, remained open. Frau Beitner glanced at him, assumed only a temporary traumatic paralysis of the larynx and turned to reach for her stone bottle. Branssler hurried on.

'I can't think of anything else that would give Freddie some sort of hand to play.'

'But … we'd be starting a war!'

'We'd be opening a Front, or giving someone else the means to do it.'

'*How* would we do it?'

'We wouldn't - *you* would. My boss wants this buried, which means that *your* boss is the only person in the Reich who'd absolutely, sincerely want the opposite.'

'It would mean some sort of … hell, an *approach*. Who …?' Suddenly, Fischer saw the cliff-edge, but Branssler clasped his shoulder and pushed a little harder.

'Who else do we know who can talk to the Big Men? You've got a record, Fischer.'

'But where would I start?'

'Speak to Krohne, he'll know. Or he'll know who knows.'

'I could just suck my pistol instead. It would save putting someone else to the trouble.'

'It won't be like that. You have an advantage.'

'You mean there isn't much left of me to kick to death?'

'I suppose so, yes. You've no handle they can turn, no family, no commitments, no reputation other than in the business that needs to be done.'

'They wouldn't know about that.'

'They do, believe me. Within three months of the Reichsführer barging into Peenemünde, Luftwaffe had opened a file. They may not know all of it - hell, who does? But they have your name. We know because someone leaked the fact back to Prinz-Albrecht-Strasse, and then Gestapo got hot about what they might have missed when they thought they were using you. It's all wonderfully business as usual.'

'Why would Luftwaffe be interested?'

'Why *wouldn't* they? Every time Himmler's tentacles extend a little further he gives more people reason to want to chop them off. And your boss is at the front of that queue. Shit, he's been looking for a way to do it since, what, 1935?'

'At least since then.'

'So.'

'Christ! We'd be starting a *war*!'

For two blocks, from *Tomi's* back to the Ministry, Fischer tried to measure the drop. The thing was fantastical; it relied upon so many assumptions not being delusions that even to open his mouth would be to sever the cord that restrained the ballista's arm. He wondered at the brazenness of Gerd Branssler to even suggest it with a straight face. He wondered if his own failure to laugh it off as a manifestation of a head injury or Frau Beitner's special cocktail (though that might have been the same thing). He wondered whether the idea could even have been conceived in a time before black had become white and catastrophe a commonplace. He didn't allow himself to wonder if it might work.

Ernst Körner looked at him strangely as he entered the Ministry. It was one of his *pointed* expressions (he had as many expressions as he had slouches), and if Fischer's attention hadn't been so consumed by the business he might have found it annoying. But when he reached his office and found almost every member of the department waiting for him with more or less the same set to their faces, he was obliged to notice. Salomon Weiss, whose already near-albino complexion was made more ashen by shock, stepped forward.

'Otto, they've arrested Karl.'

In their Germany, only one question was pertinent.

'Who?'

'Luftwaffe.'

Thank God. For a moment, there had been nothing in his mind's eye but the SD, dragging Krohne to a building just around the corner. If this was being kept within the family there was hope at least.

'Was anything said?'

Weiss shrugged. 'Not that any of us heard. They walked into his office and two minutes later everyone left. I thought they were just going to a meeting, but Detmar saw that one of them was holding Karl's arm.'

They'd tried to do it discreetly - again, that was *good.* No one was definitively, fatally arrested without a big show, the theatre of intimidation visible, clear and understood, its message not so much flagged as engraved. So unless Karl had finally put his cock into the wrong hausfrau this had to be about his fishing trip to Breslau.

Where would they do it? Fischer recalled the expression on Ernst Körner's face. He'd seen it too, so they must have left the Ministry. He told everyone to get back to work and almost ran back down to the ground floor. The old guard was standing to half-attention while his mate examined the papers of two civilian visitors. When they had gone inside Fischer tossed his head slightly, and Ernst ambled across.

'You saw it, Ernst?'

Ernst glanced around, sniffed, and nodded. He looked upset. Everyone in *LuftGeheimStelle* IIb knew that he'd been supplying Krohne with prophylactics for the best part of a year now (at only twenty percent above the entirely theoretical list price). They must have had something of a relationship.

'Three of them in a black Horch, all blue-greys.'

Horchs weren't supplied for taxi duties, so they hadn't come from or returned to an airfield. Either Krohne had been taken somewhere else in Berlin or he was being driven back to Breslau - or, God forbid, Zossen.

'You didn't talk to the driver?'

'A right surly bastard.'

'Any standard on the car''

'No.'

'What about insignia?'

'Yellow Tabs.'

Ordinary *Luftfeldpolizei*. Fischer stared across the courtyard, weighing the possibilities. Someone at *Forschungsamt* HQ had taken exception to Krohne's questions about the *HJ* - or, perhaps, to questions *per se*, it being a place where paranoia was a professional qualification, not a disease. The person to whom that *someone* reported was capable of removing a departmental head without formal notification and whisking him away to parts unknown. Had it been one of the many branches of RSHA, the casually arrogant manner of Krohne's arrest would have been expected. But Luftwaffe wouldn't play it like that, not unless Karl had been found in possession of a codebook, a pack of Player's Navy Cut and six British passports. So the order had come from stratospheric regions, and there was nothing to be done.

Ernst was standing with Fischer, contemplating the same patch of courtyard. He sighed.

'Bad business.'

'Yes.'

'A shame, really.'

Fischer breathed harder. 'Yes.'

'Still, it isn't Siberia, is it?'

'What?'

''Potsdam. I said, it isn't Siberia.'

Ernst shrugged, and Fischer stifled an urge to club him to the ground. 'The oberstleutnant gave Surly Bastard his orders when they came out with Oberst Krohne. They've taken him to Werder, the *Luftkriegschule*.'

There were no secure facilities or interrogation unit at Werder, and it wasn't far enough from Wilhelmstrasse to represent an abduction. They wanted to talk quietly, out of the office. Fischer's diaphragm relaxed slightly. He wouldn't need to tell Freddie Holleman and add to his present store of guilt.

It was obvious suddenly that a decision had been made on their behalf. The fate of the twins was now in play - it had to be, unless Krohne somehow managed to make his interrogators forget the questions he had been asking at Breslau. The first requirement of Branssler's idiotic, impossible strategy had been achieved - they had attracted attention. Of course, it could well be of the fatal variety. He couldn't see how he might begin to make a case, much less put the incentive; the chain of command was useless, in this case a necklace that would drag him swiftly to a murky bottom. Perhaps, as at Peenemünde, he would merely bypass its inconveniences. There, he had managed not only to piss in the pots of Army Ordnance, the SS, Abwehr and Gestapo *and* walk away from it but he'd also taken the love and gratitude of the Führer's favourite Generalmajor with him.

Light-headed, he indulged a gruesome fantasy. The office would be palatial, the sort with weather fronts, crossed swords to break up the wallpaper and home to more leather than the pampas. He would be ushered - or carried - in by guards with gold-braid on their shoulders, whose heels knew how to click precisely in time with the pair next to them and still sound crisp despite the half-inch of lamb's wool beneath them. Released, he would march up to the banquet-scale desk, clear his throat, clench his bowels, frown with serious intent and go straight at it - *Well, Herr Reichsmarschall, what do you think of this Lichterfelde business, eh? Yes, shocking. And who do you imagine has the juice and motive to shut down the kripos? That's right! But I think we can find a way to placing a large item into his latrine chute. All I need is three or four weeks and the help of the best assistant investigator in Berlin. The thing is, he's a bit distracted right now, what with his kids having been abducted - oh yes, by that great, close friend of the Reichsführer, Artur Axmann. What do you say, sir? Eh?*

He may have groaned, because Ernst was looking at him solicitously. 'It'll be alright, Herr Major. Worse things happen … well, just about everywhere, these days.'

Fischer feared the truth in that cliché. Without another word he went back to the third floor and tried to ignore the eyes that followed him around the office. Hushed, semi-whispered conversations killed even the pretence of work that day, and for most of the afternoon he kept to his room, the door inhospitably closed. He tried, hopelessly, to reconstruct the sequence of circumstances that had brought him from comfortable obscurity to clear sight of a firing post in less than seventy-two hours; tried to imagine what a wiser, less sentimental Otto Fischer would have done differently to wash his hands of the business. A pointless exercise - the sensible options were obvious, numerous yet elusive, requiring the application of common sense, a quality he seemed to have shed with most of his skin.

At 4.30, Detmar Reincke knocked and entered without waiting for a response. He was holding his telephone message pad - which, in a way, was Fischer's fault. When he became Kohne's second in command he had drafted an order demanding that all messages be taken on the correct stationery, rather than committed to the first scrap of paper to hand and promptly misplaced thereafter. The initiative had met with varying degrees of resistance or indifference, but a regime of constant nagging had slowly brought everyone into line, which was why the surprise was spoiled for him now. If Reincke had a telephone message pad in his hand it was because he was delivering a telephone message.

The young man looked at him with great respect. 'You've been invited to Potsdam, Otto. For a chat, they said. Don't worry about transportation, they said.'

Ernst Körner exhibited most of the recognised symptoms of idiocy, but even he, overhearing *Werder* and *Luftkriegschule*, probably hadn't assumed that Krohne was being invited to give a talk to trainee pilots, and neither did Fischer. There were other things in the deer park besides the Cadet Flying School, trees and the few clever deer that had managed so far to avoid the cull. There was Luftwaffe's makeshift General Staff HQ also, a pale, above-ground imitation of OKW's operation at Zossen, Göring's last defiant attempt to keep the former from falling entirely into the hands of the latter. But that wasn't where Fischer was delivered either. The impeccably polished black vehicle carried him to one of a group of low wooden huts about half a kilometre from the main staff buildings, with plenty of trees around them to muffle sounds that shouldn't be overheard.

He stood to attention next to Karl Krohne, waiting. The gentleman behind the desk wore a brown jacket over black trousers, without insignia or any indication of rank - an affectation of very senior men. He was stockily built, narrow-eyed and restraining himself visibly.

'You're Fischer?'

'I am, sir, yes.'

'So, the other half of this music-hall act. Your commanding officer has told me about the situation, but perhaps you can add something as it occurs.'

'I'll do my best, sir.'

'Thank you. Let me summarize briefly, then. A member of your former department's staff deserted in mid-1943, abetted by you gentlemen?'

So Krohne's nerve had given way at the first touch. Fischer cleared his throat. 'Yes, Herr Ministerial Director.'

'Yes. Applying salt to the wound, this person continued to draw his Luftwaffe service pay and rations during his retirement?'

'Yes, sir.'

'Again, abetted - in fact, *organized* by yourselves?'

'Yes, sir.'

'Yet, rather than enjoy his comfortable situation he returned recently to Berlin and requested that you help him locate his sons, in order to extract them from the Reich's youth training programme. I assume that this fraternal gesture having been discharged, you intended to find them a suitable, alternative retreat - an alpine lodge, perhaps, or a villa with a view over the Mittelmere? Will the Luftwaffe be required to bear the cost of his final choice? I ask only because the Fuhrer likes to have all projected expenditures included in departmental budgets, and I shouldn't wish to fucking mislead him!'

A response would have invited more of the same, and neither Fischer nor Krohne spoke. For a few moments the gentleman glared at them, tapping a finger nervously upon the desk's inlaid leather surface, and then slammed down the hand as if the only feasible decision had recommended itself.

'You should be shot.'

'Yes sir.'

'Beheading would be preferable, but in that case a trial would be necessary. So, I should have you dragged a decent distance from this hut, placed against a tree and shot.'

'Yes, sir.'

'Quite unbelievable! The enemy stands on the soil of the Reich itself, and I'm obliged to take time to deal with this .... *shit*!'

'Sir ...' Fischer sensed Krohne stiffen beside him, but he continued, ' ... obviously, grave offences have been committed, but I'd ask you to consider the damage. Oberleutnant Holleman's wounds are such that his value to the Reich is minimal. Also, he removed himself from our department for more than personal reasons. He was in possession of information detrimental to the security of the nation, and went into hiding partly upon my initiative. I considered it important that he not be found by ... certain parties who might use that information against the *Wehrmacht*.'

He hoped the emphasis would be understood. At least Karl Krohne took the hint.

'Major, I hardly think that Ministerial Direktor Schapper is interested in our motives!'

Fischer released his breath. *Thank you, Karl*. Gottfried Schapper, head of *Forschungsamt*, a man obliged to work for Himmler but who reported to Göring - a protégé, in fact. It was almost the best he could have hoped for.

Schapper stared pensively at him. 'You were seconded to Army Ordnance, at Peenemünde.'

'I was, sir, yes. In August 1943, for two weeks. Oberleutnant Holleman assisted me in that role.'

Fischer could almost see the beads flitting past Schapper's eyes as he calculated the time scale, the likely business, the potential winners and losers.

'And he deserted …?'

'He *left* our department at the end of that second week, sir.'

The pregnant question was which uniform was Schapper wearing, the brown or the black? *Forschungsamt* could know nothing of the real secret of Peenemünde or why Holleman had fled, but the aftermath had been obvious, and painful. Himmler's empire had acquired yet another satrapy - control of V2 production - and given notice that it recognized no natural boundaries. To many people that had been galling; to one in particular, the very highest-ranking officer in the *Wehrmacht*, it was yet another wound in a war he had been losing for a decade now. Into which ear would Schapper whisper?

The Ministerial Direktor was frowning, contemplating the view afforded by the cabin's only window. Fischer pushed a toe closer to the edge.

'If I may, sir?'

'Yes?'

'I understand that you're acquainted with Reichsmarschall Göring?

This time Karl Krohne didn't even pretend to understand. Forgetting that he was supposed to be standing to attention, he turned and stared at Fischer, astonished. Schapper's frown deepened. 'Of course I am. What of it?'

'I wonder if I might suggest that you convey certain information to him, regarding crimes committed within his jurisdiction?'

'His present jurisdiction is the Four-Year Plan, not criminality.'

'Of course, sir. But if such crimes were capable of damaging the reputations of members of the Leadership, he might regard the matter as potentially … considerable. As would any good National Socialist, obviously.'

Lips pursed, the finger still tapping, Schapper said nothing. He was close enough to the Leadership to sense the dagger, smell the poison and mistrust the open hand, but he knew better than most that they were approaching the end of things. Debts were soon to be paid, and their mutual boss was a man with epicurean tastes in revenge. He had been stripped of almost every one of his once-considerable powers, appointed Court Jester without applying for the post and become the butt of a thousand cheap thrusts from men who had once queued to kiss his chubby hand. As everything fell apart and went to Hell, would he resist an opportunity to return the coin?

Schapper sat up suddenly, leaned forward. 'But surely this is a means to distract me from your culpability in the other matter?'

'No, sir. I mean, it isn't *another* matter at all. In fact, it's very much to do with why we're here. If I might explain …?'

17

'God, Otto!'

They stood in the Air Ministry's vast reception hall. Krohne had his hands pressed to either side of his head as if practising the coming surrender. He was staring at his subordinate, horrified. During their thirty-five-kilometre return journey in that quite lovely car a tense, pregnant silence had done the talking, though one word had pressed itself forcibly in the vacuum - *camaraderie*. It was Krohne, after all, who had summoned that spirit. He probably hadn't expected it to be so brutally field-tested.

Fischer glanced around. Other than two receptionists and a brace of guards preventing access to the stairs leading to the Hall of Honour, no one was remotely within hearing. Even so, he didn't want to say more. There were some things with which even marble-faced walls couldn't be trusted.

'Karl, we'll talk about it later. I should go to Freddie, his food must be almost gone by now. Should I mention this or wait until it's certain?'

'Certain? What part of it could possibly be *certain*? What if just *knowing* about it's enough? What if Schapper has all he needs just *knowing* about it? We could be dead before it goes dark!'

'At the moment it's a theory, that's all. Men like him and ... well, they don't move on anything without checking all the holes for traps. Why wouldn't they let some lowly idiots take all the risks while they stand back, watching, keeping their cuffs unsoiled? If it works they get what they want. If not, what's their loss?'

'I can't see how we can do this, Otto. I can't see how we - well, *you* - can do anything without any access, without asking questions, without exercising the least authority where it matters. It'll be the world's first entirely powerless investigation.'

'Then we'll need to be creative.'

'What, visit the crime scenes, close our eyes, pray and hope that something occurs?'

'Every creature leaves a trail, Karl. You were in the *Wandervogel*, weren't you? Didn't they teach you that?'

'I was a hiker, not a birder.'

'That may be even more useful if we make a mess of this.'

'Oh God!'

The sitting room in the safe house was unoccupied. Fischer wasn't worried initially - there was only the one external door, and he had let himself into the house with its sole surviving key. But a quick reconnaissance failed to produce the item, and though it was obvious that abductors would not have kicked in the door, removed the occupant and then hired a locksmith to repair the damage, a missing Holleman played badly upon his nerves.

Twice, he returned to the ground floor and began the search again, knowing that there was no possibility he had missed something. It was only on his third sweep that he heard noises. He tracked the source to a wall in the first-floor dining room, where he heard muffled male voices. A door to his right opened onto an external metal footbridge some two metres long that doglegged back to the left. The door at its other extremity was slightly ajar.

Around a small-packing case in an otherwise empty storeroom, Freddie Holleman was playing cards with two civilian workers - Poles, from their chatter. Cigarette smoke hung heavily above them, and three empty herring tins of the brand supplied by Krohne lay scattered on the floor.

The fugitive looked up from his hand. 'Otto!'

The two Poles jumped up nervously. Holleman grabbed the arm of the closest. 'No, lads, it's alright! *Dobry towarzysz! Dobry towarzysz!*' He laughed, and it struck Fischer that he hadn't heard him do that since August 1943. 'They think you're the fucking Germans! Take a seat, we'll deal you in the next hand.'

But the presence of a second uniform, one with a mutilated face above it, had killed the game. Nodding, smiling, thc Poles backed out of the room, their tea break suspended indefinitely. Wistfully, Holleman looked down at his winnings and did the decent thing.

Fischer helped him to his feet. 'You shouldn't have moved, Freddie.'

'But I was going mad.'

It hardly mattered now. The interview at Werder had made discretion an irrelevance; either the offer would be taken up or by dusk the three of them would be on their way to a penal battalion somewhere on the Vistula. At Holleman's pace, they returned to the safe house. Company or the lack of it had done something to his nerve-stretched mood, and he babbled.

'This is Georg Danziger Fabrik. They make birch plywood for Mauser stocks, and they used to supply furniture companies back when people bought furniture. Georg is long dead and gone, but he and our boy Rosenthal started the local Rotary club in '33, just in time to get themselves expelled for being yids, the stupid bastards. The two firms have been in these buildings since the 1850s, that's what Leszek told me. Him and Casmir, I thought they were *fremdarbeiter*, but he says no, they started here in '37, a few weeks' work they thought, and then it just carried on. No one's bothered them since the war started except to glance at their papers. Strange, isn't it? Rosenthal, a good German employer, gets fucked because he's Jewish, but two enemy aliens ...'

'Freddie, listen.' Fischer had caught the slightly desperate gleam in Holleman's eyes. 'Karl and me, we might have an arrangement that gets us to where the twins are. But we had to promise something, and you're part of that promise.'

'Of course, anything at all, that's wonderful. Does Kristin know?'

'No. This is about as confidential as you could imagine. In fact, knowing anything at all about it is probably a death sentence if we mess it up. But if things go as we hope, you should be able to leave here tonight or tomorrow. Then you can call her, make up something.'

'Tell me, then.'

Fischer shook his head. 'Not yet, and for the same reason. If it doesn't happen, it's best to know nothing.'

Holleman breathed hard, but it must have been far more than he had hoped for. "Those herrings were the last of it. Did you bring anything?'

'Bread and cheese, something like liverwurst, a tin of Steiner's.'

The very best that Fischer had managed to find at the ministry, and it had cost almost half the cigarettes he had managed to hoard since losing the habit.

'Thanks. What's that?'

Outside, from the direction of Leipzigerstrasse, a growing, persistent roar of traffic pierced the safe house's funereal calm. It made Fischer uneasy. Civilians didn't drive any more, not without fuel coupons or tyres. He handed the bag to Holleman. 'I'll go now. Hopefully, you'll see one of us tomorrow.'

He locked the front door behind him and walked through the narrow passage out on to the street. A line of armoured vehicles -

StuG IIIs, panzerwagens, an *ostwind* and four ageing *wirbelwinds* - were moving eastwards on to Spree Island. He watched them for a minute or two, until he could be sure. Across Mühlendamm and into the ancient Nikolai quarter the column was splitting, with elements heading north and south along Freidrichsgracht. Fischer felt an unfamiliar spasm of anxiety. It was sacrilege to despoil Berlin's ancient heart with their heavy, churning steel tracks, yet also a hint of a future everyone was trying to put from mind. Even if there was no plan as yet to defend the city against the Red Army, steps were being taken to ensure that the Home Front remained loyal to the death.

18

Fischer slept as badly he could ever recall, after an evening in which the sisters did their best to make him perform two summary executions.

The latest squall was upon a point of rations. On most days, Frau Traugott had the appetite of a convalescing sparrow and hardly indulged herself the full bounty of her ration allowance. Conversely (her usual deployment), Frau Ostermann regarded sixteen hundred and twenty-five calories as being considerably short of an adequate daily portion. This disparity in the sisters' needs was regarded by one of them as an opportunity. She would never have considered it theft, merely arbitrage, a necessary adjustment in the interests of efficiency - and indeed, it would have been an insignificance to Frau Traugott had anyone other than her sister scraped half an ersatz sausage from one plate to another, or ladled slighty more oat gruel into one bowl than its twin. But the battle-line drawn upon the matter had gradually become more pronounced than the Great Redoubt at Borodino. To Fischer's knowledge, low-level skirmishing had been going on for some weeks now. He had affected not to notice the pointed re-redistribution of portions, the veiled counter-references to food wasted in cats' stomachs and the occasional practiced stab reminiscing upon a sister's once-slender figure (they reminded him of the probes into enemy positions that preceded any major offensive, when any wise man kept his head down). The final provocation had been a discreet, contented belch, expelled after supper the previous evening. He didn't even notice it, but it pushed Frau Traugott over the parapet. Her sister (having first begged pardon) met the assault head on.

Had they been men, a degree of escalation might have occurred with some further opportunity for negotiations. But the sisters fired off everything they had before the flare fell to ground, and Fischer, caught in the middle, became hideously well-informed. He learned that the mother the two women shared had never really loved Frau Ostermann, and that Frau Traugott, far from being her father's favourite daughter, had been conceived not so much in joy as drunken error, regretted immediately. On marital choices, it was put to him that the late Herr Ostermann had been a country dolt with the manners of his livestock, and Herr Traugott only slightly more eligible a catch than psoriasis. His opinion was earnestly requested as to whether it right that a refugee should gorge herself upon her benefactor's rations rather than be grateful for what the law provided, and - from the opposite trench - whether ladies with exuberant upper lip hair should consider shaving occasionally. Insults degenerated into historic injustices - childhood betrayals, thefts and deceptions were aired in turn as the sisters led Fischer through the barb-strewn wastes of their unresolved business, an ordeal he wouldn't have wished upon Generaloberst Arthur Harris. There was some relief as the battle swung away momentarily upon the matter of the ladies' respective scholastic non-achievements, but when it returned bearing children and their refusal to be conceived he fled to his rooms without excuses or even a *good night*. Wombs were not a ground upon which any man could expect to survive.

The sisters went at it loudly for another hour at least, though to Fischer it seemed like two or three. In the dark vulnerable hours he dwelled fondly upon his years in barracks and the mere inconveniences of a brutal, bloody war, slept only fitfully and woke more exhausted than if he had force-marched around his bed all night. He washed and dressed quickly, leaving the house before either of the combatants emerged from their bunkers.

It was a cold, damp morning but he chose to walk in hope of flushing out his tiredness. He stopped for a hurried breakfast at a workers' cooperative canteen on Alt-Moabit, a long-serving establishment that had been one of Moabit's many communist strongholds in the old days, a home for fiery denunciations of recidivist comrades and implausible plans for seizing the loyalties of the mostly oblivious proletariat. The *kozis* were all gone now, dead against a wall, prudently converted to National Socialism or lying low awaiting Uncle Joe's liberation express; but memories and traditions were harder to erase, and the Regime made practical gestures to keep them bedded down. Most mornings, a working man could get an egg here still, and almost-fresh black bread, and sometimes even real bohnenkaffee, diverted by a semi-official act of *legerdemain* from Wehrmacht field stores. This particular morning wasn't so good - hard bread, margarine, malt substitute - but Fischer ate ravenously, with the same brutish concentration as the hundred or so Berliners around him. When he had cleared his plate, he lit his first serious cigarette for some months and absolved himself by drawing upon it only twice before offering it to his neighbour, a much older man in a *Bahnschutzpolizei* uniform. He got a wink and no second glance at his ravaged face.

Light rain accompanied him across Tiergarten, until his uniform began to smell of the sheep it had once been. The discomfort complemented his mood, for which sisters' bickerings had been only a catalyst. The rest was an *auflauf* of his wounds' love of winter, the ever-pressing scars of a ruined city and the prospect of a war all but lost, the whole mess seasoned with his latest blessing, the resurrection of Friedrich Melancthon Holleman.

Tiergarten's relative emptiness urged him to devote forensic attention to each symptom of this grand malaise, and all the while the wind strengthened slowly to double the pleasure of a soaking. By the time he turned into the bleak canyon of Wilhelmstrasse he was wetter than the live end of a sonar array and the cold had sent what remained of his right bicep into brief but painful spasms. Had *Tomi's* opened at a civilized hour (it was now almost 7.30am), he would have been tempted to adjust course and medicate himself heroically with Frau Beitner's liquid throat extractor.

But as he entered the gate of the Air Ministry several unusual circumstances excised the longing. Most obviously, Ernst Körner and his colleague were standing more rigidly to attention than toy soldiers. Surrounding and ignoring them about a dozen heavily armed members of Fischer's old regiment, Fallschirmjäger 1, were deployed to prevent any determined assault upon the main entrance. To one side of the courtyard, three Mercedes staff cars were parked in line. They bore consecutive service plates, but he found this much less intriguing than their bunting. Two displayed the pink and black pennants of the Hermann Göring Panzer Division, which, given the identity of the men filling the yard, was hardly surprising. That on the third was a fey confection of red, silver and black with an oversized, gold-braided eagle at its centre, and it hardly required a vexillologist to enlighten its present audience. The thing was to be seen here once or twice a year at most, usually when some pointless gathering was being hosted in the Hall of Honour, a place where fanciful uniforms and grandiose grammar could best be put on show. The third Mercedes was one of Grosse Hermann's personal chariots.

As Fischer walked past Körner, the guard's heels finally proved themselves up to the challenge of clicking smartly. Two old Fallschirmjäger comrades (he didn't recognize either man) intercepted him in the reception hall and examined his papers with minute care. On the third-floor landing he went through the same ritual; this time, one of his interrogators looked him straight in the eye and gave a slight nod. Fischer couldn't recall his name but the occasion was burned - quite literally - into memory. They and three others had shared a shallow, hastily scraped-out hole in an olive grove at Maleme on a bright, late spring morning, May 1941, watching most of their unit being cut to pieces by a Kiwi machine-gun battalion. They had also shared a cigarette and a flask of filthy water, and when they were pulled out they had shaken each other's hands and acknowledged the luck of the devil that had preserved them. Back then, it could still be regarded as *luck*.

Ignoring the discomforted glances of his *LuftGeheimStelle* IIb colleagues, Fischer went into his office, took a sheet of paper from the desk drawer and wrote as quickly as his left hand allowed. It wasn't an impressive list. He recalled eight books he had retained since childhood (some stories of old German Gods, his father's dog-eared copy of *Der Struwwelpeter* and a *Hauff's Fairy Stories*), a photogravure of his parents upon the occasion of their tenth wedding anniversary, his father's pocket watch, a lock of his mother's hair (cut several years before the red turned to grey), his non-standard issue military effects, his gold Wounds Medal and Knight's Cross, his silver hip flask (long unused in case the available poisons tarnished the metal), the Fallschirmjäger plunging eagle sleeve badge he had bartered away in 1943 and then re-acquired, expensively, two months later. It was a meagre tally, and bringing it to mind was easy. More difficult was finding a name to fill the space he had left near the head of the page. It said much of a man's mortal estate when he couldn't think of anyone who might care to be his heir.

His sister had given difficult birth to a son, Kaspar, and then departed life promptly. Fischer had met the boy just once, dribbling in his crib - a christening, the summer of 1932. The widowed father had taken him back to his family home in Freiburg soon afterwards; Fischer hadn't since seen them, or corresponded. For a moment the surname escaped him, and when it returned he almost laughed. *To Kaspar, son of Maria and Louis Schmitt, I bequeath all my worldly possessions. That is: ...*

Karl Krohne arrived at 8.05, his face a study in fatal resignation. Fischer might have considered his *sang froid* impressive had he only the distance between the Ministry's reception hall and third floor in which to compose his thoughts. But the fresh haircut and dress uniform, the gloves and carefully brushed cap, the silver Wounds Medal pinned mitigatingly to his chest, betrayed a certain prior expectation of events.

Ten minutes later, they departed the Ministry in one of Reichsmarschall Göring's very nicest cars.

19

For the first thirty minutes Fischer’s mind's eye dwelled upon a ditch in a heavily wooded area, or, if their executioners’ duties didn’t include excavation, a piece of flat ground in the same with two spades waiting. A basement seemed equally likely, though the aftermath would have required an inconvenient degree of housekeeping. But then it occurred that the two pairs of shoulders in the front seats - very broad, powerful shoulders - might have returned from the Spanish War with some garrotting expertise, in which case potential venues for an extra-judicial execution were too numerous to guess at. It didn't stop him guessing, all the same.

The car purred northward, through Wedding and Pankow, as smoothly as if it were the world rather than the vehicle that was moving past. As Buchholz slipped by the cloud cover had begun to break, any number of suitable sites for a discreet killing had been ignored and his uniform had ceased to steam from its earlier dowsing. He began to breathe a little more regularly, reminded himself that the car was being driven at a dignified, legal pace as though real uniforms occupied the rear seat, and that no corners had been taken on less than four wheels. The transportation of condemned meat was done differently, he was certain.

By Wandlitz there was no longer any doubt as to where they were going. Fischer's diaphragm contracted sharply once more, and next to him Krohne tried to sit to attention in his plush, giving seat. They entered Schorfheide Forest a few minutes later. About five kilometres further on the car passed through the estate's principal gateway. It was a surprisingly modest affair, manned by a single guard, but the monumental length of the arrow-straight drive and what lay at its other end dispelled any illusion of humility. Before the war Fischer had glanced through a magazine article in which the estate’s proud owner, dressed in a heavily leathered interpretation of medieval lounge attire, had conducted the camera around the principal complex - an overpowering concoction, intended to recall some German race-memory of bucolic grandeur, a Wotan-scaled country retreat for a man who had retreated much and was determined to make up for life’s little frustrations - *Karinhalle.*

The car bypassed the epic entrance and turned into a garage block modelled upon some bygone merchant adventurers' hall, the wooden pillars supporting a steeply pitched *faux* Burgundian tile roof. A gentleman in civilian clothes emerged from a side door in the main building and waited for them. Without being handled, Fischer and Krohne were ushered expertly between the car and house. The civilian went inside a few moments before they reached him. When the door closed he turned to them, and Krohne came very smartly to attention.

'Herr General!'

For the first time, Fischer noticed the walking stick. It was a common enough affectation among senior staff officers, but its owner also sported a fine lattice of small, still-livid scars on his neck, and as he moved forward to peer into Fischer's face he winced slightly.

'So, a real soldier's wounds. I would ask you to sit, but as I'm not able to you're obliged to follow my example. Regulations, gentlemen - you don't mind?'

The General's free hand described an arc, taking in the room. It was larger than many conference rooms that Fischer had been dragged to. One entire wall was comprised of glass, yet the light that flooded in barely reached the interior corners. At about the dusk line a suite that might easily have accommodated Fafner's family gathered itself around an equally disproportionate fireplace, as if shunning its present, dwarfish guests.

'The house isn't being used at the moment. When it's full and the fires are lit, it can be quite comfortable, believe me. But not today. We'll be brief, then.'

He turned again to Fischer. 'Can it be done?'

'Yes, Herr General.'

'With discretion?'

'I hope to die in bed, sir.'

The older man laughed. 'As do we all, but there must be not the slightest indication of who is interested in the outcome. *That*, to me, seems to present the greatest difficulty. Have you a plausible story for the men who will try to beat the truth from you?'

So far, Fischer had avoided giving thought to the detail of getting it wrong. 'Herr General, I'll need to be very careful. But so will they, I think. The act of closing down the investigation was itself a crime. If the murderer hasn't yet finished his business, his protectors will need a very good story to explain why they're abetting these disgusting acts.'

The old man nodded slowly. 'Yet surely, the magnitude of the offence will encourage them to extremities, if they become aware of you?'

'It will, sir, yes. But we have certain advantages. Firstly, this *must* be a swift investigation, which will hamper any timely appreciation of it. To stand a decent chance of discovering what we're doing they'll need to be expecting it, and I don't think that's likely. They have no idea that word of the business has gone further than Alexanderplatz, which will make them complacent, or at least unalert. Also, there isn't really a mechanism in place that might pick up a sense of what I'm doing. Berlin Gestapo are hopelessly undermanned - and, of course, Criminal Investigations have been ordered specifically not to pursue this matter, so in a sense there's a self-inflicted vacuum. Finally, other circumstances will distract attention from us.'

'And those are?'

Fischer looked him straight in the eye. 'The war, coming home. But of course, there'll come a point at which we must be anything *but* discreet. Our aim isn't to find the maniac himself but those who appear to wish him well, or at least free. It would serve no purpose to end the killings without advertising the fact sufficiently to flush them out.'

'A delicate business.' The General leaned on his stick, and rubbed his thigh. 'I should tell you that I advised strongly against it, but a certain party insisted that it be supported. Your failure will be a lonely experience, you understand?'

'Yes, Herr General.'

'Well, then. Where do you begin?'

'The case files. A friend will arrange that I have copies.'

'Good. There will be no further contact between us, naturally. The price you state is acceptable. Please take this.'

He picked up an envelope from a low, broad table and handed it to Fischer.

'Now, goodbye. Abel, please return these gentlemen to the Ministry.'

Fischer and Krohne saluted and followed their driver. The other one was waiting by the car, his machine pistol keeping the front seat warm. They all took their places silently, and as the car pulled back out into the long, straight drive it occurred to Fischer that they hadn't seen or heard a soul other than the General. The estate was already easing into a state of monumental abandonment, a north German pyramid complex.

'Who was that?'

Krohne was staring out of his window. He hadn't said a word since the moment he had recognized their host. 'Hm? Bodenschatz.'

Karl-Heinrich Bodenschatz, former fighter ace and personal adjutant to Reichsmarschall Göring - his liaison with the Chancellery, when tempers frayed and old comrades ceased to speak to each other. The rumour was that it was a difficult job - that the General had been on the end of more tongue-lashings from the Führer than anyone other than Göring himself. In fact, he had taken on far more than his fair share of the Reichsmarschall's legendary bad luck. On the previous 20 July he had stood in for his boss at the Wolfsschanze meeting at which Stauffenberg and his gang tried and failed to implement their particular vision of a German future. The wounds he received there would have been much worse, had not the even less fortunate Generalmajor Brandt stood directly between him and the deadly briefcase.

Bodenschatz - they could have sent someone else, someone more used to dealing with nonentities. If it hadn't been obvious just how far Branssler's half-cocked idea had succeeded, this was enlightenment. Somehow, for the sake of a brace of thirteen-year-old boys and the demands of friendship they had set the Reich's second and third most powerful men upon a collision course, and a certain Luftwaffe major was the probable point of impact.

'What is it?' Krohne was staring at the envelope. Fischer opened it, read the single piece of paper it contained and passed it to his commanding officer. A transfer order: *Cadets Franz and Ulrich Beckendorp, currently in training under canvas with Little Flag Company no. 128, Schönefeld: to Training Company 4, Flak Regiment 22, Lankwitz*, effective ... Fischer glanced at his watch ... four hours earlier.

Krohne returned the paper, tapping its reverse side. A scrawled, very familiar reference: *3:2:42*. A fiction then, to satisfy an inquisitive *Hitler Jugend* clerk.

Krohne smiled for the first time that day. 'Let's do this stylishly.' He tapped the driver's shoulder. 'Not the Ministry', he said firmly. 'I'll give you directions when we reach Berlin.'

20

In the five-minute journey from Spittelmarkt to the Air Ministry, Freddie Holleman began to cry. Wedged between Fischer and Krohne in one of the Reich's most lavishly upholstered rides he spun the valve and let everything dissipate in a short, spectacular release. The Shoulders in the front seats stiffened visibly. They were hard men, hand-picked for certain kinds of business, fellows you wouldn't look at any way but straight, and probably they'd sooner have been on the wrong end of a reprisal than this close to raw male emotion.

Krohne's handkerchief wasn't nearly adequate to the task; fortunately, they were out of the car before it filled entirely. Holleman tried to apologize as they hurried him into the Ministry, but his mind was already accelerating up the staircase ahead of his one good leg. By the time they reached the third floor, Fischer and Krohne were almost carrying him. A vague impression of Salomon Weiss's open mouth and some falling papers registered as they rushed past.

3:2:42 was a small briefing room without internal windows or glass-panelled door, about twenty metres down the corridor from *LuftGeheimStelle* IIb's main office. Krohne raised a fist to knock, but Holleman was in the room before it connected. A Luftwaffe stabsgefreiter perched on a corner of its only desk, smoking. Two uncannily similar, near-albino boys stood in front of him, almost to attention, wearing the standard DJ uniform - khaki shirts, black tie and corduroy shorts, shoulder and waist belts, knee-length grey socks and heavy marching shoes. A single runic flash adorned their left arms, and beneath it, a green triangle. The boys - Fischer couldn't have told one from the other and didn't try - looked perfectly wretched until the moment they recognized the large object that crashed clumsily into their midst. Then it was pandemonium.

Bored, the stabsgefreiter watched the melee for a few moments and handed a chit to Krohne for his signature. It was a copy of the transfer order.

'Any trouble?

The man shrugged. 'No, Herr Oberst. I just shouted and pointed to the General's name a couple of times. It seemed to do it.'

'They're alright?'

'Haven't said a word since I got them, so I couldn't say. They've been there, what, a fortnight?'

Krohne nodded, forgetting the dignity due his rank.

'Well, they've only had time to learn the Sword Words and a couple of knots. I shouldn't worry too much. My sister's boy's been in the DJ for a year now and he still seems human. For him, that is.'

Holleman, having babbled insensibly for a few moments, was applying a double choke-grip to two young necks. The boys were comforting him as best they could. One of them managed to wrestle sufficient room to kiss his cheek, which set him off once more. Fischer patted a free shoulder.

'Come on, Freddie. Karl's room.'

Unsteadily, Holleman got to his foot and frowned through his tears. He had noticed the green triangle on Franz's (or Ulrich's) arm. 'You *volunteered*?'

The boy nodded. 'Land work, dad. It was the best thing Franz and me could choose, if we couldn't come home. We didn't want to shoot tanks.'

Franz's chest swelled slightly. 'We were learning *seeds*.'

They were probably the first Hollemans in a hundred generations to put themselves forward willingly for something, so it was little wonder their father was shocked. They each took a hand and followed Fischer out of the briefing room. Somewhere between the door and *LGS* IIb they lost the stabsgefreiter.

Most of their colleagues were long-servers who knew Freddie well, but Krohne's raised hand kept the questions at bay as the Hollemans were herded into his office. He turned at the door and beckoned Detmar Reincke.

'Go down to the mess, get milk or something. Chocolate would be good.'

When Reincke returned, Franz and Ulrich were exiled to the small corner table upon which Krohne usually stacked and forgot RSHA briefings while the three men huddled as far from them as the room permitted. Briefly, Fischer gave Holleman the details of the arrangement. The colour drained from the fugitive's face as the price of his sons' deliverance was revealed.

'*Jesus!* Where can I put them?'

Fischer had been asking himself the same question for hours, and really, there was only the single, painful option. To take them back to the Spreewald would be as good as driving to the nearest *HJ* office and handing them over. Any temporary accommodation in Berlin would require that papers be produced and the boys enrolled at the local Flag Company, which was the same as sending them home. Another mad attempt to find them a new life somewhere in one of Germany's smaller byways would require that everyone place their balls in the bear's mouth once more on Holleman's behalf - not that he would expect it of them, of course. What remained, despite every rational argument otherwise, was Jonas-Strasse 17.

When she arrived from East Prussia, Frau Ostermann had expected to take as her suite-in-exile the first-floor rooms of the late Schultz sisters, but Frau Traugott, hoping still to generate a little extra rental income - possibly from *genuine* refugees - had demurred (in any case, an opportunity to disappoint her sister's expectations was irresistible). So they remained empty, and Frau Ostermann made her bed on the large sofa in the sitting room. The Schultz apartment would do very well for the Hollemans, at least for a few days, but the flies in the honey were obvious. Frau Traugott might with some justice ignite when he suggested it; or her sister, as a consequence of one of their increasingly uncontrollable sibling rages, might say something to a neighbour about the situation - which, almost inevitably, would come to the attention of *blockhelfer* Dunst, to whom the twins would be yet another entry in the Not Quite Right column of his Judas's notebook. The arrangement was going to require discretion, personal discipline and luck, and Fischer suspected that hoping for a claret ration would be less fanciful. He smiled, lying from the heart.

'Don't worry, Freddie; they can stay with me.'

Part Two

1

Lichterfelde West - a comfortable, almost reticent place; easy in its stolid, bourgeois coat, proud of its traditions and lack of metropolitan hum, a short train commute to the metropolis yet a part of Berlin proper for less than a quarter of a century, as close in mind and body to fields as to monuments. Unlike its plainer namesake just a kilometre to the east the village had escaped bombardment to date, and Fischer could see it almost as a place outside of war, the sort in which he imagined he might end his days, swathed in stolid, old-fashioned comfort, auditing his almost-attained ambitions and mild regrets, anticipating an eternal, restful oblivion.

'Christ, it's *big*.'

Like tourists, he and Holleman had come to see the sights. First, they made a brief perambulation of the Botanical Gardens - the *locus in quo* as a certain Victorian detective might have put it. Then, the sublime *Johanneskirche*, the well-spaced villas abutting broad thoroughfares, the transplanted Alpine prettiness of now mostly-bare shops on Curtius-Strasse, and, finally, Lichterfelde Kaserne, the largest, most prestigious home base in Germany, a vast Wilhelmine complex sprawling to almost 25 hectares - conceived, designed and lavishly appointed to announce the Second Reich's arrival at the top table of war-mongering nations.

There was no possibility, on whatever pretext, of their gaining entrance. In any case the view as they approached along Kadettenweg discouraged the ambition. It was a North German Versailles, complete with a thousand-seat neo-baroque church, academies, dormitories, a fully equipped lazarett, magnificent recreational facilities (their centrepiece the world's largest indoor swimming pool) and only the division's three home battalions to enjoy it all while their comrades were busy getting themselves exterminated in the Ardennes. Like the Spartans, *Leibstandarte SS Adolph Hitler*'s active units were thrown into battle as if every stand was their last, and the few survivors were compensated with the most lavish standard of convalescence imaginable.

Holleman scowled at the principal façade, from above which Mars and Minerva scowled back, hammering home the point for anyone insufficiently conscious of the setting.

'Wasted on the fucking SS.'
'It wasn't built for them, was it? This is Willie's taste, not Adolph's. How far, do you think?'
'From the Botanical Gardens? Half a kilometre. A little less, perhaps.'
'So he could be safely home within ten, fifteen minutes. Long before anyone trips over his work.'
'That sounds right.'
Fischer watched the main gate. It was manned by two guards, to whom the perpetrator would have to present his pass both upon leaving and returning from the evening's fun - a clear record for the nights in question, a paper trail they had no conceivable means of accessing or following.
'Freddie, you wouldn't like to enlist in Waffen SS? For a week only?'
'I'd fail the charm test.'
A contact in the organization would have assisted enormously, but neither man had a single acquaintance in any branch of *SchutzStaffeln*, much less someone who had the juice to access the records of - in its own, considered opinion - the Reich's premier military formation.
'Ten minutes in the sentry office, flicking through the pass book - how many hours would it save us?'
'Weeks, probably.'
They stopped about two hundred metres from the Kaserne's entrance. Both men were too distinctive not to leave an impression should their injuries be seen clearly by the guards. Holleman was doing his best not to limp too obviously. He had a way of walking slowly, of timing the push of his body's weight upon the metal leg and back on to his own that made him seem no more than slightly intoxicated. It was agony, apparently, putting the maximum pressure on the stump at a slightly wrong angle, and he eased it with a stream of *sotto voce* obscenities, recited like a rosary. For his part, Fischer kept the unforgettable side of his face as consistently away from the direction of the Kaserne as wouldn't make him seem like a battlecruiser with a damaged rudder, or demented.
As a preliminary reconnaissance it probably unnecessary, a waste of time they had little of. But Branssler had gifted them a wraith, and until the flesh could be found they needed the reassurance of the brick and stone that contained it. Now, it felt like

a mistake. The kaserne was too vast, too impersonally intimidating, to offer comfort that the task was going to be anything other than beyond the wit of two, three or possibly four men to handle.

'Shit.' Holleman shook his head and turned away. Fischer grasped his shoulder. 'Three battalions - Training, Convalescent, Guards. About two and a half thousand men, possibly fewer after the front line losses of the past year. Most of them very committed, motivated, able to take punishment without too much complaint. Probably not too many career criminals among them.'

'You were hoping for a sore thumb?'

'Not really, no. If he were that obviously *different*, something would have happened already. Non-conformity isn't an option in there, is it?'

Holleman considered this. 'Perhaps it's all of them. Cacking old ladies is part of a field training exercise to harden them up, remove the soft, sentimental edges. I heard that *Liebstandarte* did a lot of stuff in the Ukraine.'

They retraced their route northward towards Unter den Eichen, each examining the mundane lie of artefacts with an ex-policeman's eye - the footpaths, garden borders, signs and fencing, corners, the gaps between one building and the next where one line of sight became something else - hoping to divine some sense of a play from the stage upon which it had been played out. But it was difficult here even to imagine the murderer's path. The grand villas, lining much or the northern stretch of Kadettenweg, made what they were doing seem both absurd and inappropriate, like excavating a nostril at an altar. Fischer was wearing his best uniform and still he felt shabbily intrusive, ready to admit to anything to a passing *orpo*. Feeling this out of place wasn't easing his fear that they were much too visible, too unlike the expected view from one of the prettily leaded windows.

They stopped opposite the s-bahn station, held there by a line of Army trucks, turning from Drakestrasse into Baselerstrasse en route to the kaserne. Holleman shifted his weight on to his good leg and rubbed the stump absently. 'When's Gerd bringing us what he has?'

About half the trucks were ambulances, carrying wounded men patched up well enough to be moved from dressing stations to field lazaretts and then on Germany: men with a *heimschuss*, a home wound to earn them some recovery time at their home base. There must have been dozens of them to require this amount of transport.

Another hammering, then: something that Goebbels would seamlessly shape into a rearward triumph, a decisive defeat for a still-advancing enemy. Fischer wondered how many more victories of this sort they could take before even the toughest units had had enough.

'Later today,' he said. 'Let's get back to town. This place has too much of the war about it.'

(1) Agatha Fuhrmann: 58, widow, no children, resident at Grillparzerstrasse 38, Steglitz. Body discovered 30 September 1944, under trees adjacent to Altensteinstrasse, Lichterfelde, by an anonymous caller (see B file 104/1). Probable cause of death: asphyxiation due to pressure applied to larynx, bruising, both thumbs, left over right. Some damage to inner vaginal wall, probably inflicted post-mortem. No witnesses have come forward as yet.

(2) Sigrun Ziegler: 61, widow, no children, resident at Gutsmuthsstrasse 14/22, Steglitz. Body discovered 14 October 1944 in bushes adjacent to Unter den Eichen, Lichterfelde by housewife Hilda Kempe (see B file 104/2). Probable cause of death: asphyxiation due to pressure applied to larynx, bruising, both thumbs, left over right. Some damage to inner vaginal wall, probably inflicted post-mortem. No witnesses have come forward as yet.

(3) Gisella Mauer: 62, spinster, resident at Arnim Allee 87/8, Dahlem. Body discovered 21 October 1944 in bushes adjacent to Wildenowstrasse by police patrol (see B file 104/3). Probable cause of death: asphyxiation due to pressure applied to larynx, bruising, both thumbs, left over right. Severe damage to inner vaginal wall and surrounding, outer tissue, probably inflicted post-mortem. No witnesses have come forward as yet.

Preliminary observations: all bodies were discovered late Friday or early Saturday morning (perpetrator has a particular opportunity on Friday evenings?) and at one of the borders of the Botanical Gardens, Lichterfelde. All corpses were discovered within metres of where, formerly, railings denied access to the gardens. In no instance was any obvious attempt made to conceal the victim's body. To the contrary, a general impression of casual disposal was evident to examining investigators (indifference to detection/pronounced mental disorder?). No victim's clothing appears to have been removed by the perpetrator.

Post mortem damage to (3) considerably more evident than to previous victims. Some cuts to exterior of sexual organs in addition to violent internal penetration. In all cases, evidence of considerable strength in the perpetrator was apparent, which leads investigators to believe that they are seeking a male, probably under fifty years of age, familiar with, and possibly a resident of, the area.

At this time, no importance is being attached to the anonymous nature of the discovery of (1). There is as yet no evidence of acceleration of offences, indicating that the perpetrator does not feel at risk of discovery or other intervention, or that his circumstances are likely to alter in the near future.

'Solid work, probably useless.'

They sat in Fischer's office, sifting through photographic reproductions of pages whose possession carried a near-automatic date with the guillotine. If it came to that, Gerd Branssler would be leading the procession, because no one wielding a Contax at Alexanderplatz was assumed to be working on a fashion magazine article or a photo diary. He had walked the film around to the Ministry personally and handed it to Fischer, who had developed it himself in his department's photoreconnaissance laboratory while its staff of three was at lunch. One had to play the freemason with something like this.

'They weren't given time to get the business moving.' Fischer picked up the photograph of the duty schedule. 'Look at this - at its busiest, the investigation involved two Bulls and two local *ordnungspolizei*. Someone tried to keep it sluggish.'

'When did it die entirely?'

'Gerd said they were warned off on 23 October.'

'Just two days after the third death.'

Fischer stared at the notes. 'The first one was different - an anonymous call, telling them where to find the body.'

'Do you think our boy wants to be caught?

Fischer shrugged. 'Or it was someone else, someone close enough to know him. Or it really *was* a good citizen, too sensible to give a name.'

'Do we know if it was a male or female caller?'

The statement was terse. The duty officer taking the call had no clear recollection. A gas mains pipe had exploded on Kurzestrasse in the early hours of that morning and the fire teams were coordinated from the station, so there had been plenty of distractions. He told the investigating officer that it was *probably* a male caller.

Holleman scratched his missing leg, an old habit. 'He tossed a coin.'

'I'm guessing Gerd put a boot up his arse for it.'

Three murders and not a single witness; a perpetrator apparently at ease with the early discovery of the bodies, though not careless; a confident man, certain of his abilities, exhibiting a calm, measured derangement. Mistakes weren't likely.

'The killer's helpers, then. Did Gerd have any feeling about them?'

It was the question Fischer had asked as he took the film from Branssler. 'He felt, without being able to be definite, that the order to halt the investigation hadn't come from within his parish.'

'Well, any higher up would be Panzinger, or Kaltenbrunner. We're not going to bugger around with *that* sort, are we?'

Fischer considered this. 'Need it be either of them? RSHA hardly has a formal structure. It's more a plate of macaroni than a ladder - everyone has sauce on everyone else, or knows someone who has. It could have come from Gestapo, or SD - hell, from *anywhere*.

'What's RSHA's complement in Berlin?'

'Christ knows. It's fluid, probably about two to three thousand.'

'Fine. We should be finished by lunchtime.'

'At the latest, because we aren't going to be asking any of them anything.'

Holleman grimaced. 'We have no witnesses. We can't do a door-to-door, either around the Botanical Gardens or in the victims' neighbourhoods. We can't try to find out who's protecting our man. And we absolutely can't enter *Liebstandarte*'s kaserne to interview suspects. Meanwhile, we've told one of the most powerful men in the Reich that we'll solve this in three weeks, on which basis alone he's sent my boys back to me.'

Fischer shrugged. 'And then we can think about what happens if another of the Reich's other most powerful men finds out that we're coming after one of *his* boys, and probably implicating a senior RSHA man in the process.'

'Shit. I'm sorry, Otto.'

'For what?'

'Burying you in it.'

'I could have refused.'

'Well, we're in the hands of God and Karl Krohne now.'

'God might disagree.'

Krohne hadn't been police in any of his past lives, so it had been agreed that his job would be to try to move Gottfried Schapper to assist with *Forschungsamt* resources if their investigation reached the point where no other option was available. How this might be done hadn't been discussed, because no one believed it could be. Schapper had been Göring's man since pre-Reich days and presumably wanted what his boss wanted; but at a time of widespread military collapse the chances of him using his assets to aid their lunatic scheme were all too calculable. If an investigation could call upon a bag of tricks, the bottom of theirs had been unstitched already.

'So where do we begin?'

Fischer stared at the bare wall of his office. A journeyman dauber's stab at the Zugspitze had once adorned it, and its frame's edges still darkened the otherwise pristine drabness. He missed it now, wished that he hadn't had been so quick to it put it into the bin. A death in snow was said to be merciful, almost painless, and the prospect of it might have lifted his mood a little.

Holleman nudged his shoulder. 'Otto?'

'Ladies first, I suppose. All widowed or single, obviously unaccompanied, vulnerable. None of them live near the Gardens. Why were they *there*?'

'He didn't drag them there.'

'Doubtful. They were found within metres of the road, on Altensteinstrasse, Unter den Eichen and Wildenowstrasse, three sides - north, south and west - of a rough rectangle. He may be saving the east for his next visit, but it's curious he didn't start with it.'

'Why?'

'You've seen it. The eastern boundary is just a park path, not bordered by housing for most of its length. There are a few glasshouses and maintenance sheds and then the Botanical Museum, that's all. None of them are occupied at night, so if you wanted not to be seen that would be by far the best option. But he's avoided it so far. And look where he *has* left bodies - Altensteinstrasse's a busy thoroughfare and Unter den Eichen's the ring road, for God' sake. Why would he risk being seen like that?'

'He wouldn't. He kills them in the Gardens and then drags the bodies to the periphery. If he drops them in the bushes he doesn't have to be seen by anyone.'

Fischer nodded. 'Good, Freddie, that's good. Let's talk about *him*, then. He's almost certainly left-handed, strong, knows his trade. As to *who*, I can see two possibilities. If we're right about it being someone at the kaserne, either he's been stationed there for a while and only recently experienced some trauma to trigger these episodes, or he's just returned from where there are traumas enough to bring on anything. If it's the former, I don't know how we'll make a start. But the latter … '

'Convalescent transfer records.'

'That's right. He's either rated unfit or he's getting better, in which case he's already been allocated to a CT company, and even Waffen SS have to lodge medical records with the central archive. It won't be easy. You saw it this morning - *Leibstandarte SS AH* are *the* elite, so they get to eat the first shovel-load of shit in any action. There are probably hundreds of likely candidates.'

'But not all at the kaserne's lazarett?'

'Would there be room enough?'

'So, we eliminate all the names that went elsewhere.'

'Our first job, then - the medical records of Liebstandarte wounded.'

'Where's the central archive these days?'

'I'm not sure. It *was* at Kroll Opera for a while, but when the place was bombed I heard it was moved out west, to Ruhleben. Which means Alexander Kaserne, probably.'

'Do you know anyone there?'

'No. But records for Flakgruppe South are going to be held there too. It shouldn't be difficult to find an excuse to get into the place to see Luftwaffe files.'

'More difficult to explain why you're then trawling SS records.'

'I'll think of something. There's one other thing. I don't agree with the statement that this man isn't escalating his crimes. The last one, 21 October - either he really didn't like the look of her, or it's getting that he needs to do more to satisfy himself.'

'There's something else.'

'What, Freddie?'

'The timing of this. It's been more than nine weeks since the third killing. There must be at least one, and probably two more by now. But who's been keeping count?'

3

Fischer returned to Jonas-Strasse 17 at eight the following evening, more weary than he recalled from his first day's Fallschirmjäger training. He had departed Alexander Kaserne almost three hours earlier in the Ministry's mutilated OL38 (a vehicle that was growing like a tumour in his affections), but the fourteen kilometres from there to Jonas-Strasse had thrown up a series of herculean obstacles, commencing with an air raid warning that halted traffic on Spandauer Chausee almost as soon as the last light faded. He assumed it was yet another false alarm - that two pigeons had flown in formation over the nearby Siemens-Schukert-Werkes, bringing the entire neighbourhood's flak emplacements to swivel precipitously and some idiot to slam the red button. Then, an official function at what remained of Schloss Charlottenburg had re-routed him south as far as Ku'damm, where what seemed to be most of the rest of Berlin's road traffic was queuing to admire a burst water main at the junction with Knesebeckstrasse. His only good luck was to have thought to sign out the vehicle for use overnight, so when things began to move once more he pointed the dented bonnet directly north, towards his lodgings.

At the front door he was greeted by a sense of otherness that threw him momentarily. The house had a warmer ambience than he had come to expect, and the familiar odours of cats and old women had been replaced or disguised by a heady hint of real food. He put his cap on the hall table and for once didn't advance reluctantly.

The small sitting room was busier than he had ever known it. Three adults sat around the fireplace, chatting amiably. Young Franz (or Ulrich) was carefully setting places on the small table behind them, while in the tiny kitchen Ulrich (or Franz) was busying himself at Frau Traugott's late-medieval cooker. An occasional table was supporting half a dozen bottles of Becks that almost certainly been misplaced by the Ministry (it being unavailable to any non-military entity), and there was circumstantial evidence that Luftwaffe had lost a further three tins of cho-ka-kola. Anywhere other than at a black marketeer's warehouse, it would have passed for an early Christmas miracle.

Frau Traugott beamed at him. 'Good evening, Herr Fischer. We have rabbit broth!' Her sister, winding wool from a deconstructing sweater, looked up for a moment, savoured the words and nodded contentedly. It was the first time in some weeks that he could recall a statement from one sibling's mouth not being stamped upon by the other.

So Holleman had helped himself to a brace of someone else's balcony pigs - it was hardly surprising that bonhomie overflowed. The criminal himself was relaxed, smoking a cigarette in the self-satisfied manner of a breadwinner come home to the bosom of his surrogate family. He cleared his throat, and the twin at the table smoothly took the prompt.

'Would you like a beer, Uncle Otto?'

So that was how they were going to play it. He nodded mutely, grateful for any medication that might ease the day's irritations. Holleman, satisfied that one flank was secured, continued his principal thrust.

'As I say, Frau Traugott, me and the wife made sure the boys could fend for themselves. Cooking, cleaning, any chores you can think of, just ask. They'll be happy to do the floors and windows if you like.'

Their adopted landlady nodded in time to his cadence, seduced already by an arrangement that would slow the entropy of her knees. It was a cunning strategy, but Freddie Holleman's masterstroke had been to bring three extra ration cards into the house. Six could eat far more economically than three, so the potential threat from Frau Ostermann's unruly mouth had been expunged as effectively as if her lips had been sewn together.

The rabbits shared their pot with onions, potatoes and carrots, a spectacular interruption to the prevailing culinary drought. The old women took their time over it, manhandling the larger pieces of meat and loudly cleaning the bones with the slightly hesitant swinishness that polite company calls good appetite. When they had all but removed the patterns from the plates, the boys expertly cleared the table and washed the dishes while the ladies worked the sofa, reminiscing upon every recent mouthful. The men retired to the late Schultz sisters' apartment with their beers.

Fischer described his visit to Ruhleben. There had been no problem getting a first look at the medical records index, no one had disbelieved his hazy reasoning for wanting to look at convalescent data and no one had noticed him glancing at Waffen SS entries. The disappointments had been unforced, unavoidable.

'Would you like to guess?'

Holleman shrugged. 'Three hundred?

'If the numerical sequence is unbroken, two thousand, two hundred and six. I assume that's the total for hospitalized or in convalescent companies, but not those in the ersatz regiment, certified fit or awaiting posting back to the Front.'

'Jesus! That's just *Liebstandarte*?'

Fischer nodded. 'I told you they'd been taking a pounding. This year alone, they've taken one at Korsun, at Caen, at Avranches, and, right now, somewhere in Belgium. Each time, they're the tip of the spear that our genius leaders decide to thrust at a waiting stone slab, so they get more or less wiped out and need what amounts to reconstitution. If it weren't for the name and tradition, the division would have been disbanded after Kursk. We've a hell of a job in front of us.'

Holleman sighed. 'Well, my day's been a little better, because I've been thinking.'

'As well as stealing rabbits?'

'Yes, as well as that. I may have a connection between our three dead ladies.'

'What is it?'

'People's Kitchens.'

'What?'

'One-pot suppers! All the victims were childless and living alone, so they had just the single ration card, probably no friends' network to access stuff from the black market and no serving sons to send home treats to supplement their shitty diets. They were eating at the same place - a *volksküche*!'

Modestly, Holleman lowered his eyes. Fischer thought about it, about how he wouldn't have thought of it. It made a good deal of sense. Some of the larger people's kitchens catered for several hundred needy appetites at a sitting. In a large, busy space a man could decide upon his prey without fear of being noticed.

'But the same one? Why? These women lived in different areas. Why go all that way in the dark, and in winter?'

'The food was better at the one near the Botanical Gardens. The one I'm going to find today.'

'It must be indoors, a proper dining room. They wouldn't have travelled to eat at a stall, a goulash-cannon, not on a cold evening.

But there are plenty of public kitchens, even in the suburbs. There must be something else, some other attraction.'

'It's heated?'

'But it's not the only one, surely? What else could attract old ladies?'

'Old men?'

'In a city that's crammed with them? No, it's the food, obviously, and it's always about company and a chance to warm up for a little while. But there's something more, something that makes them gather at this particular place near the Gardens, and *usually* on Friday evenings.'

'We'll find it.'

'If we don't, I doubt that anyone will find *us*.'

4

Even in the suburbs, they were a common sight - men who had marched to war and returned as something visibly less, reminding Berliners of the price that was being paid, of the sacrifices that a great destiny demanded of the nation. It was a terrible tragedy - everyone said so, as if chanting responsories to a given truth. But as their number had grown, the visibly Less had become somehow less visible. People began to resent the claims upon their compassion as if it were a rationed commodity; they reminded themselves that everyone had to fend for themselves these days, everyone had kin at the Front, everyone faced a similar prospect of seeing a father, a brother, a son come home broken, helpless. Pity, like meat, had become an occasional luxury, to be sliced very thinly.

Many of them came to the *volksküche* - men whose families had found that they couldn't cope with yet another burden. Some were entirely destitute, sleeping rough at the heart of Reich, broken soldiers who had been decently forgotten, who relied upon one hot meal every day or two to keep them just this side of death. Others were strong enough still to feel the shame of it, the sort who ate their soup with downcast eyes, hoping not to be recalled by those who'd known them in better times. A few were brazen, daring anyone to take exception to the small compensation of an hour's warmth and the pretence of company. They brought many different stories, fifty varieties of faded, neglected part-uniform and just one sort of luck.

But whatever their histories these broken veterans rarely complained, and this set them further apart from the civilians at the tables. Almost everyone else was tired of *eintopf* - the meal in a pot, the only so-called choice on offer. Even the word offended; *cabbage* or *potato soup* would have been far more accurate, with an occasional grudging admission that something else had fallen in accidentally to impart a faint flavour and a little pleasing greasiness. It was served only with bread, the gritty quality of which was particularly resented by the elderly, whose soft gums and precarious digestions wilted under the fibrous assault. If people griped about it, hadn't they the right to do so? But not the uniforms. They ate efficiently and refused to squander energy and heat that way. They didn't peer suspiciously into their neighbours' bowls to check that they weren't being cheated out of their share of gristle. They didn't talk about what they used to prefer in the old days when one could just walk into a shop and indulged a yearning. And they never gossiped about who did what, and with whom, to supplement their rations, or hinted at the diversion of foodstuffs by those who couldn't be mentioned, not by name. They just turned up, had their ration cards clipped, ate and left. It was no wonder that some folk resented them.

The one-legged Luftwaffe veteran seemed typical of the species. He had been waiting near the front of the queue when the *volksküche* opened that evening and taken a table only just inside the door. A regular diner wouldn't have been that stupid, would have known that the best of the warmth was to be found in the middle of the hall, but it was typical of wounded servicemen not to want to be seen. Some of those sitting at this fellow's table noticed that he was more watchful than the average veteran but no more friendly. He ignored a single, importune question about his wound, while a dozen comments on the awful quality of the food met only with a shrug and an indifferent glance from his cold eyes. What some of his neighbours found particularly curious (and irritating) was that he didn't seem to be hungry. After eating no more than half of what was in his bowl he offered the rest to an old lady beside him who had been pausing in her damning observations on what she was eating only to shovel in a fresh mouthful. She accepted the gift eagerly, and forgot to thank him.

They might have found his missing appetite less intriguing had they known that this was his third meal in less than ninety minutes - that his pockets were filled with ration cards, counterfeited in England and dropped over Berlin the previous week with the aim of further disrupting the Reich's dwindling resources. He had produced a new one at each *volksküche* he had visited that evening, and was beginning to regard his distended belly as a war wound. He stood a little unsteadily after the latest bout, but managed to bow formally and say good evening, which made some the older diners at his table feel slightly less uncomfortable about his unwanted presence.

At least his enforced gluttony made the winter's chill seemed less acute. He walked slowly, leaning on his metal walking stick, taking care to avoid icy patches, plotting a course towards Botanical Gardens s-bahn station. A careful observer might have noticed that there was little frailty in his movements, that this was a man who had long since come to terms with his loss and adjusted his balance accordingly. The stick in his hand was being used as a gentleman might wield one in the park. It was no more necessary for mobility than for striking down an assailant, though equally useful for both.

His latest meal had been taken in a relatively small *volksküche*, barely a dining room, on Viktoriastrasse. His first supper, two hours earlier, had been on Steglitz's southern border, too far from the Gardens to be the likely hunting ground. But it was best to be thorough, even if the extra distance tormented his stump. Still, two and a half heavy meals, abominable company and the persistent throb made the prospect of a short train ride to his adopted home a pleasant one. He began to look forward to the warmth, a cigarette in an armchair, the inconsequential conversation of his sons, and in rising spirits he started to hum something.

It died on his lips a hundred metres from the station entrance on Steglitzerstrasse, where he came to a former theatre, closed earlier that year like all such venues. It was large, able to accommodate perhaps two hundred people, the sort of building that couldn't be allowed to go to waste in these pinched times. A sign on the former billboard announced that it had been resurrected as yet another people's kitchen, open every Monday and Friday evening to provide for the district's needy or those who simply wished for company. This very evening was a Friday, and the door stood open invitingly. Slowly, without any enthusiasm, the one-legged man entered. Once inside, however, something about the hall cheered him immensely. In fact, he was probably the only diner there not to be bitterly disappointed about a certain matter, though he ate no more than a mouthful of his *eintopf* before leaving.

On the train back to Potsdamer Bahnhof he ruined the evening of an elderly lady sitting opposite him in the sparsely occupied carriage, who found it offensive that such a man, in times such as these, should regard himself as having any cause to whistle.

5

'Eddie Muntz.'

'What?'

'Eddie Muntz! A smile, a joke, a song! The Lichterfelde Reutter!'

'Not a happy comparison.' Otto Reutter's hugely successful crooning career had been built upon tugging heartstrings until they parted, but he had gone on to lose a million in the Crash and died penniless.

Holleman's hand dismissed Herr Reutter's woes impatiently.

'But they love him! They turn up every Friday, regular as bowels, to be swept back to the old music hall days. When the kitchen manager announced he'd been laid low with laryngitis the old sows almost wept! The woman next to me just pushed away her plate and shook her head like the whole point of being there had been stolen away. They come from all around south-west Berlin to see Eddie perform. And it's *only* at Steglitzerstrasse! He has arthritis, and can't travel more than a spit. He lives just around the corner on Roonstrasse and comes in about seven o'clock, when everyone's collected their food and parked their arses. He works the tables at first, shaking and kissing hands, pointing the finger, giving them the wink. Then he goes off on one of his old routines, about forty minutes of sentimental warbling and bad jokes, a few anecdotes shaped to get the tear-ducts open, and he's off home again. It all sounds hellish, but who can explain taste?'

They sat on a bench in Tiergarten, watching winter birds picking at netting over rows of allotments dug in front of the Bellevue. Excited by his discovery Holleman had wanted to talk as soon as he arrived back at Jonas-Strasse the previous evening, but offering the sisters more material to flesh out their phantom Moabit Garrotter would have been a criminal act, undiscovered or not.

Fischer rubbed his chin doubtfully. He couldn't recall having ever been this lucky as a Bull.

'I don't know, Freddie. It's taken just two days, and it stands upon your first guess being the right one. What if the connection isn't a *volksküche*?'

'I asked myself that. But the Friday opening, that fits too well with what we're looking for. And Muntz, it's too perfect! Think about how our murderer manages to get these ladies alone. Unless he's just lucky, and manages to snatch them into the bushes as they pass by him, how does he do it? He *has* to speak to them first and somehow reassure them enough to get them to go with him. And now that the bars, the theatres and just about every other social venue's been shut down, how else could he do it?'

'Someone an elderly person would instinctively trust? A doctor?'

Holleman snorted. 'Do doctors treat the elderly any more? They're all at the Front, or buried under 30-hour days in critical wards. This is someone with the leisure to choose his evenings. Besides, a doctor or anyone other local figure of authority would be known to just about everyone. Someone would have mentioned seeing his face, wouldn't they?'

Fischer agreed, though he didn't say as much. The *volksküche* idea was a good one; he just worried that it was *too* good, that it had seduced them. If they'd had a department's worth of help he would have called it their best lead and methodically eliminated the alternatives. But they had no men, no resources and no time, so whatever they chased would have to be worth it.

'Did you see many uniforms?'

'Plenty, though none with insignia of course. But it made me think. We've too many possibles in Liebstandarte's medical histories, yes?'

'Far too many.'

'Well, I think we were wrong about how fit he is. I think we can we eliminate the ones who are recovering.'

Slowly, Fischer nodded. 'It struck me, too. No leave.'

'That's right. *All* active duty leave's been cancelled for months now. So the boys in the convalescent companies and the ersatz battalions, the ones who are expected back at the Front, they aren't going to be getting out of Lichterfelde Kaserne to catch an evening with Eddie Muntz, are they?'

'He's like you and me.'

'He's like you and me - useless. And, in his case, probably messed up by it. The ones I saw in the *volksküche* looked bad, damaged and ditched by the state, their families, everyone. If Alexanderplatz hadn't shut this thing down so firmly, I'd say that any one of them had the potential to hit back at something, hard. But ordinary soldiers don't have fairy godheavies to watch over them, do they?'

'Yet you said it, *he gets their trust*. He *must* do, otherwise he couldn't have got them into the Gardens, not without noise. And even in a *volksküche* ... '

Holleman frowned. 'I know. That's the one thing I can't see. Civilians and uniforms don't mix well - at least, not from what I saw last night. The service lads kept to themselves as if they'd taken the vow, and wounds make civilians nervous, remind them of what's happening to their own somewhere out East. So even if our boy greases them with compliments about their gorgeous varicose veins, I doubt that they'd go off with him. There has to be something else.'

Fischer sighed, stood up and stamped some feeling into his feet. 'I'm going to have another day in the Alexander Kaserne records. Can you try to find any cafes that are still open for business in the Lichterfelde area? A veteran warming his stump for the price of a cup of *muckefucke* shouldn't attract too much attention. Just listen to what's being said.'

Holleman nodded. 'If it keeps me indoors in this weather, fine.' He took Fischer's arm to steady himself and stood. 'Don't bother with the leg wounds, by the way.'

'No?'

'Our boy has to walk the better part of a kilometre to the *volksküche* and Gardens, and then get home again. I could do it, just, but given the choice I wouldn't, and I've had four years' practise. The killings started recently, so he hasn't been out of the lazarett for long. Whatever's wrong with his body, he's mobile.'

6

The Kaiser Alexander Kaserne was a miscegenation of French chateau, Dutch municipal building and German university, and the sum did its best to insult each. To Fischer's eye it more resembled a Prussian Elector's clumsy response to his wife's nagging for a place of her own, somewhere to unwind with her ladies-in-waiting and their lovers. But it had the advantage of being big, and underused. Its home unit, the Kaiser's 1st Grenadier Guards' Regiment, had been disbanded after the First War, and without tenants it had gradually taken on the role of a reserve records office. Wehrmacht divisions whose home kasernes lay within Wehrkreis III military district had their duplicate records stored here. Waffen SS did not, except for medical records of their wounded personnel. In life, SS personnel went their own way; in death and distress they were statistics like any other poor bastards

Fischer showed his pass and was ordered to wait in the index office. The previous day he had been supervised briefly by a friendly *zahlmeister* looking for a way to pass the time and then allowed to examine the card indices unmonitored. He hoped to see the same man today, but after ten minutes a reserve leutnant in a neck brace came for him. From the pinched look on his face, Fischer sensed that this visit wasn't going to be a case of giving and getting the nod.

The leutnant wanted details, which he noted down. Fischer's story was credible enough - the Luftwaffe was concerned that the proportion of flak battery personnel returning to duty after convalescence was less than that of other service branches. While no comprehensive survey was anticipated, the Air Ministry wanted to compare the incidence of returns to active duty by Flakgruppen wounded to those reported in regular Wehrmacht formations. Obviously, they weren't going to be putting like with like, but if Fischer might examine medical records for, say, one reserve formation and one elite division, then the potential extremes of the equation might be covered.

There was no question that the request would be refused - it had been cleared beforehand by a comrade of Krohne's in Flakgruppe South who towered about fifteen ranks above this little snot. Even so, the leutnant took his time and gave every impression that he had the power to decide the point one way or the other. Fischer didn't mind a little arrogance - it always helped to let idiots think they were being magnanimous. He just didn't want the boy's breath warming his collar while he went about his business.

'Do you have any particular models in mind?'

Fischer shrugged and forced a smile. 'I don't really have a feel for which reserve unit would be appropriate. As for the other, we were hoping to look at Waffen SS methods. They may have something to teach us.'

The visible stiffening of the leutnant's broken neck disagreed. The Waffen SS's first call on recruits and equipment still rankled among the regular field-greys, who despite all the evidence still regarded them as not quite real soldiers. But bruised feelings notwithstanding, Fischer couldn't see how the point could be argued. No one reconstructed more quickly or effectively after a good thrashing than Waffen SS divisions. It made perfect sense to want to know just how they did it.

He was made to wait while the leutnant went away and pretended to consult someone, but a few minutes later a clerk in a gefreiter's uniform brought two card boxes and placed them on a table. The first was labelled *Landesschutzen Bataillon 316,* the second *SS Totenkopf Wach-Bataillon-Berlin.*

It was disappointing, but Fischer had already constructed the argument. *Thank you, but Totenkopf contains too many former camp guards and an increasing number of non-Germanic personnel. The results might be skewed by this fact. Perhaps the gefreiter might bring him the records for an openly recruited, purely German formation - say, Liebstandarte SS Adolph Hitler?* He had said it to himself too many times for it to sound convincing, but they had no reason to suspect his motives. Who, after all, would wade through medical records without a good reason, or orders?

He waited for the man's return while making a show of examining the cards for the home infantry battalion. It took a few moments for what he was seeing to register, and a few more to stifle the profanities that leaped to mind. He was staring into a stack of punch-cards.

Oberleutnant Holleman sat at a table in the large bay window, savouring the unfamiliar pleasure – the forgotten art - of taking time to do nothing in particular. He had discovered that the café was one of just two such establishments in Lichterfelde to have survived the extinction of leisure time; the other was a tiny place near the s-bahn, a mere hut that catered for rail workers and only between 10 pm and dawn. If the district still had a pulse, here was just about the last place it could be felt. Nursing an empty cup that had only recently held something almost undrinkable, he applied himself to it. To anyone who cared to notice he was a one-legged ex-pilot, drawing a little warmth from the wood burner in his corner of the room while making each cup of swill last as long as possible, the epitome of a tragic story being enacted all over the Reich - the wounded soldier come home. For once, acting in character was entirely instinctive.

There were three other customers in the establishment. It was a bare space with just two old film posters breaking up the monotony of whitewashed walls, an unvarnished wooden floor and a few tables that didn't match each other. The place had entertained a grand total of five visitors in the two hours since he had arrived, and only those now present had troubled to stay more than the time it took to empty their cups.

Observing such a tiny constituency took up very little of his time, and he gave some attention to the girl behind the counter. She had a pretty face, with a matching temperament from what he had observed. Except for Holleman himself she had greeted everyone who entered by name, with a welcoming comment or question for each. He found this extremely useful. Without having opened his mouth (other than to order more poison) he had learned that the elderly woman who sat three tables from him was Oliwia, who had a bad but slowly mending hip, came from Posen originally and prayed to God every day that *schwarzwalder kirschtorte* would pass her lips once more before she was summoned to His Mercy. The small man who sat at the counter was Erich, a widower with two boys who hadn't spoken to him for years; they were both at the - at *a* - Front, he neither knew nor cared where. His friend (who wouldn’t or couldn’t sit) was Albert, a former wheel-tapper on the railways whose wife Gerda was slowly withdrawing into a world where no one could follow, a journey that had begun the day *WASt* informed them of their only son's heroic sacrifice for the Fatherland.

The girl herself was Mona, and her unwitting role was that of an archivist of human misery. She had a subtle expressiveness that invited confidences, that opened wounds gently, and these people had a need to be bled. It was why they were here. They talked to each other of small things, but it was at the counter, or when Mona brought their drinks to the table, that they spoke of what frightened them, of what darkened their worlds.

It was the war, the war, the war; but also shaded hints of an uncomfortable, closer thing not to be spoken of openly. Only Albert, worrying about Gerda and not sensing his own, parallel descent, didn't try to skirt it at a distance. He used the term *monster* several times in asides that were too quiet for Holleman to do more than suspect the context. At every iteration it had the effect of stopping the conversation momentarily, of making his friend Erich and Mona herself glance around at nothing and then at the cripple by the window, the room's only unknown quantity.

He sensed that their fear was grounded upon more than the killer and his efforts, otherwise their conversations wouldn't have been so guarded. A nice collective fright brought people together, gave them an excuse to forget present problems and dwell upon its vicarious horror. But it seemed to Holleman that his fellow patrons were manoeuvring as if the subject was as unspeakable as the act itself. They gave the impression that someone - a person or persons either not known or not to be mentioned - wished it not to be spoken of. He wondered how they could know that, unless it was a thing revealed.

He tried to keep a sightless, thoughtless expression upon his face, but his racing mind made it difficult. Who would have warned them to hold their tongues? Who would have *known* to do so? Did someone from the Alex come down to Lichterfelde, stand on a table, gather the locals around it and say, *look here, we know you're worried about the old ladies Getting it, but would you please forget the whole thing?* It wasn't likely. Did a civilian spontaneously divine the workings of the RSHA by staring into the *muckefucke* dregs that stained his cup? The Reich's recent military strategies appeared to be conceived on much the same principle, so the possibility couldn't be dismissed out of hand; but to Holleman's mind the likeliest suspect was probably about sixty years old, in a uniform that didn't fit and wasn't wanted - a person who, despite his ostensible removal from civic society, regarded himself still as a part of it and was unable to hold his tongue when in the company of his non-police friends.

A talkative man, then, who either knew something or someone who did. Holleman thought quickly. He could neither leave it at that nor ask the questions that might drag out the information he needed. He opened his tunic pocket and removed a notebook. Three pairs of eyes registered the act and all conversation in the café ceased, because National Socialist Germany no longer boasted poets or diarists. He scribbled quickly, tore the page from the book, folded it, placed it on the table and caught Mona's wary eye. He smiled, raising the empty cup.

Her body shielded him from the other customers as she refilled it. He pushed the piece of paper towards her. His frown was meant to be reassuring, but whether she took it that way or as a warning, he couldn't say. She picked up the object hesitantly, and in its place he put another, blank piece that he had folded under the table.

Quickly, he drained the foul, lukewarm liquid, climbed to his feet and put on his Luftwaffe greatcoat. He turned to leave but then, theatrically, recollected the important item he had left on the table. The second piece of folded paper went into his pocket, and he sensed a slight relaxation in the atmosphere. He didn't glance back as he opened the door.

'They use Hollerith machines.'

Holleman frowned. 'So? That's for statistics and stuff. They must have files too.'

Fischer was examining the contents of his plate. To date, the Air Ministry's canteen had suffered less than civilian Berlin in the game of allocating what could be scraped from the larder's dark corners. But their definition of *meat* was beginning to surpass human understanding.

'That isn't what I mean. The punch cards were used to carry out a huge survey, two years ago. They encoded about three million medical records, just about everything they had. So I asked whether there was a quick way to distinguish between files used in that exercise and those containing data that had been entered subsequently.'

'What was the answer?'

'That it was easy; that most paper files relating to the exercise are somewhere in the upper atmosphere, destroyed the night Kroll Opera was bombed. The punch cards are all that remain of them.'

'And our fellow's likely to have been injured since then.'

'So the two thousand plus Liebstandarte casualties that I mentioned are in fact a lot of redundant punch cards and some paper files - I don't know how many, but probably no more than half the total. Our good luck.'

'You've started on them?'

'I have. So far, nothing that fits our guesses. There were many cases so severe that the poor bastards couldn't hope to hurt a wren, much less an old lady. And a lot of others where recovery was followed by a swift transfer to a convalescent company, and then an ersatz regiment, and then back to the Front. I haven't found anyone who was better than one but worse than the other, not yet.'

'Christ, I'm sure this is dog!' Disgusted, Holleman pushed away his plate, pulled a cigarette from his tunic pocket and told Fischer about the café and his *muckefucke*-ravaged gut feeling for what he'd seen there.

'You know that look, when someone realises they've been talking too loudly about the way the war's going, or the pamphlet they picked up in all innocence and forgot to drop immediately. The glance around, the hunched shoulder, the Oh Shit moment - it's like a national fucking dance-step. But talking about crime - and *murder* at that? Look at your landlady and her pretend strangler. She's been putting it around more than a ten-mark whore, and not even your *blockhelfer* thinks he should report her. It's what folk *do* when they can't talk about anything else. But not in Lichterfelde. They've been given the word - or *a* word - and it's hard to say if it doesn't scare them more than the monster himself.'

Fischer nodded slowly. 'You think he's police?'

'Who else? Who else would know?'

'If he is, we should be able to find him.'

'Gerd will know which local lads were used.'

'Dangerous, though.'

Branssler had risked a great deal already, and Holleman looked troubled. The debt he owed the Bull was already greater than he was likely ever to repay. He shook his head. 'Let me go back to Lichterfelde and speak to the girl. We may not have to ask Gerd.'

'You think she'll talk?'

'I don't know. I tried to make it clear that I wasn't testing her. I just scribbled something about whether she and the people she lived among wanted it stopped.'

'When will you do it?'

'Tonight. The café closes at eight, I'll catch her as she locks up. Have you noticed anything?'

Holleman was looking around the canteen. It was almost empty, but then it had been a long time since the building had seen anything like a full complement of staff. At about a dozen tables, diners were huddled, trying to fool their stomachs into taking nourishment. But the huddles were tight, discreet, their conversations private. Some of them seemed quite intense.

Fischer pushed away his own plate. 'You haven't heard? Orders have been moving all morning. Luftflotte 3's been ordered to throw in every aircraft they have - *every* aircraft – into supporting von Runstedt's offensive. If it fails, the Allies can control the air with carrier pigeons from now on.'

'Poor bastards. They might as well point their noses at the tree-line as they take off.'

Holleman, a pilot, knew something about air superiority and what happened to those without it. In May 1940 he had been part of the offensive that had surgically expunged the Belgian and Dutch air forces in just four days. It should have been a pleasant memory;

once they'd dealt with the handful of Hurricanes and a couple of dozen Fokker D21s it had been a matter of practising strafing runs, victory rolls and drunken songs of heroism in the squadron mess. But only his relief at coming out of it unscathed had kept the shame of what he'd done bedded down. There was no need to wonder if the Americans and British would feel the same, afterwards.

Fischer noticed the drop in morale, the phenomenon of a suddenly quiet, thoughtful Holleman. He seized the opportunity, suggested that the boys needed some time with their father, and was pleased by his prompt success. He'd found it difficult to lie to a friend, and he preferred to regret the necessity of it alone.

His second visit to Alexander Kaserne had been a remarkable success, and not just because half the records he might otherwise had been ploughing through had been destroyed. It had struck his atrophied *kripo*'s mind only as he sat between two card boxes, trying to decide how best to make a start. He and Holleman had agreed that they could forget the convalescents whose leave entitlement was now theoretical - they had assumed that men too badly injured to walk couldn't present a threat to the least hearty old woman in Lichterfelde. They were also reasonably confident that they might narrow their attention to those who were ambulant but considered unable to return to combat. All of this was sound, as far as it went. But what, Fischer had asked himself, would such men be doing? Why would they be at *Liebstandarte*'s kaserne still, when the division clearly had no further use for them? Surely, they would be at home with their families, or in a rude shelter under a rail bridge, bitterly considering their betrayal by the same as they drew their fraying greatcoats around their cold bodies? They certainly wouldn't be suspended in some form of stasis between active service and retirement, held in a barracks' stillness in which their deteriorating minds could fashion something new and terrible.

Then he recalled what he and Holleman had suspected - *he's like you and me*. A man who was finished with war, but not with service; a man who felt himself to be a soldier still, for whom loss of the life was no less to be feared than the loss of life itself. It wasn't necessary to guess how many former invalids fitting this profile might be at Lichterfelde Kaserne - the medical records would tell them precisely, because a formal posting would have been filed with the discharge sheet.

It had taken less than two hours. With a tired shrug, the gefreiter had accepted the argument regarding the unsuitability of *SS Totenkopf* records and brought files for *Liebstandarte SS Adolph Hitler* instead. Fischer had needed only to check the bottom line of each wounded man's copy *gesundheitbuch* for his last or current posting. Many of those final entries had comprised a single word: *deceased*. Others bore an equally terse *retraining*. A very few stated that the subject had been *dismissed unfit*. Even fewer recorded a re-assignment to a support unit or a training battalion, and invariably where this was the case a destination was stated also. Just five of these named Lichterfelde Kaserne.

As long as it had been a theory carrying long odds, Fischer hadn't bothered to think of what came next. But the thing had torn in from the horizon like a howitzer shell, and he had a decision to make. For the past three evenings he had watched Holleman playing with the twins and experienced a strange sense of attachment to something that wasn't his, a quality of second-hand belonging. Franz and Ulrich had been lost but miraculously restored, and he didn't believe the price of it should be that their father be lost in turn. The man they were chasing was broken - perhaps as much as they, physically. But insanity brings a more dangerous strength, and Fischer wasn't sure that either he or Holleman were up to facing it. Worse, powerful people didn't want this man's hobby causing embarrassment to his comrades or to the organization they served. If it was necessary to attempt to stop a tank assault with a stick, it was better that only one man wield it, not two.

The way that Fischer saw it, something final was in prospect. A decision had been made that the continuing deaths of elderly, socially worthless females was preferable to the publicity of an investigation, so an arrest and trial could never happen, even with the unlikely blessing of the Reichsmarschall himself. The alternative – the *only* alternative that Fischer could see - was to remove the problem informally, or be removed by it.

He was almost certain that the gaps in his memory were expanding - *almost*, because the condition itself made any accurate judgement impossible. The things that had happened long ago he was content to have gone - he assumed it was what happened over time, even to healthy minds. But to lose the recollection of decisions and acts whose consequences remained was to stand upon the edge of something terrible.

That morning he had been asked for two reports he had no recollection of having been assigned to produce. For a moment he had been angry, convinced that the man who asked him for them was playing some sort of game. But there had been no hint of it in his face, only puzzlement that the order hadn't been obeyed. He had apologized - oh yes, *those* reports; he'd produce them by noon, he promised. And then he spent the morning frantically assembling something that might pass for a job done half well, or at least not entirely forgotten.

An hour later Marx, the pay section clerk, told him that he owed almost a week's pay for his *skat* losses, a claim he was obliged to take upon trust. He wanted to ask when or how often he had played to lose such a sum, but didn't dare for fear of advertising his derangement. He was becoming convinced that some of his colleagues were looking at him more warily than previously, and he worried that he had said or done things not in keeping with his position, perhaps in moments when his concentration wandered. This was something that needed to be dealt with urgently, but he knew of no way to broach the matter to the medical officer that wouldn't create further questions regarding his fitness for what small duties they allowed him. So he spoke of them only to his particular friend, Horst.

Horst was a great fellow, a real comrade. They hadn't met in the field (at least, Horst said that they hadn't), though they had passed through the same training battalion. It had required their mutual calamity to effect a formal introduction, and what a fine feat of irony it was to have found a friend whose speciality just happened to be the tricks that a man's head could play.

Horst was proud of his metal plate. He said that it set him apart from the pansies and pretty boys - though of course, he wasn't referring to anyone in particular, eh? It was also functional, perfectly so, a service-hatch for proper field maintenance. Most men needed a hospital bed when things went wrong, but Horst just called in a mechanic to have his gearbox stripped and re-fitted. Headaches were a small price for that sort of convenience, he said.

Doctors had told him that the pain was going to be a lifelong companion, and Horst wasn't quite as amenable as he pretended. He suffered it bravely, with a tight, fixed expression that a good friend recognized immediately but didn't mention, and on his very worst days it was always better not to try to make him think too much about things. He dealt with it well, always deflected his pain by asking about yours, and you didn't insult him by saying *oh, it's not much* because there was no such thing as a little pain, not for them. God or the Devil had decided otherwise.

Horst had been quick to reassure him about his memory losses. Who, he'd asked, wouldn't want to forget some things, given the choice? Besides, a severe injury was a big thing for both body and mind, and bound to throw one's senses for while. Don't worry, he'd said, deploying one of his hearty slaps that could rattle a man's teeth in his head - let time take care of it.

But time was working against, not for his mind's peace. Horst's own head injuries were entirely physical; they caused him pain, dizziness and disorientation, but everyone knew you couldn't take a piece of shrapnel the size of a doorknob without paying a price for it. His own wounds were far from his head, and this was what made him worry that he had something other than the consequences of a chewed-up stomach to deal with.

It was Horst, trying to think of something that would allow a mind to regain a sense of self-control, who suggested a diary – obviously, not the bleating chronicle of tedium that some people imagine to be of interest to posterity, but a strict schedule of his days' events, against which he could check his subsequent memory of the same. His timetable wasn't so onerous that he wouldn't have the opportunity to keep a reasonably precise record, and he liked the idea in any case; it was a form of discipline, and it would be imposed upon a life that had lost too much of that recently. He had agreed, quite enthusiastically, to make an effort.

That was two weeks ago. Now, scanning the results, he felt that Horst had been wrong. If anything, the gap between what was written and what he recalled made his fears for his mind more, not less, acute. He read things about which he had no memory whatsoever, of conversations whose drift had drifted away entirely, of orders, given and received, that might have been carried out or not. The gaps were growing, and not slowly.

He didn't want to tell Horst about it. His friend would only try to be reassuring, and this wasn't something that could be talked away. He didn't want to hear the forced cheerfulness, the bluff, robust *never minds*; he didn't think that he could convincingly put a brave face upon it. In any case, Horst would try to get him out of himself, and that was the problem precisely. He wasn't sure that would ever be able to get back in, if he managed it.

Wolfram Busch: Born 17 March 1918, Bremen. Wounded Prokhorovka, 12 July 1943: shrapnel, removal of lower right leg at dressing station. Hospitalized SS lazarett Lichterfelde. Transfer home kaserne, Lichterfelde, 18 October 1943. Convalescent training company; rank oberscharführer.

Garin Hutmacher: Born 25 July 1922, Berlin Wedding. Wounded Gniloy Tikich River, 15 February 1944: tracer bullet, collapsed lung, liver damage. Hospitalized SS lazarett Lichterfelde. Transfer home kaserne, Lichterfelde, 26 June 1944. Quartermaster's stores; rank scharführer.

Heller Martin: Born 20 February 1921, Berlin Pankow. Wounded Buczacz, 5 April 1944: shrapnel, right ear removed, skull fracture; later diagnosed at SS lazarett Lichterfelde with personality disorders, manifested irregularly. Transfer home kaserne, Lichterfelde, 9 June 1944. Senior mechanic, motor-park; rank hauptscharführer.

Blaz Messmann: Born 29 December 1920, Potsdam. Wounded Kamenets, 26 March 1944: shrapnel, severe damage to colon, resulting in partial removal. Hospitalized SS lazarett Lichterfelde. Transfer home kaserne Lichterfelde, 2 July 1944. Convalescent training company; rank sturmscharführer.

Horst Kassmeyer: Born 15 November 1919, Hamburg. Wounded Prokhorovka, 13 July 1943: shrapnel, severe head injuries, resulting in permanent motor instability, acute headaches. Hospitalized SS lazarett Lichterfelde. Transfer home kaserne, Lichterfelde, 4 August 1944. Administrative Office; rank hauptscharführer.

The list's brevity was poignant, and Fischer could well imagine how far the definition of *fit for duty* had modified over the past two years. Even so, he was tempted to remove Busch from the list. The amputation wasn't preventing him from acting as a training instructor, so that fatal half-kilometre to the Botanical Gardens might not be insurmountable. But the date was wrong. Young Wolfram had been home for more than a year now. If he was the guilty party, why hadn't his very special symptoms exhibited earlier than 28 September 1944?

On the other hand, Martin's *personality disorders, manifested irregularly* read almost like a charge sheet. And a man who worked with his hands - how difficult could an elderly woman's throat be, after a day applying torque to battered gearboxes? If this had been a less complex series of crimes, Fischer might have set the other names aside. But broken minds weren't amenable to logical deductions.

The rest – Messmann, Hutmacher, Kassmeyer – were all equally likely or not to be the man, though the latter's lack of full motor function suggested that a degree of luck would be needed to discharge his business with consistent efficiency. Wouldn't his twitch get in the way of his hands in the middle of a choking? Then again, Messmann's stomach wound must have weakened even a …

The names blurred, and a sharp sensation - like hitting a post when riding a bicycle - emptied Fischer's mind of the jiggling odds. After a few moments he slowly, thoroughly, crumpled the piece of paper and let it fall to the floor. *Stupid.* He had tried to work it like a *kripo* and had set aside what was really needed – a sense of reality. His search for a name, his fears for telling Freddie that he had a short list and what he was going to have to do with it – what did it matter? An identification was pointless, an exercise in cleverness. There *was* no investigation; they had neither the authority nor ability to enter the kaserne and make an arrest, so a name, an identity, was irrelevant. If they pointed a finger and said *he's the one*, who would be listening? They couldn't even monitor the murderer's movements, so how were they to know when he planned to emerge from the safety of his military home? The man - whatever his name - would identify himself by the act of approaching a woman in such a way as to gain her trust sufficiently to get her into the Botanical Gardens, or nearby, without making a fuss. They had to see it happen. That was it - that was *all* there was to it.

Even a photograph (the copy medical records didn't hold them) would have offered only a brief advantage, perhaps a few seconds in which to make their man across a crowded *volksküche*, to think of a means of keeping him in sight without revealing themselves. Really, the face didn't matter - it was the uniform that would give him away with its unique *Adolph Hitler* cuff band. And even then, they had to get close enough to see it without being noticed in turn.

Of course, Fischer's own insignia would mark him out as readily as the murderer's. Most of the poor bastards in uniform who ate at *volksküche* were discharged unfit, so nothing remained except dark patches on their threadbare tunics. By the same token, if Freddie had encountered their man on his recent evening at Steglitzerstarsse he couldn't have passed himself off as a derelict, his single leg notwithstanding. They were going to have to be discreet, in a way that he couldn't yet imagine, much less think of arranging.

A knock on his door loosened the tightness in his head. Detmar Reincke shuffled into the tiny office, a thin sheath of papers tucked under his half-arm. He had parsed another batch of statistics on non-existent jet-fighter squadrons and needed them to be signed off. Fischer scrawled his signature and handed it back without reading the dubious content, but there was something about Reincke that caught his eye, something quite out of place. He looked far more … *pleased* than a crippled veteran should, in Berlin, in snow, with 1945 looming.

'What have you to smile about, Detmar?'

The young man shrugged. 'God, I don't know, Otto. It's Christmas Eve. Even in this vale of shit there's still something about the day. Report me, if you like.'

Christmas Eve - he had entirely forgotten, for very good reasons. All across Germany today there was no goose to set upon the table, no gifts to wrap, no *krippenspiel* for the kids, no good cheer to anticipate, no warmth of fellowship, no ease of spirit to set against troubles elsewhere, no hope for man's redemption with the Child's birth. He wondered what remained that could put Reincke in such a good mood. Was it anticipation of a brief interlude on his father's farm outside Flensburg, a chance to stare at the frozen fields where they used to graze livestock?

'Are you going to see your parents?'

'No. I told them that leave was cancelled.'

'But it isn't, not for Ministry staff.'

Reincke shrugged again and defiantly held his boss's eye. 'I've met a girl. She's not allowed to travel, so I'm staying here with her.'

'An ausländer? *Jesus*, Detmar! The Lord left you one good, strong hand to pull it with. Why take the risk?'

'If you saw her, you'd know.'

Love or lust, it would have to be something fairly drastic. She must have had a good heart at least, to find something worthy in a German with no right hand, a badly rearranged face and as much idea of courtship as a Simmental bull. The idiocy of it aside, Fischer was impressed. To find the wrong sort of girl at absolutely the worst possible moment and then to be happy about it was to piss in Fate's teapot and ask for a second cup. Silently he wished the romance well, knowing that it couldn't possibly be. But now he had asked the question it was too late, he was infected, too. A maudlin, senseless twinge of something better than resolute pessimism, a worm of good cheer, had stirred in his gut, and a very important matter occurred suddenly.

'Detmar, do you remember the March conference here? The one the Reichsmarschall addressed on the matter of fighter production?'

'The bloodbath?'

'Yes, that one. The place settings were unusual, weren't they? Little metal models on plinths, of famous German aircraft?'

'Something of a stab in the eye, given the news they all heard.'

'I know. What happened to them?'

'I have no idea.'

'Well, if you can find a couple of them for me, I'd be grateful.'

10

He sensed it, just, on his way back to Jonas-Strasse - the stubborn flicker of former, better times, like gas movement in a corpse; a mood, an out of place frisson, suspended amid the crowds of shabby coats and worn faces around him, whispering the day - *Heiligabend.* Queues were forming outside churches that no longer possessed the luxury of roofs; children with nothing to look forward to that night looked forward nevertheless and made more human noise than Berlin had heard in months. In the Tiergarten, he noticed that trees had been endowed with paper lanterns (though none could be lit), and a veterans' regimental band was playing the seasonal standards in front of a huge and growing crowd. Had he been Goebbels he would have used it all as material for some shit on the Indomitable German Will and spoiled everyone's evening by broadcasting it.

There was a shoe positioned very precisely on the doorstep at Jonas-Strasse 17, and he took particular care not to disturb it. In the sitting room, the twins were sticking paper stars and half-moons to the window, avoiding the dusting of fake snow they had applied already to several panes. The small dining table, too modest to be used as such by more than two diners usually, was laid with the establishment's best glasses and porcelain, all showing to their slightly chipped best upon an ornately embroidered *wiehnachten* cloth that, from the careful, loving manner in which Frau Ostermann was stroking out its creases, had probably been a young wife's labour for the marital home. Her sister and overseer had lit a small fire in the grate and was defending it with her arse, skirt lifted at the back to reveal a pair of dark green bloomers, the most festive colour in the room.

Sitting in his armchair, Freddie Holleman observed all of this contentedly, giving occasional directions to his boys as he polished cutlery with spit and a kitchen cloth. Fischer nodded him out into the hallway. There, he removed two small parcels from beneath his coat - poor efforts, inexpertly wrapped by a childless man with only duct tape and brown paper to hand. He transferred them to the parental object surreptitiously. 'Yours to Franz and Ulrich. What's that smell?'

Holleman grinned sheepishly (or perhaps rabbit'ishly) and alleged that one of Frau Traugott's neighbours had been amenable to parting with three of his stock for forty cigarettes. He admitted also to an approximation of *glühwein* heating on the stove, to which Fischer unwittingly had donated what remained of his slivovitz.

'The rest is some sort of cherry brandy and sugar water, I hope it works. Thank you, Otto.'

He was regarding the packages with watery eyes, and Fischer hurriedly outflanked a hug. 'Lichterfelde, Freddie. Not tonight, eh?'

Holleman shook his head. 'Of course not. I'd forgotten what day it was.'

'So had I. There'll be time enough tomorrow, or the day after. By the way, I ...'

There was a firm rap upon the door. Holleman stiffened and threw a panicked glance towards the sitting room. Fischer patted his shoulder reassuringly. Whoever stood outside was exhibiting an old-world reluctance to just kick their way in. He slid the bolt and pulled it open. 'Welcome!'

A heavily scrubbed Detmar Reincke nodded formally, half-turned and ushered forward a quite lovely, impeccably Aryan young woman. She tried a smile that didn't quite work, though Fischer it a decent effort from an ausländer, far from home, dragged unwillingly to a conquerors' celebration.

'This is Kalle,' her escort announced proudly. 'And this ... ' a bottle appeared from under his greatcoat ' ... is what we used to call wine, I believe!'

Against all likelihood it became a memorable evening, the meal a feast such as none present could recall, or so each of them claimed. The rabbit stew (a *winter fricassee*, insisted Frau Traugott) surpassed even that of three nights earlier, possibly due to the half pint of cream it contained. The rest was a strange, uncomplementary muddle of victuals, pillaged by Holman and Fischer (each unaware of the other's cupidities) from the Ministry's supply stores. They ate tinned cheese and *knäckebrot* as a mad sort of entrée, ersatz *sauerkraut* (fashioned from a vegetable none of them could guess at with any confidence) to accompany the main dish and *waffelgebuck* and *bohnenkaffee* to finish. The twins, forbidden the latter, each received a pack of citron drops, which they decided to ration to one per day until they could break out from their temporary encirclement (somewhere west of Bialystok) and rejoin their units.

After dinner they were allowed to open their gifts. Fischer was as nervous as he imagined parents were on such occasions - he had hoped that Reincke would find two of the same model, but all that remained in a small stationery cupboard on the first floor of the Ministry were three different types. He had chosen the Albatros and Fokker, leaving the Pfalz to some future appropriation. Politely, neither boy expressed a preference or glance covetously at his twin's acquisition. Fischer reassured himself that they could swap later, if they wanted to - but then, who would know if they did?

They were allowed to strafe the sitting room for a while before being sent to bed, and when peace came the adults gathered around the fire. Graciously, Reincke had agreed that the wine could be sacrificed in the service of making the *glühwein* drinkable, and now Fischer and Holleman carried it in from the stove in an old, misted glass tureen. Each of those present took a cup. After an awkward moment, the senior officer assumed responsibility for morale.

'More such nights, and goodwill.'

They drank, and Holleman refilled the cups swiftly. Kalle, who had remained silent during dinner except to thank everyone whenever a plate was passed her way or economically dodge over-intrusive questions from one or both of the sisters, cleared her throat.

'Peace for all.'

From a Danish *fremdarbeiter* it carried a sharp edge; in the tense pause that followed Reincke hugged her with the elbow of his handless arm, Holleman bowed in his best old-fashioned manner and Fischer started to mumble something meaningless about how all enemies become friends once more, eventually. Mercifully, he was shushed by Frau Ostermann's imperious hand. She raised her cup and waited until everyone had done likewise.

'The Führer! May God not serve him as he deserves!'

'Amen', said Frau Traugott firmly, and kissed her sister's cheek.

When they were done, Kalle became almost violent trying to clear and wash the dishes, but the sisters' rule was implacable. Holleman and Reincke were placed under orders while the three ladies eked out the last of the fire's warmth, speaking of things that on other days would have remained in the heart's bed-chest. Fischer sat a little behind them in the armchair, half-listening, longing for a cigar and a glass of something extinct to top the evening. To save her kerosene ration Frau Traugott had turned off the table lamp, and weak light from the fireplace flickered across the walls, painting the same shapes he had followed manically as a child, trying to see a resemblance before they were gone and replaced by others. In the kitchen, plates clinked against each other in the sink, masking dirty laughter when either Reincke or Holleman discreetly brought their conversation even lower, leaving the kettle to rattle busily on its hob, demanding that someone come and do the business before it ran out of steam. Above Fischer's head the ceiling vibrated slightly, disturbed by young feet mocking what was by timeless tradition the year's least effective curfew. It was all so briefly, perfectly normal that he was both enraptured and bereaved, lost in the magnitude of a recovered memory of how small contentment could be; pained by its unwitting revelation of the distance their great, poisonous endeavour had carried them. He tried to tell himself once more that he was blameless, but the flickering shapes threw that one straight back at him. He searched for some mitigation instead, a hope of redemption made possible by a faith he couldn't share upon moral reasoning he had never quite understood. It might have been there; he didn't find it.

A little after eleven the sirens sounded, and the world resumed.

Christmas Day, its larder already emptied, was overlooked. Everyone kept to their beds later than usual, trying to catch up on a mostly sleepless night sharing neighbourly odours in the basements of the courthouse on Turmstrasse. It had been yet another false alarm, but the word from Frau Speigl (who came around to Jonas-Strasse for an hour in the morning to warm her toes) was that Cologne had been hit badly, a seasonal gift from the British to their Aryan brethren. Her intelligence was usually sound, and they took it as such.

The day was cold, with a proper seasonal bite. Courtesy of Frau Ostermann's visit to the Winter Fund office on Bermerstrasse the twins now had a winter campaign kit - two scarves and overcoats, the former, outgrown property of older lads (or, God forbid, recovered from a bombed-out household). Holleman and Fischer talked about an outing, and plotted one to Flaktürm I at Tiergarten's western extremity. For two years, since the structure's topping-out, their father had been promising his sons the excursion and disappointing them, and the day seemed a proper one for amends. The twins' interrogation techniques weren't up to prising out the details. Their father just winked and promised something special.

Wide-eyed, their young breasts swelling with martial pride, they approached the monstrosity from the zoo side, straining their necks to gaze up the concrete cliff-face of the tower to the four corner escarpments where 128mm guns pointing like heroic sentries at the skies, covering the world's four corners, ready for anything. When the spell broke they looked to their father and new uncle Otto for reassurance that this was what would keep them safe, the enemy at bay. It wasn't easy. The vast state-of-the-art construction hardly belied its medieval purpose as a shelter against a stronger, more mobile threat - a bald, soaring admission of weakness. Still, the veteran cynics put on astonished expressions, pretended the same belief in what they saw.

Officially they were on manoeuvres, so field rations (black bread and one citron drop each) were distributed in the Tiergarten, and then they played football, hid and sought, learned the rudiments of juggling from an old fellow who claimed to have fought with the Boers at Spion Kop and chased birds from the allotments as numerous hand-written signs pinned to trees urged them. It was almost dusk when they returned to Jonas-Strasse. During the afternoon, Holleman had left them for an hour to go to the Ministry, to call Kristin at the Köthen hotel; when he rejoined them he was subdued, and answered his sons' excited comments sparsely. Later that evening, Frau Traugott noticed his mood and tried to interest him in anything that occurred, from the last of her apricot brandy to a carol concert at the Heilandskirche. She might as usefully have set herself to enticing a wall.

St Stephen's Day dawned dangerously clear, an end to the relatively safe, overcast conditions of the previous days. Holleman lit a small fire upstairs and set the twins a few maths exercises to keep their minds from deteriorating further under the onslaught of the sisters' renewed bickerings. When they were settled, frowning over simple equations, the two Luftwaffe officers drove through deserted streets to the Ministry in the Opel (Holleman had redesignated it the *Ottowagen*, to his sons' huge amusement).

LuftGeheimStelle IIb was a ghost department in a building full of them. Between the Ministry's main entrance and the third floor they saw only three guards, each forlornly defending the Luftwaffe's Homeland against unseasonal intruders while contemplating the empty chair at his family's table. Karl Krohne had left a brief message to say that he was putting his son on a train for Bamberg that morning and might come in later. Fischer doubted the intention would gain flesh. What was there to do here anyway?

Holleman filled a glass from the washroom sink and took two pethidin capsules, a certain indication that he planned to punish his stump.

'The café won’t be open today, Freddie.'

'There's an apartment above it. I'd sooner not be seen by her customers.'

'It may not be hers.'

Holleman took a notebook and a pencil from Fischer’s desk and pocketed them, shrugging off the suggestion. 'She wore a blouse and a thin *strickjacke* when I was there. It was a cold day, and no coat hung on the door behind the counter. She commuted down a flight of stairs.'

With Holleman gone and no one to warm it, the office cramped Fischer's mood further, but he made pretence of clearing his in-tray. All reports were from the west, where up to twenty-eight well-equipped German divisions, probably the cream of what remained to the Wehrmacht, were being thrown profligately at much the lesser of two certain evils. It was going to be May 1940 all over again, they'd been told - surprise, dislocation, a speedy thrust between the enemy's forces and a parting of the ways for those unnatural allies, the Unites States of Jewry and the British Empire. His mind went back to Zoo Tower and how adept they had all become at self-deception. One hardly needed to be a Moltke to parse movements that had become almost non-movements in the past few days; worse, the weather was clearing, so the Allies' massive air superiority was about to come into play (and *play* it would be, with an over-extended, disconnected enemy to aim for). The battle that was going to make Churchill and Roosevelt sue for peace appeared to be departing the script, another preposterous overreach misrepresented as a strategy. But none of that was Fischer's problem. All that would be required of his department was something breezy, confident and utterly misleading to convince friend and foe that the Reich had a Luftwaffe still, once it was over.

His head was down, studying the reports, and he didn't notice that he wasn't alone until Karl Krohne's office door slammed and a chair hit a wall. Gratefully, he abandoned his reading to wish his boss whatever cheer of the season remained, and to speak of killers.

Krohne's face, daubed with misery, warned him off.

'Karl?'

'I told Magda yesterday, while Peter was packing. I told her about Therese.'

Vaguely, Fischer recalled a *Therese* from a conversation they'd had a couple of months earlier. At the time, she had been merely the latest of Karl's many little adventures, a former model and bit-actress whose big break was never likely to happen - a 'looker', according to her illicit beau (who fell more often for a certain sort of woman than trees fall for tempests), the tenant of an apartment in Prenzlauer Berg where a man's ego could be warmed back to life at the cost of no more than a few minutes' diversion from his route home. But this one must have put out roots, if Krohne could still confess to it.

'It was the only way to get her out of Berlin, Otto. I've planned it for days, and couldn't do it. But Peter was going away, and it seemed …' he stopped, put a hand to his head.

It was unlikely that Magda Krohne had been unaware of several years' energetic infidelities - the implausible excuses for working late, the obvious hints of cheap scents and her husband's periodic swings between euphoria and high anxiety. Perhaps, like many strong women, she had been able to weigh things without sentiment, making do with the good in her marriage and placing the other in a secret drawer, the one that Karl had now prised open with a blunt instrument. Fischer knew her only vaguely, but had seen nothing in her that hinted at a weak temperament. He doubted that she'd be back.

Not knowing what form of words such news required, he summarized where they were - Holleman's theory of the *volkskuche*, his own decision not to tell his friend how close he was to identifying a suspect. All he got was an occasional nod, and even that might have been part of an earlier conversation Krohne was reconstructing in his head, hoping to find hints of something less final than he feared.

Fischer returned to his office, leaving his boss to torture himself in peace. He knew that he should have sympathized, said something pointlessly optimistic, but it was all a distraction. The world was disassembling, and, as with death, each of his compatriots had an individual ordeal to face, a bespoke bucket of shit to avoid if it were possible. For now, there was only one matter that they couldn't help but share. It was Tuesday, and in three days Eddie Muntz would put weight on his arthritic knees, hobble around the corner and serenade his fan club once more - three days in which to find a means of spotting, stopping and surviving the Lichterfelde strangler.

12

Holleman knocked once. An inner door opened somewhere above his head, and he heard the creak of stairs. She was wearing a coat and house-slippers - a cold apartment, not an imminent expedition.

She recognized him immediately but stood her ground, seemingly unafraid (though he might be him for all she knew). Her head tilted slightly, inviting him to state his business. He did so very quietly, making an effort to not to mislead her. She turned and went back upstairs, not bothering to check whether he followed.

They spoke for almost an hour. At one point she offered him a drink, the same *muckefucke* as she served to her customers downstairs, and he declined. Her apartment was much as he had expected - a basic, unheated three-room affair with not enough furniture and too few personal effects to give it a hint of individuality. On a small table sat several small packets, more food than one might expect had she worked elsewhere. It wasn't much of a home but it didn't look broken. If she had a man at the Front he wasn't a fiancée or husband.

At first she was withdrawn, reticent. Someone in uniform, even one missing a limb who had asked rather than demanded to speak with her, wasn't to be trusted with confidences, particularly not regarding *that* business. But that quality of *einfühlung* he had noticed in her two days earlier - of her seeing into others and giving something in return – was soon evident. It was attractive, more so even than her physical presence, and Holleman had a ridiculous sense urge not to be himself. So his questions were put as gently as he knew how, and this took a little more time than his usual technique – a very abrupt, threatening technique - required.

Her name was Mona Kreitz. She was from Kassel originally, though her family had relocated to Teltow when she was a child. She regarded herself as a local; she knew no other place as well as this, and had no wish to see more of a world she feared mightily. She was twenty-nine years old, childless, without a partner or prospect of one and with no urge to change her situation. Her parents' marriage had not been good; she preferred not to tempt fate, to test whether it ran in the blood.

Holleman didn't want to move on from the pleasant world of Mona's life and aspirations, but he had come to Lichterfelde on St Stephen's Day for a reason. It was a difficult role to play; he and Fischer had struggled to find a form of words that would extract information without giving any in return, yet a question had a way of encouraging others, and without official warrant discs it wasn't going to be easy to demand answers. So he told her that *they* – the police and certain military agencies, involved for reasons he couldn't divulge – were concerned; that every effort was being made to protect the women of Lichterfelde, and this meant that things had to be done discreetly. Panic would help no one but the monster; rumour and gossip would do no more than to bring further terror to the area, so discretion – and Holleman told Mona that he couldn't emphasise this enough – was going to be very, very necessary. He asked her if she could be trusted, and as he did so he risked taking her hand, hoping that his reading of her empathetic nature was acute and not just the fancy of a lecherous old man (which of course it was, in part).

Mona nodded forcefully, not seeming to notice his touch. She said that she often listened to what her customers had to say but wasn't the sort to repeat anything without good reason. She was happy to give any information that might help, though nothing that would get anyone into trouble. She wasn't an informer, he understood this?

He said that he did, absolutely. Their society had become soiled by informers – he was telling her this frankly, and it wouldn't surprise her to hear that police work had become much more difficult because of it. When one couldn't trust what was said, how could the truth be known? Neighbours' jealousies and spitefulness had ground many investigations into the dirt, and as he'd hinted already, the only ones to benefit from this were the guilty. So he wasn't interested in what Mona thought, only in what she thought she *knew*, and she wasn't to tell him anything otherwise.

By now, he was both pleased by the rapport he had established and astonished that such shit could pour freely from his mouth. But Mona seemed to accept his assurances at their face value and opened up a little. She had worked at the café for two years now. The owner, an elderly Dahlem man, an old family friend, suffered from a heart condition and had looked for someone reliable to keep the business going in bad times. It wasn't, of course – *going*, that is;

there were no takings these days other than ration clips, and she suspected that her employer was more sentimental about the café than common sense should have allowed. But she wasn't complaining; she had the apartment that came with the job, could eat at his expense at a time when many were going hungry and had the company of her customers.

They weren't a very mixed lot these days, as he might imagine - predominantly older folk, many with sad stories that had to be aired somewhere. Her own mother had been a worrier about small things, a lamenter of the bad and indifferent alike, and Mona had been obliged to grow up with a listener's ear which helped greatly in her present job. Not that there was much to hear that was small or indifferent any more. Almost everyone had a tragedy that could be softened a little by talking of it, and some had several. They were the fruits of any war she supposed, even when things were going well.

She paused at this point and looked nervously at Holleman, trying to gauge whether he was the sort to believe still in the nonsense of Final Victory, whether she had said too much already. But he waved a hand and made a *moue* with his mouth, to let her know that they shared a view about what they were supposed to think. Then he asked if they might speak about the *situation* in Lichterfelde. She nodded, and told him that the stories had started about three months earlier. At first, she had only half-listened. Back then they'd still had the radio on for bulletins, trying to make sense of what was happening in France and the East, and most of what was discussed more than a metre from her elbow hadn't registered. But when everyone got sick of the stream of awful news dressed up as hopeful, the radio was retired and the *stories* – if that was what they were – became the only matter that took her customers out of their private concerns.

By the time Mona noticed the atmosphere two ladies were said to have died near the Botanical Gardens. Details were very sparse; there were several versions of what had or might have happened, and countless theories regarding the guilty party were pored over. Someone – she couldn't recollect who - was convinced that the killer was a retired general officer, one of several former commandants of the Kaserne who had remained in the area. But these were old Prussian academy men, not the new lot, and she wasn't convinced that any of them were sufficiently vigorous still to do that terrible business, however it had been done. Another customer – an elderly Polish lady, long married to a respectable German – believed it to be the work of a railwayman, like the monster Orgozow. The Gardens were close by two s-bahn stations, so he could have committed his crimes and been miles from the scene before anyone discovered them. Others had suggested – very quietly, and always after making particularly sure of their audience – that only a high-ranking member of a certain organization would have the ability to move around at will without his identity being checked constantly. No one knew anything, but almost everyone had a theory.

Holleman asked if anyone had suggested it might be someone from the kaserne. They were very fit men, after all, and had a reputation …

Mona dismissed the suggestion firmly. The boys there had always been respectful of Lichterfelde and its people. There had never been any trouble from them, not even when they were still being given evening passes and allowed to visit the area's bars and cafés - when there had *been* bars and cafés, that is. They were very well disciplined, much more so than the old cadets, arrogant types who had regarded everyone else as peasants and treated them as such. Back then, there'd been many local families paid not to make a fuss about their violated daughters - at least, that was what Mona had been told by some of her older customers. No, no one was thinking it might have been one of the kaserne's boys.

But then, something strange – *stranger* – had happened. A rumour went around that a third lady had died, and talk in the café became even more single-mindedly devoted to the circumstances of the deaths and the identity of the murderer. This was the beginning of November, and everyone was sure that the village was going to be inundated with police, even if they were spread thinly elsewhere and doing their best at difficult times. Yet, almost overnight it seemed, there was a sense of something going away; it was hard to explain, but Albert, one of her regular customers, had compared it to a valve being turned below a large water tank and suddenly there being *nothing* in the place of all that former pressure. But no one could quite say what that *nothing* was, not at first. A few people wondered if they had imagined everything - that a rumour, self-feeding, had assumed far more substance than it deserved. But no, one of her customers knew Hilde Kempff, the woman who had discovered the body of the second victim. The killing was a fact, not the sort of twisted fiction that old Hans Lutze liked to make up to keep everyone listening to him.

Hans Lutze, she explained, a *rottmeister* from Steglitz, a true, pure bore. He liked to hold court in a corner of the café where his cronies would pretend to listen to his stories while giving each other the wink and the nudge, laughing into their hands at him. She hadn't seen him for a while. Perhaps their old bar – the one whose closure had brought them to the café in the first place – had re-opened, though now that she thought about it his friends still came in on their usual night, just without Hans. But he was old, and moaned about his health. Perhaps he had been ill lately, or winter was pressing too hard upon his bones in the evenings.

So a sense of quiet unease had settled upon the area. There had been *kriminalpolizei* here at the beginning, though they had interviewed no one that she knew personally. But they went away, and it was as if Lichterfelde was being left to deal with its own problem. No one could say what had happened, but some had heard – or *said* they'd heard - that there had been a fourth killing. If the police weren't interested then perhaps it was true that the killer was someone very important, so even to talk about it might be the same as being caught with a leaflet, or a Jewish surname. It was difficult to know whether to be more frightened about the monster or the silence around him.

Holleman asked if she knew any local policemen. Other than Lutze only one, she told him - a Steglitz man, Rudolph Bildmann. He used to come to the café quite regularly, but it had been some time since she had seen him. The regular *ordnungspolizei* were worked off their feet these days, too few men for too many streets, so it wasn't surprising. A couple of elderly reservists, *hilfspolizei* attached to the local station, came in occasionally. One of them she didn't know, even by name. The other one was Paul Schroeder.

Paul was Lutze's partner, a lovely man, a widower who'd come out of retirement the previous summer. He wasn't more than a glorified *blockhelfer* despite the uniform, and he had no sense of self-importance, much unlike his partner. But he too had been different lately. He was less willing to chat at the counter - a bit subdued, or frightened, like everyone else. It was the killings, obviously. If Holleman needed to speak to him she could pass on the message, but she couldn't say when next he might come to the café.

He gave her a card, listing a number at the Air Ministry, department *LuftGeheimStelle* IIb. He told her that this was a secure line, and that anyone using it would not become known to any other agency. Again, he stressed that discretion was most necessary, and he asked Mona not to repeat any detail of their conversation. In fact, if he were ever to return to her café, it would be best if she didn't recollect him - he wouldn't be offended, he said, with what he hoped was a roguish smile.

Was it true, she asked him, that the authorities had washed their hands of this business? No, he reassured her; it was just that things had become complicated, what with resources being spread so thinly, and the great reorganizations necessary to meet the coming … *challenges* from the east. But he and his colleagues were determined to pursue the matter, *if* they could continue to do so without interference, or idle speculation, or open mouths compromising their efforts. He hoped that she understood?

Mona nodded. She told him that she was glad he had come, because although she didn't know what to believe of what was said officially these days, hearing nothing at all was worse. And if he ever *did* return to the café he would be very welcome, even if she wasn't permitted to say so.

13

The flea market was closed, and although Kurststrasse was a thoroughfare almost no one was using it. It was mid-morning; civilian workers were at their workplaces, soldiers were digging in everywhere, *hausfraus* and the unemployed were mostly indoors, giving what little warmth remained in their bones a decent chance. Three men met among gravestones in the churchyard opposite the market, unobserved, unnoticed.

Gerd Branssler grinned as Holleman approached, and the two men hugged tightly. It had been seventeen months and a world ago, so Fischer stood back a pace, giving old cronies a little space for sentimentality. But the honeymoon ended the moment Branssler unlocked his iron grip.

'What the *fuck's* been going on?'

'Exactly what you set us on, Gerd.'

'Well, you've been spotted. Most of the Quality's been dragged across to Prince-Albrecht-Strasse to explain why it is that someone's asking questions about a matter that shouldn't *be* a matter anymore.'

The prospect of half of Berlin's senior police being roasted over a slow fire didn't wrack Fischer's conscience, but he was puzzled by it.

'I don't see what they can know. We've made no ripples in Lichterfelde. The only person who's been asked anything directly is someone …'

'… who wouldn't say a word, ever.' Holleman shook his head. 'I've been seen around the place, but who's going to think that a bloke with a tin leg's any sort of trouble?'

Branssler shrugged. 'Something's got them going. And then *we* were called in, me and Dieter Thomas, he was the other Bull assigned to the thing. Almost two hours of it - who the fuck have we been talking to, the wife, the kids, the mistress, the old fellow who sells us cigarettes on the way to the Alex -*anyone* who could have made sense from the wrong sort of fart, they wanted to know.'

'What did you say?'

'That the day we were taken off it we forgot it. I showed the boss my work schedule, asked him if he thought I hadn't been glad to be rid of one more mess. Dieter said the same, about he hadn't seen his family for days, what with all the stuff on his desk, so how the fuck could he have spilled the story?'

'You're alright with him? Your boss?'

'Fegmann? Probably. He thinks it's far more likely that it was some bastard upstairs, a greasy little shit in a grey suit who sold encyclopaedias or rubbers back when people had to have real jobs, boasting about stuff to make himself seem harder than he is.' Branssler grinned. 'Even if it wasn't. Still, they know something, somehow.'

Fischer frowned. 'If they do, why aren't they coming after us? Why spend time and manpower eating their own while we're busy searching out what they want to keep hidden?'

Holleman was nodding. 'They've got an itch, that's all. We'd be lying in several sewer pipes already if they knew what we'd been doing.'

Branssler sighed. 'Well, it's a mess. What do you want?'

Fischer told him what he and Holleman had to date. It took a while, and the Bull glanced around constantly as he listened. When he heard about the *volkskuche* he nodded. The *kripos* hadn't been on the job long enough to work up any ideas, but it was the kind of theory that investigators liked - one that drew together several ragged edges. It didn't mean that he fell for it.

'What about hospitals? Were the old ladies being treated for the same complaint?'

'Gerd, *no one* treats old ladies any more, you know that.'

'Some of the bethels do charity work, if it's … useful.'

He meant *experimental*. Fischer thought about it, shook his head. 'The kaserne's lazarett is the only major one in the area, and they weren't being treated there. Not unless Himmler's been organizing battalions of storm-*omis*.'

Holleman grinned. 'Don't suggest it, for God's sake. Gerd's right though, it needn't be the kitchens. It's just the thing that fits best.'

'Gerd, what about the *orpos* you used? Were they out of Steglitz?'

'No, it's a small station, reserves almost to a man these days. We've used Dahlem boys before so we borrowed a couple. Technically, Lichterfelde's not their beat, but it's close enough. I can get you the names.'

'Does Hans Lutze sound familiar?'

'Yeah, a little. Who is he?'

‘A *rottmeister* at Steglitz, we think. He hasn’t been seen for a while.’

Branssler nodded. ‘I remember him. An old sod with a real working mouth. He couldn’t stop talking about how *he’d* found the corpse.’

‘Which corpse?’

‘The third I think, the one in Wildenowstrasse. But she was under a bush, and I don’t believe he’s the sort to bend enough from the waist to spot something on the ground.

‘He had a partner, a reservist, Paul something.’

‘*He* was the one who found her, my money on it. Dieter spoke to him the next day and got all the detail the other idiot couldn’t provide. Not that it was any use to us.’

Holleman glanced around, gauging the distance between them and any strange pair of ears. All he found was a solitary civilian, hurrying east along the opposite side of Kurststrasse, oblivious to anything but his shoes.

‘Lutze has disappeared. At least, no one’s seen him for a while.’

‘I’m not surprised. They wouldn’t rank a reservist as *rottmeister*, and if he’s a career man who hasn’t moved any further up the ladder by now he’s useless. He's probably just wandered away from the job. We’re seeing more of it these days, the old ones quietly fucking off to their sisters’ places in Baden or Augsburg, shitting themselves about what the Ivans do to Germans in uniform. No one bothers to check their papers, not at that age. Think it matters?’

‘We don’t know. It may be nothing.’

‘A lot of it may be *nothing*.’

Fischer shrugged. ‘We haven’t come far. But there are just two of us, having to work with as much public face as a couple of burglars.’

Branssler scratched a cheek that didn't look to have been shaved for several days.

'So, what next?’

'We try to catch him with his hands on a throat.'

'That sounds right.'

'And…'

'What?'

'It should be me, just me. There's no reason for Freddie …'

Both Branssler and Holleman sniggered, and Fischer felt his carefully staged moment of nobility slip away. The Bull's eyebrows rose innocently.

'You're going to stake out the Steglizerstrasse *volkskuche*?'

'It's the only way.'

'And you're going to be anonymous? What, remove your insignia, blend in like a veteran fallen on bad times?'

'That's right.'

'Look in the mirror, Fischer. You can take off whatever you like, and still you'll stick out like a hard-on. That face, it's completely unforgettable - you show it in a crowd and the crowd will be able to repeat it, scar by scar, to anyone who asks. Not Freddie, though - alright, he's got the one leg, that's common enough these days among the down-and-outs. But who'd remember *his* face?'

'Thanks, Gerd', said Holleman mildly.

It had been the one matter Fischer had meticulously avoided - that of his surviving the evening. But Branssler was right; it had been almost three years since he'd enjoyed the gift of being just another face among others, of being seen without causing offence. If he sat down the following evening in the full dress and insignia of a *General der Flieger* it would still be the mutilations they'd see and remember. His place was in the dark while someone recognizably human did the public appearances. Freddie Holleman would have to be the front line.

An *Ostwind* roared down Kurststrasse past the graveyard, the turret gunner at his place against regulations. Fischer wondered if it had been one of those he'd seen days earlier, chewing up the old quarter, now redeployed to spoil the view elsewhere. The irony struck him suddenly - that its modified Panzer IV chassis was now doing to Berlin's streets what its previous incarnation had doubtless done to any number of towns and villages in the days when German forces were marching outward. Rebuilt, it was a weapon effective now only against low-flying aircraft, and the British and Americans hardly ever dropped below eight thousand metres. What was the significance of that?

Branssler coughed, hawking diesel fumes out of his throat. 'Thank Christ they never build *Germania*. That thing would rape a marble road.'

Holleman laughed. 'How would they have managed the victory parades? Rubber sheeting? Levitation?'

Fischer, a Balt, had never ceased to admire Berliners' ability to find the funny side of Hell - a wonderful, irresponsible quality, absolutely necessary in a city in which a certain Austrian gentleman had raised his standard. Where else could the native phlegm have handled the consequences of his pissing upon the World's four corners?

A bottle emerged from Branssler's overcoat pocket, and they perched on gravestones, taking turns at it like schoolkids, one eye sharp for trouble, trying not to cough as the unidentifiable liquid scorched their throats. After a while snow began to fall lightly, and even before it had settled Holleman was trying to scrape together a snowball from the eternal resting place of one Adolph Maria Gentz, who had departed his corporeal estate at some indecipherable moment during 1867. Branssler's feet, which were resting on the same gentleman, playfully scattered whatever Holleman managed to gather, and then they were on their knees, wrestling, laughing like idiots while Fischer held the bottle for them, watching from an unbridgeable distance.

A few minutes later, the *Ostwind* swept past them once more, in the same direction as before. The gunner had either fallen off elsewhere or been driven inside by the weather.

'The bastard's doing laps!' cried Holleman as Branssler up-ended him for the third time. After that, the world's several wars went away for a while.

14

Paul Schroeder was a conscientious man. His wife (God keep her soul) had said so often, and she wouldn't have tolerated anything less in a husband. For forty-five years, man and boy, he had kept the books at Grossmann and Sons' machine tool company, a tenure interrupted only by the First War, and, eventually, the creeping astigmatism in his right eye that made reading small figures impossible. Of course, Herr Grossman and his sons had disappeared from the firm years earlier and from society itself a little after that, but Paul had carried on under the new management, working scrupulously, maintaining a perfect attendance record (not a day's unauthorized absence in more than four decades), seeing other staff come, tread water and go off to more promising opportunities elsewhere, politely hearing and refusing managers' suggestions that entries might be accelerated or postponed creatively to burnish the company's balance sheet in this or that accounting period. Eventually, he had come to be seen as a near-permanent fixture, as much a feature of the former Grossmann and Sons as the ornate plaster ceiling work in the senior dining room or the iron boar that sat above the main gate. But the employment laws applied to Paul as to any less conscientious employee, and retirement had come as wrinkles do, expected and resented equally.

They had been sorry to see him go. On the day itself, one of the parent company's senior managers had himself driven all the way across Berlin from Pankow just to shake Paul's hand, present the small gold watch and entertain his colleagues with roguish anecdotes about how his shining honesty had caused more than one climbing fellow to want him shuffled elsewhere. And then he had offered Paul a lift home in his Mercedes, right to the door of his apartment block, in broad daylight. You couldn't ask for a better testimonial than that. As Paul watched the limousine disappear down Lothar-Bucher-Strasse he felt that life could offer no greater fulfilment than that a man's qualities be so correctly acknowledged.

The terrible anti-climax of retirement proved to be worse even than he had expected. He could never understand why some of his colleagues had looked forward to it, had spent years anticipating it in any number of dreary monologues about the things they were going to do with *a bit of time on their hands*. Paul really didn't see how gardens or matchstick sculptures or pigeons could adequately replace one's life's work. He hadn't looked forward to his own golden, eventless years with anything other than dread, and everything he feared had promptly revealed itself as an immutable truth.

Then Gerlinde had died - a woman as strong as a breeding sow, passing from rude health to desiccation in what seemed like a moment, the cause of it as much an enigma to the doctors as to her loving, grieving husband. He still saw her empty hospital bed as clearly as his own reflection in his shaving mirror - the day itself was impossible to forget of course, because it had been the first of the present war, the day the Führer finally lost patience with all those stupid Polish provocations and was moved to defend the Reich. Gerlinde had been worse than usual that week, off her food and barely able to listen to him telling her the news without slipping back into sleep. Still, he had been utterly unprepared when they told him she had passed away peacefully the previous evening, only an hour or so after he'd kissed her goodnight and come home. He could tell that the doctor felt the same way - the man wouldn't look him in the eye, kept shaking his head, trying to be matter of fact, but yes, it was there, Paul could see it clearly, the shame of having failed his patient. Perhaps it had been an infection not known previously. There had been a lot of elderly people dying in hospitals all over Berlin that week in September 1939, a curious, tragic thing. He couldn't blame the man.

A house emptied of its beating heart; a dragging procession of days, weeks and then months without purpose, as if Paul were suspended in a bitter jelly waiting for what remained of his life to be consumed. Neighbours brought him dishes they had cooked and asked him to join in pursuits that filled their own days, but such kindnesses only made the pain of his loss more acute. He started to do what old men did, to wander the streets wrapped up against any sort of weather, or sit for too long holding an empty cup in places where anonymous human company kept the mind from turning entirely within itself. And when he returned to his cold house each afternoon he would stare at the walls and think of other days, when there had been order and company in his life.

A former colleague from Grossmann's, someone he hadn't known well, made the suggestion. Really, he had quite urged it. Men were needed more and more at the Front (he had said this as if it were a revelation); all the young ones had been taken and then those in middle age, or what they used to call middle age before necessity adjusted everyone's understanding of the term. But now there was a hole in the Home Front, and men were needed to replace those who had gone. Of course, one could always contribute in other ways - there were, after all, those who felt they were doing their bit by telling tales on their neighbours, or monitoring their movements with minute attention, hoping to scrape together enough dirt to make stains. But wouldn't it be more worthwhile to help ensure that the streets were safe?

It was an attractive argument. To Paul, moving from a position of value to utter invisibility was a painful thing, and if there was still a useful role for a man healthier than his sixty-five years deserved, well, that was all to the good. So with his former colleague's assistance he made his application, had an interview with a rather intimidating Major and was accepted immediately for the auxiliary police force, the *Hilfspolizei*.

He'd expected no more than an armband and schlagstock, but they provided a full uniform, one that would have fit a larger man quite well. Naturally, the training was cursory, a matter of form only. It followed proper *schutzpolizei* protocols yet Paul had a sense that much was omitted, probably because of the lack of faith their instructors had in the raw material. He was, after all, patrolling the streets less than a month after his enrolment, though in the company of a more experienced man from whom he was expected to learn the practicalities of police work.

Paul quickly came to regret being placed under the tutelage of Rottmeister Hans Lutze. They had a necessary job, respected, and to do it correctly required a degree of commitment. Unfortunately, his new mentor was a man who went out of his way to display rather less than a *degree*. On their first beat together he told his pupil that there was no necessity to strain a bollock or two trying to get somewhere they needn't be if the only result was to make their station master think that they were good, eager boys. There was a way of doing things, a way they weren't taught during their training, which allowed a fellow to please his bosses and keep his feet from swelling out of their boots. He, Lutze, didn't mind sharing these revelations with his new mate, because it was only right that thirty-five years' experience should be to the benefit of those who were smart enough to learn from it and who didn't come to the job with all sorts of ideas of their own.

Paul had never been assertive in the company of other men (other than upon the matter of book-keeping), and being new to the job he didn't believe it was his place to question the way things were done. So he became the obliging dog at Lutze's heel, imitating the walk, noting the reassuring manner with which his partner greeted the perambulating citizens of Steglitz and Lichterfelde, taking his ease at the prescribed intervals determined by some arbitrary yet venerable custom that carried a man to and from his station over precisely the correct term of hours. In doing all of this he learned almost nothing of what it was that a policeman was supposed to do, though he heard a great deal of the intrepid and sanguinary career of Hans Lutze, who, in addition to many other admirable qualities, had the gift of not being able to keep his lips together for two adjacent minutes.

On their daily rounds Paul became a sort of extemporary microphone, being talked at by someone who was projecting his tale, suitably embellished at each successive telling, into posterity. He was not required to respond to any of it with other than an occasional, appreciative grunt. Indeed, it was obvious that Lutze regarded anything more as an interruption and therefore unendurable. It was equally obvious that the aspirations, opinions and even the name of Paul Schroeder remained a relative irrelevance that had scratched not so much as a mark upon his partner's memory.

But Paul's compensation was that he endured this ordeal in the open air, and in all weathers. He loved the outdoors, savoured it with a passion nurtured by more than four decades' service in a dusty, unventilated office. He and his wife had spent most of their brief holidays walking in the Spreewald or the Harz Mountains, bronzing their knees, filling their suburban lungs with God's air, and a large part of his loss of her had been the loss also of that companionable delight. So *ruining his arches* - Lutze's sour diagnosis - was ample compensation for the aural discomforts of his working day. Within weeks his body began to feel less than its age, and good, comfortable sleep came to him at nights in a manner he hadn't known since Gerlinde passed on. It was a little blasphemous to think it, but he might almost have blessed his luck to be alive at a time when a plague upon younger men had restored some occasion of dignity to their elders.

Soon, it seemed even that Hans Lutze might be taking benefit from their relationship. A persistent, quietly expressed opinion of what their duties entailed (*nagging*, Gerlinde would have called it) gradually effected a perceptible change in his partner's behaviour. At the beginning of this insurgency, any suggestion or nudging enquiry met invariably with a blunt *we don't Do It that way, watch and listen*. More recently however, Paul's near-refusal to do things that were in plain contravention of instructions or regulations had provoked little more than a sigh, and sometimes even mute acceptance. Upon one night at least, it had brought so palpable a reward - at least, that was how Lutze saw it - that Paul could imagine him drawing a lesson from it and changing his ways.

During the previous weeks, two ladies had been found murdered in Lichterfelde in the most bestial manner imaginable. Alexanderplatz was sending men to assist; in the meantime Steglitz station, already drastically undermanned, managed to mobilise only two of its elderly personnel. Paul and Lutze were ordered to patrol the perimeter of the Botanical Gardens during the early night hours, and to do it with *excessive vigilance* (their station master's exact phrase, enunciated carefully so that the message was fully understood). Obediently, Paul had paid particular attention to his surroundings as they walked, and he listened even less closely than usual to tales from the trenches. Twice, they did their prescribed circuit, trying to ignore the gentle, cold drizzle that dribbled down their necks. But then it began to rain quite heavily, and Lutze, who shared much of a hearth cat's dislike of moisture, declared the active phase of their beat to be at an end.

For once, Paul resisted firmly. He pointed out that the murder of old ladies required something more than the sort of apathetic response the police offered to misdemeanours. When Lutze sighed, he went further. He told his partner that there were some occasions when nothing less that one's best efforts would do, even if the price of it was sore feet and a soaked neck (and more implausibly gory stories, though he didn't say *that* aloud). And when Lutze refused to emerge from beneath a mature rhododendron bush on Altensteinstrasse that was giving him an adequate degree of shelter, Paul told him that he would go on alone if necessary.

Ten minutes later, even before Lutze had finished moaning about 'overtime', they found her. At a near-subconscious level, rhododendrons - their spread and dense, concealing nature - had lodged in Paul's head, and as they walked he stooped at each large bush to shine his torch beneath it. Lutze watched this performance with pitying amusement until the moment that Paul shouted loudly at him, quite out of character, at which, reluctantly, he shuffled over to see what the hell could be so interesting.

Of course, he sent Paul to call it in while he remained out of the rain, keeping company with the body, and when the *Kripos* arrived he took all the credit for the discovery. Paul didn't mind (it was the sort of thing that Lutze *did*, after all); he was too quietly pleased with himself to care, pleased that being conscientious still had its reward in the world, and he took the wink and the slap on the back from the big, thick-set Alexanderplatz Bull with some pride.

For twenty-four hours they were the toast of the station. Most of the others were a little dazed at Lutze's success, but they treated Paul now as though he were one of their own. The Bull's partner returned the following day to take a more detailed statement and even hinted – in front of the station master - that there might be a job going at the Alex for a trainee policeman with the right attitude. It was a joke, naturally, but it was for Paul's benefit rather than at his expense, and a sense of *camaraderie* almost overwhelmed him. A human life had ended terribly and he felt very bad about that; but in every other sense it was the happiest moment of his widower hood.

But then the tiresome, obtuse Hans Lutze simply disappeared, and the world's oddness reasserted itself. At first there were nudges and winks - it was suggested that perhaps Paul should go out on his own, seeing as how certain lazy bastards, having done their job for once, had decided to recover from their exertions at leisure. After a day or two there was curiosity, and then exasperation - how *like* Lutze this was, after all, to finally raise expectations and then piss upon them. Had he said anything to Paul since the incident, or behaved differently in some way? No? Then came the beginnings of an enquiry, the station master himself going around to Lutze's home, asking questions of his neighbours, and a start was made upon tracing any living relatives to whom he might have fled.

And then nothing at all, or worse - a day when they were told never mind, forget about Lutze, about the body in the Gardens, everything. A new investigations unit was being set up to chase the perpetrator, and it was now apparent that Lutze - who, after all, had known precisely where to find the third victim - was involved in some manner. Everyone had been compromised by this, particularly Paul Schroeder, though it was accepted that he had merely been an innocent dupe in the matter. It was for the best – it was *essential* – that nothing further be said, either about the killings or Lutze, until the unit had concluded its work. They were told that they were now a part of the investigation, and had to act accordingly.

Paul complied with the order, naturally. At first he was fearful that the reassurances were a ploy; that he was suspected of complicity in the crimes and had been placed under a discreet but dangerous surveillance. Yet no one came to question him further about his movements or the discovery of the third corpse, and as puzzling as this was he couldn't help but be relieved. For a little while, he thought about going into town to see the friendly Bull at the Alex to ask whether he might be of any use to the new investigation; but he realised that this would be both inappropriate and attention seeking, and someone of sound mind wouldn’t be so foolish. So he kept his own counsel, which is to say he did nothing at all. That wasn't difficult because no one was saying *anything* - not at the station, not in the streets, not over hundreds of back fences as the washing went up or came down. All the usual intercourse of the outer suburbs carried on as before, other than the matter of the killings and Hans Lutze’s part in them. Upon that subject, a silence settled loudly over Lichterfelde.

Paul continued to turn up for his shifts - a conscientious man could hardly do less, though the pleasure he had taken from his duties had disappeared as emphatically as Hans Lutze. He was switched back to the day shift, and spent most of his time separating neighbours and adjudicating such deadly matters as trespasses upon assumed reserved seats in bomb shelters. It kept him busy of course, being out and about in the company of people (too many of them some days, if he were being honest). Nevertheless, he was aware that he was merely discharging a role rather than savouring it, and to a man like Paul this was stale bread.

It was one thing to be dutiful, another to obey in his heart. Events that confused him also preyed upon his mind, obliging him to revisit what he should have forgotten. He wasn’t a real policeman, certainly, but he was troubled by what he couldn’t sense or see. An investigation, however discreet, had to have a presence. It had to ask questions of someone, take steps to ensure that all possible avenues of enquiry were followed. Most importantly, it had to offer a sense of movement, to reassurance folk that the implacable process of justice was in hand. But Paul couldn't sense *anything*. The silence was more like a shroud covering what had passed, and that would be terrible enough if it *had* passed. But there were rumours, whispered across the silence, that the creature proceeded about his business unhindered by the phantom investigation - that another woman, and perhaps two, had been found dead in the same manner as before.

Not being a real policemen, Paul shouldn't have felt that he was betraying a sacred trust. But he wore a uniform and that said something, or should have. It was a responsibility and, yes, a calling; people who passed him in the street, who asked if he might intervene in some matter (however trivial), had expectations of what stood behind him, vast and abiding - the rule of law. A uniform might be removed of course, but not the obligation it carried. A man might tell himself that he was nothing much, a tiny part of something vast, but his warrant disc said something else. He could absolve himself of the indifference or incompetence of others, and certainly, he could accept that there were some things he was not qualified to judge. But in all the silence, Paul couldn't stifle the murmur of his doubts. He was absolutely certain - he *knew* - that Hans Lutze, for all his many, obvious faults, had no connection with or part in the killings. He couldn't see how men of intelligence, with years of experience investigating the darkness in men's souls, hadn't arrived at the same conclusion.

So it became easier to believe that they *had* done so, that there was a reason for allowing the assumption to stand unchallenged. Perhaps, he told himself, it was a subterfuge, part of a plan to put the real killer at his ease and encourage some mistake that would expose him. For a while this logic was comforting, until its weakness became too apparent. If nothing was being seen to be done, if no one was being questioned, if the killings continued unhindered, and if someone was content to allow guilt to lie at the door of an old, disappeared man, then the likeliest explanation was there was no investigation at all.

Paul Schroeder was a conscientious man. Everyone who knew him said so, or thought it. He was by no means courageous, or foolhardy, and never did things without looking at the consequences as far as he could judge them. But not doing things when something *needed* to be done was wrong, as anyone with a conscience understood perfectly well. So the business troubled him exceedingly, the more so as weeks passed and the silence dragged on.

Trying to distract himself, he began to visit the Blue Rendezvous Café once more during his off-duty hours. It was Lichterfelde's only remaining enterprise of the sort, and he had spent much time there when his widowhood pressed hardest. The quality of its few products fully reflected the hard times, but the manageress, Mona, was always welcoming, and if the filth she served was a crime against the memory of coffee at least it warmed the hands while conversations - complaints, usually, of health, rations, the war - stuttered to life. For his own part he tried not to speak much, to offer his opinions. Having borne the brunt of Lutze's reminiscences for months he was loath even to mention his own, much less hold forth to a hapless audience. A customer's occasional enquiry tried to elicit something worth repeating, but he was careful to say nothing that might travel.

He couldn't speak of *the matter* to anyone, of course, and as far as the generality of Lichterfelde was concerned, Hans Lutze was merely elsewhere, absconded, gone west perhaps. Paul purposely avoided the café at times when Lutze's old cronies gathered, and he offered no comment when any of the locals speculated as to what had dragged the *rottmeister* from their midst (not that they were complaining, of course). This passive collusion with what he was coming to believe was a lie made it more difficult for him to remain silent; but as he reminded himself, even had it proved unbearable there was no one to whom he might unburden his fears.

He sensed that the girl, Mona, was trying to bring him out of himself. He always sat well away from her counter at the smallest table in the café, but still she made a point of coming over with her pot to refill what he could hardly get down the first time. He appreciated the gesture but wished that she might find other causes to take on. A sympathetic (and very pretty) ear might tempt him to say something he shouldn't, and he couldn't help but be nervous, even taciturn in her company. She didn't notice his manner, but nor did she broach the business of Lutze or the murders, and gradually their silent passages became less tense and even acquired a quality of intimacy, a mutual appreciation of company without idle, unproductive conversation. He might have been deluding himself of course (it was what older men did in the company of attractive women), but he couldn't deny that her presence warmed him more than her *muckefucke*.

On the first, cold Wednesday after Christmas, the need not to be alone pressed a little harder than usual upon him, and he was at the café early. Mona noticed his arrival, and, as had become her habit, checked her other customers' cups before coming across to his usual table. When she'd filled his cup she paused for a moment, reached down and squeezed his hand. Obviously the gesture had some meaning, so rather than be frightened by its unexpected closeness and beat a retreat he waited a further hour, until only the two of them remained in the café. Then, she locked the front door, came across to his table and sat down, taking his hand once more. When she spoke it was of something so curious, so unexpected, that he felt as though fortune was turning yet again, though towards something whose face was as yet utterly indistinct.

Oh yes, he told her when she had finished explaining what it was about, he'd be very happy to speak to the officer, and was certain the gentleman would be astonished at the things he had to tell.

Friday, 29 December 1944: RSHA intelligence briefing, Prinz-Albrecht-Strasse 8, Obergruppenführer Ernst Kaltenbrunner chairing, and Karl Krohne couldn't think of anywhere (a diarrhoea-ravaged pig-farm not excepted) that he wouldn't rather be. As usual, he had trawled his store of plausible excuses for not attending and discarded them reluctantly. It simply wasn't possible to avoid Ernst's fantasy fests, not when one occupied the lowest rung of Luftwaffe Intelligence's ladder of cowardly delegation.

He glanced around the table. The usual coterie of head-wounds had assembled - 'Gestapo' Müller, Otto Ohlendorf (Amt III: Inland SD), Walter Schellenberg (Amt VI: Ausländ SD and what remained of Abwehr), Friedrich Panzinger (Amt V: Criminal Investigations) and Himmler's pet library-stripper and occultist Paul Dittel (Amt VII: Records). Then the outsiders - himself, Martin Paetzel (*Forschungsamt* Abt VI - the 'good fellow' who almost certainly had snitched to Ministerial Direktor Schapper regarding Krohne's Breslau trip), an unnamed suit representing the Reich's strategic oil combine Kontinentale and two similarly anonymous general officers who had come up from Zossen to hear the latest glad tidings.

The format was fixed. First, matters arising from previous meetings, then a general situation report, individual department briefings on the titanic achievements of the past fortnight, and, finally, 'any other business' - all of it delightfully irrelevant to what was happening out of doors. Occasionally, non-RSHA attendees were asked to leave a meeting temporarily while special security issues were raised and discussed. Interruptions of that nature could consume an entire morning, but Krohne assumed that the other ejectees were equally content to wait mutely in the corridor, admiring the shine to their boots, rather than be enlightened as to what constituted *special*.

He had been attending these gatherings for four months now and had developed an idler's ear which allowed him to drift away for minutes at a time, comfortably certain that he would hear nothing to advantage. The occasionally relevant item he noted, asked questions regarding, begged copies relating to; but as he was invariably the junior officer at the table his input was hardly ever required, and he had little need to worry about an unexpected, embarrassing question that might drag back his wandering mind from Capri, or AVUS, or the splayed legs of his latest illicit adventure.

But some things he was careful to watch for. Whenever the words *Final* and *Victory* came together in a sentence he paid epicurean attention to the table's reactions. Invariably, Müller's head would blur in agreement with whatever the words were attached to while Ohlendorf's face would drop faster than a tart's drawers; the rest would follow the lead of one or the other, or wear the sort of non-committal expression much practised in Saturday night identity parades. Kaltenbrunner himself preferred to play the sphinx, expressing no opinion upon the likelihood of the Soviet Union, the United States and the British Empire packing their collective kitbag and going home. Still, he always had a snippet or two, nonsense that flew in the face of all reason, to flag his continuing faith in what he doubtless knew to be the most lost of causes.

Today, predictably, the lead item in the general situation report was the offensive in Belgium, operation *Watch on the Rhine*. According to their chairman the Amis and the Tommies were reeling, the former retreating into France and the latter ready to reprise their 1940 dash to the Channel Ports - at least (and at this, Kaltenbrunner raised a reassuring, knowing eyebrow), they would be, any day now. That brought very little discussion. The two OKW men glanced at each other as if they'd been told that Martin Luther would be popping in later for tea while the rest of the table either nodded sagely or stared blankly into their briefing papers. Then Kaltenbrunner swept eastwards to the Vistula, where the shock armies of Stalin's Belorussian and Ukrainian Fronts were apparently so exhausted after the previous autumn's exertions (during which they had tossed the last living German out of Russia and swallowed most of what the Führer had earmarked as *Lebensraum*, phase one) that an epidemic of dandruff would topple them. Facing this enfeebled juggernaut, a reconstituted, replenished and revitalized Army Group A was ready to administer the *coup de grace*. The small matter of the armies presently trapped in Courland was skimmed over. Contingency plans were being prepared that would clear out the Reds or extract the Germans; Kaltenbrunner wasn't entirely sure which it was to be but would get back to them when he had more information.

The correct response to all of this was of course a hearty guffaw, but Ernst was the curious sort of comedian who preferred his audience not to laugh at the jokes. As always, it was a relief when the routine ended and they could turn to the minutiae of their own departments' delusions. Krohne was intrigued to hear how Panzinger in particular would play down the matter of a maniac roaming Berlin's south-western suburbs, strangling ladies of a certain age without having so much as a single *hilfspolizei* unit on his arse.

But the head of the Kriminalpolizei mentioned nothing of Berlin operations. His report was entirely devoted to efforts, coordinated closely with Gestapo, to keep areas closest to enemy activity free from potential domestic subversion (that is, to prevent the general population either from running away or preparing to welcome the New Order). Müller jumped in with his own report on the same matter and added his usual appendix, names of the latest poor bastards to be arrested, 'examined' and executed, the dregs of the extended grudge-clearance that 20 July had provided an excuse to indulge. Everyone, including Krohne, nodded sombrely as they were read out, because on some matters it didn't do to be other than a loyal member of the herd. Ohlendorf then offered something insipid on securing communications and transport hubs in what remained of the General Government, while Schellenberg and the dry stick Dittel said nothing. OKW's men were there to listen not speak, and Paetzel (*bastard*, thought Krohne, idly) had only one item: the evacuation – that is, the re-redeployment – of *Forschungsamt* from Breslau to Jüterbog had been almost completed, though he understood that the military commander of the former was confident that any Soviet effort to take the city would fail (both Kaltenbrunner and Müller nodded furiously at this). Then it was Krohne's turn. He shook his head, frowned and continued to pencil-shade the words *Magda Krohne, 42: Lovely as Always* that he had written earlier in the margin of his briefing paper.

The last individual contribution was from the civilian, the oil man, who was attending to provide estimates of what could be done to replace oil production from the Romanian fields and lignite wax from the Reich's equally lost Latvian brown coal deposits. Kaltenbrunner, asking a single question, called him by name - *Rasch*. It rang neither bells nor interest for Krohne, though grudgingly he had to admire the man's inability to give a straightforward answer.

The final agenda item was other business, but for once Krohne's attention hadn't wandered off on to what the Air Ministry canteen was going to misrepresent as luncheon. A thought occurred suddenly, forcibly, that he might be sitting at the same table as the man who had put the lid on the Lichterfelde investigation. He glanced around, trying not to be too obviously furtive. There was Müller, a man who delighted in plots, stratagems and filthy little barbarisms. He was almost *too* suited for the hat, but Krohne wasn't sure that he could be involved. He had neither professional nor instinctive connections with Waffen SS; in any case, his speciality was Jew-removal from 'pacified' territories, and, more recently, arranging piano-wire nooses for the necks of braver men than he. Also, the palace rumour was that he had moved away from Himmler and into Bormann's pocket during the past eighteen months, so he had no reason stop an investigation that had the potential to embarrass the Reichsführer.

Kaltenbrunner himself? It was doubtful, though impossible to gauge accurately. The man committed himself to nothing that wasn't in his own best interests, and again, he wasn't really a part of the Military, his General's epaulettes and Knight's Cross notwithstanding. If he were to be involved it would be at a deniable, stretched arm's-length. Schellenberg could be dismissed out of hand; he was an overgrown boy who loved the dashing, daring thrust, running and breaking spy rings, the decisive *coup de main* that foiled an enemy strategy. Quashing an investigation into the killings of helpless old ladies would be contemptible to him, even if he could declare an interest.

The others were more intriguing. Like everyone else in Wilhelmstrasse Krohne was aware that, between stints in Berlin, both Ohlendorf and Panzinger had commanded certain *special* operations in the East that gave the lie to their seemingly bland, bureaucratic animas. Back then, however, they had been Allgemeine, not Waffen SS, and presumably they retained the habitual resentment of the one for the other that had survived the two branches' effective merger. It was hard to imagine that either man would regard the reputation of *Leibstandarte SS Adolph Hitler* as something worth taking risks to preserve. Of course, Panzinger, as king of the *kripos*, must have been some sort of party to the decision - he could hardly ignore an outside influence upon one of his operations. But he was a new boy still, his feet not yet firmly planted in poor Arthur Nebe's boots, and others may have taken the lead. Still, the swine couldn't be discounted entirely.

This was difficult. Deductive reasoning came naturally to former police like Fischer and Holleman, but as an ex-newspaperman Krohne could only think the worst of everyone and then double it. He glanced around the table, at the super-powered arbiters of all their tomorrows, and wondered if there was a professional technique for identifying a single aberration in a reservoir of similar.

Kaltenbrunner was rising from the table, about to rush away to chair yet another meeting vital to the Reich's future, and Krohne wondered suddenly if he were being short-sighted. What if the investigation had been halted from the very top, by Himmler himself? He was in the west at present, playing at being Commander in Chief of Army Group Upper Rhine, a formation that doubtless felt itself blessed by the appointment. Even if his skills weren't nearly up to that particular task, surely the Reichsführer wouldn't have the time or reach to concern himself with killing the Lichterfelde business?

Krohne felt his bowels clench. But what if the Führer had given the order? It wouldn't be so fantastical - after all, who would care more for the reputation of the division than the man whose personal safety had once been their *raison d'être*?

The thought stole the last of his courage. Four days earlier he'd had a marriage, a safe, boring job and - Allied bombers and the Red Army permitting - a fair prospect of seeing out the bloody catastrophe. Now, he was a likely divorcee and a recruit in a tiny army that had opened hostilities on its own people, with excellent prospects of no more than a scree of topsoil to cover his still-warm corpse; a fool in the company of fools, set upon finding his own private Stalingrad in south Berlin. He half-wished now that he had found the courage to tell Freddie Holleman to fuck himself *and* his kids and done what a German was supposed to do, which was to bear the yoke patiently for as long as the present ploughman held the reins. He wished his wife were at home still, forgiving him his many sins, and for what any faithless husband coveted - the gift of appreciating what he'd had before it lost hope in him.

A cough brought him back, and he looked up. The room had emptied of everyone other than himself and Panzinger, who was blocking the doorway, smirking as if contraband had been discovered in a school locker and he had a detention ticket ready. Krohne scowled, tempted to make the pig wait. But he reminded himself that Otto Fischer wouldn't have bothered with pointless gestures. He would have wanted to know the worst immediately so that he could make a start on dealing with it, on twisting it to some sort of advantage. Krohne envied that sort of spirit, however fatalistic. He was an amateur in a professional game whose rules had sharp edges, and he worried that what he was going to hear wasn’t capable of being twisted, not by him at least.

16

On Friday morning, Holleman and Fischer left Moabit before dawn and were in Lichterfelde West by seven-thirty. They parked the *Ottowagen* in a non-residential cul de sac around the corner from Sophiastrasse, the short street in which the café stood. Between the car and the apartment's outer door they saw no one, and Holleman's knock was too discreet to attract the attention of any nearby curtains.

It took a few seconds for Mona to come to terms with Fischer's face, though he thought the effort a decent one, missing any hint of quelled disgust. It took a little longer for him to come to terms with hers. He had never understood what people meant when they spoke of perfect features - the term seemed dispassionate, appropriate more to a horse's proportions or a classical façade than to something that stirred earthy desire. Mona Kreitz's face wasn't *perfect* by any means. It was constructed from a collection of individually delightful features, and they came together in a manner he couldn't imagine being improved upon by any enforced symmetry. It was a prospect that invited further examination in the way that a painting or the view from a hilltop did, and made the observer feel better for it in the same way. He wondered how someone like this could possibly be alone.

She invited them in, and closed the door quickly. Holleman asked the favour while she was filling a kettle. No, he assured her, this wasn't something that could bring trouble for her. They needed a place from which to observe the neighbourhood. Not a base, she should understand - they had no intention of putting down roots, or requisitioning her home - merely somewhere they could remain for a while, perhaps for several hours at a time during the coming days, without drawing attention to themselves. He was sure she appreciated that it was very necessary for them to be close by, should another atrocity occur? Yes, he told her, there was a reason why it should be in her café in particular.

Fischer listened to this gentle, persuasive Holleman with some surprise. It was a little like observing the same in a wolf, playing with her cubs. You knew that it must happen, but still, to see it ...

The girl was almost at ease in Holleman's company, nodding in the manner of someone unconvinced by what she was hearing but too polite to say so. The request was not a small matter, whatever they pretended, and Fischer suspected that she wasn't so stupid as not to see this. Still, he allowed it as conceivable that some people could do the right thing for the right reason, even in these times.

He had brought a small bag containing a few bribes, foodstuffs not available to civilians, but their few minutes' acquaintance had convinced him that she wouldn't react well to a clumsy gesture. He produced only a small pack of real coffee as the kettle began to rattle. She took it in the spirit it was offered, and asked them to sit. While she was busy in the tiny kitchen they perched awkwardly upon the forward slopes of an old sofa, caps in hand like country dolts in a comedy of manners. Fischer glanced around, examined the landscape. The apartment was bare, but some of the pieces she had brought to it – he assumed it had been she, and not the proprietor – were clearly of good quality, not junk that a penniless girl might find at a bombing market. The armchair by the small, unlit fireplace was ugly but substantial, a pre-Second Empire extravagance in walnut and stuffed dark green velvet, the kind of thing her mother had probably inherited from *her* mother. A hat stand behind the door held no hats but matched the wood of the armchair precisely, and a covered round table under the solitary window on to Sophiastrasse showed a leg - or, rather, pedestal - in what he was fairly sure was the Biedermeier style.

Her taste in wall hangings was far more contemporary, and dangerous. Four identically sized posters from old Berlin exhibitions of what had since been deemed *entartete* sat in matching metal frames, one upon each of the room's walls. Two of them were almost abstract depictions of a man and woman, naked and coupling, writhed into a single form. Their possession by this ostensibly sweet girl disordered Fischer's thoughts considerably. He wasn't often so forcibly reminded that his own sexuality was merely missing in action, not formally interred.

She brought out the drinks on a tray. Holleman took his and blew too robustly upon the grounds, trying to settle them, and Fischer continued the business while he wiped the damage from his lap. 'Do you know Edouard Muntz, Fraulein?'

She smiled. 'Lichterfelde's Reutter? I met him once, outside the *volkskuche* on Steglitzerstrasse. He saw me, assumed I was a worshipper and tried to autograph my hand. The old ladies love him, but it's not my sort of thing.'

Probably a Schönberg sort, he decided. *Or Berg.*

'He was a popular act around here?'

'Worshipped, rather than popular. He still is. A woman standing next to me actually swooned when he pointed a finger and gave her a line from *Dolly, You're the Apple of my Eye*. It was nauseating, like too much sugar in a drink.'

But brave, even to think of singing something composed by someone who'd fled Germany the year that National Socialism arrived. Either Muntz felt himself to be impervious or he was making a point.

'And he gives a concert at that particular *volkskuche* every Friday, doesn't he?'

He saw perhaps the beginning of a frown. She was finding his questions frivolous, irrelevant, when a monster was killing women without fear of consequences. Why did was he bothering to ask about an old fool like Muntz? She shrugged, turned her head away slightly.

'Yes, there's always a full house for him. And for the food, of course. It's dreadful, apparently, but it fills bellies. I heard that he missed one time, through illness.'

'Twice now', Holleman murmured. Fischer nodded, pretended to make a note in his book and smiled at the girl. 'So you don't go often?'

'No. As I say, I met him just once, the only time I've been there. Usually, the café keeps me here until late. In any case, I don't like to be out in the dark.'

Holleman coughed gently and half raised a finger. He really was trying to be polite. 'You gave me a name when we spoke the other day, a policeman at Steglitz. Rudolph Bildmann?'

'No - I mean, yes, he's a policeman, but he *lives* in Steglitz. He works at Dahlem station, I think.'

'We've heard his name also from a friend at the central Criminal Investigations Office. Has he returned to the café since we spoke?'

'No, not recently.'

'Can you recall the last time he was here, or when you saw him, if somewhere else?'

Mona stared down at her untouched drink, her full lips pursed, and Fischer's rusty imagination squealed around a further few notches.

'I ... think he came in towards the end of October, or perhaps a little after that. I remember because it was already dark, and that was unusual. He works the nights, so he would usually come in at about four, for an hour or so. That evening he came later.'

'Do you recall speaking to him?'

'I don't, whether I did or not.'

Two *orpos* involved in the investigation - when it *was* an investigation - now missing. According to Gerd Branssler, Bildmann was relatively young, mid to late forties, so he hadn't gone west unless he planned to end his days hung from a telegraph pole with a one-word obituary - *Fahnenflüchtiger* - pinned to his chest.

Holleman asked a final question, and Mona gave him the address. They finished their coffees, told her they might return in the early evening, and showed themselves out. A solitary civilian on his way to work had just passed by the outer door when they emerged. He didn't glance back.

Holleman fiddled with his cap as he checked the rest of the street. 'Interesting.'

Fischer nodded. 'It would be good to find him. But Dahlem ...' Dahlem station was large, and connected. It had run its own criminal investigations section until the war took most of its Bulls. Now, it was obliged to ask help from the centre, so if two Luftwaffe officers walked in and asked questions it would be like shouting down a pipe that had its other end at Alexanderplatz.

'It isn't right, though.'

'What?'

Holleman shrugged. 'Times like these, a man shouldn't just wander off. Amounts to sabotage, doesn't it? Someone should be looking for him.'

Fischer let pass the matter of Holleman having committed exactly that crime. 'It wouldn't work, Freddie. Not with your leg and my face.'

'No, but Gerd could do it. He'd have a reason, wouldn't he? He knows the man, so he could ask straight questions. If it's anything to do with this business, then someone's going to have to pull him off it quickly, and we might get a glimpse of *who*.'

Fischer took his arm, and they walked west, towards Augustaplatz. '*Very* dangerous for Gerd.'

'Not if he makes an innocent, stupid noise about it. A policeman's gone missing - well, *perhaps* missing. If he hasn't, there's no harm. If he *has* then it's a crime or desertion, and whoever doesn't want Gerd to be asking had better have some pull, or a good reason to shut him up.'

'What if someone decides to make a big point about it?'

'With a senior Bull? Not likely, unless they caught him slipping one into ReichHeini's mother. It would be a quiet word, or a slap.'

There was old bomb damage just short of Augustaplatz. The road itself had been repaired, but several frontages gaped like eye-sockets still. A small sign had been pinned to the frame of a former shop window, informing the curious passer-by that one Egon Bressler had attempted to loot the ruins and been executed promptly. It was dated the previous February. Holleman was correct about that, at least - there's was a society conditioned to pry, to watch its neighbours, to insinuate its nose into business that was not its own and to report even the smaller transgressions. If a Bull wanted to know why one of the *orpos* he'd worked with had disappeared - if he *had* disappeared - it would be entirely in order. A duty, even.

But the logic applied to normal situations, and this wasn't such a thing. It couldn't be measured, assessed, walked around or studied, and Fischer felt confident about nothing to do with it. He shrugged. 'Let's look at the one-pot paradise.'

A faded sign above the entrance to the *volksküche* on Steglitzerstrasse told them that it had once been *The Olden Times*. With a name like that, Fischer didn't need to guess at the fare that had drawn its former clientele. Someone like Muntz, even singing in double time, could hardly exhaust his grossly sentimental repertory under its roof. The doors were open, and they walked in.

A solitary female cleaner was dragging a mop between tables. The theatre's bones were still evident; its 'boxes' - a single line of partitioned booths no more than five feet above the level of the main floor - ran down either side of the hall, but the cheap seats had been removed and the space given over to ranks of utilitarian tables and chairs requisitioned from a hospital or other, similar institution. The only other token of bygone days was a small upright piano, half-covered in a corner.

Fischer glanced around, and something he had meant to ask returned to him.

'Where do they cook it?'

Holleman turned, made his own brief recce. 'I've no idea. They served it up from over *there*, but when I came in they were almost finished. I didn't see any sign of a kitchen.'

The cleaner had stopped and was watching them warily, a pool of water spreading slowly around her. Fischer nodded. 'Good morning. Could you tell me what time the *volkskuche* opens today, please?'

'*What*?' The hand cupped an ear. He was going to have to give her a good look at his face. He moved closer, into a pool of light cast by one of the small, high windows above the entrance. She stared straight at him, undisturbed by the view, old enough to remember what had come back from France during the last one. He repeated the question.

'When the food gets here. Five o'clock, if you're lucky. Six, if not.'

'Where does it come from?'

'God knows! Some samaritan, or the Führer ...'

'No, I mean, where is it cooked?'

She looked darkly at him. 'Why? You can't have the first dip, it's for everyone!'

He smiled, wanting to kick away her mop. 'Really, I wouldn't try. Does it come far? From Berlin, perhaps?'

'From Unter den Eichen, 'round the corner! The old municipal kitchens!'

Back on the street, Fischer and Holleman stood for a while, watching local life lurching arthritically into its business. Here, on the city's edge, there was less of the millenarian atmosphere that omnipresent bomb damage and the shadow of the flak towers had fostered. This was a community still, albeit one with large shrapnel tears in the fabric. People were greeting each other glumly, stoically indifferent to what they avoided mentioning; a few folk waited outside a local butcher, blue *marken* coupons ready, hoping for some good news on the slaughtered proteins situation; a few meters from them a milk-cart was offering the regulation 250 millilitres to a line of mothers standing ready with their flasks and jugs while the cart's propulsion system - surely a candidate for the butcher's slab any day now - casually dropped a large load into the street. Set aside the few damaged frontages and it might almost have been 1940 again.

'Do you have the address?' Fischer held out a hand to Holleman. His friend glanced at it. 'Lothar-Bucher-Strasse 8/6, Steglitz. About a kilometre.'

'Will your leg make it?'

'Easily, if we don't run.'

The Opel was battered and forgettable but it was also Luftwaffe grey, which might attract glances. Fischer didn't want to risk it for the man's sake. If he was willing to talk, it wouldn't be polite to get him disappeared.

Holleman had a 1934 city guide, with the street they stood on just visible on its penultimate page. That was fine; they were moving north, back into Berlin. It only occurred to them at the halfway point that they could easily have boarded the s-bahn at Botanical Gardens and jumped off a stop later in Steglitz. But the morning was clear, the terrain level and Holleman's missing leg didn't seem to be bothering him. It felt almost like a day out, if such things happened still in the world.

Lothar-Bucher-Strasse 8 was a low apartment block, a fine Mebes and Emmerich edifice of late-Twenties' vintage, the style that small, well-to-do families had sought out during Weimar Berlin's vast suburban expansion. Number six was on the first floor. Holleman rapped upon a door that opened too quickly for their approach up Menkenstrasse to have passed unobserved.

'Please come in.'

Paul Schroeder was a neat little man, an old-fashioned sort who wore a tie beneath a buttoned sweater indoors. The apartment was equally well ordered. Other than for a number of books placed in an imprecise pile on the table beneath the window Fischer would have assumed it to be unoccupied, or self-consciously preserved. A picture, prominently placed on the mantelpiece, depicted a slightly younger Schroeder with a plump, middle-aged woman, framed by a glorious view across the Harz Mountains. They were wearing walking clothes - real ones, the sort that a gentle perambulation wouldn't have required, and two large rucksacks sat on the ground beside them.

Fischer had noticed the *hilfspolizei* cap hung on the stand in the hallway. 'Your day off, Herr Schroeder?'

The older man grimaced slightly. 'I have mild but recurring *herpes zoster*, so you really shouldn't come too close. I haven't worked for almost a week now.'

Fischer made a sympathetic face. 'I'm sorry to hear it. Both my colleague and I have had the chicken pox, so we're probably safe. You said to Fraulein Kleitz that you wouldn't mind speaking to us?'

'About the murders.'

The Luftwaffe officers looked at each other. It was strange to hear it said aloud, in Lichterfelde.

'Yes. We were told that you personally discovered the body of Gisella Mauer, on Wildenowstrasse, the early hours of 21 October?'

Schroeder frowned. 'Was that her name? They didn't tell us, before … she was pretty, I think, though her face was twisted very badly, and swollen. I haven't seen someone killed violently since … there was the last war of course, but that was a different matter.'

'A bad business, sir.' Holleman was staying in character, a sympathetic face to set off Fischer's unavoidably brutal one.

'Yes. And then …' the old man paused for a moment, took a breath, let it go '… they told us we should keep our mouths closed, that a new investigation was under way, from Alexanderplatz. But I don't think that's correct. I haven't spoken to anyone since the day after we found her, and no one's been asking questions since, not in Lichterfelde. I would have known if … and Hans Lutze! They said that he was involved in it, but that's nonsense! Really, I …'

Fischer held up a hand before he lost the man entirely. 'This is the rottmeister from your station?'

'Yes. An accomplice they said, it's unbelievable. They came to this conclusion because he disappeared, but how could a man his age do such things? He wasn't a *good* policeman, everyone around here knows that, but he was with me all that evening and I assure you …'

'Of course, yes. No one has had any word from Lutze since, what, 24 October?'

Schroeder was exasperated, angry with his invisible taunters. He shrugged. 'No one that I know of. Our stationmaster went to his house, but Hans wasn't there. I've asked a few people myself, discreetly, when not in uniform. As far as I can say, he's not been seen at all since that day.'

'Do you know if he has relatives elsewhere in …'

'Ach!' A hand waved it away irritably. 'He hasn't deserted, if you're asking that. He likes his job - or rather, he likes being a rottmeister. It makes people listen to him, and my God, he loves to talk - all the time, about killings, or the war, or what he did to the Reds in Berlin in 1919. If Hans is in a place where he can't talk about himself he'll probably die!'

It sounded like the man Gerd Branssler had described. Holleman looked up from his notepad.

'And what are people saying in Lichterfelde, about the killings?'

The old man shook his head. 'They're not. Everybody must be thinking of them still, but it's as if we've all taken a vow of silence. We glance at each other in the street, or in the café, knowing that we're thinking the same thing more or less. But we don't talk about it.'

'Why do you think that is, sir?'

'I don't know; I don't know. They told us, the police, not to mention it, so nothing was said officially through us. Perhaps we were too ready to …'

'To your knowledge, no pressure's been placed upon local people?'

'As I say, no.'

'And at your station, Steglitz? Is *anything* said, despite the order? I mean, people gossip, don't they? Police are human, too.'

'No, not to me, at least. Of course, I'm only *hilfspolizei*, not a real policeman, so I don't *belong*, if you see? It may be that one or two of them, old comrades, are saying things. As you say, it's what people do. But not to me.'

Fischer nodded. 'When the silence fell upon this business - it was, what, almost two months ago - there had been three killings. Is there any sense at all, even without information, that there may be more than by now?'

Schroeder nodded. 'They speak without speaking, if you understand. One hears hints about getting home early to bed before *something* happens. I heard a rumour that half of Dahlem's *orpos* came out here at the beginning of December to search the Gardens once more, and then went away again without speaking to anyone at our station. I don't know if it means anything, but it's definitely a fear, if not a fact. I don't believe that anyone thinks it's stopped just because we mustn't speak of it. These days, we expect things not to be as they appear to be.'

Holleman, his lips pursed, glanced at Fischer and nodded, prompting.

'Do you know who we are, sir?'

'Luftwaffe, it seems. Should I know more?'

Fischer smiled. A sensible, cautious response - obviously, Mona Kreitz had been careful to say little. 'There are reasons why this investigation was closed down, but we don't know them. We certainly weren't involved in anything that was discussed. However, it seems to … *some* people in Berlin that this isn't a satisfactory way to proceed. Murder can't be overlooked, even during times like these. There's a feeling that more needs to be known about what happened, and what may still be happening. But like you, we don't know much. There's one thing, though, that's very important …'

'That you mustn't be seen to be doing what you're doing.' Schroeder smiled, just. 'I'm not a fool, Herr Major. I understand that this business couldn't have come about at the whim of someone of the middling sort. It takes a degree of power, and we live in times when power has shown that it can do anything. Am I being indiscreet?'

Holleman laughed. 'Fatally, sir. But me and my partner, we don't talk much either, do we?'

'No, and we trust that those to whom we speak do much the same.'

'Well, that won't be difficult. As I say, we've all learned not to speak of things in these parts.'

Fischer thanked the old man for his time. They were being shown to the front door when he recalled something that Holleman had asked the girl.

'Herr Schroeder, the men at Lichterfelde Kaserne, the Leibstandarte division: do you know if there's been … trouble with any of their lads?'

'Rowdyism, you mean?'

A word that covered many sins. 'Yes, rowdyism. Have there been complaints to the police, to your knowledge?'

Paul Schroeder shook his head firmly. 'Never. They're very well disciplined, a credit to the uniform. Now, the old Imperial cadets, I could tell you stories about *those* swine.'

How is it that the Air Ministry and *this* survive?'

Astonished, Holleman gazed at the central glasshouse at the Botanical Gardens, the Great Pavilion. It was vast, vastly fragile yet wantonly intact still. Only a few dozen metres to the north, the far more substantially constructed Herbarium was half-wrecked, a victim of one of the previous year's many air raids.

'It's glass. The Allied bombers probably didn't see it.'

'What a blow, if the Reich's strategic reserve of giant water lilies had taken one.'

Fischer smiled and stretched out his legs a little more. 'Bomber Command and the Chancellery must share a grasp of strategy.'

Both men breathe deeply, taking in the unseasonal smell of grass. It was almost five pm, Friday; the Steglizerstrasse *volksküche* opened its doors in little more than an hour, and, if their assumptions were correct, a middle-aged woman would be in considerable danger soon afterwards. Perhaps she was here, in front of them, one among the several small groups of people - almost all of them in their sixties or older - enjoying the same blessed air; perhaps she was hungry already, looking forward to the day's only meal, wishing that time might skip a little more quickly to the moment when a revolting mixture of rice and vegetables, greased with animal fat, eased the ache in her stomach. A poor final meal - *he* would be offered better, if he survived the day to meet the gallows.

They sat on a bench in the ornamental Italian Garden, directly facing the Pavilion. Holleman had unbuttoned his field coat for the first time since departing Jonas-Strasse at dawn. It was too warm now to wear comfortably, but the lack of any insignia on the shabby uniform beneath made its removal in daylight risky. He was perspiring enthusiastically.

'Jesus! It wasn't *this* warm in my last cockpit!'

That item had belonged to a burning Bf109, plummeting towards the picturesque Vecht River with two Hurricanes pouring fire into its fuselage and its pilot's now-fondly recalled leg, so Holleman was probably stretching it a little. But then Fischer's own coat lay neatly folded over the arm of the bench, and he was enjoying the last of the winter sunlight. It was only fair; in an hour he would be shivering, probably hungry too, standing in a darkened doorway on the south side of Steglitzerstrasse while Holleman was inside the *volksküche*, eating, watching, waiting to follow someone and give the nod to the same doorway as he emerged. That, on crumpled paper, was their master plan - the Lichterfelde Manoeuvre.

'We should try to stop him before …'

A young woman with a pram had wandered to a point less than fifty metres from the bench. Fischer grabbed Holleman's arm, faced him, spoke quietly.

'We shouldn't do *anything*. We need his hands around her throat before we even think about taking him. You watch, you make sure you have the right one, and then we follow. He needs to get her *here*, so there's time enough.'

'It isn't lit. Shit, *nowhere*'s lit. What if we can't find them? He could just pull her into the bushes and we've lost him.'

'No we haven't, and we won't. He'll be talking, or *she* will. Remember, she doesn't suspect anything, not yet. Not until she's in the Gardens.'

'Or wherever else he decides to take her.'

Fischer shrugged. 'It doesn't matter. They'll be walking, like us.'

'Do you know what the worst of it would be?'

'That it's the Führer?'

Holleman almost smiled, but the business was too close now. 'That we get him alive. What would we do with him? Who could we hand him to who won't give us a bullet from the same chamber? Fuck! *Where* would we take him?'

With no legal jurisdiction, they were about to commit what would, perversely, be regarded as a criminal act. Holleman was right - the best option would be to shoot or strangle him, ensure that his identification was prominently displayed and then make about half a dozen anonymous calls to police stations in the area. Failing that, getting themselves killed during the encounter was probably wiser than having a living method murderer on their hands, waiting to be rescued by Prinz-Albrecht-Strasse - or, God forbid, the Chancellery.

The young woman had taken a seat on the next bench. She was staring fondly into the pram, teasing its contents with a finger, cooing something. The two officers stood and nodded politely when she glanced up. Fischer made a forgettable comment about the felicity of the weather as he imagined an innocent visitor to the Gardens might. She smiled vaguely, her attention already back with her baby. She hadn't noticed his face or Holleman's leg.

They emerged from the Gardens at its northernmost point, by the little cemetery off Königen-Luise-Platz. It was directly away from Steglitzerstrasse, but they had time to waste before true darkness fell. Fischer pulled his cap low over his face, trusting the day's final light to make him a silhouette to those who approached from the east.

Dusk settled swiftly, and the streets of Lichterfelde cleared of their human presence. Promenading citizens had made the best of the unseasonable weather, but before Fischer and Holleman were more that half a kilometre from the northern entrance to the Gardens they were passing through an empty nightscape, the slight noise of their heels echoing back from half-seen buildings. Fischer had been a *kripo* for too long not to believe that things unsaid could hang in the air, poisoning it. But he had never experienced the phenomenon as a generality, a miasma.

'Like a curfew.' Holleman glanced around. They were walking down Hindenburg Damm, already too far south of Steglitzerstrasse; but the *volkskuche*'s doors would be locked still and to be early would risk attention from a queue of bored, hungry locals ready to commit new - and in Fischer's case, memorable - faces to memory. They might have waited somewhere in shadows, but Holleman happily suffered the torment of a pre-dinner walk. He had sworn to Fischer and Heaven itself that he needed a real, cut-off, encircled and unsupplied field-hunger in his belly before he could inflict another helping of *eintopf* upon it.

A few minutes later they turned right into Augustastrasse and crossed the little park in Augustaplatz. As they emerged, the old music hall could be seen directly ahead, its open doors casting a weak light into the night. The last of the early arrivals were shuffling in.

Fischer had chosen his place already, a former draper's doorway with the ubiquitous black-edged *Died for the Fatherland* sign in a side window. The shop was about twenty metres from the *volkskuche*, its deeply recessed entrance reassuringly dark. When they reached it, Holleman took off his coat and gave it to Fischer. The poor state of his uniform - that of a nondescript Luftwaffe ground-staffer - had been the work of Frau Traugott and her sister. They had rubbed and thinned the jacket elbows and trouser knees to a silvered gossamer texture and then distressed them further with a solution of weak tea. The cap, though also regulation Luftwaffe, was frayed and belonged to a different uniform, while his boots achieved an unimpeachable authenticity merely by not being a pair. When the ladies were satisfied that to do more would over-egg the pudding, Holleman had dressed and used Jonas-Strasse 17's largest mirror to practise his stoop (not difficult) and sour, hopeless expression (effortless, if not instinctive), and everyone had agreed that he made a pitiable prospect. They had even fashioned a rude crutch for him, and this he now assembled in the darkened doorway. A forlorn touch, he had also pinned his 1940 campaign medal to the jacket's breast - a broken veteran's only remaining point of pride.

'Break a leg.' In the darkness Fischer grinned. He'd been waiting to use the line for some hours now.

'Fuck yourself,' Holleman said pleasantly, and limped out into the faint illumination of Steglitzerstrasse. A couple of late diners, hardly more than shapes, hurried along the street's opposite side without glancing at him and entered the former theatre. He followed them, exaggerating his limp enormously. Fischer pressed himself back against the shop door.

The food table was already busy, servicing a queue that backed around two sides of the theatre. At its head a civilian, an old man, was marking ration coupons. Beyond him, one female volunteer passed wide shallow bowls to a second who filled them from one of two large tureens and handed them to her customers. By her side, a boy in *Hitler Jugend* uniform served out chunks of black bread. It was an efficient arrangement, slowed only by the efforts of the queue's more senior elements to get a conversation going as they took their portions. The volunteers were having none of it; they shooed on each customer with as little politeness as didn't shade into an outright command, heartily endorsed by complaints from further down the line.

Holleman formed its terminus for less than two minutes before an ex-soldier, head down, mumbling to himself, covered his rear. They shuffled forward slowly. A careful examination of both the queue and those who were already sitting at the tables offered no obvious suspects. None of the uniforms present was serving in any capacity - Holleman's view resembled more a trauma ward at a field lazarett than a military parade - and only one of the civilian males (clinically myopic, limping badly) appeared to be closer to vigorous youth than his mid-sixties. No one had sufficient killer potential to invite his attention, but he wasn't discouraged. It was early still, and the star of the evening had yet to appear.

Glancing behind, he saw that he was now roughly the mid-point of the line. He caught his mumbling comrade's eye, and noticed for the first time that the face was brutally pocked by small shrapnel wounds. The man twitched, half-turned away and found more Down in which to insert his head, but several old ladies immediately to their rear stared back boldly at Holleman, as if demanding his business. He almost wasted a smile, and then recalled who he was supposed to be.

When his turn came he took a bowl and some bread, nodded thanks to his benefactors and took the last empty seat at one of the tables to the left side of the room. From there he had a good view of the entire stretch of the queue from door to serving table and could monitor it without drawing attention. He glanced briefly at his neighbours and decided that the surveillor was not likely to be surveilled - his was the only face not set determinedly to what it was eating, to loading fuel as quickly as the gullet permitted.

The fuel itself was terrible, and there were moments when he feared his portion might stick fatally in his throat. No one else seemed to be having a problem - he was reminded of feeding time at Tiergarten, the lions and what they did to their raw horsemeat. It did nothing to sharpen his appetite. He averted his eyes, pushed the spoon down into his own mess and concentrated upon summoning the will to lift another load to his mouth.

A quite thunderous *entrance* spared him the test. As he looked up almost every utensil in the room clattered to the table, its purpose forgotten in the rush to free up hands.

'Good evening, my dears!'

From the doorway, Eddie Muntz, flanked by two beefy uniforms, opened his arms as if to sweep up his entire public in a single embrace. He looked older than Holleman had expected, an artefact of a less unforgiving age, swamped by an exuberantly fur-collared coat and soft felt hat. His face was obviously rouged and his lips painted; he moved carefully as old men do, but there was a definite *mince* there still, a relic from when such affectations weren't fatal. It might have been the Republic still, the top of the bill at one of the city's less respectable venues.

The dour, resentful atmosphere that had lain over the *volksküche* dissipated like mustard gas in a dawn breeze. A few female fans shrieked piercingly, yet they were almost drowned out by the applause. Holleman, astonished, merely stared.

'Do you know, I've missed you all! Yes! I have!' Muntz swept theatrically to the nearest set of adorers and began to squeeze hands. He could offer only the one himself as the other clutched a cane with a silver fox-head handle, but his adorers dutifully waited for it to become available before snatching a brief benediction. He had the music hall hack's habit - something that Holleman hated furiously - of speaking and then bursting into song for a few moments before returning seamlessly to dialogue as if offering a taste of his genius to parched lips, to keep them going until the real relief could commence.

But Eddie was obviously, intensely popular - and courageous too, to flaunt his homosexuality so proudly in a milieu that provided very special treatment for the condition. His guards didn't seem to be enjoying their implied association with degeneracy. They were both young but heavy-faced, men who looked to be able to handle themselves in a bad situation. They scowled, pleased about nothing, moving awkwardly in the presence of someone who more or less glided between tables, tugs in the wake of a yacht.

'Look! I'm young again!' Eddie waggled a leg coquettishly to reassure his public that his recent bout of arthritis had been slain, and they applauded enthusiastically once more. Then, still on his introductory circuit, he fired his first salvo - *In Paris, In Paris, sind de Mädels so süß*. He had a light baritone that made for a more robust version than the original, but even the audience's sole critic was reluctantly impressed. Eddie held his notes well, knew a nuance and didn't need a band to carry it off. He finished to a thunderous ovation but waved it down impatiently and threw himself into *Seeräuber Jenny*.

Christ, thought Holleman, *a fucking medley*. He glanced around at those closest to him. Even the hungry veterans, sour-faced to a man a matter of minutes ago, were joining in happily, and why shouldn't they? Eddie was singing to them as much as the older ones, patting their shoulders as he passed by, winking and pointing like a ham at people he didn't know. It was probably the first warm attention they'd enjoyed in a long, painful time, and things like that couldn't be mocked.

It was about twenty minutes into the cabaret, when Eddie had put *The September Song* to bed and was taking a little rest among some eager old ladies, that Holleman looked again at the two bodyguards and cursed himself for letting the show distract his attention. They wore the thin black *Adolph Hitler* cuff band of Leibstandarte SS - it was as plain as Muntz himself, but he had expected to see it on a black Panzer tunic, not ordinary field-grey. He had also missed their wounds. The sandy-haired, thick-set fellow bore a recent, livid scar, running from his left temple down into the collar of his tunic, while his comrade's forearm, hidden by the tunic, looked thicker than it should, and the hand at its end wore a dress glove - unremarkable, except he was wearing only one, and men of his rank didn't get to wear them at all, things being equal.

Holleman was thinking hard, wondering what he might do to get outside without being noticed, when Sandy bent over the star of the evening and whispered in his ear. Muntz looked up, smiled dazzlingly, nodded and kept his eyes on the boy a little longer than was strictly necessary as he moved off towards the door. The other hard case moved slightly closer to Muntz and placed the good arm's hand on his shoulder, as if to compensate for the halving of the maestro's aura.

Holleman almost jumped up and followed, not caring who noticed. But he could see no obvious female target, and neither of the bodyguards had spoken to anyone as they followed Eddie around the room, much less arranged an assignation.

Yet would they need to? The thought tormented him. They were Eddie's men, everyone could see that - surely, an old woman, accosted by one of them outside and offered a personal audience with the Lichterfelde Reutter, would accept gratefully, perhaps agree to take the short cut through the Gardens, ignorant of, or perhaps forgetting in the heat of her autumnal passions, the matter of his living south and east of Steglitzerstrasse, not due north? He was convinced, suddenly, that this was how it was done. An easy, friendly encounter, a lady grateful for a little attention from a man who couldn't possibly have designs upon her unmentionable parts, a brief, hopeless struggle and then eternal silence.

Only one strategy occurred. Fortunately, everyone's eyes were on Eddie. Holleman gagged once, and his stomach gratefully deposited a splash of fat-drenched root vegetables on to the table. A circle cleared precipitously around him as he jumped up, mumbled a hasty apology and hurled himself towards the door. Vaguely, he noticed the disgusted expressions, the wordless complaints of outraged fans whose dreams of yesteryear had been fouled by a lout, and he barked his best knee badly against the last table before the exit. But then he was in the street, in the pool of light cast by the theatre's entrance lamp, frantically waving at one of three darkened doorways opposite.

No one emerged. Cursing, he scanned the street each way, seeing nothing in the gloom. He forced himself to be calm, to slow his breathing, to listen. He heard no footsteps, though the bodyguard had emerged only a few seconds before. It didn't make sense. Unless the man was an Olympic sprinter in the heavily booted event he could hardly be out of range already. And then Holleman's nostrils got a clear, close scent of tobacco.

Shit.

Sandy walked out of the darkness, a matter of just three metres from where Holleman was lit up like a landing field. The soldier - his tabs identified him as a rottenführer - dropped the cigarette, stubbed it with his foot, nodded briefly at the strange Luftwaffe invalid who seemed to have a live wire up his arse about something and made as if to go back inside. This close, Holleman could see that the eye at which the scar terminated was dead.

'Good show from Eddie.' It was all he could think of, to make himself seem less suspicious, less *caught*.

Sandy shrugged slightly. 'Fucking pansy. Can't see what the attraction is.'

Holleman grinned ingratiatingly. 'Still, an SS escort, the man must be important.'

'Not to me, he isn't.' The corporal scowled. 'But he's Sepp's uncle, so I'm helping with the babysitting. The old queen got himself beaten up by some of our lads last year. Can't say I blame them. That sort should be gone by now.'

'They are, mostly.'

'Yeah? Well, someone missed Eddie. All I can think is, some of the Bosses must like that old-time shit more than they hate what he does with his cock. Don't stay out too long, mate. It's cold.'

The younger man went inside. Disgusted with himself, Holleman turned and watched the shadowy figure of Otto Fischer emerge from the gloom opposite.

'You silly bastard.'

'Sorry, Otto.'

'Well, get back inside. Look embarrassed - that should be easy.'

Holleman nodded, smiled ruefully. 'We've got two *Liebstandarten* in there. Neither looks like he's our boy.'

He turned to follow Sandy, but stopped.

'Otto?'

'What, Freddy?'

'I puked. Just by wanting to.'

'Well the evening's not been wasted, then.'

Holleman's back was to the light, so Fischer couldn't see whether he smiled before turning once more and limped back into the *volksküche*. From the open door came a faint hint of Muntz, getting the crowd going again with *Lili Marlene*. The song was obviously a matter of intense debate at the Chancellery, getting itself banned every other week and then scraped back off the list for some unstated reason. Fischer assumed that this was one of its legal weeks; that Muntz wasn't trying to arrange bed and breakfast for himself in one of the Reich's camps for retired idiosyncratics. He paused and listened for a few moments. The voice was a good one, sounding much younger than it was, and as he re-crossed the street to return to his dark hideaway he hummed the familiar melody as, he assumed, many of the audience were doing at that moment. His tuneless effort probably masked something of the approach, and he had no sense of it happening, no time to react to it, felt nothing as the hard asphalt rose swiftly to slap the bad side of his face.

Part Three

1

There had been a doctor, apparently, though he couldn't recall a face or locate any sort of memory to tie down the alleged fact. Time had passed - he could be fairly sure of that at least - but not as he expected; occasions that must have followed on from others fell into no sort of order or sense when he tried to plot their place in his fractured recollections. Several times he saw one (or both) of the twins wielding a spoon, putting something into his mouth, and he had a distinct sense of something going down when they did. It wasn't always disgusting - he had a firm sense of that, too. At one point he thought that he might have tasted chocolate without being quite sure whether this was a current event or sensory nostalgia. It didn't matter. Most of the time he thought of nothing, and whenever he realised this he assumed that he had been sleeping, or close to it.

It was the spectre of Freddie Holleman who mentioned the doctor, during one of the times its face loomed in a world which otherwise seemed to have contracted to a portion of ceiling and an intermittently pulsing headache. He was touched that Freddie had found the time to visit, though he wished that his friend might keep his voice decently low instead of assuming a state of deafness or senility in the patient and bawling every word like a sergeant on a parade ground.

Of his battered senses, only his hearing seemed to be more acute than before, however *before* might be defined. He heard birds during daylight, and footsteps moving up and down the street outside with a clarity he couldn't recall; he could most definitely hear the sisters' bickerings (though the detail often merged into the domestic mush of other voices), and the pipes conveying water around the house, and a quiet but seemingly interminable BBC broadcast, and even the soft, clandestine shuffle of cats wandering in and out to check an environment previously forbidden to them.

It must have been one of them - Marlene, or Sigi, or Chancellor Bismarck - that brought it on. From being a simple matter of ceiling, noises and headache, the world suddenly became a struggle to breath, and the arthritic pain of limbs unemployed for too long thrashing suddenly, and too much snot, copiously flaying his face and eyes, and Freddie Holleman too, getting a firm grip, pulling him upright, failing to get out of the way when the vomiting started.

'... dirty bastard!' He felt his mouth being wiped with very little tenderness, but the dizziness didn't allow him to focus too clearly on the detail of it. He could breathe again, and that was enough to make up for what lacked elsewhere. For a while he concentrated on getting as much air as possible into himself, letting the headache take the benefit of his strengthening pulse.

His found it difficult to focus his eyes. The walls of his room (which he recognized like old acquaintances, unexpectedly returned from a trip overseas) loomed and receded in a way that almost invited another bout of sickness, and he was obliged to close them out for a few moments. Opening just one of them kept the nauseating perspective at bay, and he was able to he peer around periscope fashion, until Freddie loomed once more, wiping his shirt with a corner of the blanket.

'How…?'

'Three days, almost. Tsk.' Holleman discovered a splash on his grey trousers and applied another section of blanket. 'A nice fracture. Seventeen stitches, concussion very likely, he said.'

'Who?'

'The doctor! How many fucking times do I have to…?'

'No. I mean, who hit me?'

'No idea. Our perpetrator, probably, though he must have been snug in his bed before you were found. It was an old gentleman. He wanted me to tell you that he was sorry for kicking you, but it was dark and his legs aren't that steady these days.'

'Nice of him not to run away.'

'Wasn't it?' Holleman stood up, and Fischer noticed that he was unshaven.

'Must I thank you for the tender care?'

'The boys, they took it in turn. Franz even gave you a bit of a bed-bath. He's probably scarred.'

The headache was now attacking a reasonably clear mind, and hurt much more for it. Fischer eased back carefully against the headboard and groaned.

'Soup, Herr Fischer!'

Frau Ostermann announced this from the doorway with little less pomp or volume than a toastmaster catching sight of the Emperor

Franz Josef. She advanced towards the bed, paused when she saw the mess on his eiderdown, turned and placed the tray upon the window table.

'It's pea, a Prussian recipe!'

'Dried pea, without marjoram.' From behind her sister, Frau Traugott seasoned the dish with a little deflation. 'Or speck. Is your poor head hurting?'

'A little, yes.'

'The cowardly swine! A foreigner, I'm sure of it. Did he get your papers, or wallet?'

Fischer glanced at Holleman, who nodded slightly. It was good thinking - a sensible story, believable, requiring no embellishments.

'I don't think so. Perhaps he panicked.'

'He should be shot,' Frau Ostermann sniffed, adding this to her store of proofs of the world's degeneracy. 'Herr Holleman has informed the police.'

Oh, I'm sure he has. Fischer struggled upright. He noticed that he was wearing pyjamas, an involuntary donation from the long deceased Herr Walter Traugott. Holleman helped him to the table, where he was obliged to try to eat under the minute gaze of three adults and, from the door, thirteen-year-old bookends. The best that could be said of Frau Ostermann's recipe was that it didn't taste too much of anything one way or the other, but he was ravenous and devoured it with an enthusiasm that made her beam. She turned to her sister. 'You see? A *good* Prussian recipe!'

Frau Traugott sniffed. 'There has to be *one*, naturally.'

When he'd finished, Fischer placed a hand carefully on the back of his head. It was heavily bandaged and tender, but the external pain was as nothing to the ache inside. It must have been a cosh; he had no memory of the blow, much less of any attempt on his part to react. A swift, brutally effective assault, so why wasn't he dead? There had been time and darkness enough to finish the job casually, with only the door of the *volkskuche* needing to be watched as the victim was dispatched to a happier place - it made no sense.

'We'll leave our soldiers to their business.'

Frau Traugott waved out the boys and dragged the soiled cover from the bed. Her sister, warmed by the small victory, collected the tray and followed. Holleman waited until they had gone before extracting two pethidin capsules from his pocket.

'They'll help.'

Fischer took them gratefully. His head wasn't up to thinking about how it had come to feel like this, and behind the pain, waiting its turn, was a quiet, bubbling anxiety. He had been three days unconscious, three days taking his ease while a killer went about his business and the Reichsmarschall waited impatiently to be briefed upon their complete lack of success in stopping him. It was like waking to discover that he'd fallen asleep at the wheel of a speeding car.

Holleman was regarding him closely. He had a look about him, of someone waiting to tell the patient that his test results said the very worst thing. Fischer wondered what possible twist of the knife waited to be inflicted.

'What is it, Freddie?'

'Nothing.'

'What have you been doing, while I was …'

'Nothing.'

'Nothing?'

'Karl's got an idea. You should listen to him. To put it bluntly, he thinks we've been wasting our time. He thinks it's not someone from *Liebstandarte SS* at all.'

The full, exquisite spread of damaged nerve endings on Fischer' skull bloomed horribly. 'Oh, that's wonderful. What do you think?'

'That he's probably right.'

'Sweet Jesus.'

Three men, Luftwaffe officers, stood on the north side of Unter den Eichen, a broad boulevard in the south-western Berlin, borough of Steglitz, district of Lichterfelde. A nice place, even this late in a bad war - substantial, quiet and usually leafy, though in late December only the evergreens in the arboretum of the famed Botanical Gardens were putting on a splash of colour. A handy place, too - close enough to real Power even when a green swathe had separated the village from the city, when Kings and Emperors had thought it a sufficient location for their military academies and barracks. Like Potsdam, it had been near but not *of* Berlin.

Cities grow, though, and Lichterfelde had become an outer suburb. Now, the metropolis embraced it, its arteries thrust through it, and what had once been merely handy had become most convenient. The privileged military enclave, no longer a *faux* country retreat, had opened its doors to the twentieth century and its big businesses. Some of Germany's foremost commercial entities had factories and offices here, lining or abutting the ring-road, strategically placed yet with an ease of movement denied to city-centre enterprises. Electronics, chemicals, machine-tools - every manufactured commodity that the modern warring state deemed indispensable was represented in some aspect in the area between Unter den Eichen and the Teltow Canal. And complementing that emigration from the centre, snug among its principal customers, the Reich's foremost employment agency stared into the Botanical Gardens over the heads of the three men who contemplated it.

'We didn't even *think* of this.'

Freddie Holleman spat into the road. In front of him, on the south side of the boulevard, at Unter den Eichen 126 - 135, the elegant five-storey headquarters of SS Wirtschafts-Verwaltungshauptamt, the central bureau for economic administration, preened itself modestly. If anyone needed to know how far *SchutzStaffeln* had penetrated German society, here was the place to start. Here was the money, the fruits of legislated gangsterism, directed from a building that oozed the quiet, respectable anonymity of a Swiss bank; the head office of an efficient, pervasive nest of private shell companies exploiting every resource of the vast commercial empire that Himmler's child had accumulated to itself since 1933. Under the low red-pantile roof, SS maintained and extended its grip on forestry, mining, quarrying, cement production, fine porcelain manufacture, food resources, mineral water extraction, military uniform production, camp construction, fine art acquisition-without-bidding and the supply of non-unionized, wage-free labour to a huge swathe of German industry.

Gently, Fischer rubbed his heavily bandaged head. 'Well, if he lives here you can choose your motive.'

They had chased a lone psychopath, imagining that the honour of his unit, its reputation, required that his unspeakable crimes be hidden from view. They had hoped somehow to force a gap between political expediency and insanity sufficiently to extract their man and survive the consequences. They had been fools. Here, there was no gap; within the building opposite the inconceivable was not only entertained but formalized, structured and exploited for a profit. They had believed that they were investigating murder, when in fact they had set themselves against a way of death.

Karl Krohne scowled at the edifice. 'I assume that we're not going to announce ourselves.'

Having had several days fewer than Krohne and Holleman to absorb the shock of their collective error, Fischer remained a little dazed by its magnitude. A solitary mistake could be accepted and even - given luck, a following wind and God's saving Grace – redeemed, but to be wrong in every particular invited a sense of helplessness he last recalled at his mother's teat.

If it was Gerd Branssler's fault, no one was saying so. His hypothesis had been sound enough - they had accepted it and moved on quickly without pausing to consider whether there were alternatives. Momentum had brought its usual circular logic, with each new clue seemingly reinforcing the rest, when all had stood or fallen upon just the one, untestable assumption. Looking back, they might admire how, like drugged bricklayers, they had built half-carefully and almost methodically upon their delusions until the moment the edifice crashed down.

But Branssler had been right about one thing - they had been made. Logic said the Judas had been Ministerial Director Schapper, covering his own or his boss's arse, or perhaps playing two decks simultaneously. How could it hurt to let slip a little of the detail, if the consequences fell only upon the idiots who had brought the thing to him in the first place? It might well have flushed out a response that identified the puppeteer; at the very least it would absolve *Forschungsamt* of any collusion with men who were crafting their own suicides. Fischer didn't doubt that like all professional betrayals it had been carefully neutered, an innocent comment lacking any quality of innocence, to a man or men equally divorced from consequence.

He thanked a Heaven in which he didn't believe for Karl Krohne's dreary, weekly meeting at Prinz-Albrecht-Strasse, where opportunities for petty thrusts were never knowingly foregone. Friedrich Panzinger, far from being outraged to discover their efforts, had been delighted to be one revelation ahead of the pack. *So, what are your boys doing down in Lichterfelde, eh, Krohne? Playing in someone else's sandpit? Be careful - it may not have a bottom!*

All night, three exhausted Luftwaffe officers (one of them nursing a raging headache) had stared into their ersatz coffee grounds, trying to divine what it meant, where it was leading them. Krohne's logic was sound - if Panzinger had teased rather than pounced it was because he wasn't worried about what they were doing. But that raised a whole babble of further questions whose answers none of them were eager to chase too closely. For hours, they had twisted ideas into knots, each less capable of unravelling than the last, until their meanderings and permutations of fact, fear and wild supposition could be distilled to a single, composite question - *What had been said, when had it been said, and to whom?*

At dawn, in a grubby, bomb-damaged Neukölln street, they had flung shale at a bedroom window like wild children. He came to the door in his underpants, cursing furiously, refusing to invite them inside. But when Fischer whispered the business in his ear it became a matter of dragging him back into the house before the entire neighbourhood could bear unwitting witness to what one Gerd Branssler intended to do to the entire leadership of RSHA Amt V Criminal Investigations and its collective ring piece.

The Branssler residence wore its missing *hausfrau* like a running sore. In the sitting room, several days' meals could be reconstructed from stains decorating the plates that sat upon almost every horizontal surface. Clothes, worn until they offended even their wearer, lay where he had dropped them on and around most of the visible furniture. Mercifully, the stench of stale tobacco overlaid everything, making what might have been pestilential merely disgusting. Branssler's three visitors, long used to most of war's sartorial compromises, positioned themselves carefully in the room's centre, taking pains not to brush against anything.

The foundation and cause of the mess had found a pair of his least-stained trousers and was squatting on a low wooden chair, glaring at them. His bared chest, a steppe of silver-white hair, was muscular still despite the over-generous belly sitting beneath it. The wide shoulders and thick arms reminded Fischer of the gantry crane at Swinemünde docks that his father used to operate, while the calloused hands gripped their knees as though ready to propel the torso clear of its lower half - an east Berlin Buddha, done with *dhyãna* and looking for a deal of trouble.

'It was me, then.'

Fischer nodded. 'It was a good theory, Gerd. Worse, it suited them to let it run. When did you mention it?'

Branssler sighed. 'Christ, I don't know. Probably the morning after we found the third one. It had been on my mind a while, the Kaserne so close by, Leibstandarte. It seemed to fit neatly'

'To whom?'

'Dieter Thomas, definitely. I don't think … anyone else.'

'It doesn't matter. If he opened his mouth at the Alex it would have run upstairs quicker than the clap. Someone heard it and liked it, and the moment they killed the investigation it was more or less set in stone, a neat little distraction.'

'Fuck your mother!' The Bull stared at the floor, shaking his head in disgust.

'Karl worked it out. He thought about who told him, and why. Why, that is, would someone who had good reason to stifle the investigation, who'd been told that rogue Luftwaffe officers were making noises, *not* want to fall upon them like the hand of God?'

'Panzinger *knows*?' Branssler could hardly take it in.

'He told Karl that he knew, but then he laughed about it. He said it was truly astonishing how some people wanted to make their own bad luck when there was so much of it going around looking for a home. And then he just walked away.'

'He doesn't care?'

'He cares. He cares enough to want us to carry on thinking what we think. Because if we do, then someone else stays invisible.'

'Who?'

'We have a possibility, Gerd, just that. Three ladies have died. It may be more by now, of course. The killer *must* be from Lichterfelde, or close by. And if the Alex closed down the search, then it's someone they don't want caught. Again, we *know* this. These are just about the only indisputable things we have. So, what - *who* - else lives in Lichterfelde?'

They had all overlooked *SS-WVHA* because it was an entity that in Germany whispered its presence, however pervasively its tentacles spread across the new territories. The men who worked there weren't the crowd-rousing heroes of the Reich or its fearful, shadowy watchmen; they were grey corpses, the bureaucratic, desk-bound architects of abominable efficiencies. But as individuals they could be reached, unlike their brethren behind the kaserne's walls. If someone on Unter den Eichen had to be protected, how better to do it than to allow busy minds to think that guilt lay elsewhere, in a place it couldn't be pursued?

Branssler had apologized almost tearfully, but Fischer reminded him that they were all culpable, that there was still a job to be done, *if* the Bull could get the information they needed. And of course, he could. That is, he told them he'd break heads to get it, even if it meant ...

Holleman had needed to calm him once more, which stole time they could hardly spare; but before the city's remaining commuters were on the streets in any numbers the three Luftwaffe officers were in Lichterfelde once more, standing at a new starting line, staring at a problem whose size confounded assessment.

'*If* our man lives there, we can explain at least one thing.' Fischer turned away from 126 - 135 Unter den Eichen and walked towards the Botanical Gardens' main southern entrance. Holleman and Krohne followed. They found it in less than a minute, squatting beside the much-expanded allotments of the *German Farming* section - an ugly, utilitarian structure, too new to have acquired a patina of belonging even had it not been so incongruent with the setting. Fischer and Holleman had passed this way three times previously, but it had been concealed from their eyes by a hedge. In any case, they hadn't thought to look for it - why should they? There was no secret here, every department had to have at least one. It was regulations, after all.

'He wasn't going to leave them too close to this, was he?'

Three victims had been discovered, one at each point of the Gardens' compass except the obvious east, the main driveway, abutting which the low, broad profile of *SS-WVHA*'s air-raid bunker intruded massively into the bucolic illusion.

Holleman prodded the sloping, sod-laden foundation with his artificial foot.

'Strange place to put it, in a park, a good sprint from the office. If they wait for the sirens, bombs are going to be falling around them by the time they get here.'

Fischer pulled him away. 'The tree cover makes it hard to spot from above. And it's probably intended to preserve papers, not bodies. There'll be a mort of commercial contracts needing shelter before flesh gets a turn. I expect there's another reinforced area in a basement over the road. Come on. Let's not give them too much of a view.'

'Where now?'

'To get a *muckefucke*. And to begin again.'

3

'Memory is a curious facility. We know next to nothing of how it works, or which part of the brain regulates it. We don't know why it can fail and sometimes be recovered without apparent cause. We don't even understand how, absent a traumatic event, some memories not associated with typical events recur excessively while others lie dormant for long periods. There's very little that's straightforward or uncomplicated about it.'

They were the kind of reassurances that raise doubts rather than bed them, and the doctor seemed to be directing them as much at himself as his audience. A pleasant man, but like the breed as a whole, ineffectual. So, once more, the patient tried to explain his symptoms.

'It isn't individual memories that I can't recall, Herr Hauptmann. I have entire periods of blankness, time erased, and nothing returns either soon afterwards or much later.'

He hadn't wanted to admit this, not to anyone. His work was all that remained by way of an anchor keeping his wandering head in place, and any diagnosis that removed him from it, placed him in a ward, would be worse than a clean shot to the head. But even more than that he feared not knowing where his mind might be going. Having an expectation, even of something terrible, was better than waiting like a child in darkness for something unknowable.

The doctor frowned. 'Your wounds were abdominal. We wouldn't have expected any subsequent trauma to have manifested mentally.' He glanced up. 'The physical healing is very good - excellent, even. Obviously, there will continue to be problems given the extent of the damage, but this thing, this … well, it must be unconnected. A new issue, not a new manifestation.'

'Can something be done?' The absurdity of it struck him as he asked. The doctor had already glanced at his watch twice; this was at best a five-minute consultation offered as a perquisite of the job, and there was a line of his colleagues outside waiting for the same. With half her men of fighting age killed, wounded or desperately digging in against a remorseless enemy, the Reich didn't have the time or resources to treat her heroes adequately, much less useless invalids with fascinating foibles.

The doctor said something he didn't catch and didn't need to - it was little more than a soothing noise, an aural placebo to be taken gratefully. He mumbled thanks and stood up, feeling the familiar tightness in his stomach sharpen to a brief pang. The man was right; the wound was down there, not in his head. The *problem* was one for which a convenient antidote didn't exist, not in the present age. At the door he nodded in the next man, Bedderdorf, Amt A, one of the accountants - a punctured lung, if what remained of his memory served. Another pleasant fellow; the building seemed to be full of them.

He returned to his office section. It was busy as usual, too much work for the few staff, but no one complained. Busy days took minds from dragging clocks, as … someone used to say, he couldn't quite recall. He let that one go. Missing fragments of what he might have known formerly didn't concern him; it was the broad, deep, empty places that he feared.

His section's principal business was men - and women, of course, but collectively the resource was stated in the masculine, sex being irrelevant to the statistics. Amt W controlled the acquisition, deployment, management, productivity and maintenance (food, sanitation and bedding) of the resource, so companies that contracted with *WVHA* could leave the entire business of their workforce to the SS. This modular concept, they were told often, was the future of labour management in industry, and it couldn't be denied that enterprises utilizing their manpower were highly productive. But then they couldn't fail to be. The drag-weight matters of wage negotiations, working conditions and productivity agreements weren't in point, so management was free to concentrate on innovation and meeting production quotas. Meanwhile, the labour force concentrated upon working until it ceased to be viable, at which point it was replenished by new material. Moral issues were similarly otiose; the resource was drawn entirely from races and groups that had forsaken or never possessed the rights that Germans - good Germans - might take for granted, so their work both absolved their crimes and compensated the state for the expense of keeping them alive.

Amt W's was a small office, but it maintained contracts across the Reich's industrial heart - Blohm & Voss, Junkers, Krupp, Heinkel, Messerschmitt, Stayer-Daimler-Puch, Stolberger, Salzgitter, I.G. Farben, Volkswagen, Ford-Werke, Daimler-Benz,

Opel, Seimens-Schuckert, Hugo Boss and thousands of smaller concerns, all utterly dependent upon SS labour to make up the shortfall created by the millions of men who had gone off to war and the millions of women whom a certain Austrian gentleman was too nervous to conscript for factory work. It had become the most pervasive contractor of manpower in the history of free capital enterprise, generating billions of reichsmarks, burdened by a vanishingly small wage-bill and administered entirely from a building on Unter den Eichen upon which the SS paid no rent. It would be hard to conceive a more efficient business model, or one more envied by German business and many of its erstwhile foreign competitors.

So in a sense he was proud of what he did, though it couldn't be said to be what a soldier would call a proper job. He and nine colleagues had the particular task of matching skills to needs: of ensuring that the supply of substitute labour to combines contracting with *WVHA* was suitable to their purpose. Most of these enterprises required abilities, or at least the potential to develop them. A few years' earlier, arrogant attitudes had encouraged wrong thinking: that any sort of labour would suit any role for which it was needed. They had been corrected quite forcibly on that point. Standards had slipped, targets had not been met, arses had been kicked and men in suits had come from their factory floors, stood face-to-face with WVHA staff and told them that it wouldn't do, that things had to change. Their complaints, which had gone all the way to the Chancellery, had been heeded. Now, replacement labour was as carefully graded as the system allowed, and skills were matched to the bench at which they were utilized.

But the document on his desk, an item that had arrived with that morning's post, was a product of the old way of thinking - a retrogressive, foolish order, and he was tempted to ignore it. It required, without offering any rationale, that the entire labour force of Soldau camp be transferred westwards and distributed between eighteen industrial combines in Hesse and Westphalia. It was nonsense; as the author of the order must have known perfectly well, every inmate of Soldau was employed solely in agricultural labour and was fit for nothing but more of the same. He could imagine the reception they would receive in their new workplaces, at a time when Reichsminister Speer was demanding unprecedented efficiencies and British and American pilots were doing their very best to hamper them. In fact, it was easier to believe that the Allies had insinuated the order into *WVHA* as a useful prank, such was its inexplicable, pointless idiocy.

The thing was marked *most urgent*, and came from the office of Obergruppenführer Pohl himself (though it was signed by a subordinate). There was no reason to delay implementing the order, but the disappointments of the morning had put him in a stubborn mood, a mood to hamper a stupid, ill-conceived process. The next fortnightly review of the department's work would be made in five days' time, 4 January 1945, so he removed his desk diary and opened it on the page for 3 January. He could deal with the thing then, at the very last moment. A churlish gesture, but it cheered him slightly.

A piece of paper slipped from the diary, from that same page. He picked it from the floor and read it. Other than its date - exactly one week earlier - and in missing the word *most*, it was identical to the one he had just decided to ignore. He had no recollection of having seen it previously, but that hardly surprised him. At least his reaction to the thing had been consistent - to push it back until the last moment. Yet remarkably, someone had found the delay unacceptable and followed up within the week. Usually, only the important matters, the big contracts and major deployments, were monitored this closely. From memory (he almost laughed as the expression came to mind), the complement of Soldau camp was less than twenty thousand - twenty thousand supremely inflexible workers, to be sent *most urgently* to factories where their lack of skills would seriously slow production.

This made it more difficult to ignore. An order with no sense to it demanded to be questioned and even challenged. Regrettably, his section leader, who almost certainly owed his appointment to a ranking relation's influence, was not likely to take up any cause that might get him transferred from Unter den Eichen to a siege trench on the outskirts of Budapest. If something was going to be said he would have to say it himself, but unterscharführers weren't put on God's green Earth to question orders, not in the SS. He compared the two pieces of paper once more. They were definitely identical, with the same scrawled, anonymous signature, and something else that should have been immediately apparent - they were directed to him personally, not to the section. To his admittedly imperfect recollection, no initiating order processed by the section had *ever* had a named recipient. Someone wanted this business dealt with, and they had chosen him specifically to be the dealer. When he failed to action it, *he* had been prompted to correct the oversight. So why hadn't the section leader been around to rouse him? Why hadn't the author descended two flights and deployed his own boot to get things moving?

The obvious, sensible course was to quell his irritation and process the order immediately. It would be a complex procedure, as with all transfers. Soldau's commandant would need to be issued with what doubtlessly would be a most troubling order, and precious resources would require reallocating; the Inspectorate of Concentration Camps at Oranienburg had to be notified and their agreement secured - it was *their* decision to make, strictly speaking; some sort of transportation would need to be arranged - or, failing that, a sufficient number of guards to prevent the transferees from just wandering away; finally, the various recipients of this unwanted gift from *WVHA* would require advance notification of their curious windfall, though what use they could make of it was anyone's guess. It was all paperwork, and would travel through any number of departments on its way to moving things along. But for all the stamps it acquired on that journey, it would continue to bear only one signature - his own.

He wasn't susceptible to paranoia, but this made him nervous. Having dealt with it he would no doubt ponder its meaning, over and over, distracting himself with unproductive speculation. He couldn't see what it should have to do with him when there were other men in his section, equally skilled at pushing paper, who might have done it as easily. Why had someone wanted *him* to deal with it?

He stared at the things until he could almost recite their content unseen, and decided not to make anything more of it. It was an order, and it wasn't for him to say what was best for the *WVHA* and German industry. So instead of delaying the business further he made it a priority, to remove it from his desk and attention. But the *why* stuck in his mind, all the morning and afternoon, as he made calls, drafted memoranda and put his name to the papers that turned the intention into fact. And Soldau …

He couldn't decide whether it was the business itself that brought it too forcibly to mind or something else. It was a word, a place, a minor element of a vast, interlocking system, a name that came to light very rarely and only upon a point of sugar beet or barley production. He was certain that he had no deeper knowledge of the place than any other man in the section; it had been a Polish kaserne before the war and then, following the invasion and liberation of the corridor, a holding and transit camp for Jews and other undesirables. But for the past three years it had been an *arbeitserziehungslager*, a work camp, as nondescript a facility as might be found anywhere in the Reich or new territories. He hadn't dealt with any matter specifically relating to the place in the six months since joining the section - he knew this because he took a few moments to check his schedules back to his first day with Amt W and found nothing, not the merest reference to Soldau or its labour force. And yet the name had a resonance, of the sort experienced when an unfamiliar mouth utters one's name. He said it to himself, over and over, hoping to elicit a spark of recollection, a context, and failed. By the time the papers were ready for his section leader's review, the thing had dug itself a hole in his head. It was so frustrating, and the whole business so perplexing, that when his shift ended he decided to ignore both his doctor's strict warning and his native common sense and take up Horst's invitation to *push out the boat* with his home-brewed poison.

4

Mona Kreitz had three customers, all Luftwaffe officers. It was likely that the prospect of them sitting at the window as if it were a services canteen would incline most of her regular morning clientele to walk straight past and attend to the day's other business, but that was hardly her concern. She had no stake in the café - if it could still be dignified by the term - and doubted that her boss would notice the dip in coupon clippings. Still, it made for an unusual Saturday, for better or worse.

They made a striking picture - a cripple, a one-eyed philanderer and a man whose face might have been written by Strobl. Sitting at her smallest table, sipping ersatz coffee, mumbling to each other dolorously (at least, that's how she interpreted their mood), they needed only an orchestra's lament either to melt an audience's heart or test its stomach.

Holleman had paid his customary polite respects and asked if they might sit for a while to discuss an important matter. She could hardly refuse him. The way he asked made it easier to agree, but his manner didn't deceive her; he had the look of a hardened man, the sort who wouldn't hesitate to do things that she could hardly conceive, and if he made an effort to seem otherwise it was obviously a strained one. His friend, the new one, was far more polished, and brazen. He kept glancing at her, making no pretence of not enjoying the view. She was used to that look; it had followed her almost her entire life, an unavoidable annoyance, but at least she knew how to deal with it. It was the mutilated one who defied her attempts to read him. A face like that didn't lend itself to the usual assumptions of what lay behind it - it was more of a battlefield in which one sought to find clues to the landscape it had once been. Emotionless, she thought, or sealed against further harm; a good or bad man, she couldn't say.

Of the three only Holleman was occasionally loud enough to hear clearly. Whenever his voice rose the charmer invariably turned to her to apologize with his only eye while the mutilated one - Fischer - calmed his friend, told him to speak quietly. It was to do with *that* business, of course; she didn't need to be at the table with them to know what had brought them back to Lichterfelde. Nor did she need police training to see failure, or at least disappointment. She hoped to God that it wasn't yet another murder.

She tried to dismiss the thought before it could take hold. Common sense said that it was best not to know anything, but this thing didn't have a single logic. To preserve the self in one way meant to imperil it in another; knowledge was dangerous, but ignorance was no protection once night fell and the streets emptied, not in Lichterfelde. So she paid attention to their cups and, when they were empty, filled another pot and took it to the table, hoping to hear enough to ease her mind without making her culpable.

'... follow the ladies instead.' The badly wounded one - Fischer - paused as she approached, and smiled (at least, she thought it was a smile). Hastily, he covered his cup with a hand, and the others did the same. 'Thank you, no.'

They said nothing else while she stood there. It couldn't have been more pointed yet she remained, willing some impossible enlightenment to occur, until their smiles assumed a fixed quality and the pause became unbearable. When she retired to the safety of her counter her face was burning.

For the next hour they remained at the table, speaking quietly, her only customers. At about noon, Albert and Erich arrived. They were chattering, preoccupied with something, paying no attention to anything but their gripes. A metre in from the door, they noticed the Luftwaffe contingent and stopped abruptly. Mona had a smile of welcome ready for them. It was so dazzling, so warmly welcoming, that their feet could hardly refuse to proceed. They were helped on their way a little by the one-eyed charmer, who nodded, smiled, said *good morning sirs* pleasantly as they shuffled past his table (though of course his uniform spoke much more loudly than his manners). Albert, whose career on the railways had given him something of a sophisticated man's ease around strangers, returned the nod. Erich stumbled mutely to the counter, saving his own for Mona.

In a little while, the café had two unconnected, equally artificial conversations flowing. The officers had raised their voices and were discussing the quality of German artichokes compared to the obviously inferior foreign varieties. Mona, had she a taste for wagers, would have staked a week's takings on none of them caring what the final word on the subject would or should be. At the counter, Albert and Erich, having caught the word *artichoke*, seized upon rationing with dogged determination, it being one of the few subjects about which Germans were allowed - expected, even - to complain bitterly without official censure (unless they attempted to ascribe blame, which no sane person would do). Between these culinary poles of indifference and despair, Mona considered herself unusually excluded. It was all very well to stand at a counter awaiting the next order - that was her job, after all. But usually she was invited to comment, and more often to sympathize with whatever injustice or ill fortune was being aired. Today, even the old men, cowed by the company they were obliged to endure, kept their own counsel. She felt she might have been one of the pots on the shelf behind her, inanimately monitoring the passages that flitted past them.

Her days dragged without the diversion of conversation. The café's only inanimate source of distraction was a copy of *Berliner Illustrierte Zeitung* that lived below the counter; it was dated October 1941, and she had read it so often that its content was inscribed upon her soul like the Lord's Prayer. Today, less than a minute's examination of its long-familiar tips on ladies' wear drove her to a desperate decision. On a long shelf beneath the counter sat a nest of old crockery and utensils that probably had last seen a cloth or water when she was a girl. It was something she had deferred for as long as she could recall, a chore bequeathed by the indolence of former managers. For the next thirty minutes she was on her knees, pulling out stuff, allocating it to the *cleaning* or *disposal* piles. It was hard work, and several times she caught herself muttering threats into tannin-clogged corners, or at the lower edge of the shelf against which, twice, she banged her head. Eventually, everything was dragged out, the space cleaned and the rubbish, stacked across the floor from counter to wall, almost entombed her. One of her feet had lost all feeling; she massaged it before trying to rise, and as she did so she realised that the conversation at the counter had ceased. She glanced up. Albert and Erich were sitting quietly, trying to be invisible, straining to watch the uniforms while keeping their faces safely averted. There was a fourth man at the table now, a big, thick-set fellow in civilian clothes, perhaps in his early sixties, wearing the trademark American gangster's hat and overcoat favoured by Gestapo and similar. This, she decided, was something about which to be anxious.

She could make out no more from their whispers than earlier, but then only a fool would pry into such people's business. The big civilian was bent over the table, resting his fists upon it, and the others had leaned forward to hear him. Her two old men couldn't take their eyes from the group; like pheasants caught in a net they seemed resigned to the worst - a demand to know their business, their papers checked, a false accusation made by a neighbour who objected to the fact that they wouldn't part with one of their pigeons for the pot, a small room with bars at one end and then a train to somewhere out East (one never asked or knew where, of course).

The civilian walked across to the counter, nodded at the old men (Albert almost whimpered), turned to Mona and produced a warrant disc, which relieved her fears considerably. As far as she knew, Gestapo didn't bother to identify themselves.

'Good afternoon, Fraulein. I understand that you know Rudolph Bildmann?'

Mona nodded and gestured at the window table. 'I told them. He hasn't been in for a while now.'

'No.' He took off his hat and rubbed his head. It was massive, bony, mostly without hair. He looked to be of that species of thug who invariably stood behind local Party officials when they could be bothered to attend council meetings, making them seem more important than they were. But the voice didn't fit the rest - it was like Herr Holleman's, a gruff, loud thing trying to be gentler than it could quite manage.

'I wonder if you can recall how long he's been coming to the café - that is, when he used to come, of course.'

His smile was easier than the rest of the face, and she relaxed slightly. 'For about as long as I've worked here. At least, I don't remember thinking of him as a new face.'

'And that would be…?'

'I took the job in October nineteen forty-two, so two years.'

Erich, who had been as mute as a mouse in a cat basket, coughed. 'He was in the army. But he came home.'

'Do you know when, sir?'

'Two, three years ago. You can ask at Dahlem station, that's where he works. Since the 'twenties, I think.'

The policeman seemed pleased with this information, vague as it was. 'So he was police, but then went away to war for a while and came back again? Was he wounded?'

Erich looked doubtfully at Albert, who shook his head. 'He just … came back.'

'About two or three years ago?'

Both men nodded.

'So, nineteen forty-one or two?'

If it was a test it was an easy one, and they continued to nod.

'Does he have any close friends that you know of?'

Albert and Erich exchanged another glance, perhaps thinking that they might have done well not to speak in the first place. Mona came to their rescue. 'He always came in alone. He'd talk to people, but I don't think he knew any of my customers very well. Except Hans Lutze, but that was just because they were both police.'

The big man's eyebrows lifted. 'He knew Lutze? They were friends?'

'Oh no. At least, Rudy wouldn't have said so. Like everyone else he thought he was a bore, but Hans always used to make a point of going over to say something when he saw that there was another policeman in the café. It used to make Rudy wince, but he was polite about it. He never told him to …'

'… bugger off!' Albert said it with relish, and cackled. 'Everyone who knows Lutze wants to do that!'

The big man smiled. 'He likes to talk, I hear.'

'Talk? His lips never meet, except to bounce off each other! And it's always murder, murder, murder, and the state of the bodies, and whatever filth the murderer got up to before or after the business. I'll tell you, people have been very happy since he took it somewhere else.'

'You don't know where?'

Albert slapped the counter, grateful to be offered the punch line. 'Don't know, and wouldn't want to!'

Mona noticed that the two old men were now almost completely at their ease, persuaded by their interrogator's easy manner, and imagined that this was how confessions were secured when it had to be done bloodlessly. It didn't seem to her that the answers he had been given could be at all useful, but the big man was nodding, apparently content.

'Now, do you know any of these women?'

He offered three names. Albert and Erich shook their heads immediately. Mona, whose job didn't allow her to be quite as familiar with surnames, thought for a little longer before shaking her own. She knew who the women must be of course, but they hadn't been customers - at least, not the sort to give their names, to tell her something of their lives. Again, the policeman didn't seem too disappointed to hear nothing. He thanked them and returned to the table. The four men spoke briefly, quietly, and about five minutes later they left together. Only Holleman made a point of thanking her, though the mutilated one looked at her for a moment longer than she might have considered polite, or disinterested. It was hard to know what it meant, in that face.

Albert and Erich, excited by their near-appointment with a Gestapo cellar (as they insisted it had been), remained for a further hour or more, happily recounting their adventures to the three customers who entered during that time. Mona wished that they might have been more discreet, but they were old men, starved of attention, and they couldn't be denied their few joules of limelight. Their audience thought it a good sign after weeks of silence that *officials* were showing their faces again, and seemingly wanting to do something about *the situation*. That wasn't quite the case of course, but Mona could hardly tell them what she knew. Still, it would be all over Lichterfelde before the day was done that the murderer was being chased once more. It struck her as a strange thing, that Holleman and his friends had taken such little care that day to keep the nature of their business to themselves. It went entirely against what they had said to her previously, and she didn't know whether to feel used by them or frightened - to wonder if they were being too clever for her to comprehend, or not enough to keep her safe.

All citizens of the Reich were logged. Data upon their births, marriages, divorces and deaths, who worked at what and when and for what recompense, whose opinions and actions contravened the comprehensive prohibitions of National Socialism, whose biology failed to reflect the necessary minimum standards necessary to preserve and enhance racial purity - the paperwork held it all. By a particularly sharp stab of irony the Party's ability to know everything about everyone had been greatly facilitated by the degenerate Republic's well-meaning social welfare reforms; the regime that inherited the system had merely refined and extended it, though *welfare* (whether individual or collective) was hardly a motive.

All things flowed from a citizen's Reich Personnel Number. If one had that, and the authority to access the data, all that might be known of a soul was there, recorded and stored electronically. In 1933 and more comprehensively in 1939, details upon every citizen between the ages of six and seventy had been collected, collated and entered into the *volkscartei*, the great catalogue of the people. Like all things German it nodded both to the near and far homelands - a national system of registration whose data was stored and maintained at local level under the administration of each urban and rural district's *ordnungspolizei* force. Which was why, on the afternoon of 4 January 1945, Kriminalkommissar Gerd Branssler presented himself at Berlin-Steglitz police headquarters and asked to see records pertaining to one Agatha Fuhrmann, deceased, late of Grillparzerstrasse 38.

The watch master, an old veteran who wore campaign ribbons from the First War on his uniform, scowled at Branssler's warrant disc but waved him into the back office without asking *why*, summoned his junior watch master (a septuagenarian) and told him to escort their guest to the basement. Having discharged his duty in an efficient, suitably brusque manner, he returned to the dog-eared translation of *Moby Dick* he kept under the counter for long days such as this.

He had read less than a page more when their visitor emerged into the front hall once more, his face as clouded as the sky outside. He gave the watch master (who had hurriedly thrust the book back under the counter) a curt nod and barged his massive frame out of the front door without a word.

'What's his gripe?'

The junior watch master, who had followed at a safe distance, shrugged. 'The woman's details are missing, all of them. There's nothing for that ID number at all.'

The older man shook his head. 'Can't be so,' he said emphatically, and farted loudly to reinforce the point.

His subordinate shrugged once more, already losing interest. It was a miserable January day, his seventy-two year-old knees were complaining bitterly about the flight of stairs they'd just negotiated and he had six more hours before he could scurry home to his cold apartment and the wife he wished had buggered off years earlier when first she'd threatened it.

'I know. But it is.'

As the afternoon light faded in front of the ruins of the Beyernhof beer hall in Potsdamer Platz, Fischer and Holleman watched a squad of *fremdarbeiter* workmen filling in holes that they had probably, and very imperfectly, filled a week earlier. They were ragged and ill-fed, though applying themselves in such a way as suggested that they were putting their hearts into their work. More asphalt was being scattered across the road than was landing in the holes, but their overseers, two bored *hilfspolizei* pensioners carrying even more antique Mauser 98s, didn't seem to care. Fischer wondered what purpose the guards were supposed to serve. There were thirteen men in the work detail, and the two reservists' magazines held a total of ten bullets, only the first two of which could possibly be fired before avenging spades descended upon aged German heads. Perhaps *no one* cared, any more. The conquerors and conquered occupied their familiar stations, knowing that the world was about to change drastically, not knowing what to do in the meantime other than carry on as before, doing nothing much that was useful.

Holleman nudged him. Gerd Branssler was crossing the platz from the direction of Potsdamer bahnhof, dodging the thin flow of traffic that traversed the few entirely repaired sections of road. His habitual frown gave him a purposeful look, the kind that Fischer and Karl Krohne tried conscientiously to wear each time they hurried to *Tomi's* for an early drink.

'Jesus, I'm tired.'

Holleman passed a flask to the Bull, who took it and drained it gratefully.

'Did you manage it?'

'Wait …' Branssler cleared his throat, spat, and removed a notebook from his coat's inner pocket '… because this is interesting.'

They crossed to Café Eins A, whose staff had placed two shabby tables and a portable gas lamp on the kerb outside the damaged frontage, daring the RAF, USAF or the German winter to deny the establishment its remaining shard of *joie de vivre.* As soon as they sat an elderly waitress, properly dressed still, shuffled over with a tray and placed three cups on the table. She glanced once at Branssler and withdrew without requesting their ration cards.

The Bull watched her go. 'I went to the stations at Steglitz and Dahlem. They let me see the records at each. I found the files, copied the stuff, and here we are.' He tapped the notebook.

'They didn't ask why?' Holleman was amazed. It wasn't possible that someone - even a policeman - could turn up and demand to see *volkskartei* data without a damn good reason *and* the correct authorization.

Branssler shrugged. 'I just waved my warrant.' He pulled it from his pocket and threw it on the table. The fading light caught it: a silver disc, not the bronze of a Bull's ID. Fischer picked it up, held one side to the lamplight and briefly examined the expected motif, an Eagle clasping the Swastika. He turned it over. On its opposite face were two engraved legends, the officer's ID number and, above it, *Geheime Staatspolizei.*

'Who's lost this?

'Kriminalrat Emil Brucker, only it isn't lost.'

'How the…?'

'A favour, repaid.'

'It must have been a big one.'

'Emil was photographed in a hotel room, up to his balls in a young man whom I assume needed the money badly. I managed to recover the evidence.'

'How?'

'It wasn't difficult. I'd hired the photographer.'

Fischer smiled. 'I assume Emil has Sundays off?'

'He does today. Anyway …' Branssler flicked open his notebook; '… Sigrun Ziegler, *née* Metzger, Gutsmuthsstrasse 14/2,

Steglitz. Widowed, no children. Worked for twenty-two years at Messmann-Filke-Werke, Steglitz, as a secretary and bookkeeper. Joined the Party on 12 December 1934, probably because everyone else at her place did so the same day, courtesy of a little shove from their boss. No known affiliations to antisocial elements, no association with proscribed organizations, no Jewish blood. One notable talent - she was a keen amateur violinist, playing in a string quartet until 1939, when, I assume, the joints in her fingers began to shout too loudly. Widowed in 1928, husband Alfonse, heart attack. No subsequent formal attachments. Sigrun was our second victim, found just off Unter den Eichen on 14 October, by a passing hausfrau who probably wished she'd taken another route that morning.'

Branssler turned a page, smacking his lips. Fischer couldn't understand why he was sounding so pleased. This was hardly more than they had already.

'Gisella Mauer, spinster, address Arnim Alee 87/8, Dahlem. Discovered 11 November, in bushes on the east side of Wildenowstrasse, by the famous Hans Lutze and his partner. No long-term employment record. Her family was in the jewellery business in Munich, but no Jewish blood here either, strangely. I assume Gisella had the means to work only as she felt the need. Did a few months, most recently in 1935, as a helper in a kindergarten. Special talents, none. No affiliations with naughty people or organizations but not a Party member either. No known male friends. Our third unlucky lady.'

He closed the notebook, leaned back, and smiled. Holleman and Fischer glanced at each other. 'The first victim, Fuhrmann? What about…?'

Branssler's eyebrows rose innocently. 'Who?'

'What do you mean, *who*?'

'There *is* no Agatha Fuhrmann, which is fucking strange because I have a distinct memory of her wretched, strangled corpse. But the records don't exist, so she can't have either. And this is the really strange thing - I double-checked her registration number, and it doesn't belong to anyone else.'

'But they're in sequence …'

'Right.'

Fischer got the point finally. 'She's been removed!'

'From existence, if you can call it that.'

'But didn't you go to the *volkskartei* back in October, when it happened?'

It was standard procedure in any murder investigation, and Branssler managed to look both embarrassed and defiant.

'Can you guess how many Bulls are chasing how many serious crimes in Berlin right now? The week it happened, me and Deiter had six other murders, two black market scams and a gang of recreational rapists on our dockets. *Then*, we got dragged in to one of Müller's *fremdarbeiter* sweeps as a sop to the general belief that every single criminal in the city's a fucking foreigner. So no, Otto, as it happens, we didn't!'

Holleman scowled. 'Then your eyes aside, no witness confirmed that there *was* a body. It was an anonymous report, wasn't it?'

'It was, so we're stuffed. But that doesn't matter, does it?'

'Because this means something.' Fischer leaned forward. 'You don't remove the papers of a random murder victim for no reason. She was the first, so either she knew the murderer personally or …'

'She was killed because of something else she knew.' Branssler was smiling again. 'And whoever took the papers was too late, because we already have her name and address, thanks to the old darling being just about the only civilian in the Reich who did what she was told and carried her registration card.'

'That's why it was shut down - you knew too much already.'

'It looks so, doesn't it? But the other women, I don't know.'

Holleman threw back his 'coffee' and winced. 'Well, we can ignore them now, can't we? Concentrate on Agatha?'

Fischer sighed. 'Difficult. The *volkskartei* data would have helped, given us at least a push in the right direction. But with just a name and address it's going to need a door-to-door, and to do that …' He looked at Branssler. 'Can you borrow your grateful mate's disc again?'

The Bull shook his head firmly. 'He almost said no *this* time. I shouldn't have returned the photographs. All I have on him now is memory, and he's been careful since. Station toilets, probably.'

The *fremdarbeiter* work party had finished its half-job in the road in front of them, and were formed into a travesty of an ordered line. The lead guard shouldered his Mauser and saluted the two Luftwaffe uniforms as he marched past.

Holleman nodded at him, muttered 'cock' under his breath.

Fischer laughed. 'What about the other party?'

Branssler waited until the work gang had disappeared into the gloom of Linkstrasse. 'Bildmann? I asked the Dahlem watch master. He said he didn't know anything. Said he'd been on leave that particular week and hadn't heard a word since. Made a point of saying he hadn't asked. A stupid lie, but that's not important.'

'It's that he dared say it to someone he thought was Gestapo.'

'And if he did that, he either knows or has a damn good idea who's working all of this, and it frightens him more than a *Geheime Staatspolizei* disc. So Bildmann's yet another person that someone's trying to make invisible. I'll rummage at the Alex. We'll have his transfer details, if that's what happened.'

Air-raid sirens wailed suddenly, and two waitresses rushed out to collect the tables. Fischer dropped a few coins on to theirs before it was up-ended.

'You can sit this out in our office,' he told Branssler. 'God seems to love our bit of the Luftwaffe. We haven't been touched since '43.'

The Bull grinned. 'No thanks. The Alex's taken it four times in the past year, but the cells make for wonderful bunkers. We always ask our guests if they mind company for an hour or two. No one ever seems to.'

Holleman shook his head. 'It's two kilometres, Gerd. Even the RAF can get *here* before you can get *there*.'

'If it's going to happen, let it.' Branssler looked up into the sky as most Berliners did, wondering if the clouds were low and thick enough. 'Better now than …'

'Idiot. You want your wife to have a new friend called Hank?'

'Rather than Vlad, I would. At least she'll eat.'

He went without goodbyes, as always. They watched him fade into the gloom of unlit Leipziger-Strasse, taking his time, daring some wet-nosed Anglo-Saxon kid in a sighting bay to take aim at one of Berlin's few remaining finest. Fischer reassured himself that it must be yet another false alarm, that they were probably safe above ground, that Gerd Branssler was too unimportant to waste ordnance upon. But then the city's craters and cemeteries were full of people who had thought the same thing. He and Holleman put on their caps, gave the sky a final glance and headed for the absolute, inexplicable safety of the Air Ministry.

6

The raid was a squib, like most during the previous six months. A squadron of Mosquitoes buzzed over the rail yards, dropped an irritation of explosives and flitted away without a single loss. A military inconsequence, and still it sent most of central Berlin's population underground, another precious night's sleep lost.

In the shelter beneath Turmstrasse courthouse, Fraus Traugott and Ostermann claimed the bench nearest the exit with the skill of professional early arrivers. Franz and Ulrich had brought their aircraft and were using that part of the bench not covered by elderly ladies as an extemporary landing strip from which to evacuate their failed bridgehead (eight soldiers, originally Austro-Hungarian infantry, repainted in field grey). Apart from an occasional *hush, dear* when engines revved too enthusiastically, the sisters left the boys to their war and applied themselves to knitting and surveillance. Like amiable Defarges, they cast their gaze over the neighbourhood characters, the harassed families, the officious *blockhelfers* - in their clover patch once more, counting, organizing and chastising for lateness - and the loners, the old, those dispossessed by bombing or bereavement, the secret-keepers minding some business, willing their neighbours' eyes not to linger upon them.

As the shelter filled, the usual irritations commenced. Human odours in the confined space became oppressive, and everyone made the instinctive effort to convey an impression that it was someone else, not they, who had brought them. Small arguments about the available space flared briefly between the usual suspects and subsided to discreet elbowings under the *blockhelfers*' stern gazes. A few of the die-hards tried to get a song going and were crushed by glares or hisses; one old man whose name no one seemed to know failed (as he always did) to interest a few of his neighbours in a reading from Goethe to pass the time. Even the children - the twins excepted - no longer found the experience of missing sleep an adventure. Some threw brief tantrums, others settled immediately into the state of mute resentment that their parents had taught them, or tried surreptitiously to begin arguments that might be blamed upon the other parties. As always, it was a tiresome distillation of what people found most objectionable about their above-ground lives, and they misbehaved or seethed accordingly.

In this clench of weary misanthropy the sisters sat serenely, clicking their needles, occasionally raising their eyes to the ceiling as if they could penetrate nine feet of concrete and the courtroom to ascertain the current state of RAF operations over Berlin. On other nights they had the company of Major Fischer, whose unmilitary work schedule allowed him to return to his lodgings at a civilized hour and take a mouthful of sustenance before the enemy ruined everyone's evenings. But of course he and Herr Holleman were presently engaged in their secret business, about which the sisters had already developed theories. It was Frau Ostermann's opinion that a team of British saboteurs were at large in the city, against which the Luftwaffe had deployed only a modest counterstroke in order not to create a general panic among Berliners. To Frau Traugott this was nonsense hardly worthy of comment. She considered it far more likely that foreign spies were desperately seeking access to blueprints for the wonder weapons that the Führer had promised would sweep the British and Americans from German skies, and that Major Fischer was coordinating the Luftwaffe's response from the Air Ministry - being, as he was, one of their most important people. While her sister could not argue the latter point, she felt that the remainder of the theory not so much lacked credibility as mocked it. Agreeing to disagree heartily, they had refined, embellished and repeated these assertions until each had settled several centimetres into the stonework of Jonas-Strasse 17.

But in public - and certainly, in the shelter - they maintained a truce on all matters, it being both vulgar and modern to fold family laundry under the gaze of others. Every few minutes, one of them would lean forward to glance at the boys and smile fondly or ruffle young hair. Being childless, each assuaged her disappointment by regarding other people's offspring as unpleasant creatures on the whole, failing in most of those particular qualities that her own undoubtedly would have displayed. But Franz and Ulrich were not, in the sisters' eyes, like other children. They were dutiful, pleased to help when asked, skilled at household chores and mostly quiet. Also, they were handsome (which amplified their other virtues considerably), and the ladies preened themselves as one did with attractive possessions. Frau Speigl's envy of their new situation was a peculiarly satisfying discovery, and since making it they had lost no opportunity to list to her the manifest benefits of having two such uncomplaining skivvies to relieve their domestic ordeal. The effect of this campaign could be measured in the distance from them that she had taken to sitting.

Tonight, busily reconstructing new knitwear from unravelled old, Fraus Traugott and Ostermann paid only a little attention to the company once it had ceased to file past them and the blast doors had been closed. Bickerings slowed and stopped, everyone had secured as much room as they were going to be allowed, and a general weariness discouraged conversation except among the die-hard gossips. It was the same faces as usual, though there were one or two strangers also, caught too far from their heimats when the sirens began, who could add the tension of unfamiliarity to the sum of their anxieties as they took care not to be noticed.

But one face definitely stood out as *different*. Both sisters had noticed its arrival, its casual perambulation of the filling shelter and its careful return to a seat only a few metres from their bench - a coldly neutral face, expressionless, taking in everything except the two ladies themselves and the twins. Neither Frau Traugott or her sister retained any hopes of attracting men's glances, but to be palpably ignored by someone who moved so assuredly in uncertain times, in a strange shelter, was as much as a flare going up in front of them. They observed, closely but subtly.

He was about forty, without uniform or obvious wounds, a grey man in grey clothes, hands in pockets, who wouldn't relax or try to sleep but remained alert, staring at a point that would excite no suspicion but which kept the sisters and twins within his peripheral vision. After several minutes of this, Frau Traugott glanced at her sister with satisfaction. Frau Ostermann leaned down to Ulrich and whispered. Carefully, he moved his twin's sleeping head from his shoulder, got to his feet and went to ask the time of the gentleman. The man flushed, checked his watch, said something and turned further away. Ulrich came trotting back to the bench.

'Twenty-three ten, Aunt Else.'

'Thank you, dear.' The sisters exchanged another pointed look, and Frau Traugott located Herr Dunst, who was checking one of the shelter's three fire extinguishers for evidence of anti-social imperfections. As was usually the case during real or imagined air raids, he seemed to be in excellent spirits. He carried a clipboard, upon which she suspected a myriad boxes were in the process of getting ticked to some opaque purpose other than keeping an old man occupied. She had made a point of avoiding him since his betrayal of her opinion on the availability of margarine, but the present moment seemed a good time to display an appropriate contrition. She lifted her hand. Herr Dunst's head was pointing very much away from her, but it turned immediately to identify the source of the petition. He saw Frau Traugott and frowned. She didn't take this as a bad or discouraging sign, because Herr Dunst always frowned when an appeal was made; he regarded this as a proper demeanour, signifying the seriousness with which he would consider the matter that was about to be put to him. She smiled hopefully, and he abandoned the fire extinguisher to cross the short but highly congested passage between them.

'Good evening, Herr Dunst.' She smiled again, more warmly, to let him know that even if the word *sorry* was never going to pass her lips he could rest assured that she understood perfectly her guilt in that old business and was willing to put it behind them both.

Dunst gave a short, formal bow. 'Good evening, Frau Traugott. May I assist you?'

She beckoned him closer with a finger, a gesture with which he was probably more familiar than any other. Briefly, she explained her problem - a stranger acting suspiciously, a face unfamiliar to herself and her sister. Of course, it may be nothing, but one should always be vigilant ...

Herr Dunst, taking care not to glance around immediately, nodded and increased the depth of his frown to indicate how very correct he considered her behaviour to be. He lifted his clipboard and made a short note, caught the eye of Herr Plüger - his counterpart from Emdenerstrasse - and went over to apprise him of the matter. They conferred briefly without once looking at the objective, and then parted to attend their respective duties with wildly overplayed insouciance.

The all-clear sounded just after two o'clock. A faint, weary cheer greeted it, and the shelter's occupants climbed up painfully from their makeshift beds. The stranger, who had remained upright in his chair all this time, stood quickly and moved forward to within a few metres of the sisters and the twins while keeping an indifferent eye upon an attractive teenage girl to their left. From among the impatient crowd, Herr Dunst emerged to open the blast doors. Fraus Traugott and Ostermann, each firmly holding the hand of a young

Holleman, departed the shelter quickly with only an elderly couple ahead of them. Both women glanced back at the same moment. Herr Dunst had accosted the stranger and pulled him to one side, allowing the rest to pass by. They exchanged words briefly; the man pulled his arm free, produced something and thrust it into Dunst's face, which lost all colour in a moment. The *blockhelfer* tottered backwards into Frau Speigl and her gaggle of familiars, generating a brief congestion and a stream of complaints from those still in the shelter. The stranger resumed his chase, but there were now many bodies on the narrow staircase between him and his prey. To close the gap, he would be obliged to become conspicuous, to make a noise and demand that folk stand aside. This, the sisters were certain, was something he wouldn't do.

At the top of the stairs, they quickened their pace. The man had identified himself, made public what should have remained invincibly obscure. Frau Traugott congratulated herself. An elderly woman rarely met with a single triumph, much less two, yet she had flushed out one enemy and repaid another for her earlier humiliation. Even Else was smiling at their success at having outwitted Authority. Under moonlight they hurried home, a matter of three hundred metres only. The grey man didn't follow, but as they reached the house they noticed two more strangers standing on the corner of Arminiusplatz, not bothering to conceal themselves in the ample shadows at its edge, and suddenly the victory seemed much less complete.

7

It was a street, and he was stood upon one side of it, staring at nothing, not knowing how he came to be there, fearing that the death of his mind had commenced in earnest. He could find no recollections of the day so far or of what came before it, nothing to give perspective to *now*. He couldn't breathe.

But then a fragment, a sense of time passing, pierced the blur. The details of his breakfast returned - the foul, nutritious porridge, the weak, lukewarm coffee, the stain on the table where he had set it down too clumsily. His name confessed itself to him, his wound (the sensation he'd felt but not understood), his place of work, a friend, Horst. Slowly, identity reassembled from individual, disconnected memories, wriggling up like elvers from the depths of an unlit pond while he gasped at the air and tried to calm himself.

'Are you unwell, sir?'

He'd been vaguely aware of people passing by, glancing fearfully at him, quickening their step to put distance between them; but this old man had stopped and taken his arm. There was little strength in the grip, yet it was a connection to something tangible, proven. It made him a little steadier.

'Look, here's a place to sit and rest. It's quite warm, usually, and they have something they call coffee, though to be frank it isn't.'

A café - he recalled it dimly, though he wasn't sure whether he had passed by it previously or entered as a customer. The old man smiled reassuringly, patted his shoulder with the free hand. He was a neat little fellow, buttoned up, precise in his motions and speech, unafraid. But why *should* he be afraid? There was a reason, he was certain; but among the many other slips of memory he couldn't find it.

'Thank you, yes.'

The old man opened the door and helped him over the threshold. It was absurd, when he was so much younger and stronger than his shepherd, but he went willingly with the gentle prompting, allowed himself to be guided to a table.

Paul Schroeder crossed to the counter, from which Mona Kreitz was staring back at the apparition at the table. She was anxious, naturally - who wouldn't be, offered a prospect of *that* uniform? So Paul smiled, trying to reassure her as he had the young man, and ordered two *muckefuckes* as anyone might who had just brought any old acquaintance to the café.

He had been out walking, intending only to take some fresh air after several wretched, sickly days in his apartment, when he noticed the soldier on the other side of Sophiastrasse, swaying at the road's edge as if caught in a high wind, being ignored - no, avoided - by people who knew not to make officialdom's business their own. But Paul couldn't disregard someone in such obvious distress. Even in civilian clothes he remained a sort of a policeman, an official bound to uphold the public welfare. He had crossed the road to investigate the phenomenon, and as he came closer he better understood his fellow citizens' reserve. The uniform was nondescript field grey, but the twin runic flashes upon the collar seized the attention as if an electrical current charged the air around them. They were worn by little more than a boy, perhaps twenty-two or three years old, slightly built but strikingly good-looking. His blond hair was almost white, far lighter than the face beneath it; his eyes, which Paul saw were flitting almost aimlessly, had peculiar pale blue irides that seemed almost to glow. No doubt the Party would regard him an Aryan to breed from, if his present distress wasn't symptomatic of some unfortunate predisposition.

Paul scolded himself; he had come to assist the boy, and here he was, analysing the situation as usual. *A cold fish, that Schroeder* his colleagues at Grossmann and Sons used to say, too loudly for him not to hear. They were right, of course - it was a legacy of too many years of fastidious attention to detail, of too much comfort taken from the neatness of transactions sorted and double-entered. But now he was a public servant, obliged to deal with people, and different skills were necessary.

It had been obvious even from a distance that the lad was confused. Perhaps it was a wound to the head, or a concussion. In the First War he'd seen many men become entirely disoriented under fire, and for some it didn't wear off, ever. Injuries could bring far more than the physical marks of their pain.

So now I'm a psychologist. Paul took an arm and said something bland, intended to calm. But the boy was passive, unyielding; he didn't seem to object to being bothered by an old fellow, which made his collar tabs a little less fearsome. The café was directly behind them, a good place to take time to draw breath, recover a little sense. He pulled gently to lead his patient inside, but stopped when he heard the word. It was such a strange thing that Paul wasn't sure he had heard it correctly, and he excused himself. The lad repeated it, though he did so in such a distant manner that it wasn't clear he was aware of having spoken at all.

'It's alright.' Paul told him. 'We'll just sit down.'

Mona didn't seem pleased to have the extra business. She wasn't exactly *displeased* (Paul couldn't ever recall her displaying so much as a temper), but her discomfort was obvious. He felt obliged to explain himself.

'I couldn't ignore him. He might have wandered into the road.'

She nodded in a way that suggested she didn't think the risk unacceptable, her eyes fixed firmly upon the object of Paul's compassion as they might upon a ticking bomb placed carefully upon one of her chairs. The boy was disoriented still. His gaze wandered around the café, receiving information without apparently making sense of it. One of his arms rested on the table, the hand beating an irregular, nervous tattoo; the other rubbed his stomach almost tenderly, as if it had recently stopped a football, or a fist.

Mona poured two *muckefuckes* without once easing her surveillance, and Paul took them to the table.

'It isn't too bad after the first mouthful.'

The young man nodded, tried to smile, but he didn't make any effort to test this optimistic claim. He had removed his *soldbuch* and placed it, opened, on the table, as if awaiting formal examination.

'May I see that?' He smiled. 'I'm a policeman - reserve, of course.'

There was no reason to ask. No offence had been committed that he was aware of, and even if it had the SS-Feldgendarmerie were the men to deal with it. But Paul told himself that taking an interest might engage something presently missing, something that seemed to be far elsewhere.

It was a very poorly kept document. The service entries ran only from 1943, and as young as its owner was Paul doubted that his military career had commenced as late as that. It stated that he had spent a month in a field hospital in Byelorussia, barely weeks after a posting to 3rd SS Panzergrenadier-Division *Totenkopf*. Whatever bad things had happened to them, this particular soldier - an unterscharführer - had done well enough to be awarded the Iron Cross, second class. But there was nothing about his prior training, or any period in a reserve or ersatz battalion. If this were a replacement for an older, lost *soldbuch* the former entries would have been recovered from his records and carried over into the new - unless the boy had sprung from the waves, fully formed, just eighteen months earlier.

Something was wrong here, but it certainly wasn't Paul's job to investigate. He returned the document having made a mental note of the young man's name - Lothar Fuchs - and his current posting, just up the road on Unter den Eichen.

His new friend smiled once more, took his *soldbuch* and returned it to his pocket.

'My head, I forget things.'

'Was that your wound? To the head?'

'No, a piece of shrapnel. In my stomach still, or what remains of it. I got it at Kursk, the fight for the salient.'

A bad business, Kursk - even Goebbels hadn't been able to make anything good of it, afterwards. Paul cleared his throat, a little unsure of how to play the comrade. His own memories of the soldier's life were quite dim now, and he had none of the easy way that some men felt for those who had seen similar horrors. 'I heard it was very tough there, that the Soviets were waiting for us.'

Fuchs shrugged. It didn't seem to be a matter that bothered him particularly. 'I didn't see much before …' He wandered off once more, his eyes moving to an unheard rhythm. Paul patted his hand, saying nothing, and glanced over at Mona. She was pretending to clean things, but her gaze never wandered away for more than a few moments. He nodded once when their eyes met, trying to convey dutiful regret (which was how he felt about it), and wondered how to get the lad safely back to his barracks.

'Do you have a friend I can call? A colleague?'

Dragged from his reverie, the young man frowned, thought about it. 'Yes, but you can't. It's forbidden to give out internal numbers.'

Paul sighed to himself, resigned to being the official escort. He'd planned to walk about two or three kilometres along the Teltow canal and let the air shake flush out a week's worth of apartment fever, but Unter den Eichen was in precisely the opposite direction.

He went to the counter, paid Mona for the untouched drinks and turned to offer his company. The café door was open, another SS unteroffizier blocking it. This one was obviously, badly wounded to the head, and Paul wouldn't have been at all surprised if the visible damage stopped him from thinking about *anything*. But he seemed healthy enough, or at least robust; he was laughing, pretending a sort of pantomimed exasperation, hands on hips as if performing for the back seats.

'There you are! Missing without leave again!'

Lothar Fuchs looked relieved. He grabbed at his cap and stood up, almost tipping the table with a knee. 'Horst! I was ...'

'Wandering in the head!' The newcomer winked at Paul and Mona and grinned broadly. 'Has been a nuisance? Forgot to pay for his drink, eh?'

Paul shook his head. 'No, sir. He was a little confused I think, so I brought him in off the street. Just to let him recover himself.'

The newcomer gave a little bow by way of thanks, and the glint of a metal plate covering almost a quarter of his scalp caught the light. Behind her counter, Mona gasped.

'He does that sometimes, don't you, Lothar? Going off to where none of us can find you?'

Lothar grinned, untroubled by this obviously accurate diagnosis. He looked to be at ease for the first time since Paul had first discovered him.

'I forgot who I was.'

Horst looked knowingly at Mona and tapped his steel-reinforced head. 'Hear that? What a chump! 'I'm the one who should be forgetting things, but Lothar does all of that for me! A real mate, eh?'

She smiled, nervously, unsure how much of this was banter. They both acted like nice damaged boys, but their uniforms said something else, something that no sensible German would have discounted. She had heard stories, snatches of hushed conversations, about *events* in the east from young men they'd all known as boys, the steady types your mother always hoped you'd end up with, hinting at things not to be imagined. She found it difficult to look at *any* uniform without recalling them.

But there seemed to be little that was bad here. Neither of them had looked at her the way that men of a certain age usually did, and they were showing respect to an old man (a courtesy much out of fashion). Without the need for any further evidence, her own mother would have concluded that they were *well brought up, a credit to someone*. But that was the trouble with the worst in people, it couldn't be read.

"We should be going, Lothar. We don't have leave today, do we?' Horst took his friend's arm, much as Paul had done a little earlier. Fuchs frowned and shook his head slowly.

'Not today, no.'

As they went through the door, Horst turned back to Paul. For the first time since entering the café, he seemed quite serious, even grave. 'You were very kind' he said, and closed the door gently behind him.

'Poor lads.' Paul recalled all too clearly his own generation's wounds, of mind and body both - men like him, who had marched away through a hail of flowers and hearty platitudes in August 1914, and then ... *never mind*, he told himself, and thought of something else. He turned to Mona, who was wiping her counter too briskly by way of exorcising something.

'He said something, a word. Very strange.'

'A strange word?'

'No, not in itself. But curious.'

'What was it?'

He smiled. 'Are you sure you want to know? It might be a secret, a cypher that dangerous men want to keep from us ordinary folk.'

'Oh, please don't tease, Herr Schroeder.'

'It was Soldau. He said *Soldau* - just the word itself, nothing more.'

8

'You remember what the old fellow told me?'

Gerd Branssler lifted a brass doorknocker from the overloaded table and tested the action. Its owner smiled nervously and looked down at the price he'd chalked, probably wishing he'd asked for less. But not many of these came on to the market. Incendiaries usually took care of brass fittings, leaving them all of a useless lump, and he'd been certain that someone would want it, even at thirty reichsmarks.

Fischer was pretending to be interested in a small, ivory-framed view of the Rhine, a mantelpiece item from a mantelpiece that no longer existed. By his side, Freddie Holleman pushed a few toy soldiers with his finger, trying to find a gem - two gems, if he didn't want trouble - among the poor stuff. They were the flea market's only customers at that moment, but it was a very early moment and the day was overcast, threatening rain. Were it not for the matter of the uniforms and the overcoat, the proprietor would have been delighted by the attention his wares were getting.

'Which part of it?'

'That the man went into the army *and then came back again*. No wound, no known reason. Who does that in war? Who gets the option to switch career if he doesn't like the work?'

Fischer looked up into the market's iron rafters, thinking about it. The old glass and iron roof had been covered over by wooden slats to give a false sense of protection for the space below, so he saw about as much as he sensed. 'He's a policeman.'

'Ordnungspolizei. So what was he doing in the army?'

'I couldn't say.'

'I could.' Branssler smiled at the stall's proprietor (who was determinedly not hearing a word of what he was hearing) and handed over the money. The doorknocker went into a large pocket. 'Finished?'

They left the market and crossed Kurststrasse to the now-familiar churchyard. Two rooks were fighting for a piece of worm on its low wall, hopping back and forth precisely, like starving samurai. Neither glanced at the three men as they approached.

'That's lucky, isn't it? Holleman asked doubtfully.

Branssler laughed. 'If it is, they aren't letting it rub off.' He kicked a stone at the wall. The birds rose briefly and resettled, arguing over nothing now that one of them had swallowed the titbit.

'So why did he come back?'

The Bull squinted at Fischer. 'Remember June 1941? Of course you do. A lot of our boys went east with the Wehrmacht. They needed everyone they could get out there.' He laughed again, without humour. 'Shit, they needed far more than *that*, didn't they? Fucking two-front wars! So, a lot of men from the Alex went straight into the SS. From *ordnungspolizei*, too - they formed special units, for special operations. It was good pay, about twenty percent higher than equivalent *Heer* ranks, and more leave too, and the best thing was they weren't going to be front-line troops. It was mop-up stuff, following the operational units and pacifying the locals, anti-partisan operations, police actions, making sure that the war didn't flare up again once the Front moved forward.'

Fischer nodded. He hadn't come across them, but it was no secret. In a place like Russia, the vast spaces where beaten units could hide, reform and try again, it made sense.

'For almost a year after *Barbarossa* these lads were kept busy at it. But whatever they were promised leave-wise didn't happen. I know because a few of the wives complained quietly, said they hadn't seen their old men for months, and why was it they weren't getting time at home now that everyone was being told that the war was just about won? Sure, they'd had letters, but letters don't warm beds, do they? Anyway, soon after that their men came back - not all of them, but enough to make you wonder about it, why they'd been released from active service back into the police, with pension rights preserved for the time between. Funny, we thought at the time.'

'So what was the reason?'

Branssler shrugged. 'They wouldn't say.'

'None of them?'

'None that I met. There were problems, apparently. A lot of them went on long-term sick leave, nervous conditions or lungs, courtesy of too many damp, cold forests. But it's news to me that you can get premium time off for anxiety and weak chests. There's a rumour about a hospital near Wiesbaden that's been turned over to the treatment of police with head-hurts, though no one knows anything solid. Anyway, as I say, we lost quite a few to illness. The others - the ones we *didn't* lose - don't talk about it. The only thing I ever heard was second-hand. My partner Dieter has a brother-in-law, a Stuttgart Bull who went east in 1941, came home in summer 1942 and went back to his old job. Dieter says that whenever his little girl climbs on his knee these days he shakes like a leaf in the fucking wind.'

'So you think Bildmann was in one of these units?'

'He's police. He went away in 1941 and came back the next year. You have a better idea?'

It explained Bildmann's reappearance at Dahlem police station, and not much else. It didn't tell them why he'd disappeared again.

'Will there be files at the Alex?'

Branssler pulled a face. 'Not the sort I'll be invited to look at. But I should be able to confirm the theory, at least generally. We keep duplicate records for all Berlin police.'

'He'll have a *soldbuch*, won't he? If the theory's correct?'

Holleman, who had been watching the rooks while Branssler and Fischer spoke, shook his head. 'If he was doing special stuff, if what he was doing was classified as *essential duties*, it probably didn't go into his *soldbuch*.'

'How do you know?'

'I think I've seen it. In 1940 the squadron was billeted near Eindhoven when an SS police unit came through, looking for a Jewish-Commie cell they'd had the word on. There was an RAF raid that evening and those boys were under it. Some of our ground crew helped scrape them up the next morning and brought the effects back to the airfield. We logged four intact *soldbuchs*, all of them blank for about the previous six months.'

'So what would *essential duties* be?'

Branssler looked darkly at Fischer. 'Would you want to know? We've been told often enough that the rules don't apply in this one, particularly out east. They don't say it for a laugh.'

He was right - the more essential a matter was, the less palatable the truth was likely to be. Fischer considered their options. 'Could Bildmann be ill, then? No, it's too long since he returned. If he were carrying something bad inside it would have burst like a boil two years ago. *Shit*. Do we know *anything* else?'

Branssler's invaluable notebook emerged from his breast pocket. 'Born 12 February 1898, Köln. Married 1919, Berlin, no children. Divorced, mutual consent, 1927. Joined the Party 4 March 1933, so he was *very* keen, apparently, but expelled for unstated reasons three years later. Readmitted 14 June 1940. Three commendations for diligence, the last in 1938. No known black marks or disciplinary proceedings'

'Well, see what else you can find. While you do that, Freddie and me are going to go after Agatha Fuhrmann.'

'How?'

Fischer frowned, reluctant to follow the logic. 'Someone tried to remove her from history, but they can't let it go at that. Any hint that we're looking is going to flush out some sort of reaction, to make certain that she stays removed. So, we stop being discreet. Freddie and me, we're going to drag an iron bar across the railings.'

9

Grillparzerstrasse was a quiet, residential thoroughfare, mostly of small but well-appointed apartment blocks fronted by mature trees, with narrow, ornamental strips of greenery separating the buildings from the pavement - a quiet, respectable place, keeping itself to itself, battened down against prevailing weather. Some bomb damage was apparent, particularly on the eastern stretch, but most of the buildings to the west seemed intact still.

Any number of windows provided excellent vantage points from which to observe the comings and goings at number 38, a three-storey, brown-brick building slightly overshadowed by its taller neighbours. Fischer wasted little time trying to guess which of them it might be. He and Holleman made themselves conspicuous, turning slowly, pretending to check out the neighbourhood, giving an audience a chance to commit their atypical features to memory, and then entered the building.

The post-box for apartment 2 displayed a neat, handwritten legend: *Frau A. Fuhrmann*. Holleman had the lock open within ten seconds, peered briefly into the emptied space and closed it quietly. Fischer turned. The superintendent's door faced the boxes across the hallway. He knocked once and tried the handle. As he had expected, it was locked. He or she probably cared for a dozen buildings in the neighbourhood, so it was unlikely that they would be disturbed. In the inner corridor they turned left. Holleman knocked on the door of apartment 1 and pressed his ear to it. He heard nothing. If someone was at home, they had learned that paralysis was the prudent response to the dreaded noise. Ignoring the door of apartment 2, Fischer turned to that of number 3, whose layout was oriented towards the building's rear. Before his hand could make contact, it opened as far as the flimsy chain permitted, and what he took to be an elderly female face peered out from an unlit interior.

'Frau Walter?' Fischer had memorized the names of the ground floor tenants from their post boxes.

A bony finger protruded and bent to the left. 'Apartment four.' The door began to close.

'Ah, I'm sorry. Frau Pichler, perhaps?'

'Yes.'

The affirmative had never been made so reluctantly. He tried to smile only with his face's unwounded side. 'May we have just a brief word, please? About your neighbour, Frau Fuhrmann?'

'I've made a statement to the authorities. We all have.' Again, the door moved. It was frustrating, but Fischer didn't want to keep it open forcibly and have the woman faint or worse. He knocked again, very gently.

'Yes, I know that, Frau Pichler. But if we may…? This is only to confirm a few routine matters, and we should be most grateful. Perhaps I can show you my papers?'

He pushed them through the two-centimetre space and waited. He doubted very much that she'd examine them, but the gesture might be enough. Most people assumed - knew - that the credentials of the wrong sort of officialdom were engraved upon the steel tip of a boot.

The door chain rattled and fell. Fischer and Holleman removed their caps and stepped into the gloomy apartment. It smelled stale, and the ambient temperature was several degrees lower than that of the unheated corridor - the home of a widow, probably, who was unable to afford firewood, much less coal. In the half-light, Fischer could see his breath preceding him into the small sitting room.

Thick curtains were pulled together in an attempt to retain whatever heat Frau Pichler's body could generate; even so, she moved as if carrying a full winter's worth of cold in her bones. She was a small, thin woman, doubtless made thinner by circumstances, her address the only substantial thing about her. She peered carefully at their faces and held out a hand, inviting them to sit.

There were only two chairs in the room. Fischer returned the gesture. 'Please.'

Slowly, she descended into a shabby armchair. A blanket spread over it suggested that this was where she fought and mostly lost her daily rear-guard action against hypothermia. Holleman caught Fischer's eye and half removed a package from his pocket. They had brought two *blutwurst* and half a loaf with them, to be consumed when the day's business allowed. It was little enough to forego if it loosened her memory.

She opened the bag and her eyes widened. Without hesitation or embarrassment she removed one of the *blutwurst* from the grease paper and raised it to her mouth.

'Let me get a knife and plate for that, madam.' Holleman disappeared into the kitchen. Fischer took the only other seat, a stand chair, and coughed gently.

'Frau Agatha Fuhrmann …'

'Agi.' Frau Pichler's eyes didn't leave the sausage, but she said it firmly. 'Her friends called her Agi. She preferred it.'

'Ah. You were a friend, then?'

'A neighbour.' The old woman shrugged. 'But after ten years …'

'It must have been very shocking for you. A terrible business.'

She looked up at him. 'The beast! As if there isn't evil enough in the world, to do that to a harmless woman!'

'Yes, indeed.'

'But you do nothing to stop him! Why not?'

Subtle variations in uniform did not impress themselves upon Frau Pichler. Fischer wore one so he was an official, as were the police who had spoken to her. She waved the knife that Holleman had brought from the kitchen, to emphasise her just point.

'There were certain enquiries that proved to be … unhelpful. But I assure you that we won't stop until we have the creature. That's why we've returned to speak to Frau Fuhrmann's friends.' Fischer glanced up at Holleman. 'In fact, we think we may soon have a suspect.'

'Really?' For a moment, the old woman forgot the *blutwurst*. 'Is it a foreigner?'

He shook his head firmly. 'We can't say yet. But if we can learn more about your neighbour, we may be able to bring this to a swift conclusion.'

'You think he knew her, then? A colleague, perhaps?'

The word made both Fischer and Holleman start. 'Perhaps, yes. Do you know where she worked?'

Frau Pichler chewed on a lump of meat. It was soft, but her teeth were making heavy work of it. 'Agi was … a very clever woman. She went to university, did you know? That was in the days when it wasn't done much. A degree, at twenty-three!'

'Yes, very admirable. Her workplace, Frau Pichler?'

She pulled a face. 'I don't know. In Lichterfelde, I think. It's very *scientific* what she does. What she *did*.'

The Luftwaffe officers glanced at each other, and Holleman tried the smile he usually saved for younger, attractive females. 'Didn't she ever talk about her work, Frau Pichler? I mean, she must have been very proud.'

They waited while another piece of sausage went down. The near-joy with which the old woman savoured every moment of it was not something to be interrupted easily.

'She made sure the *devices* worked. Very temperamental they were, needed a lot of *adjustment*. She used to complain about the soldiers. They are the worst people in the world to work them, she told me - all thumbs, covered in mud and dust, clumsy by nature. So they sent her to put them right when they went wrong, which was most of the time. All over the place, she went.' Frau Pichler frowned. 'Until last year of course, when arthritis got the better of her hips, poor thing. I'm very lucky in that. Nothing else, God knows.'

Fischer leaned forward. 'So, Frau … *Agi* was in the Army?'

She laughed. 'What stuff! We aren't Russians, are we? Of course not! But her company worked with the Army, so they had to maintain the stuff that that the soldiers used. *That's* what Agi did.'

'And the *devices*, Frau Pichler? What are they?'

The knife waved once more. 'Ach, I don't know. She mentioned it once, and I didn't understand a word.'

'But it's in Lichterfelde? The place she worked?'

'Yes, it's very convenient. She told me the bus went straight past the front door.' Frau Pichler cackled. 'When there *were* buses, of course.'

A manufacturer of *scientific* devices, in Lichterfelde, on a bus route, employing - and this is what made Fischer's mouth water - at least one woman in a technical capacity, and possibly more. A highly unusual circumstance, in a nation where the only devices a woman was supposed to require were cooking utensils and a birth-bed.

'That's all extremely helpful, Frau Pichler. I wonder if you know any of Agi's other friends?'

'She had none.'

'None at all? I'm sure she …'

The old lady shook her head firmly. 'No time, she used to say. When her husband was alive I think they socialized, but when he died she gave that up. Agi kept herself busy with her work. That's why her arthritis was such a blow.'

'Did you know her husband?'

'No. She moved here after he died. I think they lived in the north, Pankow or Buchholz. Before the war.'

'Ah, well.' Fischer stood. 'Let me ask you one thing more, and then we'll leave you to your lunch. After Agi died, do you know if anyone examine her apartment?'

Frau Pichler frowned. 'The police came on the Saturday, but they didn't stay very long. I remember thinking they couldn't have found too many *clues* in that time.' She shrugged. 'Since then, I think no one.'

'So it may still be as Agi would have left it, that awful day.'

'Possibly, yes. Except for what her sister took.'

'Fischer's heart raced for the second time in as many minutes. 'Her *sister*?'

'Yes, Sylvie, her sister. She came two days later, poor thing. We had a good cry together, and a glass of peach schnapps, and we talked a little about Agi. But afterwards she took only a small shoebox full of mementoes. I know because I saw it. She returned a book to me, one that I'd lent to Agi about a month earlier. She told me to tell our *blockhelfer* that the rest could be sold off for the Winter Fund, but I haven't, naturally. We all know where *that* money goes, don't we?'

'We do, yes. And Sylvie's surname? Do you recall it?'

Frau Pichler smiled and looked down lovingly at that part of her feast she had yet to devour. 'Oh, I have no idea. She lives quite locally, though. Here in Steglitz, I think.'

10

It had long been a joke between Gerd Branssler and Dieter Thomas - the sort that one respects for its age rather than its humour - that Branssler had been the lucky one, to get the view from their office's window. This was a slit, some two and a half metres above the floor, which begrudgingly allowed in a little light from the Bulls' Pen, the main Investigations Room. The *view* from Branssler's chair was that of a clutch of cables, pinned to a badly painted ceiling, making their way from somewhere to somewhere else for a purpose he had often, in idle moments, thought he should take the trouble to discover. He had never done so, but the cables performed another service that he had come to understand only some years after they had commenced their useful business - they were the instrument of his self-hypnosis, the objects upon which his eyes often rested as his mind ran off down the corridors, chasing permutations of criminal motive and method. Four cables: three black, one grey, and he knew as much of the detail of their twists and tensions - but only for a two metre stretch - as he did of the tiny blemishes on his wife's back.

He had looked at them often in the past few days, trying to bed down the feeling that things were getting out of hand. A game was being played out, and not only were the players' features obscured but he wasn't sure which piece on the board was himself. It was entirely his fault, of course. It was he alone who had caused the Lichterfelde business to rise up like Jesus on the third day when someone had gone to a great deal of trouble to put a big rock in the way. He tried to convince himself that it was an only comrade's extremity that had made him do it, but the fact was that Gerd Josef Eberhardt Branssler hadn't take kindly to having his investigation killed and wanted very much to thrust a finger up the nose of its killers. So here he was, asking the cables for yet another revelation, for some sense of the direction from which the shit might come.

Dieter was staring at him again - no, regarding him carefully, and forgetting to move on before it became a stare. He could sense it, even with his own eyes on his ceiling juju. His partner had done it often, recently; it was becoming one of his habits, like sticking out his tongue while he wrote up reports and picking his nose as he re-read them. A good bloke, Dieter. He was much too young and healthy for the job, but having an uncle in Gestapo had done wonders for his lack of suitability for a uniform. Branssler had sometimes wondered what had been entered on the service rejection form - chronic bad breath, perhaps, or red pubic hair. Still, having been given the break he hadn't become one of those bastards who just sat with his feet up, marking time and smirking about his good luck. No, he was a ferret, a good man to work a case with. He didn't cut corners, miss details or delegate stuff to people he couldn't trust, he just rolled up his sleeves and got on with it as a Bull should. So Branssler - a retired Bull dragged back to replace younger, healthier men gone off to war - didn't begrudge young, healthy, lucky Dieter his situation. They worked and drank well together, traded foul jokes and didn't make each other feel like their office was getting too small.

But this staring business was beginning to irritate. It wasn't that Branssler considered his natural beauty undeserving, but a stare was a symptom of something, not a condition like love or myopia.

'What have you done, Dieter?'

Carefully, Thomas put down his pen. His eyes didn't leave Branssler's face.

'Nothing, Gerd.'

'The innocent response would have been 'What do you mean, *done*?'

His partner swallowed. 'Well, I meant that, naturally.'

The ceiling cables got Branssler's attention for a few moments more, but having raised the point it couldn't be left to find its own way out of the building. He sighed, put his feet on the floor, both elbows on the desk and returned the stare.

'Dieter, let's play it's the end of an all-night beating. You're spitting teeth and dying to tell me something, so let it out. If it's bad, I promise I won't return the ring.'

Thomas looked down at his own desk, the blank innocence comically shading to remorse. If this were Acting School he would have been sent to the corner.

'They asked me about you. Upstairs, I mean, about the thing we were told to leave off. I should have said something, but …'

'But you wouldn't suit field-grey, I know. Don't worry, Dieter. Just tell me.'

He needed to ask - the brief grillings they'd both had but separately, about who was making noises around Lichterfelde, and who was to blame for it - of course they wouldn't have left it at that.

If *Forschungsamt*'s Ministerial Direktor Schapper had been the one to squeal he would have given them Fischer's name, and Holleman's too. It wouldn't have been too difficult to draw the line further - to Branssler himself, a known drinking comrade from pre-war days. So Dieter had been invited back upstairs for another chat, the unpleasant sort where stark choices were offered.

'I said I didn't know anything about it. Once they told us to stop the investigation, we stopped, didn't we? I showed them our cases sheet, what we were working on now, but they kept asking about *you*. Was I with you all the time? Well, no, we don't sleep together, I told them. Sometimes you went out of the office for an hour, but who didn't? You were probably fucking one of our whore informers, I said. They wanted a name.'

'They, Dieter? Who are *they*?'

Thomas swallowed again, like his throat was trying to handle a car wrench. 'Lange. I didn't recognize the other two.'

Kriminalrat Herbert Lange - another policeman who'd gone east and then come home quietly to the Alex, no questions asked. One of Panzinger's special boys, apparently, marked for a top job. Branssler had an urge to be curious, to return the favour.

'Have they finished with you?'

Thomas pulled a face. 'I think so. They told me not to say anything, obviously. I'm sorry, Gerd.'

'Not as sorry as you're going to be as you make it up to me, Dieter.'

'Make it up, Gerd?'

'Well, now that I can't fart without the Reichsführer's nose checking the smell you're going to have to do things for me.'

'Things?'

'Well, a *thing*. You can go downstairs and find me a couple of military service records.'

'For who?' Thomas seemed hypnotized by the drastic slide of events, like many who looked back upon a confession and wondered how and why it had happened. Branssler gave him the good news first, to keep his blood pressure down.

'One of them's an *orpo*, works out of Dahlem. You know him, fellow called Bildmann.'

'I've met him. I don't know that I *know* him.'

'Well at least you know who you'll be looking for. *I* need to know what he did in the East, 'forty-one to 'forty-two.'

It wouldn't be easy. If Bildmann had been transferred to an SS unit there would be a file at the Alex - two of the basements that weren't used for beatings had records on all police transfers to and from the Berlin area - but getting to see them would require something plausible, and as Branssler had just confirmed to his own satisfaction there wasn't much of the dissembler about Dieter Thomas. In fact, he doubted that the man could keep the details of his daughter's birthday gift from her. He was going to need a little help.

'I'll raise a red form on him, get it signed by someone out of town - I mean, I'll forge the signature, of course. That'll give you the reason to go looking. If anyone asks, we can always find some *kozi* connection and make it stick long enough for the question to look reasonable. Alright?'

The beauty of paranoia was that no one was safe from association by accusation. Bildmann couldn't have avoided knowing a communist at some point in his life - it was enough merely to make the point for suspicions to cling like shit to a cow's tail. Thomas nodded reluctantly. Both he and Branssler had investigated too many similar cases for the thing to seem unusual.

'Who's the other one?'

'Don't worry, Dieter. Once you're down there, it'll be easy to rummage around. The trick is to keep your eye on the duty officer.'

'*Fuck!* Who, Gerd?'

Branssler shrugged. 'The man who wants to know about me.'

11

At some point during his exertions that morning, Karl Krohne's coward's heart deserted him and he stopped worrying. There was only so much danger that one could face and continue to be terrified with the same intensity, it was just too draining. He had made three journeys when one would have been risky enough, each of them offering an excellent opportunity to be noticed by men who didn't respect rank, or honourable wounds, or the due process of law. *It should be alright*, Otto Fischer had said to him: *people not looking for things tend not to notice them*. But that particular piece of ex-police wisdom discounted the nature of a society in which the unexpected rarely passed unseen.

They had decided that to attempt it at first or last light would only invite attention, so the business had proceeded amid as much bustle as civilian Berlin could muster these days. It had surprised him that that most difficult task had been to overcome the old ladies' reluctance to part with their new nephews. In contrast, the temporary distraction of the two plain-clothed ornaments at the corner of Arminiusplatz had been as easily arranged as if a broom had been taken to litter. It was astonishing how discouraging a group of armed *Luftfeldpolizei* heavies could be, clearing the street for the alleged passage of the Reichsmarschall and entourage. Having lost an eye on only his second day in combat Krohne couldn't describe a timely retreat, but he knew when he'd seen one.

The twins didn't seem distressed by their change in circumstances. From the moment they entered their new home its mysteries had been examined with military precision, sifted minutely for their potential to distract and entertain. The sitting and dining rooms were mundane spaces cut out for adult pleasures, of no interest to them; but the large, stripped-out room on the first floor, the ghost workshop of *Werkzeugmaschinenfabriken Rosenthal*, was a potential world of adventure. Inadvertently, Krohne had intensified its lure when he told them that the partially blinded windows at its far end were being observed by the enemy and that they should approach them only on their stomachs. That was almost two hours ago, and still they hadn't emerged from their preliminary reconnaissance.

When the grey overcoats returned to Jonas-Strasse, Fraus Traugott and Ostermann could tell them what they knew, which was nothing more than a dozen or so fanciful theories. If the ladies didn't draw breath it might take two days, but that was probably optimistic. It hardly mattered. Either the business would be done before the safe house was discovered or failure would bring its own conclusion. Krohne had worried that the coats might just kill the ladies, or try to beat it out of them, but both Fischer and Holleman had laughed when he suggested it.

'They hardly have time to shit these days. And if they dare go back to the Alex with two elderly *hausfraus* they won't be able to anyway.'

He checked his Walther for the second time that day. It was always with him now, and he had used it at the Ministry's firing range on four occasions during the previous week, disastrously. His remaining eye was the wrong one for the job and he had no sense of perspective worth a damn. If it hadn't been for the uniform and war he wouldn't even have a driver's licence - it had taken all the corrupt good fellowship of his Luftwaffe contacts to 'pass' the convalescent's test. All in all, Karl Krohne was a poor sort to bring up any kind of rear in a desperate situation. But when he thought of his comrades in arms he wasn't sure that the comparison didn't depress him further. Branssler apart, they could hardly work a bath chair between them.

He glanced at the clock on the mantelpiece - a valuable item, curiously overlooked during the surgical removal of the Rosenthal family. He had wound it on the day he first came here and it had kept excellent time since, its pleasingly hollow tone a welcome ripple through the house's tomb-like atmosphere. It was striking ten o'clock. If Fischer hadn't been over-sanguine he and Holleman should have drawn attention to themselves by now, perhaps frayed some unseen nerves. The danger was that someone might panic sufficiently to be pushed to an extremity, but neither man had thought it likely. From the moment that Agatha Fuhrmann's removal from official history became apparent, they had ceased to think of their perpetrator as deranged. His mind was clear and - with whatever assistance he enjoyed - resourceful. If they could dismiss *need* as a motive for murder, then what remained, inescapably, was a reason, and reasons begat calculation. He and his shy friends were vulnerable because they had secrets. The removal of two uniformed inconveniences would be problematic - at least, that was how

Fischer had rationalized it. He had decided that this was why he'd been *warned* outside Steglitzerstrasse's *volkskuche* rather than expunged. But Krohne had noticed that Fischer, too, was carrying his service weapon, and Freddie Holleman had that bloody big P08, a gun that could ventilate a wall. Nothing was worth being relaxed about. Nothing was clear.

So this had been Krohne's idea. If everything went to hell with this business they needed somewhere more discreet than an address that sat neatly in Fischer's personnel file. He had removed every detail of the safe house from the Ministry's Berlin properties files and recovered a grand total of three memoranda, listing and authorizing the reimbursement of insignificant maintenance charges - an internal accounting sleight that, probably, no one would have noticed anyway. In every practical sense this was now a ghost address, occupying physical space but outside the bureaucratic State. Only the Führer himself and Reichsminister Speer, gazing down upon their room-sized model of *Germania*, had the ability to see it still, and then only as a tiny plywood representation of the white granite confection it was to have become.

The twins burst into the sitting room, red-faced, panting, more refreshed by a couple of hours' runaround than their elders might have squeezed from a month at Gastein. They reminded him too much of Peter, grown a little - still enthusiastic about everything, some inner coil of youth holding them safe still against what the world had become. They'd come to ask if they could do something. He couldn't quite make it out from their babble but nodded anyway, content to be shamelessly indulgent by way of amends to his own boy. When, a few minutes later, he went up to the dining room to investigate the noise and ask for a little sanity, he found a large, decorative tea chest emptied and a broom-mast rigged. Franz and Ulrich were inside it. One of them was tapping out morse code upon a small tin tray, the other waving frantically at a passing ship and then collapsing theatrically as it slipped off into a fog-bank. Krohne stifled the reproach and returned to his surveillance of the courtyard.

Fischer and Holleman returned just before dusk. The Opel was eased into the corner opposite the house, hidden to anyone passing by on the street outside. He watched them from the sitting-room window, surprised by their apparent good mood as they covered the battered thing. When they'd left that morning, no one had been smiling.

Holleman had liberated a half-bottle of Mackenstedter Korn from somewhere. They drank most of it with the field rations (which Franz and Ulrich were adamant should be eaten before the perishable stuff), and spread themselves around the tiny, cramped sitting room. Fischer, his boots off and tunic undone, sat on the floor with his back to the wall, staring into his glass.

'Karl, can you get a list of companies with Air Ministry contracts in the Lichterfelde area? Not the basic supply stuff. I mean those that have standing arrangements.'

Krohne laughed humourlessly. 'I would have to say *what* list? This is the Luftwaffe, for Christ's sake. Every department and sub-department makes its own arrangements.'

Fischer scratched his latest wound. 'Frau Pichler said that Fuhrmann *adjusted* this equipment, whatever it is. It doesn't sound like weaponry, does it? If it were, operational units would be trained up to do the adjustments. Is it something to do with support, then? The contracts obviously specify that the manufacturer continue to service their products, but they aren't going to put valuable technical staff in the way of harm. And *scientific*? What would a civilian describe as *scientific*?'

Holleman snorted. 'Just about everything she didn't understand. Which would be a lot.'

'A chemical process? Electronics? Even an old lady should understand enough from an explanation to attempt a vague description of its function. But this is something that went over her head like Scripture would a cat's. What would do that?'

'Electronics, definitely. Chemicals, I wouldn't have thought so. I mean, what chemicals need mechanical *adjustment*? You either have the right mix, or you don't.'

'Encryption?' Krohne spoke up for their own, recently much-neglected discipline.

Fischer considered this. 'No,' he shook his head firmly, 'they wouldn't give any civilian the chance of accessing codes, much less one who lived and worked out of secure quarters. A good idea, though, Karl.'

'We need her sister!'

'Sylvie Something: it isn't enough. She lives in Steglitz apparently, so we have only about thirty thousand females to check upon, and no means to do it. Of course, she might *not* live in Steglitz …'

Holleman sighed. 'It was just a thought. Let's squat on our arses instead, speculating.'

'Wait.' Fischer flicked his fingers. 'Agatha Fuhrmann didn't start this work recently.'

'No, Frau Pichler said she'd been …'

'Sorry, Freddie, I mean that she was, what, fifty-eight when she died? Setting aside the Reich's allergy to women in the workplace, she'd need technical abilities to do her job, and they wouldn't come quickly. I think she's pre-1933. *That* was when most women left skilled employment. She didn't take up a career since then, obviously. I think she was already too valuable *then* for her bosses to think of replacing her with a pair of trousers, whatever their new Führer told them.'

'And…?'

'Well, wouldn't that be unusual? A woman, in a highly technical job, at that time?'

'Holleman pulled a face. 'I don't know. Probably. But how could we trace her?'

Karl Krohne swallowed the last of his Mackenstedter. 'I think I may know.'

Both Fischer and Holleman turned and stared at him. 'How?'

He smiled, ridiculously pleased to have surprised two world-worn ex-policemen.

'Professional connections.'

It was said that Berlin's telephone system would be the final casualty of this war, the last functioning mechanism of a once-efficient nation. Beneath the shelters and the u-bahn tunnels, as subterranean as the oldest cellars and lowest sewer pipes, clusters of telephone lines passed undisturbed by all but the largest bombs - a world of busyness proceeding as if it were nineteen thirty-nine still.

A call made from a Government department in central Berlin to one of the city's southern boroughs would, for some distance, follow the Reich's principal military trunk lines linking Wilhelmstrasse and Benderstrasse to Zossen-Wunsdorf. The trunk fragmented about a kilometre east of Villa Wansee; the main lines continued due south, while lesser relays branched out east and west, connecting the outlying metropolitan nodes with their masters. These wires were never quiet, because a war going badly needed every bit as much care and attention as one that had the shoulders to carry ambitions still. So a particular telephone call, from Alexanderplatz to SS-Wirtschafts-Verwaltungshauptamt headquarters in leafy, suburban Lichterfelde, would have been lost amid the electronic mush of ten thousand daily communications. This one was not encrypted, so no record would have been made of it having occurred. Long calls can attract the idle attention of colleagues, but this, a very brief one from a private office, did not. The recipient, not mentioned by name during the conversation, said a single word in response to the unambiguous instruction and replaced the receiver immediately.

Almost certainly, his short passage from his office to the underground car-pool was noticed, but no one had any reason to recall it as extraordinary. Such was the importance of the work done at Unter den Eichen 126 - 135 that even lower-ranking members of staff were called into Berlin daily to clarify some obscure point that had worked its way under a minister's hairline. This man wasn't going to Berlin, however. His journey was to a house a mere four hundred metres distant, where he was to hand over the vehicle and its keys to another man and give him only those details he had taken himself.

He needed less than a minute to pass on the message. The man who took the keys nodded, said nothing. He waited until the messenger had disappeared around the corner at the end of the short street and then went back inside to get the necessary materials. Less than four minutes later he was driving slowly, carefully, trying to recall if there was a trick to doing it instinctively.

SS staff vehicles were rarely stopped at checkpoints, so his journey should have been relatively uninterrupted. But a self-important *ordnungspolizei* deployment at Kreuzberg had closed Schloss-Strasse's northbound carriageway, and that held him up for a few minutes. Ahead of him in the queue, several senior officers, infuriated by this interruption to their schedules, used their rank to shout their way through. He didn't follow their example. He'd been told that that there was plenty of time, and only an idiot attracted unnecessary attention. He waited, crawled forward obediently, cracked a joke with the old man who checked his papers and was on his way again before midday. By 12.30pm, he had left the car in an extemporary park on the western stretch of Konigstrasse, cleared from an erased block of buildings. It was a brisk ten-minute walk from there to Alexanderplatz, a necessary precaution.

He walked southwards, approaching Police Headquarters from the rear, and stopped at a goulash-cannon on the corner of Voltaire-Strasse and Neue-Friedrich-Strasse. The stall was doing fair business, the clientele divided between staff from the Alex and builders' workmen, probably having another attempt at repairing the mostly-ruined Bahnhoff Alexanderplatz. The two groups were fluid, though each seemed instinctively to claim one side or the other of the stall's counter.

He ordered a bowl of the day's only dish and took it to the wall on the other side of the road. He crouched there, heels against the brickwork, his back braced comfortably the way he'd learned out East to get the most from a rare pause. He ate slowly, savouring every mouthful of the nondescript mush of rice, potatoes and anonymous green vegetable. When he had finished he placed the bowl and spoon carefully on the ground next to his foot and lit a cigarette. Ten minutes - four passers-by (all with heads down), two new customers.

A little after one o'clock, three men in hats and coats walked past the stall and entered a doorway about ten meters further west. There had been a sign above it once, but time, the authorities or commercial prudence had removed all but the outline. It was a place where alcohol was available still, of the sort to be drunk at one's own risk. The trade was illegal, but no one bothered to police it any more - certainly, the police didn't. He settled further on his heels. It was going to take a while he guessed, but that was fine. He had recognized his man immediately.

An hour later, two of the Bulls emerged and crossed the street to the stall. They were slightly unsteady on their feet, though not so much as to call attention to the fact. They ate quickly at the counter, dousing the poison in their stomachs with greasy *eintopf*, loudly thanked the proprietor (an elderly lady who looked as if she would be more comfortable leading a choir), and plotted their course back towards the Alex. One of them turned and nodded imperceptibly at the squatting figure over the road, who waited until they had disappeared around the corner of Alexanderstrasse before returning his now-dry bowl and spoon to the stall. The lady thanked him, asked without hope whether he might make a donation above the cost of the food to the War Orphans Fund and gratefully placed the one-mark note he fished from his pocket into a tin below her counter. Two-fifteen pm; he said goodbye formally and followed the Bulls' route.

At Dircksenstrasse he turned left, crossed the road and entered the southernmost of the parallel alleys that serviced the rear of the Alex. It was narrow, enclosed by the walls that kept the police headquarters' business discreet. At the furthest end were twin gates, one of them framing a smaller, personnel door that allowed access to the rear entrance and loading bay beyond. The height of the walls prevented anyone in the building itself having a glimpse of who or what loitered in the alley, and only someone leaving the premises or turning in from Dircksenstrasse would see him. He lit another cigarette and waited.

Fifteen minutes late, the third Bull entered the alley. More obviously the worse for drink than his colleagues he was coming home the discreet way, through a back door and up a rear stairwell to the toilets for a swift, efficient puke and a good douching before anyone could see or smell him. He passed the uniform loitering in the doorway, nodded and carried on without a word.

'Excuse me?'

The policeman turned, and two bullets ripped into the centre of his chest no more than a centimetre apart. Loose already, he fell like an emptied sack, sloppily, onto the cobbles, one leg perched on the shallow kerb. The body twitched once, and lay still.

Quickly, the assassin unscrewed the suppressor from the barrel of his 9mm Steyr and placed them into the soft pouch slung beneath his left armpit. At the alley's entrance he turned right, walking north towards Konigstrasse and his car, taking care not to look around or move too quickly. By the time the body was discovered and identified by two Gestapo *kripos* returning from their own lunch, the alarm raised and the entire block closed off, he was back across the Spree, heading south for Lichterfelde. It was overcast still, and the hours he had spent outside had pushed the cold into his marrow. He glanced up occasionally, willing the clouds to part and warm the day a little more than January deserved. God knew, he had seen worst winters, but it was a season he had always detested – an iron-grey span of bleakness, and the time to think about what made it so.

13

It was a small world, Krohne thought, and not always the worse for it. He smiled, genuinely pleased by the coincidence.

'Bamberg? My wife and boy are there now.'

The old woman nodded. 'It seems to be a blessed place so far. I have family there, too…' she shrugged and smiled, not trusting herself to say more about them.

She had a fine, strong face, with a good deal of *no nonsense* about it but lacking any quality of harshness. Photographs didn't do her justice; he suspected that the stern, vinegar glare that had peered from a thousand of them reflected her distaste for the whole idea of self-promotion. Yet, like him - perhaps more than him - she knew the value of the Press. While he had been editing a gutter daily for the edification of steel workers she had run a political journal dedicated to the emancipation of women from expectations of them. That had ended in '33 of course, along with her political career, but unlike many others she hadn't scurried off into a hole or reshaped her opinions to suit the new world. Starting again with a women's weekly that had seemed bland by comparison to what came before, she managed still to poke the eye of Authority with inspirational articles upon the value (other than as breeding sows) of the Reich's females. Krohne had an uncomfortable feeling that their slight acquaintance flattered only one of them.

She poured real tea from a Dresdner pot while he glanced around her unfashionably stuffed parlour. There were photographs everywhere, of her with a variety of extinct species: politicians of more than one stripe, academicians who had chased knowledge rather than sinecures, writers with more than a single, authorised version of what they had to say. It was a manifest of another, lost Germany, and bearing this legacy the walls and tables themselves would be deemed subversive.

'A shame about *Die Frau*,' he said, nodding his thanks as he took the cup.

She shrugged. 'The end of paper hasn't been entirely tragic. *Frauen-Warte* is closing down too, I hear. What will good National Socialist women have for distraction now, between bearing brats and knitting for the Front?'

'And *Die Adler*, that went last year of course.'

'A pity. I always *enjoyed* photographs of aircraft.'

Krohne couldn't tell whether she was teasing him. It would be like her, he supposed. Their only previous conversation - at a conference of newspaper and journal publishers in 1938 - had been an ordeal of good humoured criticism, directed against his paper's relentless slurs upon the Democratic Party, that he hadn't even attempted to parry but rather endured, red-faced, while everyone else at the table sat back and enjoyed a professional demolition job. He recalled that no one had thought him undeserving of it.

A brief, hardly friendly acquaintance - yet here he was in her parlour, a polite visitor, pretending to be glad to talk over old times. He sensed her efforts to quell the obvious question. He was certain that the room had never before accommodated a uniform, even for tea - it seemed to be censuring him with a weight of intellectual disdain that reminded him of his father's baleful glare whenever he broached the matter of his pre-war career intentions. But she just sat patiently, politely, as if the local pastor had come to beg a small donation and didn't quite know how to get around to it. Good manners didn't distinguish whom to waste themselves upon.

'If I may …' he leaned forward and replaced the cup upon the absurdly small table between them. 'I'm seeking information on a woman, perhaps an *extraordinary* woman.'

His hostess, herself extraordinary by any measure, said nothing. Krohne coughed. 'She, um, she's dead - killed, in fact, by someone who hasn't been discovered to date. To be plain, the killer seems to have friends, and these friends have done much to discourage efforts to find him.'

Her eyebrows rose slightly. 'I would not have thought this an unusual circumstance.'

'No, but may it be that what seems to be an insane, random act is something else. Information has been … difficult to obtain.'

'You said *extraordinary*.'

'Perhaps, yes. In nineteen thirty-two how many women, would you say, held positions of any sort of authority in German companies?'

She frowned. 'Not enough, of course. But too many for me to put a number to, even with Brüning and Von Papen doing their best to get women back into the home.

'And a year later?'

'Hardly any. Policy went from discouragement to outright pressure. Most of the bosses folded, and the unions were delighted about it. You know all this, naturally.'

Krohne nodded. 'A woman who survived that process would be exceptional?'

'Unless she grew a cock, yes. But then she'd be exceptional in every way.'

He laughed, shocked that such a prim mouth would utter the word. 'So, you might know a woman like that?'

'Perhaps.'

'Her name is Agatha Fuhrmann.'

She stared into her cup. 'It's familiar. Do you know what she did?'

'She was a scientist, possibly. In any case, a technical expert upon some process or piece of equipment. But I don't know the field.'

'A pity. Science *was* the least chauvinistic discipline, so the few women in industry whose careers survived Adolph Hitler invariably had technical abilities.' She spoke the name without inflection, dispassionately, in a way that Krohne hadn't heard for years.

He nodded. 'The fact that she *is* a women makes it likely that her employer is a civilian enterprise, though probably with military contracts. We discounted weaponry for obvious reasons, and chemicals too. I don't know if that helps.'

'It doesn't. Wait.'

She struggled out of her chair and went to a small bureau in an alcove beside the chimneybreast. As the roll top retracted a mound of papers slid forward, falling on to the floor. She rummaged into the rear of the desk, adding to the mess, and extracted a shallow, neatly bound pile of papers.

'*Women in Business* - between nineteen thirty and nineteen thirty-three there were annual conferences. In the first year it was held in Hamburg. After that, Berlin. The last was a travesty, and we decided to put it to sleep mercifully. But we have a list of delegates at least, and of the papers that were read.'

Briefly, Krohne scanned the schedule of topics. Many addressed the difficulties experienced by women in the workplace and in society at large, but some were straightforward business presentations. None of the speakers in any of the four years' conferences was his victim. She took back the papers, divided them, and gave him half.

'Look at the back, the lists of attendees.' Her eyes twinkled. 'We called them delegates, to make it seem as though we had a base.'

Krohne took the lists for 1930 and 1931. The first year's attendance was sparse, but the next event had more than a hundred names appended. That of Agatha Fuhrmann was not among them. It hardly seemed to matter - the women were listed without details of which company they represented or any other means of determining their fields.

'Ah.' She leaned forward and passed a sheet to him. 'Nineteen thirty-three, the year it went very wrong for women.'

She was there, among just forty delegates who had turned up to be told that the twentieth century had just been abolished by decree. He looked up as his heart went the other way. 'This is why her name was familiar to you?'

'No, my memory isn't that sharp. Look at the list again.'

He tried to see what it was that made Fuhrmann stand out, but there was nothing - no address, no detail other than the name itself.

'It's divided, you see, with each group representing attendees from the same field, or company.'

He hadn't noticed it - blank lines, occasionally separating three, four or five names from the next group. But even so, no companies were named. Fuhrmann's name lay in the middle of a group of three, as anonymous as the rest. The old woman leaned forward, tapped the paper.

'Look at the name above hers.'

Anne van Vechten. 'A Dutch woman?'

She smiled. 'An American lady. In fact, she was the first in her company to become head of division, albeit a women's division. That's why I recall Agatha - she wanted to introduce me to this exotic foreigner. It was a most interesting conversation. I found it fascinating at the time that the Americans were a step ahead of us in this way. After all, they worship motherhood, don't they?'

Krohne sat upright. 'And Agatha Fuhrmann worked for the same company?'

'Miss van Vechten was employed by the International Business Machines Corporation. I assume that Agatha was with the company's German arm.'

IBM - a great friend to the Reich, even after the war commenced. Pearl Harbour finally severed the connection (much to the regret of senior management on both sides of the Atlantic), but its most profitable European subsidiary, Deutsche Hollerith Maschinen Gesellschaft - *Dehomag* - had survived the divorce and prospered. Like many large German companies it was both technologically innovative and culturally conservative, preferring a long-familiar environment in which to do its novel work. Ever since nineteen thirty-three, the year that most German women left gainful, paid employment to get on with the serious business of opening their legs and producing future soldiers, it had stayed put, occupying a smart headquarters complex in the one of the quieter parts of Berlin - the district of Lichterfelde.

14

'Two boys in school and a wife with shot nerves, and all they'll get is a widow's pension and the charity of a Gestapo uncle-in-law. *Christ!* '

On a normal day, Gerd Branssler could make a guard dog nervous; now, his barely-controlled rage felt like an electric charge in the air, searching for chemicals to detonate. Holleman patted a hand that squeezed a cup like it was about to extract a quick confession. The Bull hadn't noticed its surface temperature.

'Are you certain there was *nothing*, Gerd?'

'He would have said. I saw him in the morning, for about ten minutes. He had time at least to mention if he'd found something. Then the stupid bastard went on a lunch drunk, and …' Convulsively, Branssler's foot lashed out under the table, almost unseating Fischer.

'Well, we'll get the swine, no doubt about that.' Holleman was wasting breathe, but it was his fault that the sleeping dog had been kicked, that Thomas had paid the price for – another debt to add to the rest

Behind the counter, Mona Kreitz watched them carefully, too familiar now to glare away, too much a stranger to trust with even a hint of what they were discussing. She seemed nervous, and it occurred once more to Fischer that they had used her shamelessly, put her into a danger against which she could have no means of defending herself. He should have felt guiltier than he did about it, but the café was too convenient. He smiled apologetically. She didn't seem to notice.

'Well, we needn't ask whether this was part of our business.'

Branssler snorted. 'A professional execution, on the Alex's back doorstep? The bastard must have glycerine for blood. Even the *stapos* have gone insane about it, swearing they'll pull in half of Berlin and beat it to death. You'd think someone had pissed in their pots and stirred it with his dick.'

Fischer leaned closer, spoke quietly: 'Gerd, listen. When did you ask Dieter to do it? It's important.'

The Bull shook his head. 'Two days ago, the afternoon. He was nervous. I thought he'd drag his feet and I'd have to push him. But the poor sod must have gone straight down to the basement.'

'He was killed about eighteen hours later, so someone had been waiting for this, hadn't they? Everything must have been in place, waiting for the question to be put.'

Branssler nodded. 'It's someone at the Alex - it *has* to be. Even if an outsider had a pet squealer in Records it couldn't have bounced around Berlin, got the nod and been arranged, not in that time.'

'And it was just the two names, Bildmann and Lange? Nothing else?'

'What else did I have to give him?'

'But he would have *asked* only for Bildmann's records, not Lange's. So Bildmann's was the name that tripped the wire.'

Dieter Thomas shouldn't have died, but he had done something invaluable. His short journey down to the basement of the Alex, his guileless request to access a file, had forced a hand. Such a swift, extreme act wasn't a warning - it was an unaimed lunge, a self-exposing reaction of skin to a sharp stab.

'What sort of threat *are* we?' Holleman asked, bewildered. 'If we're closing on something, why are Otto and me alive? Yesterday, we ...'

Fischer grabbed his arm and squeezed it, trying to bring down the volume. 'Yesterday, we were in Panzgrillerstrasse being conspicuous. Perhaps the person who should have noticed wasn't there.'

Branssler nodded slowly. 'Not if he was at Alexanderplatz, waiting for Dieter.'

'Not a vast conspiracy, then.'

'More than one, less than ten?'

Fischer shrugged. 'What matters is that it's personal.'

Holleman glanced sideways, distracted by the sound of the café's front door opening. 'Personal? At least three women and now a Bull, dead, and it's *personal*?'

'I mean it's a matter of protecting someone, not an institution. We've had this back to front. Who'd risk ordering the killing of a *kripo* to save professional embarrassment? Wouldn't they just disappear its cause? The investigation wasn't halted to protect the killer. Both it and he were part of the same process, of keeping *someone* safe. It has to be two at the least, and probably more. But show me a crowd, anywhere, that can keep a deep secret.'

The fourth chair at the table was dragged back, and Karl Krohne sat. As he glanced around at the other faces his complacent smile faded. 'What?'

Briefly, Fischer told him about Dieter Thomas. Krohne's colour, never robust, faded further as he listened.

'Oh, God.'

Mona placed a cup in front of him and withdrew quickly. For once, Krohne didn't notice the proximity of beauty, much less react to it. His Oberst's tabs sat upon a suddenly deflated bag.

'It … couldn't have been for some other reason?'

'Oh, yes, Karl,' whispered Branssler, 'it happens all the time. Standing orders are not to leave Alexanderplatz except in panzers. Dircksenstrasse's a fucking war-zone for bulls.'

Krohne stared into the table, searching for the bottom. Absurdly in their accommodating age he was a complete stranger to violent death. As an editor he had run stories on the subject, and for all of sixteen hours he had faced it (until a French shell fragment removed his eye, his balance and his fledgling military career); but he was a virgin compared to the three men at the table, men whose civilian lives had been stained to the elbows by it. His little triumph had just drowned in someone's blood. He coughed and swallowed. 'I've found Agatha Fuhrmann.'

Too loud. Mona looked up from her cups, and the café's only other customer - an old man in a rail signaller's uniform, leaning on the counter, his back to them - shrank visibly into minding more of his own business.

Krohne winced, shrugged an apology. 'She wasn't a scientist. It was something to do with data collection, I think. She was employed by Dehomag.'

Fischer rubbed his bandaged head. 'Shit!'

Holleman stared at him. 'What? We can place her now. This is good, isn't it?'

'Is it? The old lady said that she made the devices work, that the soldiers were the problem. She must have been a calibrator of some description.'

'Well? We can't hold that against the woman.'

Fischer leaned forward and spoke slowly to make his point. '*Every* branch of Werhmacht, and *every* administrative sub-department within it, uses Hollerith machines. There must be thousands of them, in every Gau and military district, even at the Front for God's sake! And somewhere in that vast world, Agatha Fuhrmann poked the nose of the wrong person. We'd need precise schedules of her field visits, with dates, names, everything - *and* a hundred men to sift through them.'

Branssler tapped the table. 'No. Dehomag's here at Lichterfelde, isn't it? She died in Lichterfelde. Why complicate things? The murderer's here, so the reason must be too.'

'I don't think so, Gerd. Why would her life have been erased from the records if this were a local business? Someone didn't want us to know who she was, but she *was* known in her workplace, and her street. *Here*, she's known, even if people are too frightened to speak of her death. No offence to Karl, but we'd probably have discovered the Dehomag connection eventually if we'd spoken to enough of her neighbours. If the removal of her *volkscartei* data severed the link to whatever we're trying to find, how could it be a local thing?'

Krohne smiled. 'Bloody ironic, isn't it? A woman spent her life coddling the same machines that recorded every detail of it and determined whether or not she existed at all. When it disappeared, so did she.'

'That's life, isn't it? Nothing exists unless something says that it does.'

Holleman and his family were proof of Kierkegaard's error - the essence of a person was entirely external, the sum of his or her documentation. No human activity proceeded without its validating paperwork in the National Socialist state. Data was both the record and proof of an event - erase it, and what remained was less substantial than what breath did to a cold window.

Fischer stared into his cup. 'I wonder if that's what did it.'

'Did what?'

'Finished this off. Gerd, your cases were closed down, but we've been wondering what smothered talk of it in Lichterfelde after that. What if nothing did - literally, *nothing*? What if the perception of everything going away was enough?'

'Could it be enough?'

'Why not? Don't we live in proscribed times? Even ordinary matters are sifted, directed, ruled upon. Why wouldn't the excision of an enormity send a message in itself? I mean ...'

Mona had come to the table to refill the cups. Krohne, by now over his little shock, smiled at her, willing her to like him. His eyes remained on her rear as it retreated to the counter, as he leaned forward and whispered. 'But now that we know about Frau Fuhrmann, couldn't we approach Dehomag?'

Fischer pulled a face. 'A waste of time. *All* their contracts are military now, so anything we ask will be referred through a dozen liaison officers before they even think of saying *why?* or *no*. If Fuhrmann was calibrating Holleriths for Wehrmacht she *was* Wehrmacht, effectively.'

'And everywhere that Wehrmacht went, there went Agatha.'

'Unlikely, but we can hardly narrow it down. I'm sorry, Karl, it was good work. I'm just not sure it can help us.'

'So what *can* we do?'

Fischer sighed. 'Gerd's partner did us a favour. We know now just how far and how quickly they'll go, so we don't do anything alone any more. Freddie and me should look at the second lady, Sigrun Ziegler. At least *she* hasn't been erased in more than body. I was going to suggest that Karl try to get *Forschungsamt* to part with any information they might have on Gerd's inquisitive boss Herbert Lange, but that particular boat seems to leak somewhat. So, for now we leave him alone. That leaves …'

'Rudolph Bildmann.'

'About whom we know almost nothing.'

Branssler scowled. 'We know where he lives. Karl can protect me.'

15

Branssler had to settle for Fischer's protection. Krohne, unnerved still by the news of Deiter Thomas's execution, mumbled something about a meeting at the Ministry. It sounded almost plausible. He took Holleman, who would have stayed except that his twins were alone, incarcerated in a safe house that suddenly seemed far less than that. They left immediately. The past and present *kripos* lingered only long enough to check their firearms under the astonished, terrified gaze of the old railway signaller. They were in the street less than two minutes later.

Rudolph Bildmann's rented an apartment in a worn block on Kornerstrasse, its rear overlooking the railway lines near Friedenau station. It was a third floor unit, smaller than those on the lower storeys, one of six in a corridor that smelled of cabbage, neglected old people and deep, well-settled damp. Only a single window at its end allowed in any natural light, and what there was had to struggle through a patina of several years' accumulation of industrial grime coating its outer surface. The result required assistance, which a solitary, empty ceiling socket struggled to provide.

Bildmann's door was in the middle of the corridor, north side. A *sealed by order of the Reich Ministry of Justice* notice was plastered upon it at eye-level, and tape covered the lock. Branssler turned and knocked upon the opposite door. For some moments there was silence, and then a brief noise, probably an inadvertent stumble, betrayed a presence. He knocked again, more robustly. The slow drag of a chain from the inner surface of the door hinted at the usual, desperate reluctance.

A bespectacled middle-aged lady eased herself slowly through a parsimonious gap and pulled to the door behind her. Her arms crossed protectively over her breasts as she stared up the glacis of Gerd Branssler. Fischer kept his face in the shadows behind him.

'May I help you?'

She had a thin, reedy voice, made thinner by a long winter. Branssler pulled out his warrant disc and re-attempted his new smile. It didn't seem to help.

'I'm very sorry to trouble you, madam. Do you know the tenant of number 33?'

She glanced at the door across the hallway, at the reassurance of the notice pasted there. Whatever these new faces wanted, she had documentation that obliged her to know as little as possible.

'The policeman? I've seen him, but we don't speak. He isn't … sociable.'

'Do you recall when you last saw him?'

'Oh, no.' The question almost invited the negative, and she seemed grateful for it.

'How long has *this* been here?' Branssler pointed to the notice.

That was more difficult. The prohibition confronted her every time she left her apartment.

'I … don't know.'

At this point a bull usually had the option of beating out the correct answer, but it was clear already that she was going to hide cravenly behind her sex, age and apparent infirmity. Fischer emerged from Branssler's shadow, offering all too clear a view even in the hallway's dim light. She gasped, and only just managed not to cover her mouth.

'But surely you must recall when you first saw it on the door. Was it recently, perhaps? Or has it been there for a while?'

The hand that was to have hidden her disgust waved feebly instead towards the deadly item. 'It's *official*. It's not for me to say when it was put there.'

The first time it must have struck her as if it had been Himmler's bare arse, pressing through a rubber ring. But as a good German her duty was both to obey absolutely and deny all knowledge of it. Fischer stifled a smile and tapped Branssler's shoulder. The bull nodded.

'Would you oblige me madam? Should someone return, would you mention our visit and what you've seen?'

She shook her head. 'I haven't seen anything.'

'A moment, please.' Branssler lurched at the sealed door, his shoulder braced. The entire frame gave way and crashed with its documentation into the apartment.

Fischer had intended to offer some small reassurance to the lady, but he lost the thought somewhere in the foul, toxic miasma that wafted into the hallway. Quickly, the two men covered their faces as a door slammed decisively behind them. Flies - fat, young things, unseasonably plentiful - swarmed free from their life-long incarceration, mostly avoiding the large objects that stumbled through them.

He was in the small kitchen, propped informally against an ancient, grease-encrusted oven. As the smell hinted, the period of active decay had not yet passed. Maggots teemed in hollows created by earlier, now-airborne feeders, and the pool of purged fluids under the body remained slightly moist. The corpse's attitude was entirely relaxed, offering no clues as to how much of a struggle had taken place immediately prior to death. But the ligature wound tightly around the discoloured neck made the matter a moot one, and the angle of the head in relation to the rest indicated that a broken neck rather than strangulation had hurried the victim from his suddenly turned-for-the-worse life.

The apartment was cold, but winter had been winsome, changeable. There had been weeks at a time when the temperature remained slightly above freezing, others when ice didn't even try to melt. The maggots couldn't have hatched in frost unless the eggs were already safely inside their host, so it was impossible to guess at a time, or even a week, of death. The body had laid here for more than a month and less than two, but that was about all that could be said without inconveniencing a forensics laboratory.

Fischer rotated a window latch and slid the frame upwards. 'So when did the notice go up?'

Branssler shrugged. 'It went up for a reason, and here he is.'

If this was a loose end, it had been tidied very effectively. No one could have anticipated that a Ministry of Justice order would be disregarded; another week or two and even the smell would have joined its cause in the hereafter, leaving no more than a forbidding door for the residents to half-notice and then fearfully put from their minds. As good as a burial, at a fraction of the cost.

Fischer glanced around. 'We won't get another chance. You take the bedroom.'

For almost twenty minutes they searched the apartment. There were no obvious clues, no discriminating papers; in fact, there was nothing in writing that gave a clue to the life of the tenant other than an old, battered rent book (paid up until the end of 1944) and a small number of utility coupons, clipped and stamped. The man's ID papers, ration card and any personal correspondence were missing. The walls held a few cheap prints - clichéd views of famous places, the sort that 'art' studios held as their bread-and-butter stock - but no photographs. Most of the drawers were empty other than for old newspaper lining, carefully tacked to the plywood beneath. Just one held a bare selection of undergarments, clean but much worn, service issue quality. Personal artefacts were equally elusive - they found no cigarette case or lighter, cufflinks, tiepins or anything else that might have attached a character to the deceased or given a hint as to lifestyle. If someone had *lived* here, he'd been as attached as a leaf in November.

Branssler discovered the only interesting item in the bedroom wardrobe. He had missed it the first time because it was concealed behind a plywood panel, held in place by a small *S* clip. His knuckle, inadvertently exposing the hollowness of what should have been a substantial walnut surface, brought him back to it. He lifted it out and held it up for Fischer's benefit - a standard field-grey uniform with SS rank insignia - a lowly unterscharführer - but a plain right collar patch and *polizei* shoulder straps.

'Who's a clever boy?'

'You are, Gerd.' An SS uniform but without the runes or field unit markings - a uniform that, quite carefully, identified its wearer as a man not to be identified, a man with duties perhaps necessary to the safety of the Reich but for which proper recognition might not be forthcoming. Rudolph Bildmann had gone somewhere - east, probably, and returned, like many other police, with very little to tell of what he had seen and done there. There was no visible damage to the uniform, so he had been careful with it, or lucky, or he knew a good, non-Jewish tailor. But then, so many had come home in good *physical* health that one might have suspected the assignments to have been relatively untaxing. The eyes might have told them otherwise; Fischer wondered what they had said, before they went away.

The two men searched the pockets and seams carefully and found nothing. The secret was the uniform itself. Branssler smoothed it down, replaced it carefully on its hanger. 'Should we take it?'

'What for? We can't have it examined. Put it back where you found it.'

While the bull was in the bedroom Fischer revisited the corpse. Apart from the mess itself, it struck him suddenly that the *ordnungspolizei* uniform was intact, missing nothing.

'He must have been ready for his shift.'

'What?' Branssler stood in the doorway, giving the kitchen a final bull's glance.

'He's dressed for the outdoors. His jacket's fastened, the boots are laced up and even the tie's properly knotted. He must have been ready to start his shift, or just back from it. Perhaps the killer was waiting as he walked in.'

'I don't think so.'

'Why not?' Fischer stared down at the body, searching for the subtle clue he had missed.

'Because it isn't Bildmann. I know this one. He's Lutze - Lutze the idiot.'

16

At the intersection of Drakestrasse and Holbeinstrasse, Paul Schroeder stopped and smiled. It was a cold, miserable day, but a sudden warmth of nostalgia, a shimmer of past things, lifted his mood considerably. He was confronted by a spirit of old Lichterfelde, manifesting itself directly across the road from where he stood, haunting a group of elderly ladies who didn't seem to be in the least bothered by their ordeal. In fact, they were almost squealing with delight.

Conscious of his obvious Authority, he tucked his *schlagstock* behind his regulation field overcoat and crossed to investigate the fracas. Probably, what he would hear was very familiar to him, but that was the thing about a *good* routine - it didn't spoil with age.

In his daytime plumage Eddie Muntz looked almost normal, if normality could encompass a hint of rouge and a discreet touch of lipstick upon a lumpy, palpably male face. The clothes in particular were impeccable. Paul hadn't seen such a perfectly tailored, pressed suit since before the war, and the hat was perched at an angle that said *I didn't really have to try*, or Spencer Tracy. Eddie's tie was Windsor-knotted of course, to give proper effect to the English-collared shirt (Paul had one himself, carefully wrapped in a drawer, and recognized the style immediately), and the shoes had an ox-blood perfection that could have drawn tears from the Kaiser's cobbler as he contemplated his reflection in them. It was almost too perfect, and some would have considered it very wrong that the sartorial whole was so mocked by its contents.

Eddie didn't understate himself knowingly. *All the world's a stage, and all the men and women merely players* was his firm philosophy, which he declaimed - as a player would - to his audiences. The present one, if small, was appreciative, and hung upon every word of what, Paul realised as he drew closer, was nothing more than an account of a recent visit to the grocer's shop.

'… Jesus, Mary and Joseph, I said! Eight deutschmarks, for that piece of forest floor scraping? Do you know what the Fuhrer would call that, I asked him. *No*, he said. A shooting offence, I told him - profiteering! Well, darlings, his face fell further than stockings off a donkey, and he said, *Herr Muntz, please speak more quietly*. Quietly! As if I would know how! I said, don't you dare …'

At this point, Eddie drew breath and noticed Paul Schroeder, standing slightly to one side of the adoring public. He examined this apparition slowly, taking in the over-large service coat, the schlagstock held quite unprofessionally, and raised his perfectly plucked eyebrows.

'Well, the Fatherland stands proudly still!'

Paul tried but failed to suppress a grin. You simply couldn't take offence at Eddie Muntz. It was as if you had a seat at the front, in the centre, and had to accept that you'd be a butt of something during the course of a performance. As the only male in the present audience it was almost his duty.

Eddie cradled an arm, put a finger to his pursed lips and gave Paul a long up-and-down. 'But I don't recall this one. Are they drafting teenagers now?'

The taunt didn't wound as once it might, perhaps half a century ago. Eddie was being gentle, working his way to a sharper thrust, no doubt. It didn't matter; Paul and his wife had seen his routine at least half a dozen times in the old days and enjoyed every one, laughing until the tears came and then crying a little more as the sentimental songs swept them up.

Eddie's gaze lingered provocatively on the *schlagstock*. The old ladies tensed delightedly, waiting for the inevitable.

'Such a firm grip! Surely we've met?'

Paul realised that he might be killing the joke, but he couldn't help himself. 'Yes, Herr Muntz. At the *Titania-Palast*, 12 October 1937, my wife's birthday. You kissed her and signed my programme.'

'Ah,' Eddie sighed. 'The *Titania*! Even then, you see, I was reduced to singing in a cinema! And now, what do I do now? I sing my best songs while the little piggies fill their tummies - no, dear, of course you *have* to, I don't complain ...' he patted the nearest hand without bothering to check whether anyone had been offended by what he'd said, '... but it's a tragedy, you must admit! From top of the bill at the Palm Court to ... this!'

Fully aware of the wretched comedown they represented, the ladies almost brawled to reassure Eddie that they sympathized. He allowed a number of them in turn to grasp his hand while the other dabbed a handkerchief delicately against his eye.

'You know, Paul Morgan wanted me for a season - a full season - at the *Kadeko*! But Robitschek never liked me! He said I pandered to vulgar tastes - me! My dears, he insulted you, too!'

The old ladies agreed happily that Robitschek (whoever he was) had no idea of talent - was an absolute idiot, in fact. Paul caught himself nodding in agreement. He hadn't meant to worship at Eddie's altar, but the man had been so successful for a reason. He could make you *want* to like him.

'And we came to see you at the *Schlosspark*, too, Herr Muntz. That was in the year the war began.'

Eddie's eyes widened. 'The *Schlosspark*! I gave only one performance there! Of course, it wasn't meant to be a *music hall*, was it? *Much* too cultured a place for *that* sort of entertainment. But their orchestra had lost all its little Jews, so they had to book *vulgar* acts like mine if they wanted to fill seats!'

Another murmur of protest did the rounds, but Eddie was falling into memory and didn't hear it.

'The *Titania*, that was something else! I haven't thought of it for years, not even when …' he stopped in mid-declamation - a catch, something … painful? To Paul's almost-policeman's eye, the subject was exhibiting a degree of discomfort, though it was hard to tell with Muntz - his emotions were overdone for effect usually, to carry beyond the pit and into the gallery. This didn't seem to have the taste of theatre about it; he had lost that casual ease of tempo that kept his public dangling for the next line, and Paul wondered if it was his place to ask the cause.

Awkwardly, a few of the ladies moved backwards, putting a little distance between them and this new, uncomfortably unamusing Muntz. Paul nodded at no one in particular, indicating that the problem could be left to him.

'Is there something I can help you with, Herr Muntz?' Paul touched his elbow gently (he wanted to avoid an outright *grip*, now that its quality was a matter of public record).

Muntz looked doubtfully at the slight, sixty-something reservist, incompletely filling his *hilfspolizei* uniform with skin, bone and conscientiousness. 'Help? My dear, it's much too late to *help*. They're all gone now, all of them - Morgan, Robitschek, Reinhardt, Gerron, Hansen - like echoes in my heart.'

'But not you, Herr Muntz?' Paul smiled. 'You'll outlast all of us.'

Eddie shook his head sadly. 'Plague does what it does. If you don't have it, you live with the stink of those who do. It makes me so tired.'

Paul could think of nothing to say to something so profoundly unamenable to contradiction. He nodded and waited, quelling a stab of guilt for rousing an old man's ghosts. The two were quite alone, now; the last of Eddie's audience had shuffled away, resuming her morning forage for something edible that wasn't a turnip or cabbage, while the rest of Lichterfelde's sparse human traffic moved economically around them.

Muntz's eyes had been upon a point far away, but they narrowed again. He turned to Paul. '*You* were there that night. You saw her, too.'

'Which night, Herr Muntz? Who did I see?'

'At the *Titania*. She was always there, in those days. For me it was only an occasional thing, but not for her. She was a lovely, lovely child.'

Paul tried to recall the evening. There had been no child-act upon the programme, he was certain of that. His wife had detested that sort of thing, had thought the parents of young prodigies a species of grasping, pushy contemptibles, no better than Americans. If a kid had walked on to the stage she would have told her husband that it was time to go, the promise of Eddie Muntz notwithstanding.

'I … don't recall.'

Muntz took his hand, and squeezed it. To his surprise, Paul experienced none of the revulsion he imagined to be the proper response to a sodomite's touch. It was a warm, dry grasp, conveying nothing unseemly.

'Of course you don't, my dear. I'm wandering through the fields; an old man's head does that. Pay no attention to what spills out.'

That was the end of it, very abruptly. Eddie gave Paul one of his famously dazzling smiles, released the hand, and strolled slowly in the direction of the kaserne, away from the shops and his adoring female public. Paul watched him going, wondering what he should make of it. Any report of the encounter would have struggled to seem consequential, yet it seemed to his untrained mind that he had heard something not spilled but *pulled* from memory, and that it had been distressing. If he mentioned this at the station he would be mocked, obviously. *Eddie Muntz?* they'd say, shaking their heads, making obscene gestures with their fingers and palms; *what the fuck were you doing, bothering with that filthy old florenzer?* And of course, if he mentioned his intuitive feeling they'd mock him for the rest of the week, or month, make what they imagined were witticisms about anal sex and which public toilet was his favourite haunt of an evening.

No, he wasn't going to mention it at the station. But with a rare sense of certainty, he knew that he was going to take advice from someone. She probably didn't even know who Eddie Muntz was (she was very young, after all), but she had an older woman's sense of when things that were not said meant something.

17

The *Ottowagen* died just south of Monumentenstrasse. Right up to the end the engine had sounded no worse than usual and there was fuel in its tank still, so this was something serious, the consequence of one too many savagings of its clutch or gearbox coming home to roost. They were a kilometre still from the Air Ministry, two from the safe house, and Freddie Holleman's first thought was that his artificial leg was about to get some serious exercise. He had a mild curse ready, but before he could let it go someone else pulled the pin from the grenade. Lashing out with both his fists, Karl Krohne roared and flailed the steering wheel, door frame and once-upholstered ceiling indiscriminately, rocking the tired suspension violently, hurling a ripe, inventive stream of curses directed at Opel AG, its American parent company and the Air Ministry's motor pool crew - the latter as yet unaware of their postings to a punishment battalion in the Balkans that he swore by the Eternal, Vengeful God would be signed off that very day.

Holleman could have listened for quite a while before tiring of this. But two elderly *ordnungspolizei*, directing traffic at the junction of Siegfriedstrasse and Brunhilde-Gessler-Strasse, were waving them in the direction of the kerbside. He gave them an understanding, frowning nod that more or less indicated compliance, and tapped Krohne's arm.

'*Fuck!*'

'I know, Karl, I know. We'll get them to help us push it over there.' There was a space beneath the elevated railway line where the thing could be abandoned, or 'parked' as they would tell the uniforms, and then Holleman could try to massage whatever cramp had seized his former boss's testes. It wasn't the car, for certain.

Reluctantly, the elder policeman - he must have been at least seventy - gave a shoulder to assist Krohne while Holleman steered the Opel into its open grave beneath a frayed, faded poster advertising the 1938 Berlin International Handicrafts Exhibition. When it was done the old man spent several moments leaning on the battered bonnet, trying to refill his lungs. Holleman patted his thanks while Krohne gave the bodywork a final kick, stepped back and blundered into a passing citizen, knocking her bag from her hands.

His hapless attempts to help her retrieve the potatoes that spilled onto the road would have been pure comedy but for the misery painted upon the clown's face. Holleman took an arm and they left the woman to recapture the last of her supplies. A pretty *hausfrau*, she was cursing them with a welder's vocabulary, not caring if they or anyone else in a uniform heard.

Fifty metres to the south, an unmarked Hanomag had pulled in behind a parked truck. The driver waited until the two Luftwaffe officers and the woman had moved on and then got out and went to speak to the *ordnungspolizei*. They were happy to talk of course, and didn't think anything of the question. He joked with them, sympathized with their situation, told them to get indoors as soon as they could. When he returned to his car he lit a cigarette, made himself comfortable and then began to swear quietly, methodically, inventively. The two *ordnungspolizei* continued to direct traffic for several minutes more but were then diverted by a delivery truck that had parked illegally near the entrance to a yard. He watched them remonstrate with the driver, and came to a decision.

It wasn't as though he had a choice. It couldn't be left as it was, nor reacquired in such a public setting without drawing attention. He was glad now that he had decided to do it his way and not as ordered - at least, it had been *one* of his orders, and, as usual, contradicted by others. From the front passenger seat he lifted his little souvenir from Kiev, one of dozens they'd managed to find and neutralize before it was too late, before they'd done their job. The distance was fine, well within the specified radio range. He wound it three times, rapidly, and pressed the button.

Krohne and Holleman walked up to Yorckstrasse, curving east and north behind the vast space of the Potsdamer-Anhalter Bahnhof yards. For a while, neither man spoke. Holleman assumed that the recent, memorable adjustments to Krohne's domestic situation were the likely trigger, to which the news of Dieter Thomas's death must have applied a necessary kinetic energy. Some men - the lucky ones, like Holleman himself - blew quickly; others were tortured by a slow tightening that was often mistaken for self-control. Karl Krohne was easy-going, a pupil of the letting-things-ride school of life from which even a career in newspapers hadn't managed to get him expelled. Living in and for the present was what he did best, and this, to Holleman, was his biggest problem. A man who refuses to anticipate shit almost always ends up swallowing it.

They stopped at a cigarette vendor. Krohne removed his wallet, pointed a finger and paid for a small, hand-wrapped bundle of *Effekts*. 'Freddie, I'm sorry. It's been …'

'Ach, shut up, Karl.' Holleman flicked through the booth's small collection of magazines, sold and re-bought like a lending library of past pleasures, thumbed to a state of near ruin. He'd hoped for something in the hobbyist line, to relieve his boys' absolute reliance upon their own imaginations. All he found were Party-approved, Jew-baiting journals, the sort that no one had cared to read even when there had been Jews to bait.

He took a cigarette from Krohne (it seemed the most economical way to tell him to forget the whole thing). They begged a light in turn from the vendor and inhaled, letting an uncomfortable conversation avert itself. Since September 1943 Holleman had been building a debt with his former boss that could hardly be repaid, so a sympathetic ear was the least he could lend. But if silence did the job, well …

The sound was muffled, diffused across an acoustically messy urban half-kilometre. For a moment, both men imagined it to have come from ahead of them, but that was merely one of many echoes, returning. To the south, thick, acrid smoke rose from the railway lines - an attack, though neither sirens nor the familiar, dreaded drone of aircraft engines had given warning. It was an accustomed interruption, and Krohne and Holleman gave it no more than a shrug and a silent hope that the casualties weren't too heavy. They began to walk once more, as quickly as Holleman's metal leg permitted, and Wilhelmstrasse was almost in sight when the strangeness of it struck him - a single impact, in broad daylight, under heavy cloud. It was not how these things went.

He stopped. Krohne, wide-eyed, nervous, did the same. 'Can you walk that far…?'

But Holleman was moving already, dragging along the other's shoulder as a crutch, resisting a flow of humanity that moved determinedly away from the bad news. By the time they reached Siegfriedstrasse once more a fire engine was playing its hose on the upturned remnants of the *Ottowagen*. The thin stream hardly slowed flames that carried up one of the metal columns supporting the elevated section and into the wooden slats of the rail platform. Other damage was slight. The enclosed area beneath the railway had contained much of the blast, and only a single lorry - illegally parked - was burning in the street, its canvas roof already consumed and fallen in upon the blazing cargo. The driver stood nearby, gesticulating angrily at the two elderly *ordnungspolizei*, demanding angrily that something be *done* about the Eighth Air Force. The *orpos* must have been quite close to the explosion; they seemed dazed still, not quite willing to believe their luck. One of them was making tentative noises of sympathy while the other had removed his notebook and pencil but hadn't quite recovered the necessary poise to put one to the other. Beyond them, the exhibition poster was still attached to the wall, but the wall itself had been relocated to a resting position across several parked vehicles. A mess, but it had probably been Berlin's least unfortunate explosion of a very young 1945.

Krohne and Holleman stared at the spot they should have been occupying, at what remained of the extemporary coffin that somehow had failed to do its simple business.

'The fuel tank…?'

Holleman snorted. 'Twenty-eight litres, full? It wouldn't have raised a fart. This was plastique, or a shu42. The fucking thing's been pulverised.'

'Incredible, that we …'

Another snort. 'What, Karl? God? The bastard who fitted the charge probably loosened a cable and we got the benefit of it. It was sloppiness, that's all.'

Krohne shook his head. 'You think someone at the ministry, the motor pool?'

'No, I don't. It hasn't been there for three days, and no timer can be set for that sort of delay. Either it was attached in the alley outside the safe house - which it *wasn't* - or in Lichterfelde, this morning.'

'Why not at the safe house?'

'Because we're alive, Karl. If the party who wants us dead knew about the house, why wouldn't he just block the alley, knock on the door and then take his time about it? Who would hear anything? He could get *all* of us there, if he waited long enough. No, this makes me feel a little easier about Franz and Ulrich, that they're safe for the moment.'

'*Safe?*'

'A relative term.'

'Do we tell anyone about this?'

'We tell Otto and Gerd. To everyone else, it *was* the fuel tank.'

As they turned into Monumentenstrasse for the second time that morning, Krohne glanced back at the wreck of the once-despised *Ottowagen*. The flames had been subdued sufficiently for two of the fire-crew to approach. They were on their knees, trying to see into the crushed passenger compartment, ignoring the elderly policeman who was telling them that there were no victims this time. Their only remaining audience, the lorry driver, had sat down on the kerb's edge and was cradling his head in his crossed arms, as if asleep. His vehicle, ignored by the firefighters, was now little more than a chassis, an artefact, an anecdote for the shift's end at both fire and police stations, one of their few statistics that couldn't be laid at the door of Churchill or Roosevelt.

Chance, or fate, or luck, or Grace - Krohne could think only of how it might have gone the other way for any of a hundred inconsequential reasons. It was what prevented him feeling too good about breathing still.

18

Fischer and Branssler went directly from Bildemann's apartment to that of the murderer's second victim, Sigrun Zeigler. It was no more than five minutes from one to the other, not nearly enough time for the odour of the very late, ripe Hans Lutze to remove itself from memory. They breathed like mountaineers at altitude as they walked, trying to flush the corpse as much from imagination as their lungs.

Zeigler's apartment block, like most others on Gutmuthstrasse, was a substantial, mixed-use building. Shops occupied the ground floor, separated by a central, ornate portal giving access to the residents' lower hallway and post-boxes - another pre-war development expensively conceived to offer a single-package suburban habitat for the well-heeled exodus from central Berlin. The contrast between this and Rudolph Bildmann's block - an earlier, strictly proletarian edifice - was the more intense for their proximity.

An old, liveried *hausmeister* stopped them at the entrance. He was military-erect, almost as polished as his hallway, and it was clear from the moment Branssler waved his warrant disc that he wasn't to going to be intimidated. But a glance at Fischer's ruined face brought him even more to attention.

'Your business, gentlemen?'

Branssler asked to see Frau Zeigler's apartment. The *hausmeister*'s head was shaking before he'd finished. 'Impossible. It's been sealed by order of the Ministry of Justice. I have strict instructions.'

Someone had been busy with official notices. Fischer raised an eyebrow and smiled.

'Would you mind telling me when the notice was posted, sir?'

'No, of course not. A policeman put it up it on 17 October last. I made a note of it, here.' He showed them the entry in a pocket diary.

Branssler frowned. 'Deiter came the day before. That was quick work.'

Fischer nodded. 'And no one has returned since, to examine the lady's effects?'

The old man was quite definite. 'No one. I expect the foreign workers situation keeps them too busy.'

Branssler sighed, half-opened his mouth to offer the statistics and thought better of it. Fischer applied the nudge. 'Still, you may wonder why the murder - that of a respectable middle-aged lady - has not been correctly investigated?'

'It seems … wrong.'

'It is. We believe that anti-German elements are involved.'

Anti-German had meant only one thing since the previous 20 July - traitorous elements within the Reich, bent upon some form of accommodation with the Allies, a fifth-column of supply-your-own-subversives. The old man didn't wear a Party badge, but a franking machine couldn't have stamped respect for authority more plainly upon him. His aged spine stiffened yet further.

'If we could examine the apartment - in your presence, of course - we may be able to recover *vital clues*.' Branssler managed to say it without smiling. There was an argot of detective pulp fiction that the public assumed to be absolutely authentic, and he was happy to oblige it. The old man's resistance crumbled - he was being given a chance to do the right thing against standing orders, probably as good as life could get for an old soldier. With arthritic precision, he removed a large bunch of keys from beneath his coat and hobbled towards the cage-elevator.

'I'll walk.' Branssler moved towards the staircase - the elevator could hold three small persons at most, and he counted for two. By the time Fischer and the *hausmeister* emerged into the second floor hallway he was already at the door of apartment 22, his foot tapping impatiently on the jamb. As the old man fumbled with the keys he was visibly resisting an urge to snatch them.

The apartment was sparse but tastefully furnished, its colours too well coordinated to be a man's home. Lace edging adorned almost every visible piece of domestic linen, hinting at how the late Frau Zeigler had endured her long, lonely winter evenings. Next to the sitting room's only armchair, a polished stand on a low pedestal held an uncased violin. Fischer plucked the strings - they were slack, untuned, but the instrument itself was immaculately maintained. To his untrained eye the lustrous finish suggested that it had been an expensive acquisition, but *when* was difficult to say. For all he knew it was two or two hundred years old.

'Frau Zeigler was *accomplished*.' The *hausmeister*'s chest swelled slightly. Like most of his breed he regarded the quality of his tenants as no less a reflection upon himself than his tiled floors. 'She gave *recitals*.'

Branssler expressed his opinion of the lady's accomplishments with a grunt. He began to examine the room's niches, manhandling ornaments and opening drawers. The *hausmeister* winced, watched carefully, said nothing. Fischer remained where he was and observed the layout of the deceased's furniture and ornaments. Everything was placed carefully, precisely, in the way that people of modest means preserve the artefacts of a more abundant past. There was something formal here, almost as if the space had been devoted to a single purpose in a home insufficiently large to afford the indulgence. It was a music room, in a three-roomed apartment where music wasn't played, or a shrine lovingly dedicated to the memory of it. Most of the objects that Branssler was lifting and replacing were awards or memorials recognizing service, all of them fashioned to reflect a musical theme. But there were no photographs - not a single one in all the places they should have been.

'Gerd? What's the name?'

Branssler paused, and went back to the trophies he had examined already. '*Zeigler* on one, the most recent. The rest say *Metzger*.'

Adults could be blasé about their present accomplishments, but not past glories. Almost certainly, Frau Zeigler would have preserved lovingly the tokens of Fraulein Metzger's triumphs, her best link to the good old days. There would be news-cuttings somewhere, and *they* would contain photographs. Fischer went into the bedroom - it was small, plain, furnished only with a small bed, a stand chair and a wardrobe. He knelt and pulled the suitcase out from beneath the springs. It was unlocked, entirely empty, and he didn't believe for a moment that it had been so until the day the Ministry of Justice notice went up outside. Lonely middle-aged ladies had no use for suitcases other than as receptacles for their lives. This was another element in a process of erasure, of making a life invisible.

In the sitting room, Branssler was questioning the *hausmeister* and committing his answers to a notebook. It was hardly necessary, but the old man would respect the gesture like any other German. It gave weight to the exchange.

'Did she have friends in the building?'

'Only Frau Prost, in apartment 27, I think. But she moved to Innsbruck early in the winter. To be with relatives.'

With the Russians on the Vistula and her friend murdered in the street, Frau Prost would have needed a heart of ice not to flee. Fischer wondered if Deiter Thomas had asked the same question the day he was here, before she went south. There was nothing about her in the file, and he and Holleman had looked particularly for acquaintances.

'Finally, sir - the man who placed the notice on Frau Zeigler's door? Was he alone?'

'Yes. A member of *ordnungspolizei*. I'm afraid I'm not familiar with the uniform, so I can't say what rank.'

'What did he take with him?'

'Nothing! I should have asked for a receipt, otherwise.'

So the apartment had been cleaned professionally, probably at night, during a raid or drill.

'And did he give any reason why the apartment was being sealed?'

'Of course not. It wasn't my business to know. In any case, he was a quite *taciturn* fellow, and I'm not so old as not to be able to take the hint.'

Branssler smiled, the first time he'd warmed to the old fellow. 'And that was it? No one's been here since?'

'Only the gentleman's partner, to ask a few more details.'

Fischer touched the *hausmeister*'s arm. 'His partner?'

'Yes, that's how he identified himself.'

'And what were the details?'

'Questions about Frau Zeigler's life. Nothing of her death, but then, what would I know of that?'

'Do you remember exactly what he asked?'

'To be frank, it was mundane, trivial stuff. He was extremely painstaking, though. I think he was here for almost an hour. It might have been done more quickly, but he talked about the other, terrible things he'd seen as a policemen. I felt that some of the matters he mentioned were … confidential.'

Fischer didn't need to glance at Branssler. He could almost feel the bull urging the question.

'He didn't give a name?

'No, sir.'

'A man of about sixty years? Cropped white hair, a very severe style?'

The *hausmeister* smiled. 'A Lichterfelde cut, they used to call it before the First War. Because of the cadets - they were all obliged to wear the same.'

The soon-to-be-former Hans Lutze, poking his ugly face into *kripo* business, a talker, a braggart, asking questions about things that were not to be spoken of. Branssler was staring down at his notes, but Fischer was certain he was thinking the same thing - *Bildmann*.

The bull closed his notebook and replaced it in the coat pocket. 'Would you oblige us, sir? This is my number. If anyone else attempts to gain access, would you let me know? Obviously, it's very important.'

Silently, the *hausmeister* pocketed the card. They allowed themselves to be herded downstairs, moving silently, giving no occasion for other apartment doors to open. At the front door, they shook hands with the old man, thanked him for his time and assistance, hinted at how valuable his information had been in ensuring the Reich's security. It was crude, the sort of thing the public expected.

A few doors from the apartment block, Fischer stopped in front of a real estate agency window and pretended to find the sparse view interesting. There was a solitary employee inside, an old man, reading a newspaper. He didn't glance up.

'Rudolph Bildmann isn't missing.'

'No.' Branssler rubbed his face with a handkerchief that his wife would have consigned to the laundry a month earlier, and replaced it in his lapel pocket with preposterous care. 'A fugitive or a player still, but definitely our man. Or *one* of them.'

'A photograph would be useful.'

'When I've worn out my feet on his head, how he used to look won't matter.'

'We need him to talk, Gerd. To tell us *who* and *why*.'

'I'll start on his kidneys, then. But Dieter's wife has some comfort coming.'

19

Mona Kreitz's home and workplace occupied the same building, and she rarely left the premises. The café's owner arranged for deliveries - they were few enough, these days - and Steglitz's municipal services still functioned sufficiently to empty the bins from the alley off Sophiastrasse. There was little reason for her to venture out if she chose not to - she had few acquaintances and fewer friends, and if she wanted company she had her customers, nearly all of them familiar faces.

A killer was wandering the streets of Lichterfelde, so she might have comforted herself that she was being prudent, but really, that was an excuse. The creature attacked vulnerable, middle-aged women, not healthy young females who could probably put up a struggle and make plenty of noise. She had a respectable fear of meeting the man, but it wasn't what made her the way she was.

It was more the fault of her mother's genes, and how too many of them might have been passed on. Frau Kreitz's home - a beautiful home, as everyone who visited it made a particular point of saying - had been a matter of such pride to her that she had gradually lost the desire and then the ability to leave it, even for the time it took to have her hair done, to visit a sick friend, to bury a husband. Mona had lived with her during the final year in which even the house itself had become too large, when the old woman had been content to remain in her bedroom suite, contemplating the awful hugeness of the world as her body relinquished the burden of being a part of it. For her daughter it had been a bad, dangerous time, watching someone die in a perfect contentment of imprisonment, getting a tempting taste of too much safety, of the lure of a place where one couldn't be hurt by anything.

So on the days when she recognized too much of her mother in herself she urged herself to get out and see more of the world - at least as far as the ring-strasse, or perhaps even Dahlem. Sometimes the prospect of such adventures frightened her, and *that* frightened her more, made her fear that she had become too fond of places with comforting walls. Even so, there always seemed to be good reasons why it would have to be tomorrow or the day after that she made her intrepid bid to face the world. She tried to recall her childhood picnics (thought there had been few of them, and always with cousins she didn't get on with), and promised herself something similar, perhaps in the Botanical Gardens. Of course, there wasn't much in the way of variety in the German diet any more, but she was certain that she could make something adequate for a day - or perhaps just an hour or two - out of doors.

Today was Sunday, and she thought more than usual about her great project. Hardly anyone would bother to make the effort to visit the café, and if she didn't open the door to her customers who would care? She told herself, over and over until it became quite convincing, that here could be no harm in it. The morning was unseasonably bright, and many other Lichterfelders would be thinking of doing the same - she would have to be neither alone nor exposed.

She went downstairs, wrapped a piece of rye bread in a cloth and placed it in her satchel bag with the café's last bottle of Gerolsteiner. The new air-raid regulations lay (against regulations) on her counter still, so she took the time to place them in the window and remove the old, apparently inadequate version. And then she recalled that the water boiler had yet to be scraped clean of its mineral deposits, and something needed to be done still about the damage done to the wooden floor by the metal heel plates on former railwayman Albert's boots. It might take the best part of the morning to … her coat was half-removed before courage returned. She pulled it on again, buttoned it, told herself that there would be time enough for what needed to be done, took a deep breath, a final glance around her too-familiar prison, twisted the key, and then she was out on Sophiastrasse. She turned eastward, towards wide, intimidating Dahlemer-Strasse and the Botanical Gardens beyond.

The wind was the first thing she noticed. It was blowing from the south, bringing a welcome breath of winter countryside to the city - of soil, mainly, the odour of countless fields and allotments planted with the hardier greens that kept vitamins from being more than a memory in the German diet. Thank God for *cruciferae*, one of her amateur agriculturalist customers had once observed sourly - we may hate them, but the Reich can't fart on air alone.

She almost laughed to think of Erich's face as he'd said it, and crossed the wide street without remembering to be anxious. On the far side a woman passed by and nodded familiarly. She couldn't recall her name - a customer once, though not for some time now. Perhaps she could no longer spare the money for undrinkable coffee, or had company at home and no need to seek it elsewhere. But the smile had been genuine, unforced, and Mona's spirits rose further as she came to Unter den Eichen.

Her timing was perfect. A large family group, busying itself with too many little ones, was about to cross to the north side, and she attached herself to it. A few cars and military vehicles slowed politely, and they stepped into the road.

'May I, Fraulein?'

She turned as his hand touched her elbow, resisting the urge to pull away. It was the young SS man with the appalling steel plate in his head, the friend of the pretty one who had somehow found his very lost way to her café. He was beaming at her, showing at least two teeth that matched the metal of his skull. His hair - that which remained - was wet, slicked back as if he had been freshly scrubbed, and the smell of carbolic soap almost overpowered his cigarette. Behind him, a number of other SS personnel sat on a low wall fronting the WVHA building, smoking. They looked bored, as if waiting for too long for something not worth the effort. All were wearing dress uniform, their Sunday best. A couple of them leered at her without any of the energy that suggested intent. Steel Plate's confused friend wasn't among them.

'Church Parade, for atheists.' He laughed. 'At least we can sit in a pew for an hour, sleeping.'

Mona forced a small smile. 'How is your friend?'

His face fell slightly, and he shrugged. 'Not well, for two days now. His memory … well, it isn't something I can speak of, you understand.' The smile returned. 'But he remembers you! The pretty girl in the café, he won't be quiet about it, all the time, the girl, the girl, the girl! You have a conquest!'

Mona flushed. She had accepted the fact that she attracted men for almost as long as she had resented it, but being the occasion of someone's relief in distress subverted her usual irritation - it was as though she was now obliged to take an interest in his wellbeing, in whether he thrived in a world he was partly the cause of spoiling. She tried to hope the best for him, knowing what value *hope* had in the scheme of things.

Steel Plate waved at their particular stretch of Unter den Eichen. 'Shall I see you across the road?'

The offer could hardly be refused, though it seemed to be taking politeness to an extreme. As they walked he held up a hand to approaching traffic, as if his rottenfuhrer's stripe had the authority to suspend the world's motion for gallantry's sake. The driver of a military truck passed by slowly and winked, amused at the effrontery. The family who had unwittingly adopted Mona on the south side of Unter Den Eichen were still at its opposite kerb, trying to assemble their brood into marching order. The soldier released her arm as they reached them and saluted, the old way, with the self-conscious flair that Americans did in movies.

'*Auf wiedersehn*, Fraulein.'

He didn't look back at her as he returned to his comrades. So it had been a courtesy after all. She felt almost ashamed, and then she almost left her skin.

'Was that…?'

She hadn't heard him approach. How ironic that she'd feared to be alone outdoors, when acquaintances seemed to be employing themselves in shifts to ensure that she had company.

'The man with the damaged head, yes. Hello, Herr Schroeder.'

'Paul, please.' He smiled, but his eyes were tired. The *hilfspolizei* uniform was the neatest thing about him. Its contents were pallid, stooped, in need of a bench to ease the aches of a day spent mostly on his feet. He was looking across the road, watching … *Horst*, she recalled, speak to his friends.

'That young man saw me. I wonder why he didn't wait and say something?'

'He may not have recognized you.'

'No.' Paul smiled. 'No reason why he should, in *my* case.'

The tease was too gentle to make her uncomfortable. Of all her old men, Herr Schroeder - *Paul* - was the one who most filled her expectations of a father, that missing element of her childhood. A few of the others could be *too* fatherly, and indulged an urge to give advice about men and their lusts when what they were doing really was rehearsing their own, crumbling desires. But Paul had never broached the subject of how she should or shouldn't conduct herself. This was as close as he had ever strayed towards expressing an opinion of her attractions.

He glanced up and down Unter den Eichen, doing his policeman's duty, reassuring himself that no bye-laws were being broken. The family was moving off, towards the entrance of the Gardens. As they reached the open gates, a few others were entering or leaving. It was a popular attraction, even in winter - perhaps *especially* in winter, when evergreens reminded visitors that there was a world beyond greyness. It was also the only space in the area that was free of military traffic, other than the off-duty soldiers with their wives or girlfriends who were as much a feature of the Gardens as the plants themselves, a part of what made Lichterfelde what it was. But something else, the unspoken thing, strained the atmosphere here, and Mona felt it now, a slight otherness to what should have been merely a sense of wellbeing.

'Do you have *intuitive* feelings?'

'Do I ...?' The question itself seemed intuitive to the point of clairvoyance. She almost gaped at him.

'I'm sorry.' He was embarrassed. 'That wasn't quite what I meant to say. Do you ever sense that someone is trying to say something and you understand this, but without hearing the words?'

'Of course.' For a moment she was puzzled. They lived in an age that encouraged sleight of language. How else was an opinion ever to be known, that went against what was permitted?

'Will you walk with me? My shift is almost finished, and I'd appreciate your help.' He held out his arm for a moment and then withdrew it. 'Perhaps not on duty, eh?'

Mona's plan for her day was obviously doomed, but she was out of doors, which had been the point of it. She let him lead her, hoping no one would assume that she was being arrested very courteously. They walked east until Unter den Eichen became Schloss-Strasse, following its swerve to the north, and Paul told her of his recent thoughts. He was surprised that she had heard of - had actually *met* - Eddie Muntz, but that was a good thing if she better understood what he was trying to put into words. When they reached Steglitz police station he went in to make his report and sign off while she examined the sparse contents of the shop windows further north. After a few minutes, he emerged in his civilian guise (he had lost his *schlagstock* and cap) and they resumed their walk. Briefly, he told her his intention. She agreed that it was logical given his feelings about what had been said, and agreed to help if she could. It was meant more in the spirit of things, but he took it as something else, and suddenly Mona realised that she had entirely misunderstood the purpose of their encounter.

'Here we are.'

They were directly in front it - she could hardly believe that they had been getting closer, speaking of it, and she hadn't made the connection. Confronted by the test, her courage drained away.

'But how can we ask?' It would have been easy once, a matter of walking in and making a polite enquiry. Now, nothing could be passed off as innocent curiosity.

He smiled, shrugged. 'We're only lovers of the art, come to pay homage. Who could object to that? I hear that all the leadership have private arrangements at their homes, so they must be fans, too. We're doing nothing *wrong*.'

The doors were locked, naturally. He knocked again, quite loudly, and waited. The long silence that followed cheered her considerably, until a cough - a wracking, lung-deep cough - and the rattle of a key in a lock quashed her hopes for a swift retreat back to her lonely, safe café.

An old woman glowered up at them, her hands dripping water. 'Closed by order of the Reich', she intoned like a bored railway announcer. The door began to move, and Paul had to be quick.

'Please. I'm sorry to disturb you. Is the manager available?'

'No.' The head continued to shake emphatically, long after the word was grudgingly released.

'Ah.' Paul smiled apologetically and removed a piece of paper from his pocket. 'This would be … Herr Rolf Wedeger?'

'No! He's been retired for years. Since 1940.' The remorseless trajectory of time's arrow seemed to cheer her, and the scowl lightened fractionally.

'Oh, dear. We wanted to talk about some of the old shows here, and perhaps look at the programmes. Would the new manager be able to help…?'

'Him! He knows nothing about the Arts! He used to be a shoe salesman before the Poles shot off his foot.' She cackled, pleased at the irony. 'He knows the price of the tickets he can't sell, nothing else!'

Paul and Mona looked at each other. Apparently an investigation was more difficult than its cinematic representation - which, of course, was another irony.

The old lady's stared unblinkingly at them, as discouraging as a large dog at a gate. 'Do you want Herr Wedeger's address, then?'

'Oh, yes', Paul said, slightly dazed, 'that would be wonderful.'

The door closed. Given the size of the building, her age and the difficulty in finding the correct paperwork Mona expected a long wait. But it opened again within a minute, and the old woman thrust a small note into her hand. 'He lives five doors from my niece, in Lindenstrasse.'

The door slammed in their faces once more, killing the thanks on Paul's lips. Mona passed the note to him and took a step back to look up, beyond the huge concrete overhang at the ocean liner *chic* above it. In all these years, she had never set foot inside what had been the very centre of Steglitz for those seeking other worlds. She had had no girlfriends with whom to be thrilled, titillated or cast into brief, hopeless adoration by the latest Gods of the screen, no boyfriends to attempt her underwear during the darker scenes, never an inclination to have any of it otherwise. People often spoke with moist regard for the place, as if it were a portal into imagination itself. Mona thought of it rather as a substitute, for minds that couldn't make the effort unaided.

Paul seemed pleased with the results of his very first interrogation. Tentatively but very properly, he touched her arm once more.

'We can try him now, if you don't mind?'

Whereas the majestic door of *Titania-Palast* had been a cold, unwelcoming thing, the modest entrance to Lindenstrasse 14 almost left its hinges in welcome. Herr Rolf Wedeger was pleased - no, *delighted* - to be of any service he could, and demanded only the use of two willing sets of ears in payment. For almost half an hour he rummaged through seemingly chaotic piles of memorabilia, stolen or rescued from the *Titania* when he retired. Each discovery was punctuated with a knowledgeable provenance - the stars he had known, the productions variously successful, disastrous or notorious, the concerts that had challenged the Schlosspark itself with their quality. Paul listened enthusiastically and threw in his own, strictly amateur recollections while Mona put on a brave, *faux*-intrigued face and hoped that some sort of point might wander along before darkness fell.

'Eddie Muntz! Of *course* I remember!' Herr Wedeger's face lit up further, and his hands slapped his knees, dislodging a scrapbook. 'We still see each other sometimes for tea - well, you know, whatever's available - and talk about the good times.'

My God, that would be a fascinating conversation Mona thought, sourly.

'I was hoping to find a programme for a particular evening, when Eddie appeared at the Titania.' Paul pretended to search for the date in his memory. 'It was back in October 1937 - the 12th, I think.'

'Oh?' Wedeger was politely intrigued. 'Is it a *significant* date?'

'For me, yes. It was the only time that my wife saw Eddie. She's dead now, but the evening holds memories, you understand?'

'Of course. Here …' A box, nondescript among its brethren, was located immediately and lifted clear from the pile; '… this is 1937, the latter half. It was a good year for live performance, but not so much for celluloid. The *Reichsfilmkammer*, of course …'

Paul nodded. The Party's grip on German cinema had tightened considerably after 1936, when foreign films had been all but banned and criticism of the content of what remained regulated severely. Audiences had voted with their wallets, and venues like *Titania-Palast*, fortunate enough to possess adequate stage areas, had hastily put on more variety and concert programmes to entice them back. Until war rejuvenated cinema by the simple expedient of making everyone's reality unbearable, live shows had enjoyed a small renaissance.

The box's upper layers comprised neatly rolled posters and smaller bills, but beneath them sat a stack of programmes. Paul sifted through them quickly, and frowned. 'There isn't one for 12 October.'

Herr Wedeger leaned over him. 'Impossible! Wait …' He lifted one dated the previous week. 'Ah, now, this is of *historic* importance! Do you recall the Zimmermannstrasse fire?'

'The cotton bales!'

A dry autumn, a fully stocked cotton factor's warehouse and an idiot night-watchman, over fond of brandy and a pipe - a lethal combination. It had required water-engines from three Berlin boroughs to douse the blaze, and a whole stretch of Schloss-Strasse had been cordoned off for days thereafter.

'We couldn't open, so the show that should have featured on 5 October was postponed until the following week.' Herr Wedeger smiled apologetically and passed the programme to Paul. 'It didn't seem worthwhile to get them reprinted.'

Eddie Muntz had been third-billed that evening, following a mezzo-soprano and a mesmerist. There was no child-act on the programme, nor any artist who required the services of an assistant. Disappointed, Paul returned the precious object to its curator.

Mona coughed. 'Did you have a resident orchestra, Herr Wedeger?'

The old man laughed. 'We didn't have the space or funds for an *orchestra*! But we had a small chamber group to accompany singers when more than a piano was necessary. Of course, they weren't contracted solely to the establishment.'

'And was there a young girl in this group?'

'No. There were several ladies of a certain age, and two very old men whose best playing years had been given over to Viennese waltzes. But a girl? Definitely not.'

She was a lovely, lovely child. Paul thought of Muntz, saying it so wistfully. Had there been an emphasis he had missed, a gaze that was cast much further than he had assumed?

'The ladies - did you know any of them personally?'

Herr Wedeger smiled. 'I knew two of them very well. Frau Kieller, the cellist, was at school with me when Lichterfelde was hardly more than a small village. She won her first prize in music before we graduated. The other, well …' He gazed at the programme in his hands and sighed. 'A terrible thing, that such a woman should …'

'Herr Wedeger?'

'The second violin, Frau Ziegler, lately murdered by some fiend that the police - forgive me for saying it, but it's true - don't seem to want to catch.'

Paul leaned forward, trying to quash his eagerness. 'Frau *Sigrun* Ziegler?'

'Yes, though professionally she used her maiden name, Metzger. It was better known in the business - she had been a child prodigy, you see? And *Sigrun*, oh dear me, no! She *hated* that, always said that her parents had cursed her with it. She much preferred her middle name, *Sylvie*. It was what everyone called her.'

A chain of command should be just that, he thought. When he got an order, he obeyed it and that was how it *should* be. When two orders came together, he was required to use his judgement, and that wasn't so good. When two orders arrived separately and contradicted each other it was the fucking Italian Army and things needed to change. He had too many bosses, and they weren't talking to each other.

It had been like that in the old days too, he recalled. At first it had been simple, a specific job with clear goals and a sensible strategy to achieve them; but then things got complicated, as things were liable to do. Some of his comrades hadn't been able to deal with it as well as they should, and even some of the officers, too. So the redeployments had started, the search for different ways to do what was needed, and suddenly everyone had a great, different idea from the next man. That was a bad way to do things. Soon, no one knew what it was they were supposed to be doing any more. He'd heard that other groups had come to entirely different ideas about the way to go about it. In some cases, individual units within the same groups were going their own ways, making up procedures, trying out new things as they went along. How the fuck was *that* supposed to work?

At the end, it had been a relief to be extracted. A lot of them had started to hit the bottle hard, or get a little crazy and play games with their service pistols during the long winter evenings. Worst of all they were writing home, tearful stuff about how no one understood what this war was going to require before it was over. *Jesus!* No wonder the lid had come down on the whole business. It had been a shame, though, he'd often thought since.

But lids aren't always sufficiently tight to keep the maggots in. What *this* one covered was always going to need the assistance of a heavy arse, pressing firmly downward. He'd been warned about that, been told that it wasn't the kind of thing he could retire from or put behind him, ever. That was fine, he didn't even want a voice in how they dealt with it. An army wasn't a democracy, after all. But he'd given his opinion as to what might happen if they weren't single-minded, and that was the problem now - there wasn't a single mind applying itself. Too many important fellows felt that what they had to say about it should be heard and considered, and nothing done that they didn't agree to beforehand. It was like a permanent General fucking Staff meeting, with no Führer to wave a hand and shut them up.

He'd been comfortable with his initial orders. What else could they have done? But it had become messier because they'd lost their nerves, these important fellows. They'd expected surgical neatness, the clever application of a suture to contain the business entirely, and he could have told them how likely *that* would be. If he'd taken any lesson from the cards he'd been dealt, it was that everything came down to spotting the complications and handling them before they handled you.

So now, as mad as it was, he was obliged to take the initiative and do the Brass's thinking for them while *they* struggled to remove the finger from their best feature. They knew perfectly when what was happening. Things had begun to seep several ways, any one of which might lead to the detonator; yet one of them was saying one thing, and another the opposite, and the third well, perhaps or not, but either way not just yet. He - *it* - couldn't work like this.

He hadn't even bothered to tell them about the car. Like everyone else, they could suspect whatever they wanted, but proving it would be impossible. Let them complain when they heard about it. Let them tell him he was being irresponsible, or insubordinate, or showing too much initiative. He'd tell them right back, fine, *you* deal with it, but do it now - *you're* the ones with things to lose. Of course, they'd put it straight back upon him, and when they did he could tell them what still needed to be done, and then they'd say yes, and no, and perhaps. But for once, he'd insist.

Another four or five at most, he'd tell them - *if* they moved quickly. It was hardly unthinkable in the present scale of things. If not - if they waited, weighing consequences, trying to gauge what the exposures were - then the target would be a moving, multiplying one, and it would need an unusually accurate visit from the RAF to put it right. It was all a matter of dealing quickly with the odds and calling it something other than murder.

Let them decide the priorities, he'd just be happy to have clear orders for once. But the girl, that wasn't an option. The others had scattered slivers of information, too few and slight to assemble into anything meaningful (at least not yet, and how much more time did any of them have?). In their case, there was probably time to make decisions one way or the other. She *knew*, though. He'd been there when she heard it. He was almost certain that she hadn't really paid attention, otherwise everything would be fucked by now. But hoping that her ignorance would continue undisturbed was not a strategy. Whatever was said or decided upon back in Berlin, she was first - it was only prudent. And this time he was going to do it the sensible way, with help. God knew he had enough shit to scatter, if a certain party made any difficulties about lending a hand. It was time he was covered.

He admitted it, he'd made a bad mistake. He should have dealt with her at the time, rather than wait and ask for instructions. But that was always the German way, to put things through channels, to leave a trail of correct procedures. It was how things were done. It was also why they had a problem at all.

22

Freddie Holleman took a while to get it out, and then it was difficult to stem the flow. It was a big thing that they'd done, the risks they'd taken for him. Hell, that was the problem - it couldn't continue, not with the way things were going, not with fucking car bombs and dead police. It was worse even than they'd feared - if the shit coming their way had been of the official sort there'd be at least forms to be filled and a hope that a word from the right mouth in the right ear might do some good. But this way, they were as safe as geese perched on a Stalin Organ. Look, it was him and the twins - if they disappeared again there'd be no reason why the rest of them couldn't just walk away from the business. If they didn't show their faces in Lichterfelde, asking the right people the wrong questions, why would anyone chase them? It was definitely for the…

Gerd Branssler interrupted him. In a quiet, reasonable tone, he told Holleman not to talk out of his puckered end. Perhaps they'd been as dumb as Poles to take it on in the first place, but wasn't it obvious that the sort of people they were up against wouldn't be *reasonable*? If at least three old ladies, a *kripo* and (for all they knew) two Luftwaffe officers were worth cacking to keep something quiet, was it likely they'd leave loose ends dangling on the chance that the said ends had got bored and wandered off? What, he asked, was Freddie thinking? That because he managed to get away with one disappearing act when no one knew or cared he could repeat the trick when the bastards knew perfectly well that he was out there like a primed charge, ready to fuck up their best parlours?

'May I, Gerd?' Fischer squeezed Karl Krohne's arm pre-emptively to prevent another explosion. 'He's right, Freddie. There hasn't been any chance we could drop this since Bodenschatz handed back the twins. If the bastards in front don't shoot us the ones to the rear will. I know how you feel, but *this* is all we have. Either we find and stop them, or they'll do the same to all of us.'

Holleman opened his mouth but said nothing. He was outnumbered, and wrong, and he knew it. Two of them, and probably all four, had been marked out by someone they had yet to identify, who seemed to have friends sitting in some very finely crafted chairs, exercising a degree of authority they couldn't begin to guess at. That didn't count as holding any sort of initiative - there was nothing here that looked like a choice, other than to go on or get buried.

'It *must* be Bildmann.' Branssler said for the tenth time, unnecessarily. They were all fairly certain that Bildmann was involved, but who else? There had to be an *else*.

Krohne nodded. 'And your boss, Lange.'

Fischer thought about Lange. It was tempting, but … 'I don't know, Karl. All we can say is that Lange was one of the men who questioned Dieter before he died. If he'd been told that Gerd was trying to prise the lock off something they'd all been told to leave alone, he was doing no more than his job. It smells, but orders are called that for a reason. We don't have a *why*, do we? What if Lange's being prodded by someone further up the tree?' Panzinger? Someone we can't guess at?'

'Ach!' Branssler kicked the tiny office's only chair into the partition wall. 'We've got *nothing* on *anyone*! This is fucking tragic!'

No one found the better light to put it in. They had taken up a headlong chase of something that refused to show a face, a motive, a purpose, with all the misplaced confidence of blind me proposing to expose the secrets of Purple. If anyone recalled them when it was over it would be as Germany's very own Polish Cavalry, or - and Fischer told himself to check this with Holleman, a pilot, at a convenient moment - an occidental Divine Wind detachment.

In the pause, he summoned what they had and tried to put it as simply as he could. 'Bildmann - if it *is* him - reports to someone. He doesn't work alone, or on a whim. He does it for a reason, so there's a connection between the three women - the three women we *know* to have been killed. Finding that connection would expose someone who's willing to have police killed to prevent it. There *is* something to be discovered, and the women knew it.'

'But we have no idea what it is, or how to find it.'

'That's not quite right, Karl.' Fischer scratched his head. Getting it into words was as difficult as the problem itself. 'We must have the potential to uncover the thing, otherwise why would Dieter have died, and someone attempt to send you and Freddie into Space? We must be close to it, even if we can't make it out.'

Branssler pulled a face. 'So we *aren't* shit?'

Fischer almost smiled. 'I didn't say that. But this doesn't smell like any great secret conspiracy, does it? If we had access to the records we'd probably have made it out by now. Hell, if we're right about Agatha Fuhrmann and her Hollerith machines, it may *be* the records.'

'But we can't get near them. Dieter proved that, the poor bastard.'

'I know. And there aren't any more doors that we can usefully knock upon. It's frustrating.'

Krohne's office carpet, used to scrutiny, took a fourfold dose for several minutes. Eventually, it was Karl himself who said what they'd all been trying not to think.

'Well, if we don't drop it, there's the one sure way of finding our man, or men. We carry on as before, and let it all come to us.'

Fischer nodded. 'And hope that we keep breathing. But not Freddie, not with the twins to …'

'Balls. This is mad, but it's all for me, so no more talk.'

'If it's the only plan we …' Branssler paused. Detmar Reincke was peering around Krohne's door.

'Sorry, Karl. There's …'

'Not now, Detmar.'

'But …'

'Fuck off, Detmar.'

The head disappeared. Fischer turned to Krohne. 'Karl, get a message to Herr Ministerial Direktor Schapper: tell him that we'll have a name or names for him within forty-eight hours.'

'But …'

' … he'll almost certainly tell someone, who'll tell someone, who'll take it as bad news, yes. Then all we need to do is not become dead.'

'Oh, wonderful.'

'We do it *kripo*-style, Karl. You and me out front being inconvenient, Gerd and Freddie following and watching, ready to jump whoever takes offence.'

Holleman snorted. 'Jump? With this leg? No, I'll come with you, and Karl can …'

Fischer stopped him with a hand and caught Krohne's eye. 'Karl, if someone goes for Freddie and me, you'd shoot him?'

'Of course! I …'

'And your aim? The eye you managed not to lose is the bad one, isn't it? I don't think so. We'll be safer, just, with Freddie and Gerd doing the business. *You* don't mind shooting people, do you, Gerd?'

Branssler grinned broadly, said nothing.

Holleman shrugged. Shoot or be shot at wasn't any sort of choice. 'So we wait. But where?'

'We make it as convenient for them as possible. Lichterfelde is where at least one of our men is most comfortable at his business. That being the case, we ...'

'Karl, really, this is important ...'

Reincke was back. Krohne sighed. 'Jesus, Detmar, what is it? Are the Ivans in Wilhelmstrasse?'

'From Kondom Ernst at the front door, he said you'd want to know. Three women have just .... *turned up* at reception. They're looking for *you*!'

Bewildered, Krohne turned to the others for clarification. Their grinning monkey faces dropped almost instantly.

'Herr Fischer! We *knew* we should find you here!'

In the main office, Frau Traugott dismissed a red-faced stabsgefreiter with an imperious flick of her hand. She wore her best black coat, her only hat and a pair of red carpet slippers. Her sister, holding her arm, was casting a critical eye over the desks and their war-scarred occupants, subjecting Luftwaffe Intelligence to a spot inspection from which certain stringent conclusions might be drawn. Behind them, a handsome, dark woman in her mid-forties held a small suitcase and a coat. Her eyes were fixed upon a single point. Fischer, who didn't know the lady, imagined he could detect a degree of defiance - or perhaps resolution - in that steady gaze. Friedrich Holleman, who most certainly knew her, recognized it as the granite shore upon which a thousand arguments had broken.

'Oh, Kristin', he said plaintively, 'what are you *doing*?'

This one was also addressed to him personally. There was no signature, so it was either a prank or someone who expected to be known. But it wasn't Horst's hand or that of any of his colleagues, and as far as could say he had no other correspondents. And what the hell did it mean?

Lichterfelde West Station, 3pm. Manoeuvres, Blondie.

He looked at the envelope once more. It was definitely an external item, yet directed to him at his section, Amt W, sealed to keep its contents discreet and hand-delivered rather than posted. Everything about it said *joke*, other than the message. He didn't know what he was supposed to make of it.

He frowned at the thing for a while, resenting the disturbance to his peace of mind (if *mind* wasn't putting it too confidently). But he knew that he couldn't just ignore it - he had lost too much memory to dismiss what he didn't recognize. He made a decision, and then went down the corridor to arrange the obvious precaution.

Horst agreed to come, to be the moral or physical support. He liked the mystery of it, winked, tapped his nose, said something about killing two birds and then went to get permission from their watch commander, confident that there'd be no problem. And of course there wasn't. Lothar was aware that everyone in his section knew about his episodes by now, that discussions had begun already about relieving him of his duties and placing him permanently in a lazarett. But they were keen to be *reasonable*, to be amenable to any initiative that would cost nothing but might help, at least as far as to cover their arses - or, if he were to entertain a truly ridiculous thought, their consciences. So, a little after 2.30pm, when he should have been expecting half an afternoon's work at his desk still, he and Horst strolled out of the front gates of SS WHVA and into the civilian respectability of Lichterfelde West - two gentlemen at their ease, promenading like Imperial Cadets on an aristocratically-paced training regime.

As they walked west and then south, he concentrated upon the kerb in front of him, the rhythm of his pace, the sound of Horst's voice (which rose and fell according to what a particular story required but never for a moment stopped). It wasn't so bad - the day was fine and the air held a welcome freshness, and by regulating his breathing he found that he could add another prop to the fragile equilibrium that kept his head just this side of disordered.

There were few people on the streets. Horst had a *good afternoon* ready for the occasional civilian that passed them by, and invariably received a fearful, suspicious glance for his trouble. The human traffic increased slightly as they came to Curtius-Strasse and the few retail businesses that remained open in that part of Lichterfelde West, most of it either coming from or entering the railway station approach. The sudden contraflow, the confusion of several uncomplementary movements, threw his composure and he stopped at the corner of Sternstrasse, breathing deeply, trying to calm himself. Horst waited, gripping his arm, and by a supreme effort of will managed not to speak for almost a minute.

When Lothar was sure that he wouldn't embarrass himself further, he looked up. 'Sorry, Horst, I was ...'

'I know. Look, he can't miss you if you sit here. I'm going into the station for a minute, but I'll come straight back.'

The station, of course. Horst's eagerness to get out of the office hadn't been solely about his comrade's wellbeing - there was also the matter of the healthy, highly illegal flow of contraband goods between Unter den Eichen and Lichterfelde West station. Horst's home brewed poison was servicing the station master's liver on a regular basis, in return for which a rare supply of Turkish cigarettes (from the latter's cousin, a factor stranded in Istanbul since the outbreak of war and happy to be so) represented gold-standard currency back at WVHA. The latest consignment must have arrived, courtesy of some magic sleight of transportation organized by the German rail workers' mafia. Lothar smiled at his own naiveté, pleased that he wasn't the precise centre of everyone's concern.

It wasn't so cold that he minded waiting on the bench. His fragile head needed to slow down, to behave, and the weather helped. For a few moments he concentrate on watching his feet, letting their familiar shape sedate his thoughts until he felt he might risk another attempt at the visual confusion of Curtius-Strasse. Knowing what to expect was half the danger removed, and this time it wasn't nearly as disturbing. Carefully, he turned to look west, into the fading light. The illusion of warmth on his face was pleasant, though the dying sun gave off little enough of it. There were only a few people to be seen in that direction, away from the commercial heart of

Lichterfelde, towards Zehlendorf. He wondered idly if this was one of the artificial boundaries that cities sometimes had, the two places keeping their own company, sundered by the southward slash of Thielallee, whether there had been a noble estate or other obstacle here once, a natural boundary to stop them merging. It might have been a river of course, now underground or diverted. Or perhaps his withered imagination had seen few people and assumed much from it.

He turned slightly. Directly ahead of him the station approach, slightly busier with human and motor traffic both, an expected spectacle. He saw travellers and delivery vehicles, mothers and children, piled sandbags that hardly impeding the thin flow, two reservist soldiers guarding this vital hub of the Reich's transportation system and Horst, his hand clutching the precious delivery, arguing or negotiating with a man at the station's entrance. His head assimilated all of it without threatening another swoon. And then he glanced east, towards Steglitz, where the failing light was already making it difficult to distinguish what was happening in that direction.

'Still prettier than an altar boy, eh, Fuchs?'

He turned, surprised, not hearing the words. It was the voice itself that threw him, a sound of ...

And the face - quite ordinary, nothing in it that might give clues to what lay behind, only the old, familiar light in the eyes, the sparkle of what everyone had taken to be drollery before they came to know him, to understand his little eccentricities. Lothar opened his mouth. He had nothing ready to say, no sensible thoughts to supply the words, but it didn't matter - the thin, hard lips were moving again, saying things that didn't lend themselves to interruption or reason. He listened without wishing to, hoped for them to end, and gratefully surrendered to the sound of his own blood removing him from them.

It seemed then - though he couldn't be sure - that he was alone once more. For a while he thought that he was sleeping, though with little of the comfort that the state usually allowed. An unfocused rhythm disturbed him slightly, otherwise there was an extraordinary absence of feeling, as if he were already dead in all but the perception of it. What he took to be noise blocked out any sense of things around him, yet he could hear nothing that was capable of being resolved into a sound. All sensation lay in a mist, everything equally undistinguishable.

Something moved eventually, something he assumed to be his eyelids, and he was looking upwards into a distorted sky. Horst's face intruded from one side, spoiling the view, the mouth working silently at some secret message. Everything else was blurred, in a plane beyond his ability to distinguish. Data came in from his distant spine, a coldness which he took to be the stone beneath him, a slight lack of *rightness* to the position in which he lay, and a metronomic pulse of something that might be a bruise or worse, given time. But he experienced them with no more immediacy than if he was reading a circulated departmental report upon Expected Events when Falling, Unprepared. If this was the moment that had been threatening for months, he could bear it almost gratefully.

Horst was talking still, making no noise. *Good old Horst*, he thought fondly, *it's absolutely his favourite pastime*. Or perhaps he was shouting - the mouth was moving in an exaggerated fashion, the face quite flushed, the arms busy at some business, though their extremities were out of range of his partial vision. The view shook a couple of times and then modified, tipping slightly, and Lothar realised that he was being raised from the horizontal. That wouldn't do - he was quite comfortable as he was or insensible, it didn't really matter which.

Horst, please don't.

But the matter proceeded as if he hadn't been heard, and soon he was seeing all sorts of things - buildings, cars, people near and far, a dog. His skewed perspective gradually settled into what on other days he might have regarded as a kind of normalcy. *My God* he thought, thoroughly astonished. *I'm standing*.

Noises returned with other sensations, mostly painful ones. His head began to feel as if a rusty bar had cleaved it; one side of his back was stiffening quite badly, and the numbness in his left hand had taken that metronomic pulse and sharpened it to a throb. But what struck him most forcibly was what he was seeing - or rather, *how* he was seeing it.

Between ten and fifteen people were in his field of view. Three were close by, almost beside him, passers-by who had been moved to lend a hand but deterred by the uniform, perhaps. Several more stood at a distance, idly taking in the minor spectacle without any inclination to involve themselves. Those furthest from him, unaware of the drama, were going about their business as citizens did. But he was seeing them *all* of a piece, not as he had come to see the world, as isolated segments within a series of layered, dislocated planes, like sets in a child's cardboard theatre. He was taking in data instinctively - there was no longer a queue of perceptions, with his mind at the door, allowing them in one at a time or telling them to bugger off somewhere else. And his body … he stood upon feet that were a little unsteady still from the shock of the fall, but they no longer felt unsure of the contact they made with the ground. A sense of what he recalled as balance had replaced the conscious effort to achieve it.

Horst spoke, trying to prise out a reaction, but he didn't answer. Behind the other, remarkable stimulae that crowded around and in him was an echo, a trace of something both alien and abiding, a familiar thing to which he couldn't begin to put a name. He sniffed the air - it was cold, winter-sterile, nothing in it of greater interest that a hint of diesel. The sounds carrying around the station approach were equally mundane, and expected - engines approached and faded, muffled voices, a radio broadcasting a public information message, half-heard through the open door of a shop behind him. He glanced around, found nothing that might cause a damaged head to explode.

'Something ...'

'Something? What? What the fuck is going on?'

'A … ' Lothar's conscious mind tried vainly to push through gewgaws that spilled prodigally from long interment, to separate memory from now, to strip out a particular from the generality of his new, more rational confusions. But all he found was a sense of high, near anxiety - he was frightened of *something* he couldn't see or recall, but the fear had a quality that dreams brought, of things imminently falling, a … *threat.*

He couldn't imagine anything more terrible than the loss of the self, but there it was, unseen, unknown, unbearable, dragging unformed torments. He grasped Horst's arm, his fingers digging painfully into muscle. 'Quickly!'

Horst looked at him, dumbfounded. But then, as he always did, he made up his mind one way or the other, all the way.

'Well, go on!'

It was insane, but they followed a wraith, accelerating as Lothar realised that none of his pains flagged real damage. His stomach was taut and griping as always, but he had become so used to it that he no longer compensated. Ahead of them, a few civilians and a couple of uniforms moved towards or away from them on the street's south side. He saw nothing unusual, out of place, wrong in that setting.

By the time they reached Drakestrasse, he was sprinting. With hardly a glance, he threw himself across the road, half-sensing a passage through the thin traffic. Horst followed; a set of brakes squealed, a driver cursed them, and then they were across and into Steglitzerstrasse. It was getting darker, difficult to distinguish one person from another, but the hunched shapes, now almost indistinct, hid in their anonymity something that had thrust a blade into his head. He carried on, breathless almost, and hardly noticed the small group of men, moving in the same direction, who remonstrated as he and his friend forced a passage through them and swerved to the right at the corner with Kyllmanstrasse. The fear, the *threat*, began to resolve itself into words, terrible disconnected shards rising from what in other men might be called memory. He felt no surprise when in the last of the dusk he saw it, barely a hundred metres away, disappearing into another street - Sophiastrasse.

'There!'

'What?' Horst tried to slow their pace but Lothar ignored him, running on across Kyllmanstrasse, forcing his friend to follow. He felt a hand clutching his sleeve to pull him up, but he resisted, letting his momentum carry them both forward. They saw it then together, perfectly isolated against a solitary light, and all the fragmented, discordant cadences of Lothar Fuch's mind reassembled precisely into order, their deadly little tune recalled.

24

Branssler's logic was irresistible. There really was no other way - neither Kristin Holleman nor the old ladies could return to Jonas-Strasse without exposing themselves to people who had ceased to worry about consequences, which left only the safe house. Had he two hands still, Detmar Reinke would have been the obvious, discreet choice to take them there in the back of one of the Ministry's smaller trucks, but Salomon Weiss knew the alley (he had been raised near Spittelmarkt and done most of his adolescent thieving within the warren of streets between there and the Spree Canal) and he volunteered before they asked.

Fraus Traugott and Ostermann accepted their sudden change in circumstances unquestioningly. It was, as they had often observed, *war*, and their understanding of that condition encompassed a certain expectation of metaphorical winds, or tides, both of which went where they willed. In any case, as Frau Traugott admitted, they missed their new nephews, who were far less able than semi-feral cats to survive without the care and affection of a brace of aunts. A brief, frantic visit to the Ministry's kitchens, during which both Fischer and Krohne surrendered their entire reserves of cigarettes and a half-bottle of Obstwasser, secured supplies for the next two days at least. To these Holleman added a small medical kit (stolen from the office cupboard) and the Beretta 1934 he had lost to Reinke in a game of skat almost two years earlier but now requisitioned. It came with just the single magazine, seven bullets.

'Freddie, are you eating?' It was the only thing Frau Holleman said before she left with the others, but with a wife's cruel knack of conveying far more than the words. Her husband blushed deeply as she kissed him; the other men in the room made a point of being interested in paperwork or the charts on the wall while he went through his pockets, gave her every pfennig he had and whispered something no one wanted to overhear. Branssler scribbled a note and gave it to her - an address near Dusseldorf, a place to hide if things went badly.

Two guards burst into the office, their faces flushed with embarrassment, fear for their arses or the effort of negotiating three flights of stairs without touching them. Krohne halted them with a hand, a frown and a sympathetic nod, as if permitting civilians to penetrate the Luftwaffe's heartland was an entirely understandable error and nothing more need be said. When they were gone, Weiss herded the ladies the other way down the corridor, towards the back stairs that led down to the vehicle pool. Fischer went to his office, a cubicle that now seemed to him an unfamiliar space, and took his last will and testament from the drawer in which it had sat since the morning General Bodenschatz sent for them. He gave it to Reincke, asked that he post it to the address in Freiburg if necessary. The boy said nothing - he seemed uncomfortable, as though compliance would hasten the thing anticipated. Krohne telephoned the new, re-relocated *Forschungsamt* headquarters at Jüterbog, had a brief, possibly fatal discussion with an aide to the Ministerial Direktor and then the four men left the Ministry together, taking no pains not to be noticed.

Two plain-clothed SD men followed them from there to Gross-Görsch-Strasse, the temporary terminus for the Teltow line and, from a platform telephone, made a brief report to RSHA Amt III, Prinz-Albrecht-Strasse. The SD men were followed in turn by a lone Gestapo *kripo* who made an equally brief report to RSHA Amt IV, Prinz-Albrecht-Strasse from the same telephone. Both of these calls were observed by a uniformed oberleutnant from V Abteilung, Luftwaffe Intelligence, who had sprinted almost the entire distance from the Air Ministry following a hurried conversation with a high-ranking officer at *Forschungsamt*, Jüterbog. He had neither the breath nor orders to use the station telephone, and so he waited until his professional cousins had departed the platform and then walked the length of the waiting Lichterfelde-Teltow train, casually glancing at the passengers within. He boarded the rear carriage, cowed a guard into not enquiring about his ticket, and took a seat.

Later, the oberleutnant was congratulated upon his initiative and promoted to Hauptmann, his eyewitness testimony being an invaluable - in fact, the only reliable - source of information regarding the events of that day, which terminated the curious business at Lichterfelde.

25

Usually, Mona's fear of the world beyond her door was upon the broadest, most diffuse grounds - its easy accommodation of the worst in the human spirit, its iron indifference, its impervious coldness. But today those discomforts were narrower, more personal. She had opened a door, invited attention from those she least wished to know of her existence. She had made a point of being noticed, in an age in which the condition always had consequences.

Her life, usually, was an ordered place where impulses were discouraged. Her particular genius was steady and unremarkable; she preferred method, flows rather than eddies, and planned things ahead of doing them because she preferred to know what her tomorrows held. Today, she wondered whether there would *be* tomorrows. Of course, she was scared by what she had done with Herr Schroeder – what sensible person wouldn't be? But worse, she was a little excited by it, as if a small degree of intrepidity had wandered into her life and allowed her to penetrate the fearful silence of Lichterfelde. They had uncovered hardly more than a droplet of evidence, and she doubted that it was capable of interesting her unwelcome Luftwaffe customers, much less of bringing a murderer to justice; still, she struggled not to feel like one of the idiosyncratic, forceful heroines of her childhood novels - a rebel intellect spurning the 'proper' ways of doing things.

But that was nonsense. In her girls' adventures there had been no villains who could move through society without fear of harm or retribution. She recalled that they had been stupid louts, incompetents doing evil because they hadn't the wit to do otherwise. It was always just a matter of time and proper deduction, neatly paced, elegantly explained, and a satisfying denouement to put the drama to bed by page one hundred and fifty. She reminded herself that this was life, and life had a way of ignoring both neatness and natural justice.

The trouble was that she didn't - she couldn't - know what was happening. The police themselves knew nothing, while those who had followed knew little more. And yet here she was, armed only with an elderly reservist, pushing her face into a dark, deadly place, hoping that nothing would bite. Her only protection was the uniform that Paul wore, and that would preserve neither him nor his not-quite-fearless assistant if they woke a monster in its cave.

It was the uncertainty of it that worried her most of all. Without thinking, she'd plunged into something whose measure couldn't be known, and she wondered at her recklessness. This was not careful, prudent, invisible Mona Kreitz but a flighty imposter seduced by the fiction of courage, a fool.

So this morning she applied a cold compress to her condition, and made a point of doing some very ordinary things while thinking sensibly about others. Before she opened the café she cleaned it thoroughly, even the windows, and took down all the notices that were outdated or superseded. She scoured the coffee urn (a monthly chore, done only a week earlier), removed all the crockery from shelves and wiped their surfaces, and even took a wire brush to the wooden floor, her least favourite activity. By ten o'clock she was exhausted, and her mind had attained a reassuring blankness regarding the manifest dangers of places outside the Blue Rendezvous Café.

Her first customer was a stranger, a woman, who entered hesitantly and looked around with mild surprise as if cafés should have gone the way of steam baths and coaching inns by now. She ordered a *muckefucke* with a broad Silesian accent - a refugee, probably, though her neat clothes and easy manner suggested that she was one of the sensible ones who had planned her retreat well ahead of the Front. She stayed only as long as it took to drain her cup, and then Mona was alone again almost until noon, when her old dependables Albert and Erich moped in.

The boys were in a complaining mood - about their rations, the constant false air-raid alarms, their respective *blockhelfers*, the lengthening electricity cuts, Bavarians in general and several in particular, no beer or proper sausages to be had anywhere any more. For the best part of an hour they moaned like Olympic relayers, taking up each other's grumps without once dropping the baton, until Mona almost wished for an ear infection. It was something they did every so often, a symptom of the elderly male's menstrual cycle, the means by which they flushed out what needed to go. She was certain they would be back the following day, bright as buttons, laughing at everything that soured them today, asking her what she had to be so glum about - she was young and pretty after all, with all her life in front of her. For now, for Mona, the hands on the clock slowed in their passage across its face.

It was a great relief when her favourite customer, Oliwia Schenke, came in just after one o'clock. She was a slow, precise woman with no great conversation or desire to find any, but her heart spread its warmth far, and even the two sour faces at the counter lightened as she ambled to it.

'A cup of Dallmayr's and a slice of *eierkuchen*, please, Mona.'

It was an ancient joke, more used than the café's busiest dishcloth, but everyone appreciated it as though the words brought the scent of their lost pleasures with them. Oliwia was rewarded with the same thin, foul brew that everyone else endured. She shrugged amiably, removed her knitting from the large carpetbag that went everywhere with her and settled down to enjoy company for its own sake.

It was becoming a typical day. Mona could look forward to perhaps six or seven more customers before she glanced around an empty café, took her manageress's initiative and imposed her arbitrary closing time. Winter helped with its early darkness, so it would be five o'clock at the latest when she could lock the door, mark off another box on her calendar and, like everyone else in Germany, wonder how many boxes remained before the new world arrived. Today, she intended to take particular care to mark the box. It would remind her that boredom with the unchanging rhythm of her present life was wilful, self-indulgent.

Whatever comes will be worse than this. With Albert and Erich in front of her, haggling about nothing, and Oliwia tapping her needles expertly at the nearest table, Mona was struck suddenly by how close and safe her present horizons were. Silently, she pledged to herself that she was done with adventure, that the most she would lend to Paul Schroeder's business was a willing ear and then only if she couldn't avoid it. So what if her life was drifting, her days spent wondering where it was taking her? Much better a lack of purpose than the sort of resolution that three women - and God knew how many more by now - had achieved. Fate already loomed far over everyday, mundane things in Lichterfelde; it didn't need to be goaded further. She gave a little nod to seal the promise to herself, and Albert, thinking she was agreeing with his latest complaint, grimaced with sour contentment.

The afternoon dragged, but more pleasantly now. Three more customers came, stayed briefly and wandered out again. Albert and Erich finally dragged themselves away at 4pm and Oliwia a few minutes after that, and all the while Mona kept her mind directed firmly away from the unfortunate Sigrun Ziegler or Sylvie Metzger, from the other victims, from the beast who had killed them. She chatted when invited to, washed cups when necessary, made more of her unpalatable brew and savoured all the safety of her dreary, unchanging routine. After Oliwia shuffled out she waited almost half an hour more before closing the café. It was probably unnecessary, but she owed her employer a little perseverance - he had, after all, provided a wage and lodgings in return for what seemed to be half a job at most, and if he was wasting his money at least she didn't want to be part of the cause. So she watched the clock, willing quarter to five to move itself with a little more despatch.

The winter dusk had failed almost to darkness as she came out from behind the counter with the keys. Even during the peace, Sophiastrasse had been badly lit. Now, of course, it wasn't lit at all. The buildings opposite the café were residential; three had been shut up for several weeks now, their owners fled to relatives in the south or west, and the others had their blackout curtains drawn already. A few slivers of stray illumination showed, but no substantial sources of light that might have warned her of the approach of someone from across the street - in any case, the reflection of the cafe's solitary lamp in its own window removed any sense of movement outside. So it was only at the very moment she grasped the door handle and lifted the key to the lock that she saw him, a half-metre away, close enough to touch if the door had not been between them. And then it wasn't any more.

Part Four

1

The cell was small, a matter of three metres by two, furnished only with an iron bed hinged to the wall and a three-legged milking stool. A solitary light bulb hung from a wire too short to be of use to a desperate resident, its feeble wattage insufficient to illuminate even what lay immediately below it. A slight smell of bleach pervaded every surface, spoiling the occasional breeze that passed through the bars of the unglazed window opening to half-freeze the occupant. The floor, uncovered stone, was uneven and hard on his bare feet. He tried to keep off it as much as possible. It was clean, showing no obvious evidence of previously spilled bodily fluids, but he'd seen enough expert beatings, capable of half-crippling a man without breaking skin, to be wholly reassured.

Other than by the days he couldn't measure time here anymore than his future prospects, or the precise volume of the space that now comprised his world. He told himself that it didn't matter, that time was only useful to those with matters to fill it. Since first light that morning he had stared out of the small barred opening, distracting himself by trying to count a small group of winter wrens foraging in the yard's only tree. They were busy things, moving too quickly to be distinguished clearly, but the complex coordination of brainless industry was pleasantly hypnotic, and his under-employed mind had achieved an almost trance-like state in which his present helplessness felt like a release. All things were settled now. Initiative and will belonged to someone else at whose whim he would live or die, so to worry about which it would be was futile. He was as close to a sense of freedom as he had any right to expect. Everything he had done had invited this, or worse; he couldn't regret or wish it otherwise.

The key twisted in its lock and the cell door burst open. He had the presence of mind to jump down from the stool before they kicked it away (it was better not to encourage them to use their feet). They were in uniform but their tunics were elsewhere, shirt-sleeves rolled up to the elbows to emphasise how *physical* the job was or could be, if things went a certain way. It was all he had time to notice as each of them grabbed an arm and dragged him unresisting down the long, unlit corridor. At its end, they kicked open a door, crossed a narrow passage between buildings and elbowed their way into a small shower block. In the middle of a changing-room, its walls bearing the marks of lockers long since removed, they released his arms and pushed him down on to the only piece of furniture, a slatted bench. The one whose face looked as if it had gone six rounds with a truck jabbed him in the ribs, hard.

'Strip.'

He removed his uniform while they watched, smirking at his less-than-gorilla dimensions, appraising his wounds with what he imagined was professional interest. When he was naked the other one gave him a piece of soap and nodded at the nearest showerhead, a rusty disc over an immaculately clean but heavily chipped tile cubicle. The water was as cold as he'd feared, and he gasped as it sluiced over him. At that point they left him to it and went outside. After three days in the same clothes, sleeping on a lice-friendly pallet, they probably assumed that he wasn't minded to skip any of his harder-to-reach parts.

The shower came as a surprise; the neatly laid out uniform - his best, retrieved by someone and steam-pressed, for God's sake - astonished him. He wondered if they were working on his head, giving him three days to stew in his worst expectations, an hour, perhaps, of civilized handling before they made a start on his knees - a venerable, proven tactic. In this case, understanding the procedure didn't ease his mind.

He dried himself on a rough, tattered towel and dressed quickly. Piled on the uniform were clean underwear, socks and a shirt he didn't recognize. A new tie had been provided from stores, and his old cap, which had been taken from him when he arrived, had been improved with a fresh band. The mental picture of a violent interrogation faded. Perhaps it was to be a formal court martial, with a firing party immediately thereafter. One had to dress correctly for both, of course

His guards were waiting by the door. They had donned their unterfeldwebels' tunics and were smoking, their backs to him. He coughed politely. Truck Face turned, did the up and down, nodded. 'Very nice.' He and his mate crushed their cigarettes on the gravel. This time neither of them grabbed an arm. A wave pointed the prisoner in the required direction and they fell in beside him like iron bookends.

The moment they emerged from the passage between the cellblock and showers Fischer recognized his surroundings. He was back in Werder, the deer park, Luftwaffe's temporary - perhaps final - General Staff HQ. To his left, about three hundred metres away, stood the low block where Herr Ministerial Direktor Schapper had interviewed them only two weeks earlier. He wondered where Karl Krohne was at that moment - behind him, a matter only of some metres, or a hundred kilometres away? And Freddie? Gerd? It irritated him that his courage so quickly when he thought of them.

Brief, imperfect impressions of the Headquarters block's reception area registered as he was rushed through - a deal of confusion, or coordinated mayhem; dispatchers moving around each other like his avian friends in the cell courtyard; a lot of braid, talking too loudly as it passed by; the sudden, perfect peace of a carpeted corridor, too quickly experienced to appreciate fully for its luxurious otherness. Given a minute or two to himself he might have laid down upon it and made up some sleep.

He was bustled into a meeting room. Three men were seated at a large table, waiting, staring at briefing papers. Fischer noticed that four glasses stood beside the only water tumbler on the table, and he had to quell a stab of optimism. His handlers came to attention beside him, saluted smartly and closed the door behind them.

Schapper pointed a pencil at the only unoccupied chair. Fischer removed his cap and sat.

'You offered to bring me useful information, not to kill everyone.'

Prisoners do not speak unless invited to do so. In any case, he had no adequate answer.

The officer to Schapper's left - an oberst - coughed quietly and half-raised a finger. 'Information?'

Schapper frowned. The pencil tapped a slim folder that sat in front of his colleague. 'Page 2, second paragraph.'

The oberst opened the file, read briefly. His eyebrows rose. 'Oh.'

'You'll know that we're questioning your associates also, so don't waste my time. I've already had an official request from Direktor Panzinger for details. Needless to say I can't just ignore it, particularly as one of your gang of thugs is *his* man. We'll ask questions, you'll answer them, fully. Understand?

Fischer nodded.

'Let's come to the point, then. Do you have a name for us?'

'Yes, sir. But not the one we'd hoped for.'

'Go on.'

Fischer said it. Schapper considered it for a moment, took a deep breath, and dropped the pencil. The hand, released, rubbed the face.

'That's it? We gave you *carte blanche* to trample all over the southern suburbs, acting like the police agency of a state within the State, for *this*?'

'There were murders, Herr Direktor. There was then an effort not only to disguise the identity of the perpetrator, but to permit him to continue. We stopped that, and identified the responsible parties. It's what was promised.'

Schapper sighed. 'Don't be clever. You know who I had to convince, and upon the prospect of delivering something useful. The name you've given me won't raise a fart of interest.'

'Sir ...' Fischer leaned forward. He had perhaps one opportunity to put it the right way, to get something useful done '... *who* isn't the important point, but *why*...'

'Fischer, please don't think I have the patience for a crime novel. I don't want to know *why*! A few old ladies killed unpleasantly, it doesn't matter! Who would *care*?'

'And if it was considerably more than three, or four, or five? What if it's a matter of thousands?'

'Stop.' Schapper put down his pencil and closed the file. 'You can go.'

For a moment Fischer felt the firing post pressing against his back, but then the officers on either side of the Ministerial Direktor stood and gathered their papers. Neither man glanced at the prisoner as they left. Schapper waited until the door had closed. He was leaning back in his chair, studying the prisoner in much the same way as he might a man who had just volunteered his head to check for snipers.

'Let's be very precise here, Major. Who is it that you accuse, and upon what evidence?'

'The answer doesn't allow for precision, sir. I accuse one man of murder, if murder is the conscious act of unlawfully killing another human being. I accuse at least one, and probably two or three others, of being directly complicit. The evidence is anecdotal, but fairly strong.'

'But you said thousands.'

'It's a matter of definitions, sir. I'm referring to crimes in a legal sense. Killings sanctioned by an official process must be called something else.'

'What would *you* call them, Fischer?'

'Oh, murder, sir. But I'm only a layman.'

'Murder, then, for the sake of clarity. But of whom?'

'No one, sir.'

'*No one*?'

'Of those who do not exist.'

Schapper rose from his chair and stood at the window. For the first time, Fischer noticed the large portrait of the Führer that hung directly behind him. The image had become so ubiquitous that it was almost invisible to his German eye - a species of censorious, badly faded wallpaper, either shoring up what lay behind or preventing it from fleeing.

The window allowed a pleasant view out over the park, which the Ministerial Direktor wasn't seeing. Fischer had no instinct for other men's thoughts, but he had just embarked upon about a matter upon which silence was the wisest observation and against which ignorance the best inoculation. A wiser man might have left it at a body, expertly removed from a crime scene, disappeared without the necessity of further revelation. But then he recalled why it was that he still could look at himself in a mirror, *that* view notwithstanding.

Schapper turned back from the window. 'If *they* - and let us not use specific terms here - do not exist, then why should anyone care?'

'Someone does, sir. Someone has begun to believe that it matters after all, that things are moving to an uncomfortable situation in which certain … *events* may be viewed in a new and unhelpful light.'

'And this …'

'Is absolutely linked to the Lichterfelde business, yes.'

'Then you had better give me what you have.'

'Between 29 September and 20 October last year, three women were killed in or around Berlin's Botanical Gardens. An investigation commenced, run by RSHA Amt V with the assistance of a number of uniformed police out of Dahlem station. This was halted on 12 November, upon orders whose provenance we haven't been able to establish. Subsequent to that date, strong rumours circulated locally to the effect that further killings had occurred in the Lichterfelde West area. I now think this not to have been the case.'

Schapper frowned. 'Just the three?'

'We think so. At least, there's no evidence of more. All were killed in the same manner - strangulation, followed by ... embellishments. Nothing ritualistic, merely sexual, causing post-mortem damage.'

'He throttled them and fucked the corpses.'

'It looks that way. The perpetrator was a police officer, Rudolph Bildmann, who, ironically, was detailed to assist the investigation before it was closed down.'

'He confessed to the murders?'

'No, sir. He was caught in the act of trying to add to them.'

'And died resisting arrest.'

'Well, we'll call it that. A case might be made that there was a point during the beating he received from Kriminalkommissar Branssler at which he ceased to resist, but the officer in question didn't notice it. I did try to intervene.'

'Your arrest report mentions bruising.'

'My jaw, sir. Not broken.'

'The head generally?'

'Difficult to say. The stitches itch a little.'

'I noticed the wound. An ugly thing - but then, there's so little about your head that isn't. That was Bildmann, was it?'

'I assume so sir. He may have had an accomplice for the practical side of things. I can't be sure, one way or another.'

'He had *practical* help, certainly.'

Fischer's eyebrows rose. 'You know this?'

'The ladies were found in the Botanical Gardens. Bildmann didn't, as far as I can determine, have direct access to the WVHA building.'

'They came from *there*?'

'It would seem the likeliest means of getting them unseen into the Gardens. Bildmann must have killed them elsewhere, after all.'

Stupid. 'A tunnel.'

'Of course. How else would WVHA personnel reach their bunker with all those precious commercial contracts unscathed? It runs directly beneath Unter den Eichen.'

Disgusted, Fischer closed his eyes. They had been looking for clever answers when the truth was utterly mundane. The Botanical Gardens were the perfect setting in which to amplify the depravity of the crimes, but that probably hadn't been the point - they were simply the most convenient dumping ground.

Schapper almost smiled. 'So, yet another irony - that the WVHA building was your *latest* theory on the killer's home yet you absolved it of any part in the mechanical process. I assume that your dramatic encounter with the deceased occurred as the result of some other brilliant deduction on your part?'

'No, sir. We'd intended to be discovered by him, to flush him out by inferring that we were close to a resolution. Which is why we told *you* the same thing.'

Schapper flushed slightly. 'You knew that Panzinger would pass on the message?'

'We hoped so, though we had no reason to think that the Direktor was involved in the business. Not at the time, anyway.'

'And now?'

'May I come to that?'

'Soon, if you please.'

'As I said, the encounter was lucky, in more than one sense. Bildmann was intending a further crime, which we shouldn't have been able to prevent were it not for the intervention of two courageous young men. Sadly, one of them didn't survive the encounter.'

'Both of them, in fact.'

Fischer stared at the Ministerial Direktor. 'No! Really? I thought the wound ...'

'Someone else might have lived, but it was a gut shot, to a man who didn't have much gut to spare. He died yesterday morning, at Reinickendorf. Peacefully, if it matters.'

'Reinickendorf? Didn't his people object?'

'We didn't tell them immediately. Luftwaffe officers were involved in the incident, so all injured parties were removed to a service lazarett. They seem to have accepted the explanation. I doubt the boy would have received better care elsewhere.'

'He must have told you …'

'He said nothing, nothing at all. Apparently you had his first and last word on the business.'

Fischer felt a stab of genuine regret. 'He was anxious that we should know. Whether he wanted absolution or understanding, I can't say. He didn't excuse himself.'

'Of what?'

'Of the mass-murder of civilians, and rape, and other familiar sins of war. Of allowing orders to substitute for humanity.'

'*Special* duties?'

Fischer nodded slowly. 'An Einsatzgruppe, the Ukraine. Something of a traumatic experience, it seems. It was his part in operations there that his memory refused to file, or lost, and was then damaged by.'

'And yet the memories returned? Somewhat convenient, given the timing?'

'Not really sir, no. It was Fuch's encounter with Bildmann that triggered the recollections - or at least, pulled back the bar from the mind's door. What's strange is that it took so long for the reunion to happen, if one considers that the two men lived and worked in such relative proximity. If they'd met earlier, several women might be alive still.'

'So Bildmann was a member of the same unit in the East?'

'He *was* the unit, from what Fuchs told me - not its commanding officer, but certainly the biggest dog in the pack. He was the liaison, the one who involved Ukrainian groups with the unit's *work*. They were undermanned, perhaps a couple of hundred men operating across thousands of square kilometres, so they needed to recruit help. Bildmann spoke the language well enough to flatter the locals, and he shared their enthusiasm for settling old scores. They watched our men deal with undesirables, copied enthusiastically and added their own adornments. As their contact man, Bildmann was often a witness to what was done. I suppose it's not surprising that he adopted his new friends' ways in turn.'

Schapper leaned back in his chair, putting distance between himself and what he knew he was going to hear. 'What ways?'

'His personal preference was females - young girls, older women, it didn't matter. He got into a habit of playing with them in front of an audience before he killed them - a grope, making them grab his cock, humiliating them by getting them to strip. This became rape, eventually. In fact, his tastes continued to mature. Courtship wasn't really his style, and he found it more convenient - more satisfying - to kill the women and *then* use them.

'Of course, personal gratification wasn't enough. It's common with men who indulge extremes of behaviour that they make a point of incriminating others. Some of the younger men in the unit - the milksops, the mother's boys - were put through initiations. Needless to say, these did not involve drinking a quantity of beer, wrestling or singing fraternal songs. Fuchs was one of them. He admitted to me that his fear of exclusion, of his comrades' contempt, overcame his self-respect. So he did what he was told to do, and became one of them, a good fellow.'

'Do we know how many ...'

'The killings, sir? Difficult to say. Fuchs said he stopped counting, but he was certain that it ran to tens of thousands over a period of months. It was Jews, politicals, anyone who'd worked in or for government, anyone Russian - they didn't know what to expect on any particular day. Local commandos carried out many of these actions after the initial period, but the unit coordinated everything, made sure the sweeps were well-organized, filed the reports, took credit from Berlin. Of course, it couldn't last. Apart from a hard core, Bildmann and his ilk, the men started getting ill, requesting leave, writing maudlin stuff to their wives. I don't know for sure, but Fuchs told me that the group was withdrawn at the turn of the year, and largely stood down after spring 1942.'

'Yes. A decision was made to discontinue the actions *in that form*.'

Fischer wished that he hadn't caught the emphasis. 'He recalled that Bildmann left the unit some weeks before the rest and went back to Berlin, his old job.'

'So that's it? Rudolph Bildmann came home, became bored on his *orpo*'s beat, missed the old days and decided to bring a piece of the Ukraine to the suburbs?'

'No, sir, not at all.'

'Then what have we been speaking of?'

'Only poor Lothar Fuch's memory, why it went, why it came back again. The business in Lichterfelde has nothing to do with the Ukraine.'

3

Schapper checked his watch. 'I mentioned that time pressed…?'

'Sorry, sir. I'll get to it, then. Soldau, 1940.'

'Soldau?'

'East Prussia, nice countryside, sir. A *konzentrationslager* was established there after victory in Poland, in a former barracks …'

'I know *about* Soldau! What of it?'

'It started by being a place where dangerous Poles could be dealt with - *dangerous*, as in intellectuals, nobility, politicos, churchmen and the like. It went on to become something else.'

'Jews, yes.'

'Some, sir, but that isn't my particular point. For a short time in spring 1940 it was used as a sort of sanatorium.'

'Really?'

'Not really, no - not in the generally understood sense of the term. A lot of mentally ill Germans were transferred there - Prussians mainly, I understand. Not many were cured, but none of them became a burden on the facilities, if you get my meaning, sir.'

'Tell me.'

'A *Tiergarten Vier Aktion* - one thousand, five hundred and fifty-eight of the poor bastards were done away with over the space of nineteen days.'

'Who told you this?'

'The boy, Fuchs. He wasn't there himself, but Bildmann was. Later, the pig used to boast about it, that he'd been a member of the sonderkommando charged with the job. A very clever lot of lads, apparently - they'd perfected a technique for the business and tried it out in hospitals all over East Prussia. I suppose it might be called a sort of mobile public service. Soldau was their first official contract, so to speak.'

'You make it sound like a commercial arrangement.'

'That's exactly what it was, sir. Bildmann told Fuchs that the unit was paid ten marks for every mental case they offed, so that particular job at Soldau netted more than fifteen thousand marks, shared between a hundred men or so. Their commander - a lieutenant - was a good sort, didn't take a slice for himself. I think he was in it for the joy of the profession.'

'Do we know who this was?'

'Yes, sir - Herbert Lange. More recently to be found in a suit named Sturmbannführer Herbert Lange, RSHA Amt V. One of Gerd Branssler's bosses.'

'Ah.'

'You'll have noticed the excellence of Lothar Fuch's memory on this business - the numbers, I mean. Bildmann told him that the job had been run like a machine, and very precise records kept in a *scientific* manner. That wasn't his unit's doing, of course - they were modest lads, happy to do their wholesome work, take the extra money and have nothing said about it. But the officer who ran Soldau at that time insisted on efficiency. He was great admirer of modern ways of doing things, and liked to set the pace. I'm told that his was the first camp to use data-processing techniques.'

'Holleriths?'

'Yes, sir - two of them, pampered like crown jewels in the camp's administration block. They used them for everything - inventory, personnel records, wages, operational statistics. As I said, the camp commandant was a stickler.'

'A name?'

'Otto Rasch - late SS-Brigadeführer, now a director of Kontinentale Oil. Coincidentally, between June and October 1941 he was commander of Einsatzgruppe C, Ukraine.'

'So he recruited Bildmann subsequently?'

'He poached him, sir. Obviously, he recognized the man's excellent qualities, his enthusiasm for doing a job properly. Lange more or less made a gift of him to Rasch. The two officers had become great comrades at Soldau - drinking comrades, in fact. Lange could handle it, but Rasch was draining bottles too hard and fast for it to be for pleasure's sake. I suspect the job was getting into his head already. The subsequent business in the Ukraine seems to have finished him off. He made himself very unpopular out there, insisted that all his senior officers shoot at least three or four Jews personally, just to let them know that they were all in it together. Probably, someone with connections in Berlin complained about it. In any case, Rasch wasn't reassigned in October 1941. He was dismissed, unfit.'

'But he had friends?'

'He has two PhDs, so they could hardly keep him out of a job. They call him Doctor Rasch these days.'

'Your source?'

'Oberst Krohne attended a briefing at Prinz-Albrecht-Strasse eight days ago. Rasch was present. The Oberst thought it a little strange at the time, him being a civilian gentleman, and synthetic oil production figures not in the way of normal RSHA business.'

'He was observing Krohne?'

'*Damage assessment* is what he would call it, no doubt.'

'You still haven't explained the point about Soldau.'

'No sir. We mentioned Hollerith machines. Rasch's administrative staff at the camp were regularly sent back to Berlin to learn operating procedures - to Dehomag's headquarters in Lichterfelde.'

'Again, Lichterfelde.'

'It keeps coming up, doesn't it? But while Dehomag are pleased to teach our boys how to operate their machines, they're very wary of chalking up their commercial secrets on a blackboard. All training and repairs are kept firmly within the company. Their machines are delicate, of course, and things go wrong often. When it happens there are only two options - either send them back to Lichterfelde for repair or send out one of Dehomag's boys to fix the problem on site. You'll appreciate that the first really isn't an option at all.'

'*Forschungsamt* has the same arrangement. I imagine that most of the Wehrmacht does likewise.'

'Yes, sir. So clearly, Dehomag employees get out of the office a lot. The first of Bildmann's victims, Agatha Fuhrmann, was one of them. According to her neighbour, she worked for the company in a *technical* capacity.'

'Unusual. But not a repairwoman, surely?'

Not quite, no. According to Fuchs, Bildmann and his *Lange Kommando* cronies were astonished when a 'tart' turned up at Soldau to supervise the equipment's installation and carry out initial adjustments. Apparently, there were no females on site other than among the poor devils getting the kommando's professional attention, so she must have stood out like an amputation. I don't have any evidence that this woman was Fuhrmann, but I find it inconceivable that Dehomag employed *two* female technicians.'

'Unlikely.'

So, we have a prior occasion of contact between the murderer and his first victim. I can't establish a motive, of course, because I don't know what - if anything - passed between them. Whatever it was, Bildmann had some reason to kill her.'

'And this incited his unnatural instincts once more?'

Fischer shrugged. 'Perhaps it did, but I doubt that personal indulgence was the point. There's been a very precise strategy here, intended to misdirect. Three killings of a particularly bestial nature, a brief investigation mysteriously halted and an inevitable, muddying flood of rumour regarding further deaths - the murderer duly mythologized, blurred into folk memory.'

'This was deliberate? Could it be done?'

'Why not, if someone had both the will and the authority to see it succeed? He, or they, worked upon an audience for which the unseen and the unspoken are to be expected. As for rumours, they'd be harder to prevent than facilitate.'

'And yet you pierced this monstrous conspiracy within days ... wait.'

Before Schapper could respond to a tap upon the door a clerk was almost at his desk, holding out a sheaf of paperwork. The Ministerial Direktor took it, examined each sheet briefly but carefully.

'Yes; yes; not yet; most urgent; yes; yes; get out.'

Fischer cleared his throat as the door closed. 'Again, we were lucky, sir. We acquired a history.'

'From whom?'

Must I name the source?'

'Of course.'

'It was the man who brought me in. Paul Schroeder.'

Schapper filled and lit a pipe - a long, churchwarden-style briar, entirely out of keeping with the uniform. He waved the match slowly to extinguish it, puffed on the thing, kept his eyes on the prisoner. Despite the crudity of the technique, Fischer moist palms told him that it was working.

'Why *did* you run, Fischer? Your friends seemed resigned to the situation.'

'I didn't run, sir. It was rather that the investigation wasn't yet concluded.'

'You'd killed the perpetrator. I'd say that represented a conclusion.'

'Bildmann was discovered at the Blue Rendezvous café, his hands around the throat of a young woman. He believed her to be aware of what he was doing, though that was almost certainly not the case. However, she *had* come upon information he would have been willing to kill to suppress, albeit by chance.'

'This information?'

'An identity, of a woman whom we thought we had identified already - Bildmann's second victim, Sigrun Ziegler. She was Agatha Fuhrmann's sister.'

The pipe almost fell from Schapper's mouth. Fischer paused while he brushed his jacket.

'So now we can say at least that a motive *existed*, even if we can't guess at it. We can say why Ziegler died, if not her sister. One of them knew something, so the killer assumed that the other knew it also. We discussed this briefly, at the café. It was decided that I should pursue the matter while Krohne informed you of the incident.'

'In the meantime allowing me to clean up your dirty business?'

'Yes, sir.'

'You pursued what? The third victim?

'No, sir. I suspect - though I doubt I'll ever *know* - that Gisella Mauer died only to create the fiction that this was a method murderer, acting out his perversions indiscriminately. Certainly, Bildmann gave full vent to his peculiar tastes once she was dead. Damage to the body was quite extensive.'

'Wouldn't two poor wretches have sufficed?'

'Almost certainly not. He removed Fuhrmann's *volkskartei* data from Dahlem station to prevent us from connecting her to Ziegler, but even so any assiduous *kripo* would have looked for a link between the two. A third, absolutely unrelated victim added a necessary disparity, an impression of casual selection that was sealed when the investigation was called off.'

'So, again - you were pursuing *what*?'

'Understanding, sir. I still wanted to know *why*. The young woman at the café, Mona Kreitz, told me that she and a friend had obtained this information regarding Zeigler. She offered it quite freely, but I felt that the other party needed to be questioned also.'

'And this was Schroeder?'

'Yes, sir. An excellent policeman, if only by circumstance. And by way of an interested party to this business, though he doesn't know it.'

'In *what* way?'

'His wife had emphysema. Like so many others, she died prematurely in hospital on the day the war broke out, though I doubt we can blame Lange or Bildmann for that particular job.'

'How did you find him?'

'Initially, we interviewed him regarding his missing colleague, Hans Lutze.'

'The corpse Lutze?'

'Yes. Schroeder wasn't happy about the investigation - specifically, that there wasn't an investigation. Like me, he applied himself to the matter of *why*.'

'A courageous man.'

'And fortunate, too. I'm certain that Lutze died because he knew, or discovered, that Fuhrmann and Ziegler were sisters. Perhaps he was at school with one of them - they were all locals, of roughly the same age. He was a very *talking* man, of course - a loudmouth in fact. So Bildmann must have regarded Schroeder as another potential exposure. He wasn't, as it happens.'

'How do you know?'

'Because he knew nothing of Fuhrmann. But he was able to direct me to a man who did.'

'I'll need this name also.'

'Edouard Muntz, sir.'

Schapper gaped at Fischer. '*Eddie* Muntz?'

Fischer returned the gape. 'You know him?'

'My mother considered him to be semi-divine. I thought he was dead.'

'He should be, given his proclivities.'

'Ah. Not one for the ladies?'

'Not in *that* sense, no. But he has a prodigious memory for them, particularly those in the theatre. Sigrun Ziegler had been a violinist, an extremely accomplished player, apparently.'

'And her sister?'

'Another musician, but no more than adept. An amateur pianist.'

'Interesting, I suppose ...'

'It's the crucial circumstance, in fact. We thought we'd identified a link between the three victims, a *place* where the killer made his choice. We were wrong in that as in so much else, but only in the detail. I now know at least why Agatha Fuhrmann died *when* she did. Bildmann saw her on the evening of 29 September, and almost certainly for the first time since their encounter at Soldau. I know this because Eddie Muntz was not present at their meeting.'

'I detest riddles, Fischer.'

'Muntz had - *has* - a standing engagement every Friday evening, one that he's most eager to keep. He's failed to do so only twice in the past six months - most recently a few days ago, when he suffered a mild bout of laryngitis. The previous occasion was upon a matter of arthritis, of whose symptoms he had more notice and was able to organize a substitute to attend the appointment in his absence. That was 29 September; his stand-in was Agatha Fuhrmann. She wasn't a singer, but her piano repertory consisted of many of the popular tunes from what I'm told were the good old days. The venue, as always, was the *volkskuche* on Steglizterstrasse, Lichterfelde. I believe that Bildmann was there also. He saw her, and, for whatever reason, decided that she had to die immediately.

'A people's kitchen?'

'Muntz sings for the old ones, sir. They love it, and I suspect that for him it's a link to a happier past. It was the opposite for Fuhrmann. Perhaps she recognized Bildmann from her time at Soldau and allowed him to escort her home, or at least to engage her in conversation. He was in uniform after all, a policemen, and to be trusted. The next day, Bildmann was one of the *orpos* who searched her apartment for clues to what he'd done, and why. There, no doubt, he found something that identified Sigrun Ziegler and condemned her to the same fate.'

'If Muntz was acquainted with the two women he must have known they were sisters. Why didn't he report it?'

'Would you have gone to the police, if you were Muntz? He's seen enough of his friends disappeared as it is. Whatever luck's kept him from the same treatment I doubt he'd want to push it. In any case, what would it achieve from his point of view? By the time the information was relevant they were dead - in Zeigler's case, quite pointlessly.'

'Why?'

'Muntz told me the sisters had been estranged for years on the matter of their respective talents, so it's highly improbable that Fuhrmann had the opportunity to tell her anything about …'

'About what?'

Fischer rubbed his damaged head. 'I don't know, sir. Something about Soldau, perhaps what she witnessed there. It was enough to deliver a death sentence and for powerful men to abet the crime. I know only what Bildmann told Fuchs, and that doesn't seem … sufficient. T4 Aktions are no great secret, are they? Even the public got wind of them, eventually. That's why they had to stop.'

For a few moments Schapper stared at, or through, Fischer. Then he tapped a button on his telephone's exchange pad. The same clerk returned.

'Ten minutes, no interruptions.'

The head nodded, withdrew. The Ministerial Direktor breathed deeply. 'We assume that Lange is one of the abetters, and possibly Panzinger too?'

'Lange, certainly. Panzinger must have *known* of the business and colluded, because he had ultimate responsibility for the investigation. But since Otto Rasch's name came up I've wondered whether *his* might have been the guiding hand.'

'Very well.' Schapper paused, tapped out the bowl of his pipe in an ashtray. He frowned, weighed something, cleared his throat.

'Have you retained your *faith* in the Cause, Fischer?'

The question was so remarkably dangerous that the prisoner didn't answer for several moments.

'I suppose so, sir. In the same way that most people have. As I still have faith in sky, and sausages.'

'Well, you may wish it otherwise. I needn't stress the confidentiality of what I'm going to say, because it will be all too obvious. I'll give you a motive, and I promise you that once you have it you'll wish you'd kept a distance from this thing. When I've finished, you'll go. Your colleagues likewise, I don't care where. We'll have no further business together, *ever*. You will mention nothing of *Forschugsamt*'s involvement, nor that of the senior persons whom you managed to convince that this disaster was a good idea. Acceptable?'

It sounded like a question without remotely being one. Fischer said nothing.

Schapper closed his eyes. 'Almost certainly, Herbert Lange is the principal cause of this business, if not its mover. You'll forgive me if I allowed you to tell me much of what I know already, but it was important to understand what you had. You mentioned a *technique*, employed by Lange's unit at Soldau.'

'Yes, sir. Something that helped them to kill off the lunatics a little more efficiently, or economically.'

'Quite. This was largely Lange's doing, apparently. He didn't invent the technique, but it was perfected during *Lange Kommando*'s mobile operations in eastern Prussia during 1940. His expertise was noticed and appreciated in certain quarters. In the following year, when his friend Rasch went east to the Ukraine, Lange was posted just a little way down the road, to Kulmhof. He took his skills with him. In fact, he was encouraged there to further develop them. With the help of others he did so, to a quite incredible degree. Now listen carefully, and keep this to yourself, always …'

5

Fischer's watch told him that the explanation had required a matter of eight minutes to deliver. Afterwards, he would always consider the time to mark a vast boundary between one state and another, between oblivious ignorance and infection. The impulse of his gut, churning even before enlightenment was complete, was to dismiss it as a vicious calumny that even Germany's enemies would have been ashamed to devise. But Schapper's flat, matter-of-fact voice, laying out something beyond comprehension as if it were no more than a statistical report, ripped apart his doubts.

Considered dispassionately - if that were possible - the feat was unequalled, and Lange had been one of its principal midwives. In a mere six months, from October 1941 until the following April, he had obtained modest resources, applied his practical expertise and breeched a new Age of Deformity. How many men could claim to have done as much, to have conceived the means - the *technique* - necessary to remove an entire strand of human history?

Unbelievable, and yet not - to have done *that* and then returned to Berlin to take up an ordinary policeman's job, to investigate cases, attend meetings and fill in forms, to go home to a family at the end of each day and dwell upon its mundane passages, imbued Lange's eastern interlude with a horrific ordinariness, as if it were no more than a line item upon a hellish curriculum vitae.

Lothar Fuchs's story had disturbed Fischer, but it hadn't the power to shock. The killings in the forests, the appalling torments that had preceded them - it was the behaviour of men carried beyond normality by abnormal times. After years of pummelling the national psyche with the Jewish threat it would have been surprising had excesses not occurred. War made animals of all soldiers, given sufficient goading - he had his own shameful history, a part in two reprisals in Greece when he had helped to pull men out of houses, men who had made the mistake of owning weapons but not uniforms, and, with his comrades, shot them in front of their families. And his had been an elite unit, men who were proud of their warrior ethic. Something *less*, something conditioned to regard Jews, communists and other undesirables as undeserving of decent treatment, could easily have gone much further. They had been told that the rules weren't to apply in the East, that theirs was an existential struggle in which *civilized* behaviour would imperil the safety of Germany itself. It didn't shock him; it was the shame of all crusading wars.

But it was not *war* that Herr Ministerial Direktor Schapper had described but an industrial process, carefully conceived, plotted, equipped and authorized, a process devoted to a single end - the extinction of a species. More than three hundred thousand souls at Kulmhof alone, and God alone knew how many more elsewhere, moved from life to death with no greater moment than if they had been inedible fish in a fertilizer factory. He had no vocabulary, mental or physical, to do justice to what he knew he should feel about it; he heard only the unbearable voice of a worm, wriggling in his inner ear, recalling the years-old rumours, the half-thought suspicions, the stories the Soviets had been pushing, their *lies* about the sites they had found in liberated areas.

You must have sensed something.

'You knew?'

Coming from anyone else it would have sounded self-absolving, but Schapper didn't flinch. His autopsy upon his own soul must have been unsparing. 'This is *Forschungsamt* - listening, understanding, it's what we do - it's *all* we do. Do you not imagine that we turn our ears inwards also? Of course I knew. I know almost everything. And I can effect almost nothing.'

'But the Russians are rolling right over these places! Surely they'll unearth real evidence?'

'Certainly. You can't imagine the effort that's being devoted to erasing the traces, but it's futile. Our leaders are cursed with contrary qualities - an ability to step outside human boundaries and a congenital blindness to the consequences of doing so. Had I organized this … *thing*, I should have been busily dismantling it since last June at the very latest. You won't be surprised to hear that the process was actually intensified at about that time, notwithstanding the appalling success of the Soviet summer offensive. What they're doing now is far too late in every sense. I can only imagine that some idiot proceeded upon the assumption that once the Jews were made extinct nothing would remain to speak of it. Absurd, isn't it, that so many past and future policemen were involved in the business and yet no one considered the forensics? This, your thing, has been part of Lange's personal exorcism - the three women, Lutze, Kriminalkommissar Thomas, even Soldau itself. Did you know that the entire camp was evacuated and closed last week? Twenty thousand inmates, herded westwards like cattle to market - it's fantastical.'

'Fuchs told us that he received the Soldau transfer order personally.'

'Naturally. Bildmann and Lange weren't to know about his failing mind. They must have assumed they were using a man stained by many of the same barbarities as themselves, a comrade whose own best interests would be served by helping them.'

'And Kulmhof?'

Schapper waved a hand. 'They dismantled the ovens last September and shot the surviving Jews. But the wonderfully efficient SS sonderkommando that carried out the exercise buried the corpses on site, so the Reichsführer's been obliged to despatch another, very, very special unit to dig them up and burn the remnants before the Red Army arrives. They're at the site now, carefully counting, one by one, the bones of those who weren't allowed to be individuals in life. It would be laughable, if …'

'So it's Bildmann, and Lange, and…?'

'You may take your pick. Rasch is an obvious possibility, though as a civilian his influence can't be what it was. Perhaps he enlisted others who shared the experience - God knows what a brotherhood it must be. There's Panzinger too, of course. Among much else he commanded an Einsatzgruppe - in his case Gruppe A, the Baltic States. I understand that A was the most *enthusiastic* of the Einsatzgruppen, and met or exceeded all of their targets well ahead of schedule. But then, we mustn't overlook Direktor Ohlendorf of Inland SD. For some months he headed Group D, south Ukraine and Caucasus, and probably holds the record for the single most efficient operation, at Simferopol. All these men did their part, came home and slipped easily into posts where they can cover themselves against all but God's fury - until the Allies arrive, that is, and then there'll be any number of Judgement Days. Your problem, Major, is that you have too many options and no ability to test them.'

Fischer had lost the urge to scan the options from a far horizon, much less *test* them. For the killing of three women he had hunted someone who had been complicit in the deaths of thousands of innocents, processed into smoke and ash under the full authority of law, a law in the service of which he had passed the greater part of his adult life. The crimes of Lichterfelde hardly counted as a consequence of the other; they were a mere stain, the mark of soil-life caught beneath the tracks of a great machine passing obliviously over all of them, crushing and implicating. It was too much to bear.

This is guilt, his worm told him, and it brought back what Schapper had said earlier. Major Otto Fischer was free to go, which was an impossible finale to the business. Negligible though he might be, he had done a deal with a very big Devil indeed and entirely failed to deliver what he had promised - failed, and become horribly visible in the process. It couldn't now be a matter of calling it quits, never mind, you did your best.

'You're allowing us to leave?'

The Ministerial Direktor receded slightly in his uniform, as if the shrug had released a valve. 'I have no further business with you.'

'You're going to let someone else get dirty hands?'

'I doubt it, not now. I gave Direktor Panzinger the most precise details of the unfortunate events in the Blue Rendezvous Café. I particularly emphasised the unprofessionalism of his man, Gerd Branssler, who beat to death a suspect in a murder investigation without first effecting an interrogation. I also mentioned the *three* bodies you discovered upon your arrival there, of the two SS men and the young woman, the manageress. And, of course, I stressed that you were suspended from *all* investigative duties, of whatever nature, forever.'

'And he was satisfied with that?'

'I took the sense that he was delighted. No doubt Bildmann would have been another *exposure* that needed attention once the business was done. Branssler did the job for him and put a great distance between it and the guilty parties.'

'We've made them safe?'

'You were never close to touching them. As I said, these men are armoured.'

It still didn't make sense. Why would they no longer see Fischer and his friends as worth removing? Surely, they didn't imagine that their secrets were wholly secure? Bildmann was dead, but they must have had access to a pool of similar men, any of whom could finish the job. They wouldn't leave it at this.

His head turned, Schapper was looking out of the window once more. He exhaled, too loudly for it not to be a sigh. 'You think they care still? They don't, any more than I. And for the same reason.'

'I don't understand.'

'When were you taken?'

'Three days ago.'

'11 January, yes. Are your guards talkative types?'

'No, sir.'

'No, I don't suppose they are. Well, at first light on the 12th, the allegedly shattered Red Army threw what we estimate to be one hundred and eighty divisions across the Vistula. Two thrusts, south and west; more than two million men, four to five thousand tanks and God knows how many aircraft and artillery, we can't begin to count them. It's quite incredible. If we'd used the same for *Barbarossa* we'd have been in the Urals within six months and the war would be a fond memory by now. Naturally, we can't contain the breakout. Army Group A is trying desperately to re-establish some kind of front, Fourth Panzer Army appears to have disappeared entirely, Warsaw's ruins are now officially a fortress, Krakow's gone, Breslau is next. More importantly for certain people, almost every one of the remaining facilities that never existed is about to be overrun before the evidence can be extracted fully. So you see why you're no longer an exposure, Fischer. To care about *you* would be like giving further attention to a ship's rat as the bulkheads parted. You may go. I'm sure that one of the dispatch trucks can offer you a lift to the Air Ministry. Mention my name. It might help still.'

Mutely, Fischer stood, turned and went for the door, a distance that seemed greater now than when he'd been dragged in, fearing the worst. But of course, he hadn't then been remotely aware of what constituted *worst*. His hand was on the door handle when Schapper coughed.

'Fischer ...'

'Yes, sir?'

'Berlin? Your decision of course, but we've intercepted urgent requests from Moscow to London. You may imagine what they're asking by way of support for this offensive. Try to get yourself assigned to a small airfield, a place that doesn't service more than one of our alleged squadrons. Or a weather station, perhaps.'

'Thank you, sir. But I'm assigned to the Air Ministry.'

Schapper smiled, barely. 'Ah, yes. *LuftGeheimStelle* IIb, the Reichsmarschall's little joke.' He waved his pen. 'Off you go, then. If you see my orderly as you leave, please send him in.'

6

All cities die.

Staring out of the truck's side window, he could pretend for a while that it might be otherwise. He clung to the fact of Berlin's physical presence, its central, defining role in the history of northern Europe, and tried to convince himself that a past might guarantee a future. He told himself that the city was *big* - enough to make its destruction problematic unless it was already a matter of policy in London, Washington, Moscow. Perhaps then the magnitude of the task would deter them from going as far as they might - and after all, hadn't his old tutor dismissed the possibility that intent alone could destroy an *urbs*? But he couldn't rid himself of the fear, the certainty, that destruction needn't be complete to be irrevocable. This was a place that had never loved the Regime, had fought harder to preserve its idiosyncrasies than any other part of Germany; but in the world's eyes it had become the form and soul, the living guilt, of National Socialism. When he recalled what his compatriots had done to London's docklands, to Smolensk, Kharkov, Vitebsk, Minsk and Leningrad, and even more to Stalingrad and Warsaw, the last of his illusions faded. The Allies were going to make of Berlin what Genghis Khan had made of Baghdad. If he were the enemy's single head, it's what he would do.

For longer than he cared to recall he had shared the peculiar German vice of unreasonable, unreasoning hope - hope that memory was malleable, that wars came and went in the old way still, without consequences beyond reparations and the loss of a province or two. His subconscious had put its money on another generals' coup, or a damascene moment for Roosevelt and Churchill, or even a mundane accident - the Führer succumbing to one of his many ailments, or Blondi pulling down a rabid fox at Berchtesgarten. The precise circumstance didn't matter, as long as they were given time and room enough to offer something that could be regarded as sufficient, short of annihilation.

But a muzzle had been stuffed into Hope's mouth. He was privileged to share information that erased any possibility of mercy, a final goad to the most civilized nation to be salutary. This wasn't going to be 1918 in the West any more than it was in the East - the

Ivans had only to circulate photographs of the *facilities* they had overrun, to make plain what appalling, unthinkable purpose had created them, and the German people were set up for an ending to make Wagner moist. This, his adopted city, was about to die for a reason that even his tutor had not conceived - because it would be judged a life unfit for life. And who after all had given the World that concept?

Rain slid down the window, the first for several days. The truck's driver switched on the windscreen wiper and cursed under his breath when it refused to move. That was fine, Fischer decided - if it came on heavily and they crashed on the way to the Ministry he wouldn't have to worry about what was coming. *Poor Otto*, they'd say, *almost at the end, and he died like that, stupidly, upon a matter of bad wiring*. Or perhaps *Lucky Otto, he probably didn't even see that bollard coming - what a wonderfully normal way to go, and just before the real shit fell upon us all*. Who knew what to wish for, anymore?

He wondered why he was alone, why the others weren't with him, and that made him wonder if they *had* been released. Schapper couldn't be trusted - the man was up to his neck in lies and manipulations, a spider whose weavings extended far beyond Fischer's capacity to understand. To expect him to do what he said was more than naïve. Really, what did Bildmann's death matter? The killings in Lichterfelde had run their course before their 'investigation' had started, so why should the Ministerial Direktor and his masters regard themselves as anything other than cheated by this weakest of retributions? Even if the final crisis were upon them, wouldn't they sooner crush an irritation than dismiss it?

Too many questions, abetted by a cosh, confusion, three days' lack of sleep and a profound understanding of his failure tormented him - he felt dull, stupid, detached from everything except the guilt that was building in his stomach like a bespoke Calgary. More than anything he craved a bath, a beer, a bunk and the same blessed malady that had emptied the cupboards of Lothar Fuchs' memory; but time seemed to slow, to accommodate the passage of every tortured permutation of things that couldn't be measured. Outside, traffic crawled. It was heavy, all military, the whole resembled an ongoing convergence of several startled herds of cattle. The few traffic policemen he saw seemed stunned, overwhelmed by their abrupt promotion from civilian duties to rear-echelon support. They attempted to do little and achieved less; most of them were content to stand there, letting a vast moment in history pass slowly around them, honking its horn furiously.

The journey from Werder to Mitte - a matter of forty minutes, usually - consumed an entire morning. When finally Fischer climbed out at the Air Ministry's main gate the city's functioning church bells were pealing noon or farewell, he couldn't say which. He nodded his thanks to the driver. The man looked at him blankly for a moment and then pressed down upon the accelerator.

Ernst Körner, the failing Reich's least military resource, appeared to have been placed in charge of operations during Fischer's absence. A large number of packing cases were assembled in the front courtyard, awaiting transportation to where the Russians couldn't hinder their destruction. As new ones were being brought out Ernst was sternly directing their deployment in order to keep several access paths clear. Fischer watched an unteroffizier place down two boxes down in a spot of his choosing and be whistled back to try a little harder. On any other day he'd probably have applied his boot to the old man's rear, but Ernst had a clipboard now, and such things were not to be disregarded.

'Herr Major!' Ernst's heels clicked smartly, and the board was thrust to a militarily correct angle at his side. Fischer returned the salute formally.

'Beg permission to report that Oberst Krohne asked to see you at the earliest opportunity!'

It was the first good news in a bad day. Fischer turned away towards the main entrance, but was stayed by a meaningful cough. Had the old reservist not been stood to attention a finger almost certainly would have tapped his nose.

'Top tunic button, sir. Reichsmarschall's in the building.'

The third floor was a maelstrom of paper and bodies, all being rearranged according to some unspoken crisis protocol. Untouched by it, like a *polynya* in a shifting, clashing ice field, the office and business of *LuftGeheimStelle* IIb had come to a halt. All fourteen members of staff were present, doing nothing; desks had been cleared of paperwork (none of which had contained information of sufficient verity to require removal, concealment or destruction) and replaced by feet or arses, schedules by the search for news or hearsay on what was coming next. Fischer didn't need to hear the conversations; the faces said everything worth knowing.

A phone slammed loudly into its receiver. Fischer went into Krohne's office. His boss sighed, closed his real and donated eyes. 'Thank God.'

'Did you know about all of this?'

'Not until we came back to Berlin yesterday.'

Yesterday. Then Schapper probably hadn't interrogated them. They wouldn't know; they could be innocent for a little longer at least. As soon as the thought occurred Fischer dismissed it, angry with himself. Ignorance of guilt was no longer going to constitute innocence, either in this world or any of the threatened next.

'Freddie and Gerd?'

Krohne shrugged. 'I sent Freddie to the safe house, told him to get the family out of Berlin. The twins aren't safe here for sure, now that everyone who can hold a gun's being given one. If he can get them back to the Spreewald or far enough West, I doubt that anyone will bother them before …'

'Gerd?'

'Gone home to the Alex, to make his report. He said he wants them to see him at his desk, like it's a normal day. Actually, I think he wants someone to say the wrong thing.'

Fischer recalled the force he had applied to Branssler's arm, trying to stop it crashing down on a disintegrating face while Freddie Holleman had stood back calmly, watching, asking him what the fuck he thought he was doing. He might as usefully have pulled upon a wall that had decided to go the other way. If anyone at Alexanderplatz intended to take issue at the fate of Rudolph Bildmann they'd need to bring grenades.

'Schapper gave him something before we left.'

'What?'

'Herbert Lange's address. Not his home in the city, the place he has near Rathenow, to which, I assume, he'll slink off ahead of the Russians arriving. Gerd handed it back, told Schapper not to worry. Said he wasn't going to make it out of Berlin.'

And all for the sake of one man, Dieter Thomas. Branssler knew nothing of the rest, the hideous, uncountable rest; he was going to avenge humanity upon a point about which it could hardly care less. A beautiful irony, if it happened.

Krohne looked drained. 'Why are we free?'

'I don't know, Karl.' After three days in a cell, Fischer found the walls of the small office difficult to bear. He went to the window and opened it. The view had never been much to dwell upon, and had been getting less as bomb damage rearranged it further. The old ministerial gardens on this block were long gone, buried beneath enough concrete to park a squadron of Dorniers; but a pleasing hint of Tiergarten's treetops remained visible to his right (a hint that had slowly been getting stronger as what remained of Leipziger-Platz got lower). To his left, the grandly outdated Prussian Landtag was almost intact still, and on one of its higher ledges a uniformly wretched line of Berlin's feathered citizenry had congregated to preen what remained of their winter coats. As he watched, a pair of crows entertained themselves, each taking a turn to bounce one of the pigeons off its perch, sending it into an outraged tailspin towards the lower storeys. The line gradually grew shorter, but the remaining targets continued their business obliviously, heads under wings, busily digging out the enemies within, reassured by some mindless process that their perch, safe the day before, must and would continue to be so. Fischer watched until the ledge had been cleared, and wondered how obvious a metaphor could be before it disqualified itself as such.

'*Jesus.*'

'Hm?'

'Nothing.' He turned back to Krohne, who was staring determinedly at a photograph of his wife and son.

'Perhaps Schapper's boss is indulging one of his famous whims.'

'Which boss? The fat one or the weasel?'

'Or it may be a matter of putting right the small things that can still be effected.'

'Small things?'

'I can't say, Karl. You wouldn't thank me if I did.'

'A message, Otto.' Detmar Reincke stood in Krohne's door, his only hand holding the ubiquitous telephone pad. 'It's a strange one, came yesterday.'

'Who?'

Reincke glanced down. 'Standartenführer Alex Neidermann, Service PR, *Reichsjugendfuhring*, Lothringerstrasse 1. It makes no sense. He says he's managed to find a concert flautist and three pairs. You're welcome to interview them any time, if you're still interested. But he thought that you might not be, things being what they are.'

Fischer took the pad. There were seven forenames, four surnames. The second line of Reincke's painful, left-handed script read *Franz & Ulrich Beckendorp, Little Flag Company no. 128, Schönefeld*: *twins, identical, very blond.*

Monday, 23 April 1945

Almost precisely in the middle of Drakestrasse, Unterkorporal Paul Schroeder came to attention and raised his right arm as high as he could manage. Absurdly, he had an urge to glance down to check his uniform once more, but he reassured himself that it had been presentable on the five previous occasions he'd inspected it that morning after carefully removing the swastika collar tabs. It didn't matter; he wasn't here to impress anyone.

'What should we say?'

'I'm not sure. It's difficult to know what's correct. I haven't done this before.'

'Nor me, obviously. Am I neat enough?'

'I told you, perfect.'

'Would *The Song of the Volga Boatmen*...?'

'Wait.'

As far as Paul knew, this was what was known as a medium tank. Close up, there was nothing *medium* about it; it was enormous, terrifying, and the noise made any further conversation pointless. He was extremely relieved when the thing stopped. He'd heard that they didn't, often.

The turret hatch fell open with a loud clang and a head emerged wearing the characteristic padded helmet that Paul had seen in so many newsreels. Beneath it, an officer's tabs and European eyes raised a small, undernourished flicker of hope in his feeble heart.

The enemy - the Beast that was sweeping unstoppably across the civilized world, drawing down a curtain upon a thousand years of German culture, the one they had awakened by kicking it, hard. Paul swallowed with difficulty, stepped forward a pace, switched the white towel from his right to left hand and saluted the old way, as correctly as he could recall. The officer lifted himself clear of the hatch and returned it casually.

'Do you speak German, sir?'

The officer nodded. 'Little.'

Approximately a hundred well-armed Soviet infantrymen were moving northward on Drakestrasse, keeping well in on both sides, coming up behind the small, three-tank column. Paul pressed on into the little time remaining to him.

'Sir, this is Lichterfelde West. German forces have withdrawn from the kaserne. The village is not defended. May we ask that you spare it?'

The officer was listening, but his eyes had moved on to Paul's companion, the other half of this embassy to the *Rus*. They'd widened slightly.

Eddie Muntz had taken particular care with his capitulation ensemble. The dark grey fedora - set at an even, sober angle - could have been cut from the same cloth as his suit, while his light lemon shirt contrasted the crimson tie and oxblood shoes elegantly. The gloves - also grey - remained on his sideboard at home. They were his only decent pair, and he hadn't wanted them looted, or pillaged, or whatever it was that conquerors did with calf's leather accessories. For the same reason his silver-topped cane had been excused duties in favour of an old, badly scored walking stick upon which he leaned more heavily than necessary, taking comfort from the support. He had been careful not to over-rouge his cheeks, and the slightest hint of lip wax (Paul had assured him) was not wholly inappropriate to the occasion.

As the tank's commander took in the view, Eddie removed his hat and bowed formally. 'Muntz.'

Coarse laughter could be heard through the driver's plate. With difficulty, the officer returned his attention to Paul's uniform 'Unit?'

'*Hilfspolizei*, sir - reserve police. I'm not a soldier.'

'Who is authority here?'

Paul and Eddie looked at each other. It was the question that reluctant volunteers feared the most.

Eddie swallowed visibly and squared his shoulders at the tank's eighty-five millimetre business end. 'I'm the Mayor - *Мэр*.'

Paul stopped breathing and tried to detain a neutral expression on his face. The officer spoke slowly, carefully shaping unfamiliar words. 'All with weapons, *soldats*. Yes?'

'No one has weapons, sir. All have been told to stay inside their houses.'

The officer stared at Eddie for a moment longer and then squinted into the sky to his right. From the direction of Lankwitz, heavy artillery had been beating out a remorseless tattoo since before dawn, when the Red Army had forced its way across the Teltow Canal, the Third Reich's southern border *du jour*. Fortunately for the remaining residents of Lichterfelde West the extreme left wing of the Russian pincer was pressing directly northwards through poor, smashed Potsdam, and so far the village was being spared that enduring nightmare of the German General Staff, a war on two fronts. Whatever vast assault group this tank company belonged to it had thrust itself between battles.

Eddie adjusted his hold on the cane and swept the view to the north with his fedora. 'Sir, the way through is clear. Most have fled. Only old men, women, children are here. No one will fight.'

'No *volkssturm*?'

'They went with the soldiers, sir. North, to the new Front.'

Soviet infantrymen had reached the lead tank. The officer waved one of them over, scribbled a note, muttered an order. The man saluted smartly and ran back towards the canal.

'You two and fifty more, together in ... *hall*, yes?'

Paul nodded. 'Hostages. Yes, sir.'

'Everyone good, you go home. If not ...'

'Yes, sir. Of course.'

No one moved, and Paul was at a loss to know whether to raise his arms or turn and walk away. He sensed that they had come to one of those terrible moments when a breath of wind could turn *up* into *down*, an expectation of life into a swift, workmanlike execution. It dragged, unbearably. Eddie made a small noise in his throat (Paul prayed he wasn't going to sing), stepped forward and offered up his silver cigarette case.

'Please, keep the rest.'

The Russian officer removed a cigarette and lit it with a German lighter. Briefly, he examined the case and without embarrassment slipped it into his tunic. It was a poor, adulterated blend but he drew deeply, holding the smoke for several moments before exhaling and shouting another order. The infantry began to move forward, skirting the stationary tanks, separating into units of six to ten men, scouring the flanking alleys for suicide units.

The morning was bright, warm for April, the air fresh after night rain. Only the sounds of war, the haze of spent propellants and a hint of domestic gas from a broken mains pipe nearby spoiled the illusion of other, better days. A few hundred metres to the north, barricades had been erected in front of the rail lines and then abandoned when someone realised that the Reich was no longer sufficiently expansive to require trains. A little to the south, hastily scoured earthworks disfigured those stretches of the canal that had not been obliterated by pontoons thrown across it to aid the Soviet advance. Here, though, on this stretch of Drakestrasse, one might have ignored the sound of artillery fire, taken in the pleasant view of villas and low apartments, the plentiful budding trees, the air of stolid, comfortable anonymity, the lack of visible damage and imagined the fight to be a thousand kilometres away, as it had been so recently.

Paul and Eddie kept their eyes on the officer's face as he examined this fortunate terrain. He was unreadable, impossible to judge for good or bad. Everyone had heard the stories from Prussia and Silesia, the atrocities committed by Red Army personnel upon the guilty and innocent alike, the mass rapes and random killings, the plundering, the systematic destruction of a lifestyle so palpably superior to their own. But there were other stories, perhaps too readily believed by those who waited for the tide - of Russian tanks halting to avoid doing hurt to German children; of some commanders demanding standards of their men and shooting those who fell short of them; of Soviet soldiers entering homes with evil intentions but settling instead for a wristwatch, or a wedding ring, or a gramophone. It was difficult to know what to expect, to fear or hope for; it was going to be hell, or merely purgatory, or something *else*, something as yet unknowable. All that Berliners had was rumour and runes, and they acted as people do in the face of a thing unknown. Some had fled, most waited; a few had exercised a last, awful degree of initiative. During the past hours Paul had wept for one of the latter, a kind, beautiful girl who had dared neither to run away nor stay, who had innocently caressed an old man's self-regard and then squeezed the last, thin drop of hope from his heart. He had found her the previous evening, sprawled on the floor of her café, poisoned by the stuff with which she kept the place immaculately clean - beyond all fear now, untouchable, eternally young.

The officer stubbed out his cigarette on the turret plate and regarded the elderly fascist supplicants who waited patiently for the inconceivable *next*. One of them hummed very quietly, trying to find a first note; the other was wondering for the second time in his life whether protocols existed for when war ceased to be such, for when men were allowed to be so once more. Before an answer could recommend itself the Russian's hand moved left to right, encompassing the view behind them, and in his red, exhausted eyes

Paul Schroeder's desperate imagination found a hint of something, a ghost of what the world had been, too long ago now to recall fully.

'Here?'

'Here, sir?'

'This. Good place to live?'

Paul nodded slowly, feeling his own eyes betray him.

'Lichterfelde, sir. It isn't really Berlin at all.'

Author's note: the part-time exterminators

Friedrich Panzinger was arrested by Soviet forces in Linz in 1946 and sentenced subsequently to twenty-five years' imprisonment for his part in anti-partisan operations in Latvia during 1941. He was released in 1955 as part of the general amnesty for surviving German prisoners still held in the USSR. Recruited as an agent by the Soviets (and subsequently 'turned' by the Americans while employed by the West German Federal Intelligence Service), he was protected from further investigation of his wartime activities. However, a communications breakdown between his handlers resulted in his re-arrest for his alleged role in the (January 1945) murder of French General Maurice Mesny. He committed suicide on 8 August 1959 while awaiting trial.

'Doctor Doctor' Otto Rasch was indicted with other former senior officers prior to the Einsatzgruppen trials of September 1947. By then he was in the advanced stages of Parkinson's disease; brought to his arraignment on a stretcher, the court found him unfit to be tried. He died less than two months later.

Otto Ohlendorf was tried and convicted at the same trials. Alone among the senior officers prosecuted for their role in special operations on the Eastern Front, Ohlendorf did not deny his guilt or extreme anti-Semitic convictions. Despite pleas for clemency from former colleagues and businessmen (with whom, during the war, he had planned for the resurrection of German industry following a defeat he had long believed to be inevitable), he was hanged in Landsberg prison, Bavaria, on 8 June 1951.

SS Sturmbannführer Herbert Lange died in April 1945 during the final battle for Berlin. It is generally assumed that he was killed in action or while attempting to flee the city, but the precise circumstances of his death remain undetermined and his body was never formally identified. Lange's role in the development of the first large-scale, fixed site extermination facilities (at Chelmno/Kulmhof) is well documented. However, Einsatzgruppen personnel had also experimented with the mobile sealed-van killings that Lange employed at Soldau, and his 'achievement' in this respect has been magnified here for dramatic effect.

The Third Reich died in the ruined streets of Berlin's government district, the Soviet forces advancing inch by inch across a field of blood and rubble between Invaliden-Strasse and Belle-Alliance. On the morning of 2 May 1945, little more than a day after Adolph Hitler abandoned the nation whose fate he had ensured, the guns fell silent across the city. Almost alone at the centre of that devastated landscape, from which the most bestial conflict in modern history had been launched and directed, the *Reichsluftfahrtministerium* - the Air Ministry - stood virtually unscathed.

Printed in Great Britain
by Amazon